WELCOME TO HELL . . .

Zeno peeked, spreading his fingers. Through them he saw Satan, not a don now in human robes, but a gigantic fiery-eyed thing with horn and tail, beset by a great serpent and by winged clocks with spearlike arms. He saw chariots with wheels of flame and mushroom clouds on which they rode. He saw creation and dissolution. He saw the sun swallow up the sky. He saw the earth charred to a cinder, deep within the corona of that sun. And he saw a cloud of gas in which angels darted—hundreds, thousands, wing brushing wing as they worked. He saw a huge ball forming in the midst of pregnant gasses. And around all of this wound the serpent, and in the serpent's coil the Devil toiled.

And in the Devil's arms Michael was cradled, fangs bared at a hungry sky as the serpent's widespread jaws came closer—jaws that contained an entire universe within the maw they circumscribed.

Zeno's fingers closed of their own accord, shutting out the awful sight.

JANET MORRIS
CRUSADERS IN HELL

CRUSADERS IN HELL

Copyright © 1987 by Janet Morris

A Baen Books Original

Baen Publishing Enterprises
260 Fifth Avenue
New York, N.Y. 10001

First printing, May 1987

ISBN: 0-671-65639-2

Cover art by David Mattingly

Printed in the United States of America

Distributed by
SIMON & SCHUSTER
1230 Avenue of the Americas
New York, N.Y. 10020

CONTENTS

THE NATURE OF HELL

Janet and Chris Morris

Sinday, Moanday, Duesday, Weptsday, Tearsday, Frightday, Sadderday . . . the weeks rolled on, time without end, and the Devil rolled with the punches. Usually.

Time in Hell is an endless series of infinitely divided instants, as Zeno of Elea would have put it. Did put it, as a possible solution to the paradox of Achilles and the tortoise. Infinitely divisible or singularly indivisible; either any moment, no matter how small, could be divided into an infinite number of smaller moments, and so on ad infinitum, or not: these were the Original Choices in the quandary of time.

Now that Zeno had all the time in Hell to work out the solution to his problem, it seemed not to matter. At least, not until the Devil came to call.

"Hello, Zeno," said the Devil who looked, that Sadderday, rather like an Oxford don. Zeno hadn't been familiar with Oxford dons or atomic clocks before he came to Hell. Now, he worked at the Infernal Observa-

1

tory, in the department of Apparent Time. Here he was
in charge of the Diabolical Dialing Department, which
dispensed, by phone, the exact Satanic Mean Time to
all callers.

When the phones were working, anyway. If the tape-
machines were running properly. And assuming that
the Demonic Day and Dating Service wasn't screwing
around with the intervals between Paradise-rise and
Paradise-set.

Which they were today. Or someone was, today. If
the term 'day' had any meaning—beyond that of a
mathematical standard 24+ hours—when your hours
were on the fritz.

Zeno had known that something was amiss with the
hourly rate of time's passage in Hell for some . . . time
. . . now. He hadn't known, however, that the Fault-
finding Forum would decide that he was to blame,
which it must have. Otherwise, why would His Infernal
Majesty be visiting up here, on Mount Sinai—coming
to Zeno's monastic little cell in the observatory?

"Ah, s-s-sir," stammered the philosopher to the donnish Devil, a man in black robes and a powdered wig.
"D-d-do sit d-d-d-down." Zeno gestured to the sole
wooden chair that, with the single writing desk and
feather pallet on the floor, made up his cell's furnishings.

When the Devil crossed the cell to take his seat, a
black, scaled and furred creature with wings folded
against its back scampered in after him. The door,
closing on its own, nearly caught the thing's tail. It
hissed, its back arched like a cat's, its tail fluffed to
twice normal size, and it looked Zeno straight in the
eye.

Then it opened its jaws (the size of a big cat's) and
hissed again, showing ivory fangs. Next, it pronked in
mock-threat and bounded into the Devil's lap with a rip
of his robe.

The Devil winced and, from beneath his seated person, smoke began to rise from the wooden chair in
which he sat. Grabbing the familiar by its ruff, he

settled it roughly into his lap and said, "Greetings, Zeno of Elea. It seems we have some sort of problem."

"Yes sir, Your Satanic Majesty, we have."

" 'Nick' will do, Zeno, at least until this crisis is over."

Zeno of Elea, whose sins had been the inventions of dialectic and the technique of finding paired, contradictory conclusions in other men's premises, had never imagined himself on first-name terms with the Devil. He could only mutter, "Yessir, Nick, sir."

At the mention of the Devil's name, the furred and winged beast in his lap fixed Zeno with a baleful stare, then growled on an ascending note.

"Michael," chided the Devil, offering a finger to the beast who immediately took the appendage in his jaws and began contentedly to munch on it. "Michael's my . . . eternal companion. Pet. Friend. You get the picture. Have you some milk around?" As he spoke, the Devil grimaced intermittently as the beast gnawed.

Zeno could hear the sound of fang scraping bone. "Yes, sir—Nick. Around here someplace." And went to fetch the pot of newt's milk cooling outside his single window in the snow of Sinai's peak.

When he returned with it and a bowl to pour it in, the beast deserted the Devil's lap with a bound. And its master said, "Now, then, Zeno, I'm here because you're the man who argued that every magnitude is divisible into an infinite number of magnitudes, and yet self-same and indivisible. Do I have it right: 'both like and unlike, at rest and in motion, one and many'?"

"Ah, well, that's a good paraphrase, Sir Nick."

"Just a paraphrase, then? You don't consider yourself responsible for the human concepts of infinity, continuity, and unity?" said the Devil with deceptive casualness.

But Zeno was not fooled. This might be the beginning of infinite punishment; so far, he'd avoided the worst that Hell had to offer. He said carefully, drawing on all his philosophical skill, "Surely no human is responsible for the concepts of infinity, continuity, or unity. Unity is a precondition for all existence . . . something must *be*, indivisibly and wholly, to differentiate itself from 'nothingness.' Once 'being' is established, one has two states, being and nonbeing. As—"

"I'm not saying you created the concepts—just that you're guilty of first explicating them," Nick interrupted impatiently. "Now cut to the chase, you long-winded pedant."

"Yes s-s-sir," Zeno quavered, trying to stifle a pained look. The 'chase' had been his life's work; was his eternal vocation; he could not 'cut' to it, he was eternally and entirely engaged in it. And continued: "As soon as there are two states, there is also duration, from which follow all relations of space and time: forward and back, up and down, to and fro, before and after. Thus the assumption of 'being' and 'non-being' create a primary divisibility which, in and of itself, generates the 'concepts' of infinity, continuity, and unity, since none of the aforementioned can exist without its opposite. Therefore, *differentiation* is the Initial State, the First Moment, the Root Casuality . . . and the culprit you seek." Zeno smiled, having gotten himself irrefutably off the hook.

The Devil did not smile. The Devil stared at Zeno unblinkingly and then leaned forward, elbows on his knees, his white, curly wig swaying gently against powerful shoulders. "Regardless of your pettifogging, you, you alone, first rubbed Mankind's nose in this particular brand of philosophical bullshit . . . What would you say if I told you that something is disturbing the very fabric of your assumptions, here in Hell? That forward and back, to and fro, before and after are threatened at their very center? That the forward-moving arrow of time and the backward-moving arrow have collided in midair?"

"I would say," Zeno replied very softly, "that you are better at creating paradoxes than even I am. But since my clocks are not reading the time in concert—not simultaneously, if I may add a loaded term to this discussion—I will admit that there does seem to be some . . . disturbance in the procession of time. In the length of what had previously and conveniently been uniform instants. In the . . . fabric of time itself."

The Devil nodded morosely. He looked at his hands between his knees and then at his familiar, Michael, lapping from a bowl of milk which was still as full as when the two men had started their conversation, or when the creature had first begun to lap. "I'm told that Hell is in danger of becoming temporally unstable—of having no duration and all duration simultaneously. I ask you, Zeno of Elea, is this a syllogism, or a real threat?"

Zeno had a sneaking suspicion that the Devil was trying to trap him into speaking some blasphemy so terrible that it demanded infinite punishment of indeterminate duration. He said slowly, "Sir Nick, if that were so, then it would always have been so—at least once it starts, or started, or will start. So we wouldn't know the difference, since there would only be a single moment in which to realize, cogitate, remember and predict. Therefore, also, because danger is a transient condition which leads to a result, there could be no peril in the true sense, because there would be insufficient duration to lead to any denouement . . . no result, no crisis or shift or event to which what the New Dead call catastrophe math could apply. There could be no catastrophe whatsoever, since there could not be, in an indivisible instant, any shift of states—no events, if you like. There would be simply stasis, in which everything was poised to occur simultaneously, but nothing whatsoever did occur. And stasis, of all states, demands the single condition consciousness cannot meet: peace. Thus, my answer is no, such a threat is not real, because such a threat, if it became reality, would be imperceptible and so unreal. Unreal for as long as there exists consciousness. And if consciousness does not exist, then nothing—"

"Stop!" howled the Devil, his fists balled over his

ears, his wig's flaps pressed against them like earmuffs. "You know, you smartass word-monger, you really do belong here! Some of them don't, I'll admit . . . bureaucratic muck-ups and the nature of big systems to malfunction. But you're as bad as Aristotle, who told me that his precious *geometry* proved the threat false in as masturbatory language as you're using."

"Sorry, Sir Nick, but you asked . . ."

"Asked!" This time, the yowl was so loud that Michael flattened himself before the bowl of milk and began to choke. As Zeno watched, the cat/bat/familiar seemed to bloat to twice its size as every hair stood on end. Its whole body convulsed from back to front. Then, its neck stretched to double its former length and its tongue sticking an inch out of its mouth, it vomited all the milk it had drunk back into the bowl.

And this was a very interesting phenomenon, because the bowl was still full before Michael began to vomit. And yet, as he vomited and *after* he vomited all the milk he'd drunk back into the bowl, the bowl did not overflow. When the animal lay exhausted and panting beside the bowl with its eyes glazed, having vomited into the bowl the entire contents of its prodigious stomach, the bowl was exactly as full as it had been before the beast had begun vomiting. As full as it had while Michael had been drinking. As full as it had been when Zeno first brought the bowl, sloshing milk against its rim, to place it on the floor before Michael in the first place.

Zeno had stopped listening to the Devil, who was yelling. He said quietly, "Sir Nick, do you realize what this means? The bowl . . . the quantity of milk in the bowl was unchanging throughout the entire interval of not-drinking, drinking, and regurgitating. And after." When Zeno again looked up at the Devil, the face he saw was as red as the sky above New Hell when Paradise was trying to set.

"No. Tell me. What does it mean?" said the Devil,

spittle riding his words as he expelled them from purpling lips.

"It means that your informant was correct . . . at least partially correct. In some places—for example, where Michael and the bowl are, but not here, only a few feet away on either side, where you and I are—spacetime is becoming anomalously subject to different laws."

"No shit," said the Devil as he rose from his chair in disgust. "Michael!" The call shook the very rafters of Zeno's cell.

And the familiar rallied to it—or tried to. It twitched its ears, it got up on its hind legs, it sought to back away from the bowl. But for every moment away from its bowl, it exhibited an equal and opposite movement toward the bowl. To Zeno, the cat seemed trapped in a tape loop. First it went forward, then it went back, but it never managed to execute more than a circumscribed set of motions.

And the Devil, watching the familiar, began to rage. "Michael! *Michael!*" he screamed as if the beast were his only child. And strode forward, toward the bowl.

"No! Don't! Sir! Nick!" Zeno called, and lunged for the Prince of Darkness, hoping to stop the Devil from becoming stuck like a fly on flypaper, as the familiar was now, in some temporal glitch.

The familiar was yowling, intermittently, whenever it reached a forward instant in its forward/backward/forward/backward minuet.

Now the Devil was cursing so horribly that demons started appearing—coming out of the walls, the ceiling, the floor, the very air. These were horrid creatures and Zeno (seeing acid spittle drip on floorboards and begin to smoke, spittle that dripped from gaping jaws which could chomp him in two), covered his head with his hands and sank down to curl himself into as small a ball as possible.

He heard noises his ears couldn't sort into sensible

sounds. He heard the ripping of the firmament and the fundament.

And then he peeked, spreading his fingers. Through them he saw Satan, not a don now in human robes, but a gigantic fiery-eyed thing with horn and tail, beset by a great serpent and by winged clocks with spearlike arms. He saw chariots with wheels of flame and mushroom clouds on which they rode. He saw creation and dissolution. He saw the sun swallow up the sky. He saw the earth charred to a cinder, deep within the corona of that sun. And he saw a cloud of gas in which angels darted—hundreds, thousands, wing brushing wing as they worked. He saw a huge ball forming in the midst of pregnant gasses. And around all of this wound the serpent, and in the serpent's coil the Devil toiled.

And in the Devil's arms Michael was cradled, fangs bared at a hungry sky as the serpent's wide-spread jaws came closer—jaws that contained an entire universe within the maw they circumscribed.

Zeno's fingers closed of their own accord, shutting out the awful sight. His head bowed down until it touched his knees. He curled up, hiding from the chaos he had seen. And though he could no longer see a struggle that his mind could not comprehend, he could still hear it.

He heard the Devil snarling that Michael was his, and no Power had the right to take Michael from him. He heard a chorus of demons singing songs to sear the inner ear.

Then he heard nothing. Silence. Utter peace.

Unutterable peace. He couldn't even hear himself breathing. He couldn't hear the pulse in his ears. He couldn't hear the wind whipping Sinai.

Then he did hear something. He heard the squishy sound of a terrified man losing control of his bowels. Himself. And he smelled his fear in its most base form.

And he heard a clearing of someone's throat. Then: "Zeno?"

He raised his head and the Devil was there. Alone

but for his familiar, riding now upon his shoulder, wings unfurled. The Devil had wings now, also, great leathery wings and deep-burning yellow, slitted eyes.

This horror made Zeno raise his hands before his face.

But out of the gaping, sharp-toothed jaws of the Devil's new aspect came the same cultured voice of an Oxford don: "Now that we've determined that there is a threat, I'd like you to work on some solution. Now that the physics are clear to you." And the Devil began to laugh.

Squinting, Zeno saw why he laughed: the familiar had sunk its teeth into his neck and was gnashing them there. Blood began to drip from the wound, down over Satan's shoulder.

"A solution?" Zeno gasped. "Me?"

"You. A way to keep the clocks right. I'll deal with what's throwing the larger temporality out of balance . . . it's, ah, certain mischievous souls among the dissidents and elsewhere who're to blame." From a pouch at his stomach, of the sort nature gives a marsupial, the Devil brought forth an object and held it out to Zeno.

Zeno scrambled to his feet to take the artifact. "But . . . it's just an hourglass. A mere hourglass, big, but not the sort of thing I need to keep—"

"*Just* an hourglass?" boomed the Devil, his wings moving restlessly. "This is *the* hourglass. The primal standard. If you lose it, you'll find yourself with firsthand experience of a multi-temporal hard time. For now, your job is to keep the observatory running like . . ." White teeth gleamed. ". . . clockwork."

"But. . . ."

"*But what, mortal?*" thundered the Father of Lies. "It's the nature of Hell to give every man a problem he can't solve. I'll leave a few demons here to make sure you've got the proper motivation."

And in a puff of black smoke that smelled hideously charnal, the Devil was gone.

But the demons weren't. They were outside Zeno's

cell in the hall. They were outside his window, making obscene snowmen from the white caps of Sinai. And they were waiting, Zeno knew, for the hourly chimes to toll.

He didn't need to hear that first ragged, imprecise and tardy announcement of the approaching hour to know what the demons were going to do to him, every hour on the hour, for howsoever long he failed to make the clocks toll simultaneously.

The snowman outside his window looked just like him, and what was happening to it was so awful, and so graphic, and the demons were having so much fun doing it, that Zeno's hands were trembling like leaves before he'd even gotten down to work.

It wasn't so much the fear of intermittent punishment that made him shake, but the fear of getting caught in one of those spacetime glitches while he had a demon up his ass.

GILGAMESH REDUX

Janet Morris

"To the end of the Outback, and back again."
    —Silverberg: *Gilgamesh In The Outback*

"The lord Gilgamesh, toward the Land of the Living set his mind," chanted Enkidu, hairy and bold, trekking beside Gilgamesh up to the mountain peak.

And Gilgamesh, gasping for breath because the trek was hard and the air was thin, interrupted, "Enlil, the mighty mountain, the father of all the gods, has determined the fate of Gilgamesh—determined it for kingship, but for eternal life He has *not* determined it. . . ."

These lines, from the epic sung as *The Death of Gilgamesh* for ages, shut both men's mouths.

But in the inner ear of Gilgamesh, the poem continued, fragments sharp as spear points in a wild boar's heart: *"Supremacy over mankind has Enlil granted thee, Gilgamesh. Battles from which none may retreat has he granted thee. Onslaughts unrivalled has he granted thee. Attacks from which no one escapes has he granted thee . . . in life. Be not aggrieved, be not sad of heart.*

11

*On the bed of Fate now lies Gilgamesh and he rises not
. . . he rises not . . . he rises not."*

On the top of the mountain peak now stood the lord
Gilgamesh and his servant—his friend—Enkidu. And
Gilgamesh wondered if Enlil inhabited this peak even in
Hell.

It was silly, it was foolish, to have climbed this mountain in search of more than he could ever find in Hell.
For that was where Gilgamesh now was, who had sought
Eternal Life and now sought Eternal Death—the peaceful sleep that had been promised him while all around
him were the lamentations of his family.

In life. So long ago in Uruk.

For a time the presence of Enkidu had soothed him,
but now it did not. Below and behind them was the
caravan they had joined because Enkidu had seen a
woman there he craved. And because the caravan was
well supplied with weapons that were to Enkidu like
toys to a greedy child: plasma rifles, molecular disruptors,
enhanced kinetic-kill pistols that fired bullets tipped
with thallium shot whose spread was as wide as Gilgamesh's outstretched arms.

Cowards' weapons. Evil upon evil here at the end of
the Outback. Such was behind Gilgamesh, down on the
flat among the covered wagons of the mongrel caravanners with whom, for the sake of Enkidu, he'd fallen in.

Before him, on the far side of this mountain whose
peak Enlil did not inhabit, was a shore and a sea and an
island off that shore, an island belching steam and gouts
of flame from its central peak—the destination of the
caravan Gilgamesh had left behind on the flat. Pompeii
was the name of the island, and whatever awaited there,
neither Eternal Life nor Eternal Death was among its
secrets.

Gilgamesh knew this because he was the man to
whom all secrets had been revealed in life, and some of
that wisdom clung to him even in afterlife.

"To the Land of the Living," Enkidu took up his
chant once more in stubborn defiance of the murky sea

and burning isle before them, "the lord Gilgamesh set his mind."

As if it made any difference to Fate what Gilgamesh wanted, now that Gilgamesh was consigned to Hell. Enkidu's mind had been poisoned by the woman with the caravan, by nights with her and the thighs of her and the lips of her which spoke the hopes of her heart: that there was a way out of Hell.

So now Enkidu sought a way out of Hell through tunnels; through the intercession of the Anunnaki, the Seven Judges of the Underworld whom Gilgamesh had seen in life; through perseverance and even force of arms. Myths from the lips of a woman had seduced Enkidu and put foolish hopes in the heart of Gilgamesh's one-time servant and beloved friend—hopes that were, with the possible exception of intercession by the Anunnaki (whom Gilgamesh had seen and knew to exist), entirely apocryphal.

If Enkidu and Gilgamesh had not so recently quarreled and parted, if Gilgamesh had not missed his friend so terribly when they did, the lord of lost Uruk would have argued longer and harder with Enkidu. He would have refused to join the caravan. He would have stamped out Enkidu's vain and foolish hope of escape from Hell.

He should have done all those. But there was no one in the land like Enkidu, no one else who could stride the mountains at Gilgamesh's side, whose stamina was as great, whose heart was as strong, whose hairy body pleased Gilgamesh so much to look upon.

There was no companion for Gilgamesh but Enkidu, no equal among the ranks of the damned. Thus Gilgamesh put up with Enkidu's foolish hopes and hopeless dreams. Enkidu was not the man to whom all secrets had been revealed.

Only Gilgamesh was that man. Only Gilgamesh had known the truth in life. The truth had less value, here in afterlife. It had no more value than the carcass of a feral cat or a rutting stag or a rabid demon—all of which Gilgamesh had slain while hunting in the Outback. It

had no more value than the skins he cut from those
carcasses as he had in life. It had no more value than
the flesh beneath the skin of those animals, dead while
he dressed their carcasses, dead while he ate—when he
must—their flesh.

But not dead. Death was rebirth here. Death was
forever elusive. Death was merely a hiatus—and a short
cut to the teeming cities of Hell's most helpless damned,
among whom Gilgamesh could not breathe.

In Hell's cities, Gilgamesh felt like the lion caged to
please the king. In Hell's cities, his limbs grew weak
and his spirits low.

This city before them now was no exception. It dried
the chant in Enkidu's throat. It dried the blood in
Gilgamesh's veins. Pompeii, the caravanners whispered,
had come whole to Hell, so purely iniquitous were its
very streets. Its dogs had come. Its dolphins had come.
Its whores had come. Even Pompeii's children had
come to Hell.

And it was a city, so the tales ran, where everything
was as it once had been—where outsiders were unwel-
come and never settled, where a language neither Greek
nor English was the norm.

Gilgamesh looked at Enkidu out of the corner of his
eye. Enkidu had brought them here, from the clean
violence of the Outback, because of his loins and his
lust for modern weapons.

Gilgamesh had never asked Enkidu if the former
servant got pleasure from his copulation with the woman,
or only frustration, as was the lot of so many men in
Hell. Men whose manhood was too dear, too often
proved, too important to their hearts, often could not
consummate the act. Gilgamesh and Enkidu had met
because of one such woman, centuries ago in life.

He shook away the cobwebs of memory, so common
lately, and said to Enkidu, "See, the city of ill repute.
Let us leave the caravan now, Enkidu, and return to
the Outback, where the hunting is good."

"Gilgamesh," replied Enkidu, "the animals we hunt do not die, they only suffer. The skins we take . . . are these not better left on animals who must regrow them? And the haunches we eat, which distress our bowels? Let us go with the caravan into the city, and explore its treasures. Are you not curious about that place, which came to Hell entire?"

This woman was destroying Enkidu, rotting the very fiber of his mind, Gilgamesh realized. But he said only, with the patience of a king, "We will not be allowed into the city, Enkidu, you know that. The caravan must camp on the shore and its people go no farther."

"Ah, but the lord of the city will come to us and then, hearing that you are Gilgamesh, lord of the land, king of Uruk, he will surely invite us there . . . to see what no outsider has ever seen." Enkidu's eyes were shining.

Gilgamesh had never been able to resist that look. He said, "If you will put away this woman—who will not be allowed to travel with us to the city in any case—and separate from the caravan thereafter, Enkidu, I will announce myself to the lord of the city and demand the hospitality due the once king of Uruk—and his friend."

"Done!" cried Enkidu.

High above the caravan, in a helicopter hidden by Hell's ruddy clouds, an agent of Authority named Welch reviewed the background data that had brought him here, on his Diabolical Majesty's most secret service.

Welch had become a member of the Devil's Children, Satan's "personal Agency" among a dizzying proliferation of lesser agencies, without ever meeting Old Nick face to face. Agency was special, privileged, demanding and unforgiving of failure.

Agency was not, however, infallible, and the briefing material before Welch on the chopper's CRT was no better than what Welch's own spotty memory could provide. Worse, perhaps, since bureaucracy in Hell functioned but never functioned well.

Tapping irritably at a toggle to clear his screen, Welch mentally recapped the "secret" analysis he'd just read:

Mao Tse-tung's Celestial People's Republic had spread quickly along the tundra of the Outback, stopped only by Prester John's border to the south and the Sea of Sighs to the west. New Kara-Khitai had already been invaded by the collectivizing hordes of the CPR, led by Mao's Minister of War himself, Kublai Khan.

Communist troops in the Outback didn't bother Authority—as Mao had said, revolution wasn't made in silk boxes. The misery Mao's CPR fanatics brought with them like bayonets on the barrels of their ChiCom rifles would have been allowed to spread unchecked, at least until it overswept Queen Elizabeth's domain and the entire West was Mao's *if* Mao could have been content with that.

Unfortunately, Chairman Mao had greater ambitions. He sought to export revolution to every socialist crazy who could say Marghiella, and that included Che Guevara (or what was left of his soul since Welch had called in an air strike on Che's main Dissident camp north of New Hell). If the export of revolution had stopped with rhetoric, perhaps Authority could have looked the other way.

But Mao was using drug money to fund his ideological allies—from Che on the East Coast to the Shi'ite bloc landlocked in the Midwest. Once his revolutionary exports reached New Hell, reached as far as the very Mortuary itself, then something had to be done.

Narco-terrorism wasn't to be tolerated. The poppy fields of the Devil's Triangle reached from Idi Amin's southern frontier to the Persian holdings in the Midwest, and over to Mao's capital, the City of the Fire Dogs. From Dog City, "China White" made its way south and east by boat and caravan, dulling the sensibilities of the damned.

Communism was one of the Devil's favorite inventions, and that made Welch's assignment harder. Agency couldn't simply nuke the emerging Western ComBloc back to the stone age—Authority wouldn't permit it. Welch's assignment was to stop the flow of drugs East, especially into New Hell, where the Dissidents were attracting too much attention. So it was overflights in this Huey, piloted by a hot-dog Old Dead, Achilles. It was a covert crusade against drug smugglers.

And it was going to take one hell of a long time to show any results.

Welch sat back from the computer bank in the belly of the Huey and reached sideways for his pack of Camels and a swig of beer.

Machiavelli had done this to him: vendetta. More precisely, Machiavelli had done it to Nichols, Welch's one-time ADC—sent Nichols out on a search-and-destroy mission aimed at a specific caravan master who did business out of Pompeii; sent him with an Achaean relic for a pilot and Tamara Burke, whose sympathies in life and afterlife were questionable. (Whether she'd been KGB or CIA, even Welch wasn't sure.)

Rather than let Nichols spend the rest of Eternity fighting Mao's considerably greater resources, Welch had pulled every string he could think of to secure command of this mission—even called an air strike on Che's base camp to clear his decks in time to board Achilles' Huey.

Welch shouldn't have been here, fighting the Yellow Peril out in the boonies when Agency had bigger fish to fry, not when he had so much unfinished business with Julius Caesar's crew back in New Hell. But he owed Nichols this much and more: Welch's miscalculation on their last mission had gotten Nichols killed.

If Welch had been doing his job right—before and directly after Nichols' death at Troy—he wouldn't have owed the soldier anything. But Welch had come back from the Trojan Campaign with a case of something very like hysterical amnesia. It had been Nichols who

found Welch, sloppy drunk with Tanya—Tamara Burke—
in a New Hell bar and offered aid and comfort.

Aid and comfort in Hell were hard to find. Aid and
comfort coming from a junior officer rankled. Welch
had been the case officer on the Trojan Campaign;
Nichols had been one of many weapons Welch had
employed there.

So it was all backwards, to Welch's way of thinking.
He had to get things back into a perspective he could
live with. Or die with. In Hell it didn't much matter,
but case officers thought in terms of human coin—debts
owed, favors done, responsibility and trust.

Trust was a big one: whether betraying it or ratifying
it, it was the fulcrum on which all operations turned.

This mission, on the face of it, was simple, if Achilles'
assessment was correct: strafe the caravan with the
Huey's chain gun until nothing moved; firebomb what
was left once they'd made sure that Enkidu and
Gilgamesh were among the dead . . . or the missing.

That was a little addendum to the main mission:
separate Gilgamesh and Enkidu, and send or bring both
Sumerians back to Reassignments.

There was nothing in the orders about how, though,
and Achilles was right: death meant the Trip; the Trip
ended you at the Mortuary (except, sometimes, if you
died on the battle plain of Ilion, a couple of dimensions
away from here . . .) and then at Reassignments.

Even Tamara Burke had voted for the easy way, until
Welch had put her down with a carpetbag full of femi-
nine accouterments and detailed her to infiltrate the
caravan and seduce one of the Sumerians.

Tanya had a field phone, tracer jewelry, and a chopped
Bren Ten that could be heard to New Hell and back if
she had to shoot it. She was an experienced field collec-
tor, as well as a proven seductress.

But the look she'd shot Welch when they'd let her
out a hill away from the caravan had been scathing.
Only Achilles was pleased with that.

So now it was Welch and Nichols in the belly of the

chopper, alone but for their data collection equipment and each other, bathed in sweat and running lights and trying to keep their equipment cool as they waited for a signal from Tanya that the caravan had picked up its load of drugs and was headed toward the hinterland. The low-shrubbed boonies. The damned no-man's-land of buffer-zone that was so undesirable even the commies hadn't claimed it. Yet.

"You know, something about this doesn't feel right," Welch said to Nichols. Arching his back in his ergo chair, Welch put one foot up on the padded bumper of the "mapping" console that could show him how much spare change Enkidu had in his pocket or how much ammo was in one of the caravan guard's Maadi AKs. "Tanya should have called in by now. The caravan should be loaded up and on its way out by now. And I can't find the right heat signature for Gilgamesh and Enkidu to save my soul."

"Umn," said Nichols with illuminating voluability. "Me neither." Nichols was still hunched over his tracking console, stripped down to a black t-shirt that showed the screaming-eagle tattoo on one muscular arm. "Think maybe they've gone off on their own? The OD's, I mean?"

The OD's: the Old Dead—Gilgamesh and Enkidu. One of Nichols' little rebellions was a feigned inability to pronounce either name. "Tanya would have let us know," Welch said, because it was his job to say that, not because he really believed he knew what Burke would do in any circumstance that might come up during field work.

"Yeah?" Nichols was more blunt, the sneer on his square face eloquent as he shifted to lock eyes with his superior. "What if Achilles and her have cooked up a little something of their own? That's lots of money, lots of power, lots of anonymity, down there." Nichols' gaze flickered to his feet on the deck, below which was the caravan camped on the shore in sight of Pompeii. Nichols didn't like Achilles and the feeling was mutual.

Achilles liked Tanya, though. Anything with a dork would follow Tamara Burke anywhere, sniffing and wagging its tail and leaving its common sense behind. Welch ought to know.

"What are you getting at?" They knew each other too well for Welch to take umbrage at the "Sirs" missing from Nichols' badinage. When you were sweating it out in a com truck on the battle plain of Ilion or in Caesar's private office at a New Hell villa or in a chopper flown by one of the biggest egos in Hell, you wanted a man like Nichols to have your best interests—and the success of your mission—at heart.

"A little recon. If you don't mind. You don't need me here right now. What these babies ain't sayin', you can handle." Nichols' chin jutted toward the electronics displays.

Maybe it wasn't necessary, but it was logical. And it was what Nichols did better than he did anything but exponentially increase body count.

"Okay, you're go," said Welch absently in their familiar shorthand, and unwound from his chair to give the order to Achilles on the flight deck. He could have patched into Achilles' helmet-circuit from here, but if there was an argument—and there almost always was with Achilles—he didn't need Nichols hearing it.

Standing, Welch had to slump to avoid hitting his head. Stooped over, he said: "Finish my beer for me. And take more than you need down there. Including this." He reached into his hip pocket and pulled out one of the miniaturized black boxes he'd requisitioned for his recent sortie into Che's camp. "You get into trouble, or just want extracted, push this button." He turned the match-box sized oblong in his fingers until the red nipple on one side was facing Nichols. "I'll be waiting."

"You expecting this kind of trouble?" Nichols frowned at the black box before he took it.

"I'm expecting a real good reason why Tanya's not checking in, yeah."

Damned women, you could never tell what they had in mind. But it wasn't so much that he didn't trust Tanya, it was that Welch knew Nichols. Nichols had a disdain for the Old Dead that might cause him to underestimate the opposition.

No matter who the antiques were, the opposition here was really Mao. And Mao was nobody's friend, nobody's fool. Welch promised himself that, when he got back to New Hell, he was going to get Machiavelli transferred to Sanitation Engineering.

Up on the flight deck, listening to the inevitable "better idea" that Achilles had, Welch made a mental note to include the Achaean in Machiavelli's Sanitation squad. Then he pulled his 9mm off his hip and, flicking suede lint from its barrel, said levelly to the pilot, "You fly 'em, I'll call 'em. Understood?"

The chopper pilot began landing procedures without another word.

Nichols had scrambled thirty feet away from the Huey before he looked back. Even knowing where it was, he couldn't see the damned thing. Stealth technology had come a long way since Nichols died, not in the Med during the Big War, but on an island off America's coast in the aftermath.

Didn't matter. Nichols shook his camouflaged head. Didn't mean a damn thing, Welch was right.

But it made him queasy, looking back at the electro-optically distorted field which masked the chopper so well you could have walked right into one of its rotor blades and gashed your head open.

Okay, he thought, so Achilles knows his job. Ought to give him one point. But Nichols couldn't do that; his gut knew better. And Nichols, unlike Welch, remembered every minute of the Trojan Campaign—up until he'd died during it. They'd scaled the very gates of Hell on that one, and Welch, with his partial amnesia and his officer's attitude, just wasn't applying enough good old-fashioned suspicion to the events that had brought matters to their present turn.

Nichols had died in Troy, but been held in limbo, somewhere, awaiting Achilles' pickup—for this mission. On whose orders? To what end? Welch, meanwhile, who would have gotten Nichols out of limbo if he had to use a P-38 to do it, was afflicted with convenient amnesia and watchdogged by Tamara Burke, whoever and whatever she was. If all this was coincidence, Nichols was a Persian eunuch.

If it was just luck, it was bad luck. And Nichols didn't like bad luck. If he had a god, it was the one that got you out of wherever alive, stepping three inches to the right of a cluster bomb that would have blown you to perdition; ducking your head to swat a mosquito just when the round that would have smashed it to jelly sped by.

Nichols knew damned well that Achilles was trouble— always had been, always was, always would be trouble, for friend and foe alike. He'd mucked up the first Trojan War and tied the commanders in knots during the second. If Caesar and Alexander the Great couldn't get around the jinx that Achilles put on any mission he was attached to, what chance did he and Welch have?

You couldn't talk to Welch about Achilles, beyond operational talk—Welch didn't believe in luck. Welch took everything personally. Which was fine, most times—it made him an officer with whom Nichols was proud to serve. But it made him touchy about certain things, like what he didn't remember about Troy.

And Welch didn't remember one very important thing about that mission: he didn't remember that, when Achilles came flying into the middle of an already complex situation, nobody—not Caesar's crew, not the opposition down there, not his passenger Judah Maccabee, not Agency itself, and most especially not Welch— would admit to dispatching him.

Achilles was a damned wild card and even the Myrmidons hadn't had a real cheery survival quotient (so the unit's vets said), serving under him in life.

But Achilles knew his ECM. He could cajole stunts out that Huey like Nichols had never seen—or heard.

Blinking hard and listening harder, Nichols could barely focus on the chopper as it lifted, purring no louder than a happy cat. Stealth, you bet. Better than it had any right to be, like Achilles was better than he had any right to be. Nichols was willing to bet, all that capability was somebody's doing. Like maybe the Pentagram faction that was supporting the dissidents.

Achilles and Tamara Burke: neither of them had put a foot wrong the whole time they'd been in Hell. He and Welch had called up their jackets, and there wasn't a single negative notation or disciplinary action in either of their files. Too damned perfect not to be trouble.

But you couldn't convince Welch of that, not without proof. Tanya failing to check in wasn't proof, not in the mind of a guy who'd been laying her flat while Nichols was on ice somewhere for . . . how long? Long enough, that was sure.

Nichols checked his webbing and what he'd hung on it. He could probably have done the whole job himself, with what he was carrying. He had an Alice over his back with a SADEM—Special Atomic Demolition Emergency Munition—that would end any argument, except how he'd come by it. He had every electronic gizmo Welch could come up with. He had a det cord bracelet around his wrist and a high-pressure chemical delivery system next to the survival knife in his boot.

Recon had a tendency to turn into more than that, every now and again, and Nichols wanted to be ready.

Crouched among bushes bending violently with the chopper's take-off (even Achilles couldn't alter physics), Nichols checked his weapons-belt—front-line kit was ninety rounds of 7.62 NATO in life, and that was what Nichols took with him on a mission like this, whenever he had a choice.

Then he started scuttling through the bushes on the

slope, beyond which he could see the caravan making camp. Get in there without being seen, find Tamara, make sure she didn't have a problem she couldn't handle, and give her Welch's message that she was to maneuver one of the two Sumerians to the pick-up sight and bring the OD onboard, nothing more.

Welch didn't see any reason to kill the two Old Dead, probably because Achilles was so intent on just that. So it had become a command decision, an internecine struggle on which command authority in the field depended.

Personally, Nichols didn't think you could teach Achilles nothin'; he didn't even see a reason to try. Nichols could get the Huey back to New Hell, if the one lesson Achilles might possibly understand became appropriate. Hand on his M14, Nichols prowled, pumping himself up for a covert entry where there was no night or cover to shield him and plenty of nervous sentries around a caravan expecting to pick up a fortune's worth of drugs.

He had a suppressor on his customized auto-rifle, because that was the way you did this sort of mission, and he kept checking it as he scrambled down the rocky slope. He also had a button in his ear and a mike on his collar, so that he could voice-actuate communications with the chopper.

The odd sky, here where Paradise seemed skewered in place among clouds too dense and too low not to generate ground fog, threw him back in time and place, among the lush fauna of this volcanic, mountainous shore.

Jungle it wasn't, not the real sort, but it was close enough and Nichols had been Sniper Research, despite interdepartmental hassles, for a while when he'd been alive.

He was trembling with chemical hype from his nervous system by the time he reached the edge of the caravan, stopping on an overhang spawning a waterfall that generated some serious white noise, this close.

Stopping to take a look-see, wriggling on his belly over rocks and past rocks and over lush grass, getting closer. . . .

"Yo, Nichols!"

The sudden sputter of Achilles' voice in his ear-piece made Nichols flinch. His foot dislodged a rock, which hit another that tumbled down toward the water and fell over the falls. . . .

"Not now, droolface," Nichols muttered into his collar, where his mike was. Idiot or spoiler, Nichols was going to kill this guy, no matter what it cost him, and get Achilles reassigned somewhere where bugs were the only things that flew.

Below, the stone, cascading down the waterfall, then bouncing, had flushed something unexpected. Short guys in black outfits came running out from under the falls, gesticulating, chattering to each other.

Damned monkeys, or worse . . . no wonder this place sent his mind echoes of Ho Chi Minh trail. Bunch of Asiatics, hiding behind the waterfall. . . .

Nichols looked again, with all the acuity his trained eye could muster, and this time the waterfall didn't look natural. But it sure was convenient, and well-engineered. Nichols would give Mao's boys that.

Recon meant you were supposed to get back alive to detail enemy troop strength, he reminded himself as two parts of his being conflicted.

Sniper Research meant that you shot whatever you found out there, so that you could do your damned research uninterrupted. . . .

Head count, in this situation, was approximate, but Nichols was willing to bet that behind the waterfall he'd find lots more ChiCom troops—smugglers for the sake of the Revolution, in this case—and a tunnel entrance that would explain why no previous unit with this assignment had been able to find the transship route that Mao was using.

Whistling soundlessly, Nichols rolled over onto his back and very carefully, scanning the terrain around

him, wiggled his arse until he'd gotten upstream far
enough that he wouldn't kick any more stones into the
water.

Then he began unwinding the det cord bracelet on
his wrist, combining it with other necessaries from his
kit until he had a time-detonated explosive device that
ought to block the tunnel entrance, as well as stop the
flow of water, when it blew.

He sat there a few seconds, considering his handiwork. You had to use the faults in the rock strata, judge
it just right. . . . Deciding it was right enough, if nobody messed with it, he fixed his little trap to blow if a
careless foot stumbled onto the det cord, which had
enough RDX in it to be trouble by itself, and went on
his way.

He'd known he'd find a use for all this stuff he was
packing. You don't deplane with ninety pounds on your
back and haul it over enemy terrain for nothing. He'd
cannibalized one of Welch's black boxes, but Welch
wouldn't mind.

It was going to be such a nice, satisfying bang. If the
ensuing explosion didn't stop the drug traffic from Mao's
fortress in Dog City, it was going to slow things up: re-
routing, redeployment of personnel, rebasing . . . all
these things took time, men, resources.

Content that he could give Welch what the officer
needed to report a successful mission, with or without
Tanya and the Sumerians—and without setting up a
semi-permanent staging area here which they'd have to
man—Nichols scrambled down the slope and headed
west.

He had no intention of getting caught in the act, or
anywhere near here. What he'd left behind was more
important than what remained for him to do: score one
for on-site decision making.

It took the better part of two hours to circle the
camp, find Tamara Burke's wagon, and slip over to it
from the rear. He knew he should have reported what
he'd done, called in and let Welch know. But then

Achilles would know. And he didn't trust Achilles worth a damn. Or the com line he checked in on.

Welch, who didn't like "excess" casualties, might have given him an argument, Nichols knew. Welch had a message for Tanya that underscored that forgivable, but very real, flaw in the Harvard man's nature.

The camp was easy enough to negotiate—nobody here asked questions when strangers came around, especially strangers with backpacks in unfamiliar, non-standard, camouflage.

Finding Tamara's wagon was no problem—they'd scrounged it for her; there wasn't another like it in the caravan. Tapping on it with the butt of his survival knife, Nichols had a moment to worry.

He didn't like those sort of moments, wherein possible problems that might never occur popped up like phantoms and scared him witless. But he sat out the flash of anxiety stolidly—he knew how to manage field jitters. You just kept telling yourself, "So what?" and they passed.

Because there was no answer to that question, beyond the simple answer: you handled whatever came your way.

It was taking her too long to respond, and he risked a low, "Hey, Burke, you in there?"

From somewhere, a desperate scramble became a barking dog, launching itself at him.

Reflexively, Nichol's service pistol came to hand. The dog was big, brindle, a decent target. Deciding, as he watched it bound toward him in a slow motion his adrenalin-prodded physiology provided, that a two-shot burst would beat a headshot in this situation, he drew a bead. Then the gold silk of the wagon parted hurriedly and Tanya Burke said, "Don't you dare, you bastard." And: "Ajax, down!"

Ajax slid to a slavering, unhappy halt and, paw-before-paw, stretched out on the ground, whining.

"What are you doing here, Nichols?" Tamara Burke demanded angrily.

Everything about her was too damned perfect. She was too pretty, too rumpled, too obviously roused from sleep.

"You alone, Burke?" Suspicion kept Nichols alive.

"At the moment." The women crossed her arms over breasts whose nipples were rising in the cold under her thin chemise.

"You didn't check in," said Nichols uncomfortably, his eyes still riveted to her breasts, pressed firmly by her arms.

"This is the first sleep I've had," she said with a strained, game smile. "Enkidu . . . well, I'm doing my job, what I was assigned to do." She shrugged. "Gilgamesh doesn't like modern equipment, and he's not the only one around here who's suspicious, so I ditched the lot."

"That was dumb." Nichols wanted to get out of here, give her the message and be done with it. But the woman was showing signs of stress, real or feigned, and he had to know which.

"I knew you wouldn't leave me. I can't guarantee anything. . . . They went up the mountain, Gilgamesh and Enkidu. They haven't come back. I think Enkidu will, though—for me. He promised." She darted a look at the dog, then at their immediate surroundings. Content that no one was paying undue attention to them, she leaned closer, her knees now up against her chest.

Nichols leaned in too, and put a hand on one of her bare knees. "Welch wants one Sumerian aboard the chopper—he doesn't care which. Doesn't want to kill 'em. Can't imagine it's more than ethics, though, if things get tough—" He safed his service pistol, still in his hand, and held it out to her, butt first.

It was a sacrifice she obviously didn't understand, or appreciate.

She shook her head; her hair flew around her face; she bit her lip: "No, Nichols, if Gilgamesh found that . . ." Then the rest of what he'd said sank in. "Look, I haven't seen anything more incriminating that lots of pack animals with nothing to carry. We might be way off base here. And what do you mean, 'wants one Sumerian aboard the chopper'?"

"Let me explain," Nichols suggested. "We don't have much time."

The timer on the explosives was set for ten minutes from now, if he didn't intervene with a radioed signal. And he didn't think he would. These primitives were going to read it as a minor earthquake; they were out of sight of the blast, anyway. And, whether Achilles was somebody's spoiler or not, this mission was going to go perfectly, or Nichols was going to know the reason why.

When luck had given him a handle on the ChiCom problem at the waterfall, pajamas and all, he'd known he was going to win this one.

All that remained in question was whether Tamara Burke, here, and her Sumerian boyfriend lived through it or got back to Reassignments the hard way.

Nichols didn't really care which. It would be interesting to see the look on Achilles' face, however things turned out.

He returned his attention to the business at hand: briefing Burke; getting out unseen; using the extraction beacon Welch had given him from a safe LZ as far as possible from the waterfall and the imminent destruction there.

A few minutes later, headed upslope on the far side of camp, he heard and felt the explosion and his heart lifted. Behind him, the caravan folk were running around nervously and dogs were barking, but there was no attempt to mount a show of force, no sign that foul play was suspected.

He'd have liked to have some drugs to show, but he had an ex-waterfall, a blocked tunnel, and a new hole to show, and likely some dead guys.

And, most important, it had worked: nobody had found and disarmed Nichols' explosive ordnance; nobody had stopped his show. Now he just had to make the other side of the hill and wait for pickup. Sometimes, Hell wasn't any worse than life had been. At least, not life as Nichols remembered it.

Enkidu was among the chaos of the caravan when the bird descended on a roaring gale from Heaven.

He had been down on his knees, talking with a dog; barking at the round-eyed hound who barked at him. The dog belonged to the woman of the caravan whose wagon was painted red and gold, with golden silks draping it.

This dog had been barking, "Enkidu! Beware! Danger! Intruder!" Enkidu, who had been like a wild beast in life, who had been lord of the forest and ravager of its game, had barked back, insulted. He, Enkidu, was no intruder and at the dog's bark he had taken offense.

So they had been readying to battle it out there and then, Enkidu and this impolite dog who called him an intruder, when the bird began its descent and the silks on its owner's wagon blew wildly.

If Gilgamesh had been with Enkidu, things might have gone differently. Enkidu would not have been down on his knees in the dirt, barking loudly about how he would bite out the throat of this impudent dog as surely as he, Enkidu, was covered with hair. Enkidu would have been standing upright, like a man; thinking canny thoughts, like a man.

But Gilgamesh had gone to the edge of the Sea of Sighs to greet the magnificent boat with its dolphin's prow and scarlet sail that had come from Pompeii. Gilgamesh had gone aboard the boat to secure passage to the city for them both, leaving Enkidu to wait alone.

Long hours had Enkidu waited, and then gone back up the shore to where the caravan made its camp. Gilgamesh, king of long lost Uruk, would come to find Enkidu when he was ready. And then Enkidu must put the caravan woman by, forget her ivory thighs and pommegranate lips, and go with Gilgamesh onto the boat and into the wondrous city beyond.

Until then, Enkidu had it in his mind to make love to

the woman upon her flocked couch. But the dog of the
woman had scratched at his spiked collar with a clawed
hind foot and bristled his brindle fur and barked harsh
words at Enkidu, while his mistress stayed inside her
wagon, as if she heard nothing of the argument taking
place outside.

So now, as people scattered and hid their faces in the
dirt while the dog tucked his tail between his legs and
his furry body underneath the wagon, only Enkidu
remained in the clearing to brave the buffeting wind
and howling cries of the black bird that descended upon
them, scattering dust and scraps and detritus in every
direction.

Enkidu put a hairy arm over his hairy brow and
squinted at this manifestation, wishing that Gilgamesh,
to whom all secrets had been revealed, was beside
him to read this omen.

Since Gilgamesh was not there, Enkidu did as he
pleased in the face of the unknowable: he straightened
up his great body, like a wild beast protecting its territory in the forest.

Enkidu spread his legs wide and crossed his mighty
arms and leaned into the gale come from this black bird
from Heaven—or from some other Hell—and then he
waited.

Enkidu did not need Gilgamesh to tell him what was
right. Enkidu did not need the cowardly dog who whined
behind the wagon wheels. Enkidu could protect this
woman, this dog, this caravan, this territory, by himself.

Privately, Enkidu wished he had a weapon, for the
bird was twice the height of Gilgamesh and as long as
three caravan wagons. But he did not have a weapon,
because Gilgamesh despised the weapons of the New
Dead and Enkidu loved Gilgamesh, whom the gods had
decreed was wiser than he.

Not even Gilgamesh, Enkidu thought as the belly of
the bird opened wide, would have known this bird by
name or what words to say to gain power over it.

Nor was Gilgamesh here, Enkidu reminded himself,

wishing he was not wishing his friend was here to tell him what to do as a man came out of the belly of the bird whose awful breath was blinding and whose terrible roar was deafening.

Because the bird's roar was so loud, Enkidu did not see or hear the woman come out of her silk-topped wagon until she touched his arm.

He looked down at the woman whose red lips said, "Enkidu, come with me. Ask no questions." Her hands tugged on Enkidu's mighty arm, pulling him toward the bird out of which the man had come.

And that man was running toward them, gesticulating, yelling: "Tamara, come on! Bring him or forget him. Time's up," in English.

The woman jerked hard on Enkidu's arm and pleaded with him, saying, "Enkidu, my hero, you are not afraid of that chariot without horses, are you? Come with me, where wonders abound, if you are brave. But if you are a coward, kiss me goodbye and stay behind!"

Her blond hair whipped around her face in the gale as her pale eyes searched his for an answer and behind them, the once-proud dog began to howl.

"But Gilgamesh . . ." Enkidu shouted back as the man stopped and waved again—a man dressed in the colors of the land and with furrows on his brow, a man as tall as Gilgamesh and as bold, for he had come from the belly of the bird.

"Enkidu," pleaded the woman, releasing his arm and running toward the other man. Halfway there, she halted and looked back: "Enkidu, come! Let me save your life!"

The man beyond the woman wore weapons about his person, fine weapons of the most powerful kind. In one hand he held a plasma rifle; around his neck hung far-seeing goggles.

His other hand was outstretched, beckoning Enkidu with a gesture all men understood. Then he grabbed for the woman and jerked her abruptly toward him.

Words were exchanged between them and the man

dragged the caravan woman away, toward the belly of the bird while, all around, the caravanners huddled in fear and none lifted a hand to help her.

Behind Enkidu, under the wagon, her dog began to keen.

Enkidu ran toward the black bird with wide strides, strides that ate up the distance and brought him to the bird's side as the other man and the woman reached it.

There the noise was too great for speech and the wind too fierce for open eyes. Squinting, Enkidu saw the woman clamber up into the dark belly of the bird and reach back with her white arm, her fine fingers outstretched to him.

Her mouth was open. She was calling his name. She wanted him to jump into the belly of the bird with her.

And while all the people and the dog with whom he'd just argued were watching, Enkidu made his decision. He went up to the bird. He touched the bird's side, and found it to be metal. He grabbed the bird's feet, and found handholds there.

He climbed into the bird of metal, into the dark and stinking shadows of its belly, and there he took the woman in his arms.

"Nice job, Tanya," said the man who wore the colors of the land. "Better get him away from the window. He's not going to like the rest of this."

The woman from the caravan cooed at Enkidu and pulled him gently toward a couch among a magical wall of temple lights while, outside, the noise became unbearable.

Enkidu jumped up from the couch and ran to the place where he'd entered the belly of the bird, but there was no opening there. He ran along the wall until he came to a window, and there he paused.

Outside, the ground was becoming tiny and on it people were falling. From their bodies, blood was pouring. From the wagons, flame was spouting. From his vantage in the belly of the bird rising up into the sky, Enkidu could see it all.

And he could separate the sounds now, those he heard. One sound was that of the bird rising toward the sky, but the other sound was more terrible. The other sound was that of chain guns and cannon, of automatic-weapons fire strafing the caravanners' camp below.

When the bird had risen high enough, Enkidu glimpsed the island where Gilgamesh had gone. It was beautiful and magical and colored like a rainbow; in its center the mouth of a demon belched smoke and fire.

Enkidu felt remorse that Gilgamesh was not with him, in the belly of the bird. But the caravan woman was telling him how lucky he was to be alive, and how many wonders he would see when the bird reached its destination.

"And weapons, Enkidu, such as you have never had in your hands," said the woman called Tanya.

"But what of Gilgamesh?" said Enkidu. "My friend Gilgamesh was to come back for me, and we were to enter the city together."

"You're lucky you're alive, buddy," said a man whose torso was black to the tops of his arms. "Stay away from drug runners in future. As for your friend, Gil,"—the man bared the perfect white teeth of the New Dead—"Reassignments'll decide when and whether you hook up with him again, because that's where you're going, Mister—Reassignments in New Hell." As he said this, the man took out a pistol and began fondling it. Behind him, Enkidu could see shifting lights and glowing ob-longs, like windows into other worlds.

"Reassignments?" asked Enkidu with a frown.

"Nichols!" protested the woman from the caravan at the same time. Then she put her hand upon Enkidu and began to soothe him, promising all and everything she could do to make life better for him in a strange new land.

When Gilgamesh was put ashore by the dolphin-prowed boat of the Pompeiians, he looked everywhere along the beach for Enkidu and did not find him. So

Gilgamesh trekked up the shore, toward the caravan's encampment, where Enkidu surely must have gone.

Joy was in Gilgamesh's heart. He was anxious to find Enkidu and tell him of the wonders he had seen. Behind him, the boat awaited, compliments of Sulla, Pompeii's ruler, to bring both heros over the water to the city.

Gilgamesh had learned that Pompeii had not always been an island; parts of its shoreline were now submerged, a danger to ships. This Sulla was a Roman who had designated the city a colony for his war-weary veterans. There were many heroes on the island, and people of magical inclination like Greeks and Etruscans as well.

Quickly did Gilgamesh stride the distance to the camp, imagining the joy in Enkidu's face when he told him of the warm welcome they would receive in the city.

And when Gilgamesh told him another thing: this Sulla had said to Gilgamesh, "Gilgamesh, great king of Uruk? What are you doing so far from home?"

In the eyes of this Sulla, a Roman of soldierly bearing with a head nearly bereft of hair, had been no treachery, only a politician's caution.

Startled, Gilgamesh had replied, "What do you mean, Sulla? Uruk is lost to the ages. I have not seen its streets or slept in its fortress since I . . . died there." A sadness was in his voice, thinking of lost Uruk, the city of his life.

At that, Sulla queried him piercingly until, satisfied that Gilgamesh spoke the truth, he said, "I believe you, Gilgamesh. There is a false lord in Uruk, then—or another lord, at any rate. My men are tired, biding on this island, of small squabbles and small adventures. Should you and your friend, Enkidu, decide to return to Uruk, to regain your rightful places there, I might be persuaded to help you." And then a canny glimmer came into the eyes of Sulla. "Of course, we would have to know just where in the land this Uruk lies."

So Gilgamesh had replied truthfully that he did not know where in all the land Uruk was situated, that he had never come upon it in his wanderings.

And the Roman had told him then of the fabled treasures of long-lost Uruk, and offered again to help him find his home.

Such good news did Gilgamesh have for Enkidu, that he did not notice the quiet until he was upon the very camp itself.

There he saw scattered bodies, ruined wagons, and such destruction as made him cover up his eyes.

Taking his hands away, Gilgamesh ran through the camp, calling out for Enkidu.

But Enkidu was nowhere in the camp. It was if the ground had swallowed him up, as if the demons had taken him, as if he had never been. Body after body did Gilgamesh turn face up in the dirt, but none of these were Enkidu.

After many lamentations, when Gilgamesh was exhausted in his grief, he sank down beside the ruined red-and-yellow wagon of the woman Enkidu had loved. And there he waited.

Perhaps Enkidu had gone hunting. Perhaps he had not come back to camp at all. Perhaps he would come back, if Gilgamesh waited long enough.

With a throat raw from lamentation, Enkidu sat there in the dust and watched the bodies of the dead around him disappear: some burst into flame, and those moved as if alive while they burned; some became like water and soaked into the soil; some melted like tallow over a flame; some simply disappeared.

While he was waiting for Enkidu to return, thinking of the dolphin-prowed ship at anchor, ready to take them to the island of Pompeii, Gilgamesh heard a sound.

A cry. A whine. A mewling sob of pain.

Up rose Gilgamesh, searching out the source of this heart-rending cry, and found a dog, underneath the woman's wagon, bleeding from his neck and from his right forepaw.

Gilgamesh knew this dog, whom the woman called Ajax, although Enkidu had told him the dog did not recognize that name. He said, "Dog! Ajax dog, I am Gilgamesh to whom all secrets have been revealed! I can heal you if you let me touch you. Do not bite me, dog."

The dog raised his muzzle and bared his teeth as Gilgamesh reached for him. Then he sighed a heavy sigh and put his head down on his unwounded paw so that Gilgamesh could touch him.

When Gilgamesh touched the dog, it quivered and then it closed its eyes. When Gilgamesh cleaned the dog's wounds and dressed them with unguents from the woman's wagon, the dog cried but did not bite him. When Gilgamesh bound the dog's wounds with strips of yellow silk from the wagon's curtains, the dog wagged its weary tail.

When it was clear that Enkidu was not returning to the caravan, the king of Uruk picked up the dog called Ajax in his arms and carried it to the boat waiting to take them to Pompeii.

So did Gilgamesh set sail for the magical city, with a wounded dog for his companion, and from there, perhaps, to trek to long-lost Uruk. And because Enkidu was no longer with him, Gilgamesh stroked the dog and told it everything he would have told Enkidu of the adventures awaiting them.

Gilgamesh did this with a heart that was heavy, but not unbearably heavy. Enkidu had gone off with the caravan woman, this was certain: neither of their bodies were among the slain.

Gilgamesh, like Enkidu, was not alone.

CRUSADERS IN LOVE

Bill Kerby

Hey, wait a minute, who the hell is this Lefty Armbruster, anyway? Am I suppose to know him? My answering service is about to go ape; he just keeps calling.

This is not exactly the choicest time to be bugging me for favors, either. I'm not the kind of guy who doesn't remember who he's been, believe me. But all of a sudden Robin and I are flooded with attention—we are on the "A-list," everybody's new best friend. We go down to City Cafe and every head turns. They want us to be celebrity judges on *Dance Fever*. We stand in a movie line and the guy comes out and takes us right in. Free popcorn, too. My lawyer finally returns my calls. Suddenly, it doesn't seem to be my turn in the rain barrel anymore, as the old saying goes.

When I came to this weird beard town, I hadn't exactly fallen off the turnip truck. I'd been in the Marine Corps standing tall (I will walk my post in a military manner, keeping always on the alert, and observing everything that takes place within sight or hearing, sir!), struggled in New York as a starving actor (my hottest moment was when Morty himself, drunker than a skunk, tried to pick me up in F.A.O. Schwartz), plus I got involved in some semi-shady stuff which I'll tell you about later, okay?

But how the hell can you prepare yourself for L.A.? It's sixty-two miles wide at one point, every living soul in it is on the make if we're going to be honest about it, and there are—by actual count—more Mercedeses than there are Plymouths! Go figure. The weather's always nice, and half the people give you that empty grin and tell you to have a nice day, while the other half are cutting your heart out with a rusty hacksaw. They got championship sports, championship business, and championship pussy. If it's Wednesday where you are, I don't care, it's already Saturday out here! At the top, you can go anywhere, do anything, be anybody. And at the very bottom, you know in your soul that you've come as far as you can go in continental limits before you've run out of plans. This is IT, babeee. Last chance saloon.

So you get a car, you start hanging out, and you do the breast stroke through the panic and dead dreams of the jerks at the bar. Everywhere you look, mirrors. You can see yourself. Or you can be yourself.

Bo, it's sad.

Time: 3:30 A.M. Monday, April 10. Los Angeles Police Department, Officers Fishbeck and McConnell, North Hollywood Division. Automobile A was traveling south on Laurel Canyon Boulevard at a high rate of speed. It was a 1958 Triumph convertible, red in color with a tan leather interior. It was not equipped with safety belts. Skid marks indicated that automobile A had crossed the double yellow lines just south of Croft Street, which intersects Laurel Canyon Boulevard to the east. The weather was clear, the pavement was dry. Automobile B was a 1984 Jaguar X-6 sedan, green in color, with a green leather interior. Safety harnesses were employed. Vehicle B was traveling north at a normal rate of speed when it was impacted by vehicle A. There were two witnesses, whose names and statements are listed below. After the emergency paramedics were summoned by Officer Fishbeck, and the fire was extinguished, a cursory search was conducted of what was left of vehicle A. A bottle of Herra Dura tequila was found, still intact, along with cocaine paraphernalia. Also in the glove compartment was what appeared to be a large electric dildo with the inscribed words, "Look, Ma, top of the world!"

Robin and I had just bought a sensational old mock-Norman Tudor castle-type house—small, but pasta perfecto—way up on Laurel Canyon in the Hollywood Hills. Three bedrooms, a steel spiked portcullis, a cathedral ceiling in the living room, hardwood floors, a ten horsepower disposal, a view to everywhere, and a pink and black marble master bath with a Speakman shower head! It's only heaven, pal.

But it wasn't easy finding it. I mean, you got Iranians in track shoes trying to get the good ones. Or developers laundering drug money, or the worst: the trust fund casualties. They buy them up, maybe redecorate, and just sit on them until the price is right. Robin and I must have looked at two hundred houses, from the Valley to Olympic, from the ocean to Pasadena. We'd get the *Times*, make a big pot of double French roast coffee, and let our fingers do the walking through the real estate section. That was back when we had dreams. Before all this meshuga.

When I got to L.A. I had trouble, just like everyone else. But with some hard work (so to speak; more about that later) and some good luck, I found myself taking care of some kids who belonged to this old-time producer in Beverly Hills.

He was a sweet guy—looked like a leprechaun, stole like a bandit, and drank like the Commies were rolling into Santa Monica. The guy'd won an Oscar for some movie that I never saw, but my buddy, who did, told me it was short and boring with no tits and no gunfights— just two fat-ass losers from Brooklyn sitting in a kitchen talking. Different strokes, I guess.

Anyway, this producer guy didn't know how to deal with his own kids. He loved them true but, like most power brokers out here, he was scared of them. So I took over the education of three of the meanest, best looking, smartest little ferrets you ever saw. They had names, but I called them "Moe," "Larry," and "Curly."

I taught them how to climb trees. I taught them how to play tennis. I taught them how to roll joints. I taught them how to make crib sheets. I taught them how to swim, how to ride, and how to lie so even your own mother couldn't tell. Hey, these were good little cookies, and they deserved my best shot. Besides, accidentally, I was getting pretty tight with their mom, a wild Norwegian broad who taught me not to carry a wallet because it ruined the bun lines on my tight whites. She should've been a pro, not a mom. Definitely.

One day I came over and the house was locked up. My boss was sitting on the front porch, drinking out of a bottle of aquavit, grinning into a bright, chirpy morning. He said his wife and a small hit squad of lawyers had gotten there at sunup. They had served him the divorce papers, then seized the house and contents. He showed me his Oscar, proud they hadn't got that, too.

That afternoon, we went to work at Warner Brothers. He had two tiny offices in the Writers Building, where he made phone calls, drank, coasted on his dimming reputation, and tried to put together projects for which Warners got "first look."

I started out as a reader for him. I read novels, magazines, plays—anything with print, it seemed—to see if there was a movie idea in it. Hollywood is the only economic system I ever heard of that is this suicidal: They have the basis for their life's blood—screenplays—read and analyzed by unqualified, jealous, illit-

erate jerkoffs like me. Then, the studio's current
high-rolling bigshots scan the one-page "coverage" which,
by the time they get it, has been Xeroxed so many
times it's dark gray. After they see whether it's a project they might shoehorn one of their play-or-pay stars
into, they then commit somewhere between ten and
thirty million dollars and two hundred lives to it. All
because some pear-shaped wimp in a windowless room
who, basically, gets paid by the cord, says yes or no.
Smart, huh? And get this—the bigshots, who may be
buttholes but are not stupid, know exactly how kami-
kaze their system. They chuckle about it to each other
over sixty dollar hot lobster salads at lunch. It's a great
business. If you're a moron.

Anyway, after a while, I got bored reading; they
never made one of MY movies. I recommended this
one to them—I did everything but go in and tap dance
it—and they passed. It went back to its producer on
turn-around, he took it to Universal who made it, and it
grossed over a hundred million. By law, I can't tell you
which one it was, they could sue me. They would, too.
Movie executives can be real snakes, especially the
piranhas in legal and business affairs.

My office was nice and all. I made my own hours, I
liked my boss, and the work wasn't that hard. But it
sucked in the rewarding department and the bottom
line is that you have to dig what you do, if you're going
to do it well.

So when Bart Lopat, the famous old stunt gaffer-
turned-director came in for a meeting with my boss, I
struck up a friendship. Time passes. One day, I get a
call from Lopat, who is shooting this flick in Portland.

I liked being a stuntman lots better than being in the
story department. For one thing, it was mostly out-
doors. They started me off slow—fight scenes, simple
one-story falls, like that. I doubled Burt Reynolds up
there in Oregon and later, Jim Garner down in Mexico.
It was great. Real guys (none of your Volvo-driving Alan
Alda types) doing real-guy stuff like jumping off trains

or falling off cliffs into icy rivers. Drink all night and sit around all day. That's pretty much what studio movie-making is all about. But it was good money and that's where I met the Fatman.

He was a legend, even among the stuntmen. He had been one of the great ones, way back when. But he'd fused half his spine on a high fall gag in *How The West Was Won* and had to retire. That's when he discovered food and began getting fat. He didn't begin to get rich until he discovered his housekeeper, who had a real good set on her and the morals of a Moroccan goat. He changed her name to Sheenya Deep and turned her into a porno star.

Now, the Fatman was (outside of the Mafia) the biggest producer of adult films in town. He did *Citizen Kum* and *The Maltese Phallus*, among others. The guy's famous.

One afternoon (he'd come down on location just to hang out with the old gang), we were taking a whizz together in the honeywagon porta-potty, and—what can I tell you—the next day, I was in pornos.

When I started out, it was only on weekends. The bucks were good and I hate Sundays, anyway. Everything is closed and TV is mostly golf (barfo-matic) and political shit. The big surprise to me was that the folks who did dirty movies are nice. They are kind (if not real bright), and considering they screw for a living, they are decent, honest people.

I had a few fairly rare attributes, which I don't think is really necessary to go into here, but suffice it to say, pretty soon they wanted me full-time. So, what the hell. First I did five days. Then, seven. It's easy work and all, but when push comes to flog, it's demeaning.

So when that rag, *The L.A. Express*, published my daily diary in weekly installments, my phone didn't stop ringing. They called me the new Nathanael West, whoever he is. All I did was tell the truth, pretty much. I was tired of being a sex object! Plus which, my real sex life was beginning to drag. And I was getting bored with in-and-out, in-and-out—an endless routine only broken up by pompously dramatic blow jobs from girls with the mentality of an after-dinner mint.

So I took an early retirement and went to work for this guy, a real Hollywood operator, who I met at the Farmers market. He wore a pinky ring and had a hotcomb plugged into the lighter of his midnight-blue Eldo. He bragged that he'd been on every Writer's Guild strike-list since 1967.

He'd read in the trade papers about some movie about to be made that sounded good. Like one about an earthquake or soldier ants that take over Dayton. Then, he'd go to one of the typing services, the ones that specialize in scripts, and he'd bribe some 100 word-per-minute dork typist and he'd come home with a copy. Here's where I came in.

I rewrote them, scene for scene, changing all the names and places and dialogue. Where it would say "thousands of people are killed," I'd change it to "five people are killed." And where some poofter writer would be describing the hero as Clint Eastwood, I'd change it to Brad Dillman or George Maharis. Then, my boss would take and sell it under the table to some TV company for ten grand and they'd try to make it. We averaged three of these a week. Slick, huh?

But it got grueling, even though I learned to type fast. So, as my sex life got back to normal, I began to look around again for something new. That was when I got into network television.

I had some things on *The Mod Squad*, *Starsky and Hutch*, and a few movies-of-the-week. I did the pilot for "Manimal," even though I lost the credit in a screwjob arbitration. They fucked the show up. My script was incredible.

Anyway, these days, I sell a little coke, although the business is not exactly growth anymore. Not like it used to be. Before Jane Fonda's belly muscles and that workout tape, before tofu and Perrier got hip. But it still keeps me in enough bucks so I don't have to steal

scripts or do wet loops anymore. Those days were the
pits, I mean it. You look at those hunkie guys hunched
over and covered with baby oil, blowing their rocks all
over the place, you probably think they're just country
boys with a double-digit I.Q. and no dream. But hey,
one of them was me. So now you know you were
wrong.

My life turned a corner into daylight the night I met
Robin Lamoureaux.

I'd seen her, sure. Who hadn't? Three Emmys for
Nighttime; she was so great, it gives me goose bumps
to think about it. Remember her on the Donahue show
when she got him to sing "Danny Boy" and he cried?
Robin had been a semi-well-known character actress for
years. She'd show up in the middle of the second act
and get all the reviews by critics, who always forgot her
name. They called her Cloris Leachman or Katherine
Helmond or Kim Stanley. But until *Nighttime*, her
series, she was just another sagging pair of tits with a
haunting look and crow's feet.

Robin is older than I am. It's no secret—lots older.
But, bubba, I am here to tell you, when we are on our
new deck in the late afternoon, looking across the brown
stink to where Catalina used to be, when I have my
arms around her, whatever years may have separated
her and my birth don't mean squat because this woman
is my mother, my lover, my pal, my advisor, my slave,
my master, and I don't see any wrinkles or scars or
bridgework or anything on this beautiful creature who
basically saved the life of one ex-stuntman porno star
who was about to get ate by the coyotes and shit over a
cliff: me.

Did I get double parked in that last sentence?

Shawn, our real estate guy, told us our house was
originally the guest house or gate house or something
for Errol Flynn. I had to change pants. I've seen *Captain Blood* maybe fifty times. Know every line, say 'em
right along with Flynn. Folks love it at parties when we
all get ripped. I even starred in a take off on it in the

old days, called *Captain Wad.* I'll let you figure out
why.

Robin and I needed some help decorating the place
when we moved in. We'd just come from a tiny studio
apartment on Sycamore that looked like a hamster war-
ren that tunneled through cardboard boxes. If we hadn't
been so much in love, we'd have axe-murdered each
other. In the old place, if you put the key in the door
too hard, you broke a window. I'm serious.

So anyway, when Robin's lawyers finally called and
told her the network had settled out at just under a
million five (she had to sue for her points when they
syndicated her show, those goniffs), we decided to go
for the gusto. Everybody else we knew had a house.
So, this lookie loo became a buyie loo. Our real estate
agent was primarily dealing hot antiques; the poor guy
didn't even know how to fill out the papers. And, I
mean, you won't believe this luck—he was just getting
evicted from his place, so we told him that he could live
in the little mother-in-law apartment in the back. Shawn
was so grateful, he kind of stuck it to his client by
blurting out that it was some guy who was about to get
dragged through a greasy divorce and wanted to unload
the house for bupkes just to piss his ex-wife off. What a
break for us. You hear about these things but it always
happens to somebody named Ed you don't even know.
Me and Shawn probably screwed his old lady out of
a hundred grand! But I didn't see any reason to tell
Robin. She's such a softie. It's one of the reasons I love
her so much.

The only thing wrong with the place were the tel-
phones. It was crazy, Marx Brothers. Lines would cross.
You'd be talking and you'd hear some guy in German,
or it'd just go dead. The phones would ring and there
wouldn't be anybody there. Your friends would tell you
they'd called and it rang and rang. One night, somehow
I got patched into a call between these two chicks; one
sounded like Candy Bergen with those funny "r"s she
has. Jesus, they were slagging some guy who had fucked

their sister or something. They were dishing, I tell you! I'm gonna put it in a script. Just grist for the mill. It's the price you pay when you're a writer. Nothing seems real.

Especially anymore.

Robin and I had been coming pretty fast up the valley side of Laurel Canyon. It was about three in the morning. Maybe I was a little drunk, so before we started out, I sharpened up with a tootsky or two. I don't generally drive when I'm blitzed. In this city you got to be careful of the wackos who turn in front of you or cut you off or just jam on their brakes for drill.

We were in Robin's cherry '58 Triumph, a red four-banger with leather seats, and I was singing along to Don Henley like always. Robin was smiling, happy as a clam. Everything was jake; I was on top of the world. Only we never even got to the top of Mulholland.

Some buttface in a Jag crossed the line—one of us did, anyway—and when we woke up, we were out of surgery, out of danger, and out of our minds on Percodan. Wheee-ow! They had me and Robin in the same hospital room, me closer to the door, which was a good thing because everybody and his brother had to come get a look at the Emmy-winning star of *Nighttime* and I finally had to get tough. When Robin was asleep (which was much of the time), I collected five bucks a crack. People are ghouls, in case you hadn't noticed.

Both of us recovered unusually fast. Three broken legs between us, assorted cuts and bruises, and my scalp was lacerated, but in back where it didn't show. Robin's face was untouched. Which was a good thing. Suddenly, her agent began to call every day; when it rains it pours.

Seems the wreck had made the papers. Her little Triumph was so mooshed they were actually thinking of taking it on tour, a Be Careful Or This Is What Happens kind of thing. When the reporters found it was THE Robin Lamoureaux, the star-making machinery went into overdrive. We drew the line, though, at *Life Styles of the Rich and Famous*.

Suddenly, with all this new-found pub, the network wanted her. Bad. One of their over-educated young salvors, fresh from Stanford or Harvard, with history's mysteries still in his mind, had come up with an idea for a new show. The network had a big, big hole on Thursday night at ten. Faced with *Hell Street* and *Dallasty*, they had taken nothing but gas for two years. The trades began calling the slot Suicide Alley. Until this kid and his idea. Later I saw a Xerox of his treatment. This was it:

"RICHARD & BLONDIE

The Crusades! . . . . . Insanity! . . . . . Mayhem! . . . . . Family against family—BANG—children slaughtered wholesale in color—BANG—they love, they kiss, they betray—BANG—Richard the Lion-Hearted rescued from his dungeon by Blondie de Nesle, the wandering torch singer from France— BANG—they ran, they searched, they killed, they made love on the fly—BANG—as the crusaders hacked and slashed their way to hell's very gate in the name of Goodness and Mercy—BANG—exteriors to be filmed on location with a cast of thousands and interiors shot in studio, three camera, live audience! A love story for all time. Especially ten o'clock, Thursdays."

I hated to admit it, but the guy was a great writer. And it was a killer idea. It was the one area that series TV had never used—probably because of the mammoth costs involved. But they hadn't had the idea to use the long-shot battle scenes in the old Crusader movies they owned from the fifties, like *Black Shield of Fallsworth*, *Ivanhoe*, and them. Then, with a technical trick they call roto-scoping, they "blend" the star into the action. He's half a mile away, slashing through Arabs and shit, who sees details?

Why hadn't I thought of this? Sometimes I'm really kind of a tight-ass; I should have taken more acid in '70, loosened up the brain cells. I mean, you can't think of these quantum jump jobbies just eating your basic food groups.

When the network guys looked into the Crusades, they began to get horny in spite of the costs. Richard the Lion-Hearted was a historical cross between Dirty Harry and that Shakespeare guy who ended up carving up his whole family. I don't have to tell you; TV majors in this kind of stuff.

They wanted Robin for the part of Blondie de Nesle. It didn't matter to them that they would have to make a sex change, switching it from a "he" to a "she"—that in actual fact, Blondel de Nesle had been a male ballad-eer. They figured, probably correctly, that America was not quite ready for a costumed action-romance show costing three million an episode that was about a couple of historical turd burglars.

Which was lucky for us, huh? In a few days, the network started sending flowers, and before the casts were changed, our hospital room began to look like Forest Lawn or Graceland, maybe. It was weird. Robin had pretty much made up her mind not to do *Richard and Blondie*. She wanted to stay home, help me out on my porno exposé novel, be my baby, my inspiration, and like that. It all sounded tits to me until I got an idea one afternoon between *This Was Your Life* and *As the World Burns*.

Maybe we could have our apple pie and eat it, too. We wanted to be together, creating. It was our destiny, what can I tell you. I figured if the network wanted Robin bad enough, hey, they could hire yours truly for the first-draft teleplay! I had credits, I had network visibility (having sold blow to most of the execs at one time or another), and I had their Blondie!

Needless to say, Robin thought it was a sensational idea. I mean, if you can't blackmail a television network, who can you blackmail? Those quaking, suntanned, excitable smurfs wouldn't know writing talent if it jumped up and bit them on their collective blue-suited ass. They don't want it good, they want it Tuesday.

I was going to be the kid who saw that they got both. Little did I know . . .

Witnesses to the accident were David Holman and his wife Judith Mabry, both from Hollywood. Holman and Mabry were in their nonoperative Porsche coupe, which had been pulled off on the west side of Laurel Canyon Boulevard, just north of Croft, where they waited for the auto club tow truck they had summoned. At approximately three A.M., they heard a loud engine noise and turned to observe the accident.

Holman: "We were just sitting there, talking about the vicissitudes of show business in general and the disastrous party from which we had just come in particular. When we heard the howl of an engine and the squealing of tires behind us, of course we both looked around. We were terrified. I mean, we were sitting on the side of the road where the whole section of streetlights had been taken out by that mudslide last month. We were in darkness, and my Porsche is so old it barely has headlights, much less safety flashers. I thought we were going to be annihilated when I heard that car!"

Mabry: "Where David usually tends to overdramatize, like most writers, this time, he is being completely accurate. That party had been rotten. And we were chilled by the sound of the car. I think I screamed, I don't really know . . ."

Holman: "When the little Triumph crossed over the double yellow lines and headed toward that poor schlamozzle in the Jag . . . it was like slow motion . . . I knew this was real life and not some special effect. For a moment, I thought I could see the faces in the Triumph; they seemed so happy, so bright—they were laughing. . . ."

The witnesses both identified vehicle A and vehicle B on the hastily drawn map that Officer McConnell had

prepared as a standard amendment for this report and
they were signed and witnessed by Officer McConnell
and myself. The attached standard Polaroids were taken
as soon as the para-medics had removed all parties and
before either of the two vehicles in question could be
moved. Vehicle A was subsequently pilfered and stripped
clean by party or parties unknown as that vehicle contained a person classified as a class B celebrity, one
Roberta Wankowski, a.k.a. Robin Lamoureaux. The driver
at the time of this report is still unidentified.

Me and Robin's meeting at the network was for lunch,
there, at 2 P.M. We parked the rent-a-wreck down in
the bowels of the underground parking garage, level H.
I always remember what level we're on, even though
they're all identical; Robin always bets that I won't
remember and always loses. It's easy. A stands for
asshole. B stands for bastard, C for crap, D for damn, E
for euphemism, F for fuck, G for goddamn, H for hell,
and so on. That day we were in hell.

The network reception area is open up to the fourth
floor—glass from the parquet floor to the vaulted oak
ceiling, and so many plants and trees and stuff that it
looks like a John Wayne World War II movie. That day,
the light in there was stranger than usual, too—sort of
thick, it hurt our eyes. It didn't seem to bother anybody else, but Robin and I had to keep our Vuarnets
on.

Through the big double maple doors, the network's
inner offices are sort of like if Hugh Hefner was going
to rebuild the Palace of Versailles—opulent space vistas
with little doll groupings of modern oak desks and
chrome and black leather couches. Famous French artists like Picasso, and I mean original, too. Not prints.
My theory is that it's all designed to get you to feel like
shit, like you're not worth being there in all that money
and class and taste. Once they see your eyes fall and
your head dip, they jump on you and ream you out.
You're dead meat before you hit the floor.

So, here's how a meeting with the honchos of What You See on Television goes. Ready? First, everybody mills around out in front of the office, bumping into each other, shaking hands (a few air-kisses, maybe), while the secretary finds out who wants what in the way of coffee. Then, when the one-line jokes and light ribbing about the new sport coat or the new poundage stop, everyone files into the office and quickly looks for a Power Seat. One near a phone if possible, not too low—you don't want to be peering up at them through your knees—alone, not on a couch but next to a table where you can take notes and set your coffee and, finally, someplace where you can eyeball the door so that if anyone is about to come in, you know who and when.

Then, right after the embarrassing pause that always follows the Big Sit Down, you (or someone on your team) should lean in and say, "All right, guys, here's what we want." And then, you run it down to them, quick and sweet. This direct approach lets everybody know that you are there to help and are willing to wait until a quick, simple deal is cut. Then comes the exit japes, with a few departing light social promises which no one intends to keep, while everybody lines up at the receptionist's desk to look at her tits and get a parking ticket validated.

Some guys at TRW or somewhere a few years back figured that this approach works 78 percent of the time.

And it worked that day.

"We are willing to begin discussions about the Crusader project," said Stu Rosenberg, Robin's new agent, "but only if we have a verbal agreement for a quarter million dollars per episode."

Chip Russell, the WASP network exec, looked up from his Bass Weejuns. A smile crossed his face.

Stu went on. "There is something else that will impact the project and you might as well know right now." Stu turned to me.

"I'm in . . . and I'm gonna do my own deal," I said

(my agent had disappeared; I think he went down in a coke bust), "which is real simple: as long as Robin is involved, I write every word."

Our side grinned, their side went bugfuck.

Apparently, they thought I was just along for ballast. One network guy, Buddy Wickwire, a squeem with a weight lifter's build and bad breath, had been a honcho on a movie-of-the-week of mine and we hated each other. Besides having his, uhhh, roommate rewrite me, Buddy had burned me in a gram deal. The guy was a sleaze; I even heard he had AIDS. He glared across the mohair carpet at me, wanting to get those bone-crushing hands on my throat. I could tell. Definitely. But cooler heads prevailed—Chip Russell's to be exact, who simply pointed out, "We have the makings—right in this room, now—of television history. So let's make it work."

Ahhh, the magic words. Robin shot me a little smile; I was already beaming. See, when they say "let's make it work," you've got them. Because what happened (only you're not supposed to know) is they already SOLD IT to their bosses—the whole package. They went in and laid their asses on the line—the concept, the ideal casting, the budget, everything. The head honcho had, apparently, creamed his Armanis. These two guys were in for a pound. And I was going to be at least five ounces of it.

"I think you're right, Chip," I said, shooting Buddy Wickwire a look. "And I'm the man who can write the shit out of it. Can't I, honey?" I turned to Robin.

With that, Robin shot me a look of such love that, I swear to you, I almost got down on my knees right there in that office and thanked God for the day He delivered my tormented and cheesy soul into her magic.

"We're beginning to look like a hit," said Chip.

I thought I ought to sort of cap the whole thing off with a little brown-nose. It never hurts. "Who is the guy who thought the Crusader thing up? I'd like t'meet him!"

Wickwire grinned a real power grin; my heart froze.

For just a second, I saw actual danger in this guy's bonded teeth. "Devon thought it up. He works here, now."

I almost lost it. Devon Converse was Wickwire's, uhhh, roommate. The same guy who'd rewritten me on the TV movie. He was supposed to have AIDS, too.

"Yeah," Chip said brightly, "Devon's heading the team now. He'll be in any minute with the director! I guess we could talk about writers—look, here they come!"

But in my power seat, I'd already seen Devon Converse and I had to admit it, the sonofabitch was cool. He looked to be in good health to me although he was leading a man who looked old enough he probably should have been in an iron lung, maybe two.

When they came in, I led everybody in jumping to their feet. Yet, it seemed like I was the only one in the room who didn't know who the old dude was. Finally, Devon Converse turned to me and said, "Have you met Reed Savage?"

I thought he was shitting me at first. Wasn't Reed Savage dead? Or was that Walter Reed? Or Jessica Savage? Hell, I didn't know, but I covered it okay. Even though he looked old and stooped over, his ice blue eyes had enough life for a small town.

The deal was set in stone by the close of business on Friday. The only smoke that had to disappear up anybody's ass was me as non-replaceable, non-rewritable, pay-or-play writer for the run of the show. They were thinking of some hack named Thornton Wilder. Puhleeze. Did you ever scope out that wimpola high school play he wrote called *Our Town?* I mean, get real, Thornie; all Emily needs is a good horse-fucking.

The weather had been hot and nasty; it never seemed to cool down and the smog hung pale red in the air, night and day. But in Hellywood, stuff like that never matters.

The meetings started as *Blondie and Richard, Cru-*

saders in Love went into high development. The network put half a dozen researchers to work on the old time period, castles and armor and stuff. They hired a costume guy to do preliminary drawings, real wild and feathery, especially the dresses that Robin was going to use. They looked good. The network also sprung for a couple of drug-crazed comic book artists to create a picture book to sell the affiliate stations. It was all part of a kit: tee shirts, bumper stickers, contest suggestions, the whole megillah, and all around the centerpiece, a three-minute video cassette teaser!

Misty smoke cleared and there was Robin, a close up, set against our living room wall, which was fake castle-type stonelike, and while this neat old-timey music played, she read a speech of Blondie's. Mammamia, that woman can act! I know her, I now the wall, I know the words because I wrote 'em, and still, when I see that tape, damn if I don't go boo-hoo. It's semi-embarrassing.

Here's the setup: Blondie has just discovered Richard the Lion-Hearted in this French jail. They've whipped the dog shit out of him. The guard lets her radar Richard out and then drags her away. He was just teasing her. They throw her out of the jailhouse and she goes over to her girlfriend's. Blondie's wiped and she takes a couple of drinks. Who wouldn't, right? Then, she leans back against the cool stone wall, looks into nothingness, and begins to talk.

"I saw him, and yet, I did not. I heard him, and yet, I did not. I love him, and yet, I do not. He is cruel—a murderer, a warrior king whose heart belongs to steel alone. He is a hawk at the well. And, dying of thirst, I would give my life just to lie by his side one night . . ."

I told her to go ahead and write her Emmy speech; she told me she couldn't have done it without the poetry. See how perfect we are for each other?

Well, needless to say, the *Crusaders in Love* kit was a hot ticket. Some stations around the country did their own paintbox graphics and ran the clip, plugging it for their upcoming season. The big thing became: Who Will Play Richard?

You probably saw it in *People*. We got them all except *Foreign Affairs* and *Candlepin Bowlers Journal*. Who would be Richard? that's all anybody could talk about. We ate it up. You can't buy this kind of pub.

Robin and I talked about it plenty. *Crusaders in Love* had (for TV) some pretty hot love scenes (a tasteful scarf-job, two reamouts, a gang rape, and lots of nipple) that I had done, and I was of two minds about who I wanted to see play Richard. Somebody who was a good actor, sure, but not too sexy. I didn't want to sit there in the dailies with them, seeing take after take of some hot, throbbing dick in armor home in on my squeeze. I will only go so far for Art, Bo. I wanted Anthony Hopkins. He'd played Richard in *Lion in Winter* (a little heavy on the lavender) and was the physical type that would have looked good with Robin. Also, I read somewhere that Hopkins was happily married and didn't fool around. Robin favored Richard Gere. I didn't.

When the network (who hadn't even told us) finally announced the actor they had cast as Richard the Lion-Hearted, the whole country caught its breath. We were utterly flabbergasted.

Because they had just signed James Dean!

For a while, I admit, I was a ways north of confused and only a little south of certifiable. I had thought Dean died in a car crash back in the fifties sometime. I'd seen a few of his movies on TV. They knocked me out of course, but I thought the guy had passed away, expired, gonzo, gravesville, dead and buried. You can laugh now, but didn't you think so, too?

As usual, it was Robin who scraped me off the wall and explained it all to me. Dean (like Judge Crater before him and President Kennedy after) had reached his personal vanishing point right after *Giant*. It usually happens when a celebrity reaches critical mass; everybody's pulling every which way, the ex-wife and the

I.R.S. are at the door, the ink has turned from honey to piss, and one day, the stress of the responsibility and the lives and the history just shuts them down. Sometimes alcohol and dope plays a part, sometimes no. But whatever it is, they are looking square into the squinty red eyes of a personal melt-down.

So they fake their death, get a new identity, and, saving their life and what's left of their sanity, they glide into chapter three. It is the only real vacation you can ever get from fame. And if you work it right, it's forever. Like that what's-his-face for the Red Sox that pitched the three no-hitters back to back and the next season couldn't throw a strike. He was supposed to have blazed out in a car crash. They had witnesses, the wrecked Caddy, and dental records, right? Wrong! The guy has a Jeep dealership in Portland, Oregon! I met him on the picture I did up there with Burt Reynolds. If you don't believe me, call Burt and ask him. He knew the dude, too. I call them Living Dead Legends. Hey, someday, I'm going to do a book about them. You think Jim Morrison is actually dead? How about Clark Gable? Or Hitler? Amelia Earhart? Hell, no! I know this chick who SEEN HER. Case closed.

Robin and I met James Dean in kind of an unusual dealie. Normally, it would have been in some network office or at his agent's house or like that. Only about two days after the announcement of his signing, Robin and I get this mysterious call up at the house (I thought it was just the weirdo phones acting up again) from a semi-familiar voice that tells us to get in a car and drive east on I-10 toward Palm Springs. Now, me and Robin hate that town. All they have is old people and bad French restaurants where the air conditioning is turned so high you could hang meat. But that's not where we were supposed to go.

Joshua Tree is a little north of Palm Springs on the map and light years from it in all other ways. It's this little town on the edge of one of the more oddbod national monuments around. You probably heard of it:

half the Sunset Desperado rock and roll songs were written there by whichever dope burnout was still awake or alive. They all went up there and got naked, ate acid, howled at the moon, and then killed themselves. It's some kind of bent spiritual rule; at Joshua Tree, everything goes. And it had gotten weirder.

When Robin and I pulled the rebuilt little Triumph into the lot at Heartbreak Hotel, we knew we were near the Twilight Zone. For one thing, the light in the sky was different. It was a deep blood sunset and the puffy clouds were sailing across the sky fast, fast. There was only one other car, a seldom seen Von Tripp Porsche (the one with the P-38 engine, too), with a few bullet holes and a light coat of road dust. The license plate said "REBEL." It didn't exactly take Einstein to figure out whose car it might be.

We checked in the hotel with this geezer who had an Adam's apple out to here. He made a big fuss over Robin.

Our room was clean and spare. King-size bed, a dresser, two night tables, two chairs, and a picture of a cow with five legs. I thought I was seeing things, but we counted them. I told you this place was weird. There were plenty of fluffy towels in the bathroom, and one of those old shower heads that would be like Niagara Falls. Oddly, the tile floor wasn't cold. I liked that. I went back out into the room and gave my honey a great big old hug. I don't mind telling you, we were feeling pretty spiffy back then. That was before we knew what was going on.

I pulled open the curtains. One wall was a glass sliding door which looked out on a small swimming pool which was empty. There were a few chairs around it in the deepening dusk. There was somebody in one of them. Smoking a cigarette. I looked at Robin, she looked at me. We took a big breath, pulled up our socks, and went out to our destiny.

*   *   *

Los Angeles County Paramedic unit #5837 took the two automobile accident victims from their disabled vehicle to the emergency department of Our Lady of Light Hospital in North Hollywood on Van Ness. The time was 3:34 A.M. One victim was identified as Robin Lamoureaux, 51, a Caucasian female who had a possible punctured spleen, broken clavicle and scapula, possible rib damage, compound fractures of the right femur. Her blood pressure was 80/50. She was secured to a gurney after first aid was completed, and placed in the mobile unit. The second victim was an unidentified male Caucasian, approximate age 35, who exhibited no vital signs upon our arrival at the scene of the accident. Whereupon we performed mouth-to-mouth resuscitation with no visible results. Whereupon we performed cardiovascular electro-shock. The victim responded with a measurable heartbeat. The victim had apparent kidney damage, chest cavity damage with probable lung involvement, lacerations about the torso and left arm. Further, both his right and left femurs were fractured, along with the right tibia. He was secured to a gurney after first aid was completed and placed in the mobile unit. Time in transit from Laurel Canyon Boulevard and Croft to the emergency department of Our Lady of Light Hospital was 6 minutes and 39 seconds.

I should have suspected this was going to be different from anything I had ever done or imagined. But I was so stoked with the possibilities of it all, I never really got it. Dean turned out to be just about the most incredible human being I had ever met. Robin thought so, too.

When we walked out of our room, up by the empty pool that evening, it was damn near dark. Just a thread of crimson snaked along Joshua Tree's horizon. But it was enough to see Dean's face. He hadn't changed, yet he'd changed completely. He had grown into the years in a way that research doctors should take a break from cancer and study this. It's more important. Because, somehow (and don't think I'm nuts until you see his movie *Hell's Gate*, okay?) Jimmy Dean had finally conquered time. He'd turned the pain and sadness in his life to a kind of glory. He'd gone from a suffering kid and BANG, here he was with Bogart eyes, between 35 and 55, I guess—who could tell?—and a face that still held both sadness and joy in it, a punim that was still so hot it would give a corpse a railer.

He flipped his cigarette butt out into the desert darkness and got up, stiffly. "Hi," was all he said with that little grin that broke your heart. In my whole life, I never identified with a person so quick or was so shook about it. Robin was blown away, too, I could tell.

We sat out there under a billion trillion stars until dawn. It was like swimming in a river of light as we talked about being alive, about being kids, being rebels, being nowhere, being driven, being talented, being famous, about being dead. I think all three of us—I know I did—said things that night we had never said to a living soul before.

We talked until the three of us became one person. And that one person became a force. It didn't even look like the network could stop it. Because out there in the magic, three lost artists found an ammo dump, a hundred-ton tank named *Crusaders in Love*, and they found each other. This is too rare and I can't really talk about all the things that happened that night. Mostly because I still don't understand them. Like the part where Jimmy said we hadn't been completely wrong when we thought he was "dead." Is this weird or what?

When we came back to earth, we drove to L.A. The network was skinning it back into overdrive for us. Everything was geared around our show. Like if one of their half-hour pilots came in looking good, it was "where do we put this in relationship to *Crusaders*?" We had calls from every agency in town; our clients want to help, they want to be involved, they'll do anything. It was like we had woke up one morning and become Steve

Spielberg or something. In that way, Andy Warhol is right. Even though I wouldn't let him paint my garage.

There was only one little problem. The network over the last ten years had sort of flamed out. It was a combination of bad luck, mismanagement, and the generic stupidity that goes with a business that keeps on thinking its customers are mostly brain-damaged children. The network had developed some real shit. *Nutty's Buddies*, *The Orgone Exchange*, *Hell on Mars*, *Camp Wammatamma*, and that bondage show, I forgot the name of it. Stuff like these plus that series on the insurance business, and then, the Rollerball League collapses on them; Bo, they were sucking canal water.

So, last year—hell, you read about it—that Okie corporate raider, Lefty Armbruster, came in with the cavalry and took over the place. Heads rolled (how Buddy Wickwire ever survived is a major miracle), deals were amputated, and budgets were gone over with a fine-tooth chain saw. Overnight, everything got cheap.

And our little problem was that the numbers dorks in Production had told us "no way." They'd done boards, projections, computer models, the whole nine yards. The bottom line was that evidently the United States Government hadn't printed enough money since the Second Continental Congress to pay for our show. Which was not only a problem for us. See, now, in the public's mind, the entire future of the network was tied into it. Everybody was calling *Crusaders In Love* the end of darkness or the saving stroke or the long-awaited dawn, or I don't know what-all.

Which put the numbers guys in kind of a bad place. Which only made us feel tougher. Which only made the situation harder.

Lefty Armbruster even looked like a corporate raider. He wore a two thousand-dollar English suit, shaved his head, and had an eyepatch of blue velvet. He wore snakeskin boots, and his little gold cufflinks had the name of his take-over company, "666," on them in

diamonds. The guy was heat, no question. He drove to
the meeting at Reed Savage's house on Tower Drive on
his motorcycle, a black BMW 1000. Whew.

"Boys, Imo tell ya," he started. "We can do this one
of two ways. The first is the smart way: we take and
whittle this overblown battlewagon down to destroyer
size, lean and mean, and then, the network will make
your series."

We nodded. All of us in that room—Dean, Reed,
Robin, Devon Converse, and me—were waiting to hear
Option Two. Lefty chuggalugged his Tab.

"The other way is for y'all to just sandbag me and
say, 'fuck you, Lefty!' This way is more interesting,
probably the way I'd personally go, but it'd be guaran-
teed to get you fired. Now, which way do you vote?"

"FIRST WAY!" four voices said at once. Lefty
Armbruster smiled. Then, James Dean, who had said
nothing, leaned forward with that little grin.

"How about you, Reb?" the raider asked the star.
"Which way do you vote?"

"I'll go with my friends," said Dean, very softly.
Lefty smiled expansively in victory and got up, ready to
leave. Dean stopped him with his voice. "But there is
someone in this room who is acting unnecessarily like
an asshole." Suddenly, it got real quiet. "I don't want to
name any names. But I've been at this too long," Jimmy
continued, "so if that person doesn't knock it off, I'm
gonna CLOSE HIS OTHER EYE."

James Dean was looking right at the blue velvet eye
patch of Lefty Armbruster. There were a few seconds,
it could have gone either way. Neither man gave an
inch. I was there, I saw it.

"I smell a hit, boys," Lefty said. "Get this thing down
and we'll all be champs." When he went out, get this—he
left the door open behind him. It was so cool, I've
taken to doing it, although it doesn't look quite as
bitchin'.

Robin and I got to Dean at the same time. The three
of us hugged each other; he had just saved our life's

project. Devon Converse was white. He had seen death and hadn't liked its face. But we were back on track.

We went back to the drawing board, determined to cut out the fat and save the fire. I had some experience with this from the old days, as I may have told you. But going through the script now, it was major agony time, because suddenly it wasn't some pompous, overpaid screenwriter I was carving up, it was me.

And when I had done the first draft, in love and happy in our new castle on the hill, I had given Blondie and Richard the Lion-Hearted everything I had. I was writing for the ages. I put all the poetry—the agony and the ecstasy of my whole and entire life—into the 700-page teleplay. It was incredible, even if I do say so myself. A real "read," a jaw dropper. I mean it. I would show you some scenes . . . but by law, I can't. It's too hard emotionally, anyway.

The director, Reed Savage, and I waded into the script with stump pullers and a buzz saw. We cut two major battle scenes, a masked ball for a thousand, the coronation of the Holy Roman Emperor, and a passion play made up of trained dogs. We cut Eleanor and Henry, John and Phillip, Saladin and Berengaria. We were right at having to cut the storming of Acre, when I finally had to take a stand. Flat out, I drew the line. Enough was enough. If they kept cutting, they would have just about the right amount for a small series of medieval greeting cards. Reed agreed with me; now it was time to pull the loose ends together and see what we had.

It wasn't much. I guess if you'd never read the first draft or ever heard of history or ever used a word with "R" in it, it looked okay. Kind of like an infidel-bashing romance novel as seen by a meteor just before it crashes into the plot of a seventh-grade geography movie.

But I knew the network wouldn't care. Their "wisdom" was that nothing mattered except the pre-sale, the ink, some spectacle, and a few good scenes. The trailer department would cut a flashy two-minute teaser using all the good stuff, and then the sales department could get to work and sell all the spots. It's like a weenie factory; sorry to have to tell you. How anything good gets done is usually by certified excitable A-types whose insane vision accidentally explodes (usually taking a twenty-year marriage with it) into a show that is only one tenth as good as the one they saw in their mind and yet it's still better than anything else on. They are generally rewarded with Emmys, a nice office, and fraudulent profit reports where they discover they have been cross-collateralized with a network series on the heroes of Canadian golf. About this time, the visionary gets canned because he tried to resist having the show's characters all go on *Wheel of Fortune* or something.

When Reed and I put all the scenes on those little 3 x 5 cards, it was obvious that something was going to have to be done. So I did the old trusty narration track (the TNT, we call it) and, given the legendary skills of Jimmy Dean and my Robin, I went ahead and wrote them a few more limbo-set love and sacrifice scenes that made tears run down your leg and chills run up your back.

The network loved it. This guy told me that his sec heard from her boyfriend in development that he heard from Chip Russell, who had been in the office that day, that Lefty Armbruster cried when he read it!

And STILL they were looking for cuts. I didn't remember them being this cold, this hard. They got down to nickel-and-dime stuff and, no matter what we did, it didn't seem to be enough. We were still over. It was starting to be panic time. Then, I sort of saved the day.

They had budgeted the castle interiors (both French and English) at nine million. That was just to build and paint. The continued rental of the space and refurbishing was hidden in another column. All of a sudden, it came to me.

I told them they could shoot at our house!

Not bad, huh! And it worked! That nine mil was just

under their worst-case budget and they tentatively approved us. I think Reed wanted to adopt me and Jimmy was glowing. The only one who didn't seem too thrilled was Robin.

She was right, as usual. I learned the lesson and this is it: never, ever let your house or anyone's house you remotely know or like be used in the movies or TV.

I'd had this big vision of us getting paid a grand a day for the rental, plus which, we would just roll out of bed and start to shoot while everybody else had been up since four going to the network to be driven out to the location. I thought they would be careful when they shot. I assumed, if anything bad happened, we would be reimbursed. I figured that our castle looked just like crusader stuff. Robin had warned me. Still, it pissed me off royally.

First, they held the rental money in escrow (all accrued interest to them, of course) for the run of the show, which could be years! Next, because of a mob-ridden union stranglehold on the entire business, it turned out we would have to get up early and drive to the network, so we could be driven back to our own fucking house! And when the camera department first came in and was doing color balance tests, they broke a mahogany mantle. Then, the bastards spackled and painted it over, claiming it had never been there. Shawn, down in the little apartment below, had to move out when his ceiling fell in, knocked over his stereo, and almost electrocuted him. Also, some prick or pricks unknown kept stealing everything that wasn't nailed down. On top of everything else, even in preproduction, it was so noisy with the skill saws, the electric nail-drivers, and the yelling and screaming, we couldn't ever get to sleep. Or cook. Or watch TV. Or even go to the bathroom. You'd go in, close the door, and in the toilet would be floating yesterday's *Hellywood Reporter*, a styrofoam coffee cup, cigar butts, and half a prune danish. There was never any toilet paper.

They tore out walls, they built walls. They lifted the

roof, they moved furniture, they rolled rugs, they emptied closets, they hauled stuff away, and I still haven't found out where they took it.

Our bedroom became Richard the Lion-Hearted's dining hall. The kitchen served nicely as Blondie's bathroom after they ripped out the Chambers range along with the St. Charles cabinets we'd just had put in. They tore up the deck outside so they could set in trees and stuff. Our trees weren't right. They brought in jack-hammers and stone cutters so they could dig cable trenches; the dolly space had to be tabletop smooth. They dismantled the sauna and capped the plumbing to put in the sound guy's booth. They cemented up the flue in the walk-in fireplace because they had converted it to craft-services area and the coffee urn was getting chilled. Forty tons of fill dirt were dumped on our lawn because you couldn't take a chance and see mowed grass out a Crusader's window. The plasterers clogged up all our drains washing their trowels and boards. The electricians rewired the house for 220; I plugged in a lamp to read by, the cord caught fire, and then the whole dealie exploded! An hour later, it was still glowing red-hot. Does this give you some idea of what fun and glamor show business is? *Crusaders in Love* hadn't even started yet; first day of principal photography (the day I would get a hernia-making cash bonus) was still three weeks away! I wasn't sure my relationship with Robin would even last that long. She had warned me and I hadn't listened. Her shrink pointed out that it sort of characterized our dynamic (whatever that means) and although I'd like to cut that sucker, he was right to the extent that I HAD been sort of headstrong. It got so bad one night when we were in the hotel room, I put *Soldier of Fortune* down, and I just started crying. I thought about the days when my only worry was what scheme to teach that producer's kids, or how I could get the head stunt-gaffer to give me a three-story fall, or how to keep it hard when the donkey was on camera.

What the hell was a simple, low-life kid like me doing in a complicated, grown-up place like this?

Robin, saintess that she was, took me in her arms and sang my favorite song soft in my ear. "Hush little baby, don't you cry . . ."

To watch a major TV production start up, especially this one, is to know what God meant when He invented the word "wow."

Casting began to see hundreds of people; *Crusaders in Love*, even with the cuts, had 90 speaking parts. Assistant directors were hired, production go-fers, costumers, sound crews, wranglers, construction guys, honeywagons, Winnebagos, gaffers, stuntmen, grips, historical technical advisors (who got a little bent out of shape when I had Richard cut down on Geoffrey with a Winchester), scenic and matte artists, prop guys—it was like watching your dream turn to water, running down a mountain made of glass. You could almost see it . . .

And the closer we got, the more nervous and difficult the network got. Something was wrong. Real wrong.

We didn't hear that Devon Converse "had decided, mutually, to leave his position at the network, to explore the opportunities of independent production" until a week after the fact. This means he had been sacked—the guy whose idea the whole thing had been! This didn't look like a good omen to either me or Robin. Reed was too busy to mourn. Jimmy just shrugged his shoulders sadly. "It figures," he said, "they'd fire their savior." I had come to like Devon after all we'd been through with the rewrites and the cuts and all. Besides, it turned out that he thought Buddy Wickwire was a buttface, too. I tried to call Chip Russell's office for four days about it, and he never returned my calls. This, by itself, was not a good omen, either. When I called Wickwire's old office extension, I got some frosty bitch who told me that Wickwire had been promoted to senior vice president. Instead of Chip Russell.

Who had quit. Which is why he hadn't called me back. He was probably at the Brentwood market in tennis togs, having espresso; what did he care anymore?

As Lenny Bruce used to say, even though you may be paranoid, that doesn't mean they're not out to get you.

We had fifty million committed for a new series, we had a start date, we had good pub on us, and yet for some reason, we had a network that was acting in the manner of a crazed Doberman in a maternity ward. It looked like the brass was trying to sabotage us, like our own guys didn't want us to succeed. What was going on?

Chip Russell lived in a small, wonderful house in Rustic Canyon. We had taken several story meetings over there when we first started the major cuts. Lots of wood and glass, and the outside seemed to come right in. From his place on a little cul-de-sac off Lattimer, you couldn't see any other houses.

Jimmy, Robin, and I got out of my beat-up old Rambler. Even though the birds were singing, it seemed unusually quiet. In fact, it was a boss weird moment; a dry, hot wind came from the oak trees, and yet, none of the brown leaves even twittered. It hadn't rained in I couldn't remember how long—since the wreck, maybe.

We went to the front door. It was open a crack. We looked at each other. Chip had a dog, one of those awful schnauzers who always barks. It was silent. Which, to me, was the blow omen of the year.

"Sometimes I wish I was ten years old again, back in Barberton, Ohio, not knowing diddly," said Robin. I knew just what she meant. None of us had a good feeling.

We found him, sitting in his leather Eames chair, reading a book called *A Hollywood Education*, by some guy named Freeman. It was a prophetic-type thing: Chip Russell, dead as a doornail, had just got his Ph.D., it looked like. He was smiling in spite of the little black

.22 hole in the middle of his forehead. Robin went outside to barf. Jimmy found the drugged dog shut in the projection TV drawer. I closed Chip's eyes.

I'll be honest with you. I'd never, ever seen a dead body before. I've lied a few times and said I had, but I hadn't. It gave me the willies, and for a weird reason that I never would have suspected. Chip Russell did not look dead. I mean, it looked like he was just about to laugh at one of my jokes at a script meeting. I wanted to touch him, so I did. The skin was still soft. I pulled one of his arm hairs gently; it made a little hill of skin. I lifted one of his fingers. Up it came. I let it go; plop. I thought to myself, this is a body whose heart is not beating anymore, whose blood is just sitting there. This is a dead guy. And that's when I almost lost it. Because I wondered what was in this thing that made it go—made it live—made it the Chip Russell that went the thirty years in his life with the friends and hot days and cold beer, and I got real scared because I was thinking that whatever it was, was the same dealie inside of me and Robin and Jimmy, and just as sure as it was there—unmeasurable, unprovable—it could be gone forever. Just snuffed out, and I would end up to be like Chip, like this body which was starting to get cold.

"We're in deep shit," said Robin very softly.

"And we're outta here," said Jimmy. "Wipe off anything you might have touched." We booked it.

The last day of rehearsal there was flat-out the most powerful thunderstorm anyone had ever seen. The clouds were damn near purple with rage and lightning, and yet, not a drop of rain fell. Billion-amp blasts split the strange darkness, and all of us sort of creeped around, playing like we thought this was normal or something.

The last tech run-through was a real goon show. People were jumping around like it was the end of the world or something. And in the middle of all the technical madness, there were the director, the writer, and

the actors—along with the camera and sound crew—
trying to block the hard, long dolly shot that would
open the show, tomorrow morning at six. Little did any
of us know.

Jimmy was blowing his lines, over and over, in the
scene with his ministers, William of Longchamp and
Hubert Walter. I had written the scene in Latin (more
like Pig Latin, actually)—you know how high-toned
those meetings go—but it was just a Peter Piper Picked
a Peck of Pickled Peppers thing. So I was making
on-site changes on my little Epson lap computer, just
racking it out, being semi-brilliant, even if I do say so.

Robin had had an uncharacteristic fight with Reed
Savage and had gone downstairs to cool off in what used
to be Shawn's little apartment. She told me later what'd
happened.

She had slipped through the door, not making any
noise, and had caught Buddy Wickwire, toying with his
platinum Dunhill lighter, talking on the phone to Lefty
Armbruster. Even though figuring out a conversation
from only hearing one side is not always easy, she got
enough. One of Buddy's lines had been, "Don't worry,
Lefty, they'll never get the first shot in the can."

The two victims: a white female Caucasian, identified
as Robin Lamoureaux, age 51, of Hollywood, and an
unidentified white male Caucasian, approximate age 35,
with tattoo over right nipple—"Milk"—and over the
left nipple—"Tequila"—were admitted from paramedic
mobile unit #5837 to the emergency room of our Lady
of Light Hospital at 3:35 A.M. The two victims were
pronounced dead at the time of arrival. See death cer-
tificates below. Notification pending.

It must have started sometime early in the morning.
I got a call at the hotel from our neighbor, who thought
she had heard a window break and then, when she
went to eyeball it, saw a little flame or something in the
upstairs bedroom.

Fortunately, our hotel was only over the hill. I told Robin to stay there, I'd go check it out. She wasn't too thrilled with that, but I took off.

When I got to our castle, I stood outside for a few seconds. It seemed okay. At least, sort of okay; a night that was not quite dark, a smell of rotted jasmine and garbage, a sky of stars that had smooshed into kind of a big river of light. Across the mottled gulch on Amor Drive, a coyote yipped. The castle was quiet. Still, I thought I'd better go and scope it out. I let myself in with my key.

Holy Jesus. I looked upstairs and I could see the flames reflected in the Crusader armor statues. Wisps of smoke were crawling down the stone steps like snakes. I tried to call the fire department but the goddamn phones—I told you about them—didn't work. The only thing left for me was to do it myself. I went running upstairs, terrified.

Our bedroom was wall-to-wall fire; I never saw anything like it. The floor was a lake of flames. Richard the Lion-Hearted's throne—the one with all the gold scroll and jewel work—had gone up like a torch. The noise of the licking flames was beyond belief. Above the throne (right where our bed had been) the lead in the St. Michael stained glass window was melting, running down the glass, popping the panes out like rifle shots.

And then I saw something which made my heart go cold. A medieval tapestry, one of the for-real museum jobbies, had been hung over a closet door. It was on fire, and from behind it came a man walking right through the flaming image of where this knight guy was! Holy shit, it was Jimmy!

"What the hell are you doin' here?" I yelled as I threw my coat over his smoldering tee shirt.

"I was rehearsing late last night. I just went t'bed—I always try to sleep somewhere on the set, the first night. It's good luck for me!" We both had to laugh at that one. He told me someone had cold-cocked him in his sleep and heaved him in the closet.

We ran into the bathroom. There was a faucet in the steam room and a short hose under the sink. Jimmy attached them, I turned the faucet on full, and he began hosing down the flames. For a little while, it looked like we might beat it back. The red light dancing on his incredible face was eerie.

The neighbor had finally called the fire department and now they came in like an army. I looked out the hall window. Must've been a dozen spotlights hit the house at once. Red truck after red truck roared up, all crackling with their CB intercom talk which had been turned up full volume. One guy yelled up to me, but I didn't hear him. Suddenly, I remembered the costume room.

I hauled ass down but somehow, the fire had got there first. Seemed like every costume I grabbed, them flames would take the tail of it, and by the time I would run to a window to toss it out, the whole thing would go up. I almost got caught a couple of times.

Everywhere you'd look, there would be these harmless-looking little sparks, cutely winking, settling down like hot feathers, you know, only whatever they landed on would burst into flame. Somebody had opened all the windows so the hot Santa Ana winds came roaring through, taking fire into every corner in every room. Outside, I heard a woman screaming.

Inside, Jimmy and I were trying to save the Nagra sound equipment, the mikes and mixing board. We no sooner got them tossed out into the bushes when we were back trying to wheel the Chapman dolly with its big old Panaflex camera out.

That was when Robin came running in, her nightie flying out behind her in the firelight. We yelled and the three of us hugged real quickly. The dolly tracks headed out toward our huge two-story oak front door which was already starting to blister from the heat. The three of us really doubled our backs into that dolly as the flames walked up the walls. To complete the craziness, the superheat had managed to fry some wires and turn our stereo on, loud—the Eagles, "Take It to the Limit." Can you believe it?

This looked like it wasn't even real, like I had written it for a scene or something. And it damn sure was taking it to the limit. We had turned out to be Richard and Blondie, for real, there with the dude who'd dreamed them up. *Crusaders in Love* were trapped in Hell, Bo.

The fireguys were bashing their way through the back with their axes and pike poles and hoses. But it was too late. The TV company, in the interest of over-art-directed "realism," had put so many false fronts, had done so much construction, used so many 1×3s and plywood and lathing, everything seemed to explode when the flames hit it. You never want to see anything like this, believe me.

Suddenly, the ceiling in the back hall caved in, cutting us off from the fireguys. There were timbers and exploding water pipes and shorting electrical cables that were snapping around in the smoke so much you could barely see anymore. Still, we pushed that dolly toward the front door. Only now, it wasn't to save any movie camera. We were trying to build up speed and use it as a battering ram.

Just then, there was this ungodly howling laughter. The three of us turned, and across the huge smoky room, coming through the flaming portals of the porch, spotlights playing all over their backs, were Buddy Wickwire and Lefty Armbruster!

"I thought you'd be here," was all Dean said as he drew himself upright. I stood in front of my Robin when I saw Wickwire pull a .22 pistol.

"Boys," yelled Lefty, "it's done. Time to call in the dogs and get the insurance adjusters. I've saved the network fifty million with a match. All they'll find is your bridge-work and some belt buckles."

Lefty laughed the laugh of a big winner and nodded to his next in command, Buddy Wickwire, who lifted his .22 and pointed it dead at us. He cocked it as

Jimmy, Robin, and I joined hands. I jumped from the shock—

Wickwire fired—

The hammer snapped down as the ammo in his pistol exploded from the heat! I took his arm off at the elbow. He had just enough time to feel the first wave of blinding pain before a two-ton flaming timber fell on him.

If Lefty Armbruster ever even noticed, you couldn't tell by his face. With that victorious smile still there, he seemed to come toward us, growing bigger and bigger and bigger, right through the fiery timber and his minion's melting body. I guess it was Jimmy who sort of led the way, pulling us forward. Or maybe it was Robin, I don't know.

But in the middle of that pyre, in the noise and heat and insanity, the three of us, joined at the heart, met something that had become so big not even this fire could hold him, too big even for the whole wide world!

Just at the very moment when I thought we would be enveloped by the roaring size alone, the slowly lumbering dolly and Panaflex camera crashed through the flaming black cinders that had been our front door and this howling blast of icy air came through. It seemed to take the three of us, still holding tight to each other's hands, away on its wings of cold out into the night, where we could look down and see the castle below us, getting smaller and smaller, as the fire jumped to the hills around it. The wind fanned the flames that shot hundreds of feet into the night air, which showed this little guy with a blue velvet eyepatch come running out the door, stamping his feet and howling some shit that none of us would ever work again in that town, that we'd never work again in movies or TV. But HA! that doesn't include writing books, does it? Fuck no, it doesn't.

And now that me and Robin have this neat little place in Vermont and we hear every couple of months from Jimmy, who is happy as a clam living a new life (he has kids and everything), and now that you know just what happened to *Crusaders in Love*, if that asshole corporate raider Lefty Armbruster thinks he can stop me, I say let him try.

I am dead flat serious, let him try.

Anyway, our wonderful life goes on, and while I'm upstairs doing this, Robin is out in the garden watering the rose bushes, since we had this sudden weird hot spell (she loves roses). And from downstairs I can smell the apple pie (the gooey kind with the crumbly stuff on top) that I'm baking in the oven. I hear Robin come in and I yell down to her to come up and see me write "The End," (a writer's two favorite words, unless they'd be 'timefor dinner') but she doesn't answer. Hmmm. Then, I hear her on the stairs OKAY!, only the sound her step makes is too loud. "Robin," I call out, "honey . . ." This is weird—I don't like this—hand on the door, knob turns, why am I so scared? Awww, it'll be her and I'll edit this and the door is opening and HEY, **WAIT A MINUT**

BETWEEN THE DEVIL AND THE DEEP BLUE SEA

Michael Armstrong

Nuliajuk, the seal woman, came to Qavvik in his vision. He was swimming deep below the pack ice, down where the *tungai*— animal spirits—lived, paying his respects to the souls of the sea animals. Qavvik was swimming with a seal, diving and turning, and when he looked at her face she smiled at him—woman's face, seal's body.

"Nuliajuk," he said.

Nuliajuk smiled. "It is time for you to go to the surface. You must push the water aside and rejoin your people."

"I am dead," Qavvik said. He tugged at the woman's knife, the *ulu*, stuck point first in his skull. The knife would not come out. "I cannot rejoin my people. I am dead."

"You must go to the surface," she said. "Now. Push the water aside. Go. Go."

Qavvik shook his head. Nuliajuk stared at him, and then he yielded.

"Go."

He rose. He kicked, fought, swam through the cold water, up and up. The darkness gave way to light. The ice thickened, became a great mat of dark dirt, roots shooting down, timbers and old houses in the permafrost. He pushed. The dirt cracked and groaned and split apart. He floated on his back. He looked at his hands: flesh reformed on the bones of his fingers. There was a squirming around him, a twitching. His legs flew back to his body. He watched as a wolf spat out his liver, saw the liver fly back into his groin. The muscles spun and wove around the skeleton, the skeleton grew back into his body, his body became whole.

His parka came back out of the dirt. The spots of the reindeer hide grew together. His sealskin mukluks wrapped his feet. His cheeks grew back around the quarter-sized labret in his left cheek, the dime-sized labret in his right cheek. His scalp itched as his hair grew back. He licked his lips and tasted cold dirt. Qavvik spat, kicked, and rose out of the ground.

Above him was a great whale's jaw. As he watched, the arches of the mandibles leaned into each other and collapsed, settled into the mire, and sank. He blinked his eyes, squinted; the world was a blast of bright. He breathed, one deep lungful, another, the air filling his whole body.

Qavvik coughed. The air smelled like rotten eggs, humid and thick, the smoke from a dying blubber lamp. He spat, breathed again, coughed.

Nuliajuk flopped around in the swamp, mud dripping from her flippers, mud on her face. She shook her head and drops of bloody mud flew out of her long black hair. She sat up on her hind flippers, smiled, and with one flipper waved her arm at the great swamp.

"Welcome," Nuliajuk said. "Welcome, Qavvik, to Hell."

*   *   *

78 *Michael Armstrong*

"Hell," Qavvik asked Nuliajuk. "What is this Hell?"

"The world below," she said. "The place where the tungai live. The land of the devils."

"Ah," said Qavvik, smiling. "That Hell. The missionaries spoke of it often. Is this where Satan lives?"

"Satan does not live," Nuliajuk said. She turned from him, drew her seal body behind her over the mud. "Satan exists. It is not life so much as . . . so much as something else. We do not live here. We . . . well, you will see soon enough."

"Why am I here?" he asked.

She shook her head, scratched at her neck with a flipper. "Always with the why, eh? You humans: why, why, why?"

"Why am I here?" he asked.

"You are here, *Qavvik*, because you are a heathen and a sinner. Didn't the missionaries explain that to you?"

Qavvik followed her across the mud. "I was baptized," he said. "I received the good news of the Lord. I accepted his spirit into my body." He stopped. "That was shortly before I became an angatkok."

"An *angatkok*?" Nuliajuk stopped, sat, furrowed her brow. "Ah: a shaman." She crawled on through the mud. "You were baptized. You must answer to God." She turned, looked at him with intense green eyes. "That is why you are in Hell." She swatted at the back of her seal body. "Oh, Heaven. I am sick of this body and this goddamn swamp. Take my hand."

"Hand?"

"My fucking paw. Take my paw." Qavvik reached down and grabbed her paw. "Close your eyes, babe. We're going to New Hell."

She twirled and oozed and the swamp went white, then gray, then became a whitewashed room that smelled of disinfectant. The walls and floor were bare, except for a metal chair bolted to the wooden floor, and an alcove along one wall that held a great granite throne. Two lanterns hung from hooks on either side of the throne; the wicks hadn't been trimmed in some time, and the chimneys of the lanterns were black with soot.

Nuliajuk squeezed his hand. Her paw felt warm, soft; as he watched, the flipper wiggled into a hand. He looked up at her: same face, but no more seal body. She was a little shorter than him, but fleshy, big, the way a bearded seal looked. She wore a sealskin parka, sealskin boots and breeches; the black and white spots matched her old seal body. She had braided her hair into a complicated coiffure, two plaits from above her ears that joined below her chin into a long red braid that came to her waist.

"Nuliajuk?" he asked.

She shook her head. "No, not the seal woman. I am the Welcome Woman. This is my real body," she ran her hands over the parka, "though I do like this coat." The Welcome Woman pointed at the metal chair. "Sit," she said. "The Lord Satan will pronounce your sentence."

"Satan?"

"Sit," she said.

He sat, and when he turned to her again, she was gone.

"*Qavvik*," a voice said from the throne. "Qavvik?"

Qavvik looked up. A man sat in the throne—not a man, an *inua*—a naked man with the head of a bear; an immense cock dangled from his crotch almost to the floor. A tungai, some spirit, sat on the man's broad shoulders; the tungai had the head of a bat and the body of something that looked like an ermine, with a long tail and small hands. The granite throne glowed dull red, and the inua's skin sizzled like caribou steaks frying in fat.

"Satan?" As the words came out, the chair shocked him, and Qavvik winced.

"*Lord* Satan," the inua said. Satan's teeth clicked as he spoke. "Christ, how I hate these primitive religions. Yes, I am Satan, Prince of Darkness, Lucifer, all that crap. You call yourself Qavvik. But I see here," he

waved his hand and a long yellow parchment unrolled
from his fingers, "that you have other names, too."

"I am also called—"

"*Don't* say it," Satan said. "It's probably one of those
godawful names that only *He* can pronounce. Qavvik.
You will go by Qavvik here. It means . . . Oh, blast, it's
here somewhere."

"Wolverine, Lord Satan," Qavvik said. "Wolverine."

"Ah, yes," he said. "The Arctic hyena. Eats dead
things. Well, your name may be appropriate, little wolverine. Tell me, what are your sins?"

Qavvik smiled. "I have no sins." The chair crackled
with light. Pain shot up his spine and his back went
straight. "Lord Satan," he added through clenched teeth.

"You have the sin of pride," Satan said. "You damned
heathen, you are sinned for that."

"I am not a heathen," Qavvik said. "I was baptized—"

"—baptized by Presbyterian missionaries on April
13, 1861," Satan said. "Had you never been baptized
you might not have come here—might not have sinned
under less rigorous rules. But you were baptized, Qavvik,
and so you are *mine*."

"What are my sins, Lord Satan?"

"Ah," said Satan. His thin lips spread back, showing
the long yellow teeth. "Ah, now we are getting somewhere. Your sins? Your sins are many.

"You are a murderer. You killed twenty-five men,
two women, and one child in your life. You took four
wives—I see the last one left her mark—" Satan pointed
at the ulu stuck in Qavvik's head "—and had many
other women. You stole. You took the Lord's name in
vain. You honored other gods before Him. You lied.
Shall I go on?"

"No," said Qavvik. "I have sinned, I suppose." He
smiled. "I killed twenty-*six* men."

"Twenty-*six*, twenty-*seven*, what the Hell difference
does it make? Pride! That is your greatest sin. Pride."
Satan reached up, petted the tungai on his shoulder;
the familiar nuzzled against the thick fur of the bear's

head. "Okay, I'm supposed to read you this passage down here at the bottom. It's from the Big Guy upstairs— God, Lord of the Universe. God says, 'For these sins, you—' and he has your real name here, but fuck if I'm going to say it, '—also known as Qavvik, are forever damned to Hell.' There you go, buddy: that's your sentence. You're in.

"Welcome to Hell. Enjoy your stay."

And Satan vanished in a cloud of yellow smoke.

"It's not so bad."

Qavvik got up out of the chair, stood, and turned. The Welcome Woman was standing by a door that had not been there before. She had taken the parka off and was wearing a brightly colored dress that hung loosely around her porcine body. Images of some strange buildings were printed on the dress. Her hair was cut shorter and arranged in a style that looked like a loon's nest. She had purple eyeshadow that clashed with her green eyes.

"Don't let Lucifer scare you," she said. "Hell's a swell place." She held out a hand. "You want the tour?"

"What the Hell," Qavvik said. He took her hand and walked with her into the dark.

The door from the sentencing room led into a long hallway; the walls of the hall were whitewashed stucco. Screams and moans and sounds of general torment came from behind the walls. Once, a door materialized out of the hallway, and a tall blond man in black leather stepped out. He slapped the Welcome Woman on the ass with his swagger stick, jumped as she swung a fist at him, then turned, whistling, down the hallway.

"Goddamn Goering," the Welcome Woman muttered.

"Who?" Qavvik asked.

"After your time," she said. "You died in, um, 1889? Goering was just a pup then. You'll meet him soon enough. He's running the Fallen Angels while Hadrian is on sabbatical."

"Hadrian?"

"I guess you're weak on Roman history, huh? Hadrian built this wall in Britain about 125 A.D." She slowed, leaned close to Qavvik, and whispered into his ear. "Rumor has it that Hadrian has been captured by this gang of crazies, the Dissidents. The Dissidents say they'll grind Hadrian up into hamburger and cast his body to the end of Hell if Satan doesn't meet their demands."

"Can they do that?" Qavvik asked.

The Welcome Woman nodded. "Hell, you can't *kill* anyone down here, but you can make it hard to put them back together again."

They turned a corner in the hallway, came to an alcove. In the middle of the alcove was a small kettle on a block of red marble. Steam rose from the kettle—steam that smelled like boiling shit. Beyond the kettle was a door with two buttons beside it. Loud banging came from the other side of it.

"Help!" someone yelled from the other side of the door. "We're stuck! Let us out!"

"Shit," said the Welcome Woman. "Elevator's broken."

"Elevator?" asked Qavvik.

"Oh, yeah," she said. "This room you go inside and it gets lowered down and when you come out you're in a different place."

"Like a dancehouse?"

She laughed, sort of a snort. "No, no. We're in a building and there are lots of floors to it. We take the elevator to get to other floors."

"And the elevator is stuck?"

"Yeah. The guy who builds things around here—Mr. Hughes, you wouldn't know him—has a real hard time getting good help."

Qavvik pointed at the kettle. "What's that?"

The Welcome Woman snapped her fingers. "Damn! I almost forgot. Thanks for reminding me. That's your torment. You haven't received your torment." She waved down the hall. "The Hall of Torment. This is where you are assigned your punishment."

Qavvik looked around the corner, heard more screams of anguish. A small bead of sweat was forming on his nose.

"Torment?"

She smiled. "It shouldn't be too bad. And you can always appeal. Stick your hand in the kettle."

"In the kettle?"

"The pain won't last long. Stick it in there. It's God's Grace. A part of God has consented to honor us with His Presence. Stick your hand in there."

"It smells like *anak*," he said.

"Shit? You've denied God. You think He's going to smell like roses? *Stick your hand in there.*"

Qavvik shuffled to the kettle, closed his eyes, and thrust his right hand into the burning Grace. A terrifying cold gripped his hand, froze it in His embrace. Pain, pain like blood that was molten metal, flowed up his arm, into his heart, through his body, through his brain, through his soul. He opened his eyes and saw a wisp of a demon, a white angel, a great inua floating before him, blue eyes blazing. The Grace hovered over the kettle, flowed in and out of it, a face that was neither man nor woman, human nor beast. The face bared its teeth, and spoke.

"Qavvik, you are damned," the Grace said, "and this is your torment." The Grace waved an arm, and a whaling harpoon, a bomb gun, and a cloth bag appeared in the air. "You are to hunt whales in the Sea of Purgatory." Grace smiled. "And you will never catch one."

The wisp fell back into the kettle, and the harpoon, bag, and gun clattered to the floor. Qavvik's hand began to burn. He pulled it from the kettle, shook it, watched drops of steam fall to the ground and burn their way through the floor. He rubbed his hand. It was raw, red, but whole.

Behind the elevator doors there was a snap, and a

great rushing sound as something fell past the doors. There was a long scream that went on for half a minute, dwindling until it became a low moan. The doors slid open, revealing an open shaft, and a frayed cable slapping against the side of the shaft. Brilliant sunlight streamed down from above, and icy fog fell down the shaft.

"Ah," said the Welcome Women, "the elevator seems to be working now." She walked over to the open door, poked her head through the doors, ducked back quickly. Her red hair was rimmed with hoar frost, and little icicles hung from her drippy nose. "I think we're in the inner latitudes."

"The inner latitudes?"

" 'North,' you would call it. Hell's Arctic. It's like this big pit, only it's flat . . . well, it's hard to explain. Anyway, there are cold places in Hell and this is one of them. You've arrived, pal. This is it. Your new home for the next couple of eternities."

"But this room that goes up?"

"Oh, that. It, uh, seems to have descended a little faster than it should. A new system Mr. Hughes is trying out. 'Express Service,' he calls it. Anyway, you climb." She picked up the harpoon, the bomb gun, the cloth bag. "You'll need these." She handed him the weapons.

"Climb?" he asked.

"It's not too far," she said. "Probably a thousand vertical feet."

Qavvik stuck his head through the door, saw a rusty ladder to the right, felt the cold air fall down on him. "But what do I do when I get to the top?"

"Like the Grace said: hunt whales."

He swung his leg around, put a foot on a rung, tested it. The rung bent, rust flaked away, but it held. He put another foot on the rung, grasped a rung above. The Welcome Woman poked her head through the door.

"Have fun," she said. "Look me up when you're in New Hell." She added, "When you file your appeal.

See you." She ducked back into the hallway, and the
door shut behind her.

Qavvik climbed, one hand up, a foot, grasp a rung,
again. He climbed. And climbed.

He came up into the cold.

Icy snow, snow that was the color snow looked when
blood dripped into it, swirled around the surface of the
shaft. Qavvik grabbed the last rung, pulled himself up,
crawled onto the surface. He crawled away from the open
shaft and lay in the snow, his legs like slugs, muscles
like rotted sinew. The ruddy snow blew into his face,
down his neck, over his body; he was embraced by
cold.

The ground groaned behind him. Qavvik turned his
head, watched as the open shaft moaned shut. One foot
was dangling over the edge. He lifted it, and the hole
closed shut like a deep sphincter, until the dirt was
healed.

The wind stopped.

Clouds near the southern horizon glowed pale gray,
but the rest of the sky was deep ebony—no stars, no
moon, only low clouds. The south grew brighter, and
the dark shroud over the sky fell back into the dawn. A
great red globe rose over the horizon, a light-giving
globe. Warmth washed over Qavvik's face. The globe
rose higher, and the warmth turned to cold, to agony,
to pain—the same feeling he felt when his hand was in
the kettle of Grace.

"Paradise," a voice said.

Qavvik looked to his right. Fur-clad feet stood next to
him. He looked up: feet, polar bearskin breeches, a
reindeer parka, a head, a body . . . a person. He
squinted, stared at the face. The face had a labret—a
face plug—under the lip: a black labret, with a red
bead, a blue bead, stuck in the plug.

"Ukalliq?" Qavvik asked. "Little rabbit?"

The man smiled, held out a hand. "Qavvik."

Qavvik grasped Ukalliq's hand, let him pull him up.

He stood, stared at Ukalliq, hugged him. "Ukalliq. Little Rabbit."

"Do not stare at Paradise," Ukalliq said. "Her Light is too painful for the damned, though Her Heat is merciful."

"It is a short-lived mercy," a man said. Qavvik turned.

He was six feet tall or more, dressed in a parka and breeches like Ukalliq's, but his face had a savage countenance, due, perhaps, to the quilt of purple squares tattooed across his cheeks. He had no hat, no hair, except a little top-knot at his crown.

"I am Queequeg," he said, "late of the *Pequod*. I am your harpoonist." He held out his hand, and Qavvik reached behind his back, unstrapped the darting harpoon, and handed it to the giant. Queequeg hefted it, tested its weight, and smiled. "Is good," he said.

"We heard you were coming," Ukalliq said. "The Fallen Angels swept through several sleeps ago and told us a great whaler would come."

"But where are the whales?" Qavvik asked.

"Out there." Ukalliq turned, and Qavvik followed his gaze. "The Sea of Purgatory."

The Sea of Purgatory was one great flat plain of pink ice. Great ridges thrust up against the land, mountains of ice pushed against the coast, peaks along the horizon. The air flickered beyond the ridge; as Paradise rose, water and whitecaps could be seen glinting on the horizon.

"The leads are opening," Qavvik said.

"Ai, the channels will be filled with whales soon enough," Ukalliq said.

"Arviq?" Qavvik asked. "The whale?"

"No," Ukalliq said, "not Arviq. Arviqluaq. The gray whale, the whale that fights back."

"Az-zah," said Qavvik.

"Leviathan," Queequeg said. "The Great Whale."

The whalers took Qavvik to their village, a small mound at the end of a spit that thrust out into the Sea of Purgatory. They called the village Qitiqliq, which meant "middle finger." They were building sod houses for the days when Paradise would not shine, but the huts were incomplete, only depressions in the ground. For the moment, they lived in old canvas tents and warmed themselves by small blubber fires.

There were ten whalers—men, women—all tied to the sea in some way. They sat around a small fire, working on their whaling tools, trading tales. Pat, a small woman with short-cropped hair, dressed in a bright orange parka, asked Qavvik why he was in Hell.

"Pride," he said.

"Qavvik was a great man in our village," Ukalliq said. "He was a great shaman, a good hunter. He killed . . . how many whales?"

"Twelve," he said.

"You killed twelve whales?" Pat asked. "I do not understand you. The whale is a noble animal, with a language, intelligence. How could you kill a whale?"

"I was hungry," Qavvik said. "Who are you to judge?"

"I worked for Friends of the Whales," Pat said. "After your time. Our organization fought to keep the whalers from decimating the great herds."

"Pat's a suicide," Ukalliq said. "She boarded a Soviet whaling ship and jumped in front of a harpoon gun." He shrugged. "Ask her to show you her scar sometime." He smiled at her.

"Assholes," she said. Pat got up and walked away.

"Never mind her," Ukalliq said. "Qavvik, I want you to know that after you died you were a hero to our people. In my old age, the children feared and respected you, Qavvik."

Qavvik looked down. "That is good to hear." He pointed at Ukalliq. "But you? Why are you here? You never sinned. You were a deacon in the church."

Ukalliq shook his head. "I did not worship God," he said. "All that was a lie. My whole life, even in the church, I was praying to the whale." He fingered a charm around his neck, an ivory carving of a bowhead whale. "And I was wrong. My god does not exist. And God does."

"But your sin is less than mine," Qavvik said.

"All sins are equal in the eyes of God," Ukalliq said.

Pat came back with a slab of meat, handed it to Qavvik. "Eat this," she said.

"What is it?"

"Whale meat, from a stinker. We found Leviathan's body washed ashore last fall."

"No," said Ukalliq. "He hasn't eaten."

Pat glared at him. "*Eat.*"

Qavvik took the offered meat, held it to his mouth.

"No," said Ukalliq. "You shouldn't eat it."

Qavvik smiled. "You should know that it is wrong to refuse food offered by a woman." He bit down on the meat, chewed. "This is good."

"It is done," said Pat. She held her hands to her hips, laughed. "How do you like Hell food, whaler?"

"It is good," said Qavvik.

"I'm sorry," Ukalliq said.

"Sorry? Why?"

"Is this your first food?"

"Yes," said Qavvik. "It is good."

Ukalliq looked down. "I'm sorry. I tried to warn you."

"Warn me? Why? I was hungry." He turned to Pat. "Thank you."

"Do not thank her," said Ukalliq. "Now that you have eaten, you can never be satisfied."

"I do not understand."

"You must satisfy your hunger, and you will. But the food . . . the food will never settle."

"You cannot shit," said Queequeg.

"You will feel like you have to shit, but you cannot." Ukalliq winced. "Your groin feels like it's on fire. The only time you can shit is if you, well, if you—"

Queequeg held up his left hand; he was missing two fingers. "If you eat human flesh, you can shit. Little

tiny turds, but it's shit. The flesh grows back." He
rubbed tiny nubs growing from the stumps.

Qavvik put the meat down, stared at Pat. "I will eat
your *flesh* someday, little bitch."

Paradise rose in a high parabola, each day rising
earlier and earlier, until one day Paradise did not set.
The whalers could hear the ice creaking and groaning.
They had put watchers out, and one day Pat came
running into the camp.

"The whale," she said. "A pod of them beyond the
ridge."

They had a boat, an old wooden Yankee whaleboat,
built by a man named Wade. Wade had built the boat
so he could get to Purgatory. Like others, he had
believed that Purgatory was across the Sea of Purgatory, and that if he rowed long enough he could reach
the continent and make his way out of Hell. Soon after
he finished his boat, his work had been discovered and
the Fallen Angels fell upon him, flaying him alive and
casting his flesh to the whalers. The whalers said that
they sometimes saw Wade wandering the beach, a man
with no skin, searching for his flesh.

Wade's boat leaked, was heavy in the water, but it
could crack through ice. The whalers dragged the boat
out onto the ice, over the ridges, to the edge of an open
channel of water. And they waited.

Leviathan rose. The great gray whale burst through the
ice at the edge of the open channel of water. Ice cracked,
heaved, fell in great blocks around the hole. Leviathan
slipped back down, sank, came up again, hitting the ice
again. He popped out of the open hole, 80 feet of
whale, danced on his flukes, and then slammed down
onto the ice.

The shuddering ice woke the whalers from their sleep.
Qavvik got up, slipped on his mukluks, grabbed the
bomb gun, and ran for the boat. Queequeg was in the
bow, holding the harpoon. Qavvik jumped in, Ukalliq

joined them, other whalers came aboard. Pat climbed into the stern.

"No," said Ukalliq.

"I must witness this awful destruction," she said.

"Let her," Qavvik yelled from behind. "We do not have time to argue."

Pat climbed in, the whalers grabbed oars, and they shoved the boat over the ice and into the water. Twenty yards ahead Leviathan thrashed in the water, leaping up, slamming down, his belly flops like fifty elephants thrown onto the sea.

"He teases us," Ukalliq said. "Some say Leviathan is the Devil himself."

"Devil or not, we are going to catch him," Qavvik said. But he remembered the Grace's proclamation: you will hunt whales, but never catch them.

The boat crawled through the cold water, chunks of ice thumping against the sides. Water leaked through the cracks of Wade's crude boat, and Pat was put to bailing. They rowed, awkward strokes, but Leviathan was slow, and they closed the gap.

Leviathan swam slowly, his great flukes rising up and down like flapping bellows. They paddled gently, eased up ten yards, then five, then two yards behind the beast. Queequeg flicked the safety off the harpoon, raised the shaft. He took a quick breath, raised his arm, and thrust the harpoon into Leviathan.

Below the head of the harpoon was a small rod. The rod hit the whale and triggered a shotgun shell that drove a barbed bomb into the flesh, a bullet for behemoths. Queequeg counted; one thousand one, one thousand two, one thousand three. The bomb exploded, and Leviathan rose.

He was a mountain of flesh, a titan of tonnage, eighty feet of power and might and horror. Leviathan turned, head facing the whalers, and opened his great mouth. Teeth like swords—row upon row of teeth—gaped at them. Dead things oozed from the beast's mouth: demon fish, green slimy things, the battered pieces of the damned.

"Azah," said Qavvik, "that is not Arviqluaq. This is a beast I have never seen."

"It is Leviathan," said Pat. "It is the whale of all whales. He has come to get his revenge."

Qavvik hefted the bomb gun, a great gun with a barrel an inch-and-a-half wide, a barbed bomb down its barrel. "Perhaps," said Qavvik. "We will see what Leviathan can do against this."

Leviathan rolled over, dove, and went down. A line was attached from the harpoon to the boat, and when the whale dove, the line sang from the boat until all five hundred yards were strung out. The line yanked, and then the boat began moving.

"A Nantucket sleigh ride!" Queequeg yelled.

Qavvik shook his head, looked at Ukalliq. "It is not how we do it. We throw our floats, and let the whale drag the floats, not the boat." He stared at the great open leads. "But there is enough water. Perhaps the whale will not sound under the ice."

Leviathan towed them over small cakes of ice, through the open channel of water. The whale rose twice, lay gasping for breath, then sounded again. The third time the whale rose, Leviathan surfaced in a great red cloud of blood. He rolled over, began spinning, winding the line around his body.

"He's reeling us in," Ukalliq said.

"No," said Queequeg, "I think not. Qavvik, move up to the bow."

Qavvik traded places with Queequeg, stood at the bow, bomb gun ready. Leviathan rolled, blood oozing from a great wound in his back. Qavvik raised the gun, clicked the safety off, sighted down the barrel.

"Closer, closer," he said. "Okay, okay. Just a second . . ."

"My Lord," said Ukalliq.

Leviathan turned, great head facing them, and opened

his mouth. He rose up on his flukes, and fell back, yanking the boat toward the cavern of his mouth.

"Kill it!" Pat screamed behind him. "Kill the beast!"

Qavvik squeezed the trigger, fired at twenty feet. The bomb flew towards Leviathan's great eye, hit it, sank deep, and exploded. The whale fell back, pulling the boat toward him.

"Cut the line!" Qavvik yelled.

Ukalliq grabbed a hatchet, swung at the line, and cut it. Pat turned at the sound, screamed in horror as the line tightened around her foot and yanked her into the sea.

The boat drifted away. Pat thrashed in the water, was pulled to Leviathan, closer and closer, into the maw of the great beast. The whale opened his jaw, bit into Pat's chest, and speared her with his teeth. He shook her like a rag doll and spat her out. Leviathan rolled, eye streaming blood, kicked his flukes, and dove into the deep blue sea.

"A good hunt!" Qavvik yelled. "A good hunt!" He began singing his whale song, a low guttural scream.

The whalers rowed over to Pat's body, pulled it into the boat. Queequeg stared at the disappearing cloud of red. "But we did not catch the whale," he said.

Ukalliq smiled. "It does not matter. It was a good hunt. Next time. Next time we will catch the whale."

When they got back to their camp, they found a new darting harpoon, and five hundred yards of new line. They cut up Pat's body and feasted on her flesh.

They hunted Leviathan. Qavvik was never sure if it was the same whale or a different whale. The whalers would go out to the leads, set up camp, and always the whale would come. He came to them; they never had to hunt him. He came in an explosion of ice, or they would hear him moaning in the distance, or they would see him thrashing in the middle of the open channels. Whalers would come and go, and they would lose a whaler to Leviathan, and eat it like they ate Pat, but they never caught the whale. They would come close, but they never caught the whale.

Qavvik would stare at the open leads, at the vanishing bubbles, at the harpoon sticking from Leviathan's back, at the great wounds the bomb gun made. But he never caught the whale. They hunted well, but never caught the whale.

And he did not mind.

"Doesn't it bother you not to catch the whale?" Queequeg asked him around the campfire.

"Never," Qavvik said. "It is the hunt that is good. If the hunt is good, that is what matters. Perhaps I am not worthy of Leviathan. Perhaps that is why he does not come to me. Perhaps Leviathan does not wish to yield his body."

"I do not understand this," Queequeg said. "Why should you not be worthy? You are a good hunter. Is that not worth enough?"

"It is not enough to be a good hunter," Ukalliq said. "We believe that the whale gives up his body—his parka, we call it—only if we are worthy. We must please the whale. If we pleased Leviathan, then we would catch him. Obviously we do not please the whale. But we are in Hell. How can we please anybody?"

"True," said Queequeg. He smiled, neat white teeth in the patchwork of tattoos. "But we can try, right?"

So they tried.

Once they rescued a man from the jaws of the whale. They had harpooned Leviathan and were coming up on him for the kill. Leviathan rolled over, mouth agape, and a man swam out of the maw. They cut the whale loose, rowed over to the man, and pulled him out of the icy water.

He was blue and almost dead, and before his soul and body slipped back to Lord Satan for a new torment, he told them his story.

"I am Jose Marti, Cuban revolutionary," he said. "I

was swimming for Purgatory when Leviathan ate me.
You must help us. You must kill Leviathan."

"We are trying," said Qavvik. "You said 'us.' Who is
this 'us?'"

"We are the Revolution," said Marti. "We are led by
a great man, Che Guevara. There is something terribly
wrong in Hell. People who should be in Purgatory—or
even in Paradise—are damned to torments they do not
deserve. We have appealed to Satan, but our appeals
fall on deaf ears."

Queequeg smiled. "His ears are not deaf," he said.
"He simply likes to ponder these matters for a great
time. You should know that."

"We beseech God, but He does not listen to us. We
must get out. Many of us have tried to swim to Purgatory. But Leviathan gets us."

"That is true," said Qavvik. "We see many bodies
pierced on Leviathan's teeth. And when one of our own
falls into the water, Leviathan crushes their body, and
sends their soul back to Satan."

Marti sat up in the deck of the boat, clutched Qavvik
by his parka. "You must kill Leviathan. He cannot live
anymore." Jose Marti let go of Qavvik, fell to the deck,
and his soul went to Satan once more. They lifted his
body over the side and dropped it into the water.

Qavvik stared at Marti's body as he fell into the
depths. And an idea came to him.

"You are mad," Ukalliq said.

"Perhaps," said Qavvik. "Still, I see no other way to
kill the whale."

Qavvik and Ukalliq sat in the unfinished iglus of
Qitiqliq. Qavvik was greasing the barrel and stock of
the bomb gun with fat from the body of a man who had
gone back to Satan, one of the corpses that Leviathan
had spat back up. Ukalliq was sewing a watertight bag
from the man's skin.

"Do you know what happens to those who go back to
Satan?" Ukalliq asked.

Qavvik nodded. "I have heard stories."

"Stories! No story can match the reality. Did I tell you of the time when I first came here?"

"You have hinted."

"Ah, let me tell you more than hints. When I first came to Hell I was shamed at my torment. I went out on the ice, took off my parka and my boots, and let the cold take me. Paradise was not out, and I went quickly. I passed away. It was a great peace, a great sleep, but it did not last long. When I awoke, I was back with Satan. I had returned to New Hell. And there I met the Undertaker."

"The Undertaker? The man who puts bodies back together?"

Ukalliq nodded. "A horrible, disgusting man, with breath worse than shit—breath that smelled like walrus bile gone rancid for ten winters. When you awake, the Undertaker hovers over you, and tends to your wounds, and makes your body whole. He is very worried about you, and so gets very close, so the whole time you are smelling this awful, disgusting man. He looks like a great lemming—a lemming shaved bald. It is disgusting. But that is not all."

"What more can happen?"

"You enter Hell again. You must receive a new torment, and you must listen to the awful whinings of that fat pig, the Welcome Woman. When I met her again she was at the Undertaker's, watching my body become whole. When my penis grew back, she—you do not want to hear what she did."

"It sounds bad, Ukalliq."

"It *is* bad," Ukalliq said. "Qavvik, you are content with hunting the whale. Let us keep hunting."

"It is not enough anymore," Qavvik said. "I want to destroy Leviathan."

Ukalliq put the final stitch in the bag. "Done," he said, holding the bag up for Qavvik to see. "Do you think your plan will work?"

He smiled. "God's Grace told me that I was to hunt

Leviathan, but that I would never catch him. And so I will not. But God's Grace said nothing about destroying Leviathan. And so I will."

Qavvik slipped a bomb into the greased bomb gun, and handed the gun to Ukalliq. Ukalliq slipped the gun inside the bag, squeezed as much air out of the bag as he could, and stitched the bag tight. He walked over to a great tub of water, and held the bag and gun under. No air bubbles escaped, no water got into the bag.

"It will work," Ukalliq said.

Qavvik grinned.

Leviathan came to them on the edge of the ice, with a gentle moan that rose into a high squeal. The whalers jumped into the boat and gave chase. Leviathan swam slowly, let the whalers catch up with him. Queequeg stood in the bow, raised the darting harpoon, and drove the harpoon deep into the beast. The harpoon held, the bomb exploded, and Leviathan sank into a red sea.

He rose from the deep. The line flew out of the boat, whipped the boat around as it came to the end, and Leviathan towed the boat through the open channels, through the lead in the ice. Cakes of ice slammed against the side of the leaky boat, water sprayed over the bow, mist whipped through their parkas. Leviathan surfaced once, twice, three times, and then floated calmly on the surface, flukes flapping feebly.

"He tires again," said Queequeg. "Ah, his old trick."

The whale began rolling, wrapping the line around his great body, reeling the boat toward him. Queequeg and Qavvik changed places in the bow. Qavvik took out the bomb gun, still in its waterproof skin bag. He felt through the folds for the safety, switched it off, slipped a finger around the trigger.

"When we're within ten yards, cut the boat loose," he said.

"Aye," said Queequeg.

"You do not need to do this," Ukalliq said. "You can back out."

Qavvik shook his head. "I want to do this, Ukalliq."

"Satan may not send you back here."

"I will return," he said. "This is my home." Qavvik turned to Ukalliq, smiled. He reached up, tugged on the ulu in his head. The woman's knife came free. Qavvik smiled, handed the ulu to Ukalliq. "See, Little Rabbit? The blade comes free. It is a good sign. I will please Leviathan."

"Fifteen yards," Queequeg said.

"Goodbye," said Qavvik.

"Goodbye, Wolverine," said Ukalliq.

"Ten yards," Queequeg said. He cut the line.

Qavvik dove into the water, bomb gun held tight in his arms. He kicked toward Leviathan, swam toward the mouth. Leviathan opened his great jaws, and the water sank down his throat, a whirlpool sucking Qavvik into the maw. Qavvik held his head high, took deep breaths, and ducked as he was swept over and under the knifelike teeth. He sank down into the throat of the whale, into darkness.

He swallowed one last gasp of fetid, sulfurous air, puffed out his cheeks, kept his lips sealed. The whirlpool drew him down, down over the tongue of the monster, down toward the gullet.

As he swept down the whale's throat, under the brain, below the skull, Qavvik raised the bomb gun. He jammed it up into the soft skin at the base of the whale's skull and pulled the trigger. The gun kicked him back against the side of the gullet. Qavvik grabbed, hung onto a flap of flesh on the inside of the throat. He looked up, saw a great explosion above him, saw blood stream out from a hole two yards wide at the bottom of the whale's skull. Torrents of blood, torrents of gray slimy brains washed over Qavvik. He licked at the blood, let it wash down his throat, as the blood washed Qavvik down Leviathan's throat. Qavvik fell into the stomach of the whale, into darkness, into the deep blue sea.

The body of Leviathan, the parka of the great whale,

sank to the bottom, Qavvik in its stomach. Qavvik felt the breath go out of him, felt the cold wash over him, felt his body crushed by the deep. He went down and down and down, and sank into Hell. Darkness fell over him, and his soul passed on.

The horrible stench of the Undertaker's breath wafted over him, a fart from the ass of a corpse. Qavvik woke up, looked down at his body, looked up at the rat eyes of Satan's mortician. The Undertaker smiled.

"Ah, you are back," he said.

Qavvik looked down at his body. He was all cord and sinew, muscles and bones and blood vessels. He held a red-raw hand up, clenched and unclenched his fingers, winced as the muscles rubbed against each other.

"No need to do that," the Undertaker said. "We have a new skin for you—a new 'parka,' as you might say. Would you like to try it on?" He waved to a large slab, thirty yards long—a slab upon which there was laid out a great black bag. Qavvik felt his legs walk over to the skin, felt his body wriggle into the huge bag of flesh. He felt his muscles and bones and body grow and expand, fill up the skin, grow into the flesh. His body wriggled and oozed. When the skin was tight, he wiggled his arms, kicked his legs, felt the fins slap against his side, and felt the flukes slap the ground.

"Ah, a perfect fit," said the Undertaker. "I think you shall like your new body, little Wolverine." And he smiled, that awful smile of rotting teeth.

"Or," the Undertaker said, "should I say 'Leviathan?' "

SHARPER THAN A SERPENT'S TOOTH

C.J. Cherryh

The boy still slept, in that twilight world where he had rested much of the time since his return, in the broad bed, in the room with the record player and the rock and roll posters and the magazines and the pictures of green earthly fields and horses. He was seventeen. A little bit of a mustache and a touch of beard was on his face, shadow of a manhood he might never reach, in Hell—a down of beard which the sycophants zealously shaved away, as they tended him in these several days and nights; but they did not disturb his rest. Locks of black hair fell on his brow, about his ears; one well-muscled young arm lay across his chest, picked out like marble in the single stripe of light which came in from the door. His father stood looking down on him, and at last, carefully, settled on the bedside.

Brutus did not stir at that shifting of the mattress, and Julius Caesar reached out ever so gently and touched the boy's face, back of his forefinger tracing a line of bone which he saw in the mirror daily. It was a theft, that touch, stolen from time and Hell—a moment he had never managed to steal from life; and his hand trembled now, which had not trembled at many things on earth—not out of fear: it took more than an assassin to daunt him—but out of the enormity of what he stole from the Devil and from his enemies, and out of the sense of vulnerability he found in himself. The Devil had a hostage—here, in this bed. And he, Julius, veteran of plots and counterplots through centuries in Hell, possessor of vast power—risked everything in that touch.

"This isn't about Caesarion at all," Welch had said, that day in Julius' office—when Julius' second son had proven twice the fool and threatened Hell to pay if Julius did not retrieve him quickly from the allies he had chosen. Welch, the American, was an expensive man—unbuyable in coin. And from that moment and that observation Julius had looked on this recruit with doubt.

"It is," Julius had assured him, playing out the role, "most especially about Caesarion. My son the fool. My *son* who runs off to the Dissidents. Who compromises my interests."

"So make up your own family quarrels," Welch had said. "Put your own people on it."

Is that what they want? Is that the name of the game—bring my resources out of hiding? Who are you working for, Americane? It was Mithridates sent me Brutus. I know that. Sent me my bastard son—my assassin, stripped of memory, Marcus Junius Brutus, thinking he died on the Baiae road, all of seventeen . . . because it's as far as his recollection goes. Mithridates, in the Pentagram, the power who pulls Rameses' strings, keeps my murderer out of time, lo, all these centuries, and delivers him to me an innocent. The Dissidents take out Hadrian, the Supreme Commander who was, whatever his failings, Roman—and in comes Rameses and the East. Arrives Brutus, helpless and seventeen, on my doorstep. Exit Caesarion the rebel, from that lecher

Tiberius' den—to join Dissidents we know are a front for the Eastern faction.

And put my own people on it, this American says.

Was it Mithridates sent you last time, Welch, to work your way into my regard like this bastard son of mine? And have I made a fatal mistake?

"Augustus will kill the boy if he finds him," Julius had said, dour-faced. It was plausible enough. Augustus had indeed done it once and long ago. "Then no matter what strings you think Niccolo can pull, we may lose him forever."

"So." The American locked his hands behind him and paced a bit, looked at him with a curious turn of his head. "And you can't stop that? You got a real houseful here. Another son, what I hear. *Besides* Augustus. Rumor was true, was it? You. Brutus' mother."

Too many questions, Americane. *Far too many questions.* "Brutus was—is—a seventeen year old boy. Do you understand what that means? We just got him back. We don't know from where." *But we guess, don't we?* "He doesn't remember anything. You, of all men, ought to sympathize with that—"

—knowing that Welch himself alleged gaps in his memory. If it were so. If anything regarding this American was credible, this should be.

"Fine," Welch had said then, "I'll take Brutus with me—I need someone Caesarion can relate to, somebody he'll trust. Another one of your sons ought to do the trick."

That he had not expected; Julius had been, for once, caught facing the wrong flank. *Not* information. A challenge and a trap. "He . . . Brutus doesn't know Caesarion; they've never met here. Anyone but Brutus, Welch. Anything but that." And that was wrong to have said. Once into it, there was no way out but forward. He foreknew that little look of satisfaction on Welch's face, foreknew the demand, foreknew that he was compelled then, trapped, to make a play within a play, feigning Caesar feigning grief, which in fact was true, but he made his face hard and shot a calculating look which he well intended Welch to see—

If you are Mithridates' man; and Mithridates sent Brutus—

Beyond the play, beneath the double-layered grief and harshness, snake swallowing tail, that thought had come up like a foul bubble out of the dark. *If you ask for Brutus, if you seek him out—is it not that Mithridates thinks it time to throw the dice? Bring me back Caesarion. And what do you bring back in Brutus? Trojan horse, my Greek-loving American?*

But I dare not call a bluff—not of those that may pull your strings.

No, you will not lose them. You will not fail me. Not fail Mithridates, who will bring Brutus back himself— how could he fail a revenge he's planned . . . all these centuries? If Brutus should die there—Mithridates himself would bring him back.

"Yes," he had said to Welch. And thought: *I will have both of them returned. And you, too, Americane, into my hands. A man who can surprise me is too clever to leave to my enemies.*

The boy shifted, a turn of his head against the pillows, a movement of his hand, and an opening of confused eyes. Julius took back his hand, as Brutus started upright, eyes wide and his face a mask of terror in the stripe of light from the door. "Ah!" he cried.

Do you know that I know? Julius wondered. It was fate he tempted, sitting here within reach. Or it was his enemies.

"Father?" Brutus said then, a shaken whisper. "Father?" Desperately, the way a frightened boy might ask; the way a guilty boy could *not* ask, not with that tone of vulnerability.

Then Julius drew a whole breath, and rested his hands on his khaki-clad knees as he sat there on the bedside. *Not corrupted, then. Innocent.* But he distrusted what was so attractive to believe; and hardened his heart against that frightened face that peered at him out of drugs and the dark. "Who else?" he asked. "I didn't mean to wake you."

"I'm s-s-sorry—"

"Sorry? What for, boy?"

"I d-d-don't know."

"Don't stammer." He reached and patted the side of Brutus' arm, fatherly reproof. "Feeling better, are you?"

"I—"

"Thought it was best to let you sleep."

Brutus heaved himself further upright in bed, swung his feet for the side and caught himself suddenly against his arms. "Uhhh!"

"Dizzy."

"*Di 'mortales.*" Brutus' head hung. He shook it and groped after balance, looking up, shadow-faced ghost, the light falling across taut muscle of shoulder and side. "I'm weak."

"It's the medicines."

"I flew—"

So the memory was intact. Lethe-water had confused it, dimmed all recent recollection, but it had not uprooted the event itself. Rope-burns on his arms. A fear of falling. Damned American had parachuted the boy out of a plane, during which Brutus, who had never seen a plane close-up, much less contemplated jumping out of one, had managed to stay sane. And then the damned American snagged him while he was still shaken and tied him to a tree—when Brutus had thought he had come along to help.

So he had understood then, surely, that his father had turned him over to an enemy.

"I had to do it," Julius said. And then, cruelly, because he was old in Hell, far older than Brutus, in the way Hell's time ran—and knew how to manipulate: "I knew you could do it. I knew you were man enough."

A shudder ran through the waxen body. "I fell. I jumped like he told me to—Welch. He said I had to find my b-brother. He said th-th—"

"Don't stammer."

"Th-that he was your enemy."

"He. Welch?"

"Caesarion. My—*b-b-brother.*"

Julius drew in his breath. Truth, from Welch to Brutus? That fell out of the stack, untidy, distressing in implications of miscalculation about the American.

"He's K-klea's s-son. I know th-that. Is he m-my enemy? Or y-yours? "

Too much bewilderment. Too many changes. There was no chance that it was an act . . . unless one of Hell's friends had made a switch, and bedded down in Brutus' stead.

"Both, maybe," Julius said.

The face that stared back at him—gods, out of a mirror, so many, many years ago. A little of him. A little of the woman he had loved—in his own callow youth. The boy was terrified. Starkly terrified.

"What are the D-Dissidents?"

Clever lad. Right to the mechanics of the thing. Not a shallow question: Brutus knew *what* the Dissidents were; they were the nuisanceful folk who had kidnapped the Supreme Commander, Hadrianus, whom Julius' own agents kept in hiding; they were Hell's recent difficulty, and the stated reason for Julius' treks into the field—which was a lie, but never mind; most of Hell accepted it. Except, perhaps, Brutus, who had seen Scaevola raving about the towers of Ilium.

Well. . . .

"Which answer do you want, boy? What they've got to do with Caesarion?"

"That. First."

"You know Augustus is my son too. Great-nephew. Adopted."

Brutus nodded.

"Well, I married Klea. Egyptian law. Never mind that I had a wife in Rome—" Julius made a face. "It was legal—in Egypt. And null and void in Rome. Smart man, eh? But Klea turned up pregnant. Gave me a son and a tangle . . . because he was the only damned in-wedlock son I'd gotten. But he was half Ptolemiades and half Julian; half foreign and half Roman; and illegitimate in Rome but heir to Egypt. Klea's little maneuvering. My softheadedness. That was Caesarion. I'll tell you something. When you're old, and I was old, yes, and that was my last chance at a son—"

"And I was long gone."

Julius did not let the wincing show. "It was long past that summer in Baiae. My last chance, I say. I didn't live to see him grown. I knew—" *Knew about the conspiracy, son, that I wouldn't last the week; I knew Rome couldn't survive, and Caesarion couldn't, not a boy made heir to an unwilling Rome. So I kept my will—adopting my nephew. Gods, how that galled Antonius!* "Knew I had so little time. Augustus succeeded me in Rome. But it was Antonius who brought up Caesarion in Alexandria. He married Klea then. And Augustus' sister in Rome. Damned mess. Eventually Rome went to war—again. Antonius died in it. So did Caesarion. And Klea." He rested his hand on the sheet where it covered Brutus' ankle, gently, ever so gently and matter-of-factly. "Caesarion was a rebel even then. He threatened Rome. I don't say Augustus was right. It was a hard thing to do. But the whole damned East could have peeled away from Rome. Lives lost. Wars upon wars. In fact it was a soldier killed Caesarion, for Augustus' sake, because that soldier understood the way it was; did it in the heat of things and then knew that Augustus might kill him, you understand; but he did it partly for Rome and partly because he was Roman and Rome hated Caesarion. I'm telling you all the truth now. It was an ugly business. Augustus could have executed that soldier and kept his hands clean: but so many died, it was so quiet, you understand. It was just too easy to say nothing at all. And if the rumor got out, well, that was Augustus' style: no official statement. Just regrets. And Rome, you see, Rome wanted to take it at that, didn't want the blood on its hands; was glad

Caesarion was gone. Was guilty to be glad. So they took
the regrets and made up rumors. Maybe Caesarion
walked off into the desert. Maybe he was still alive.
Who knew? So many did and so many died. Do you
understand? Do you understand why Caesarion doesn't
forgive me?"

Brutus only stared, his mouth slightly open.

"And why he hates you?" Julius asked.

Brutus gave his head a little shake, as if any movement was too much. Julius closed his hand down hard
on the ankle.

"Politics, son. It's politics the way it was played in
those days. And look now: Klea's here, under Augustus'
roof. They understand. They're fond of each other.
Share a little wine. Talk about old times." He shook at
Brutus' leg. "Perspective, son. Klea's my wife. She's
Antonius' wife too. My wife, my adopted son, my old
friend. They don't live the past over and over. I don't.
Only Caesarion is stuck at seventeen. Never gets older.
Never any wiser. Seventeen is all his understanding,
just those years he had and who killed him."

"I'm s-s-seventeen."

"Don't stammer. There's a lad. Irony, yes." Marcus
Junius Brutus, assassin—thought that he had died falling off a horse, while thinking about a girl in Baiae.
Marcus Brutus who had suffered the whispers of bas-
tardy all his young life. It was all he remembered . . .
and none of the later, more tangled truth, nothing of
politics, and civil war and a disillusioned, hurting man
who had committed patricide. *For hate of Caesarion?
I never got to ask you. Never could ask you why.
Surprised hell out of me, son, seeing you with the
assassins. Hurt like hell, too. Damn, where you hit.
Did you aim? Or was it a flinch on your part?* "You're
shivering, boy."

"C-Cold." Brutus drew his foot up, pulled the sheets
up to his chin as he sat there in the shaft of light. "I
j-jumped out of that plane. W-Welch said I should
j-just fall out and c-count."

"Brave lad. I'm sure I wouldn't have had it in me. Seriously. Airplanes are bad enough. Jumping out of them—I wouldn't like that."

"You s-sent me with him."

There. The accusation. The hurt. "Do you want the truth?" The lure and the bait. Brutus stared at him with glistening eyes and a mouth clamped tight. And nodded then, shortly, defensively.

"I had no choice," Julius said. "I trusted Welch. Welch didn't trust me. I knew he'd get you out. Caesarion was the one at risk. Caesarion—was the one who could lose himself to my enemies. I trusted *you*. I thought—one of my sons could reach him. I didn't know that Welch would be a fool. I didn't know that he'd throw away the chance he had. You could have helped. You might have made a difference. You never got a chance."

It was a lie, of course. It aimed at a boy's self-confidence in his father's sight, at a consuming desire for love. It burned in him. It knotted up the muscles of his shoulders and made him shiver again.

"Is C-Caesarion—h-here?"

"He's in our hands. He's safe. It all worked out. Most of all I'm worried for you. It was a damned mess. I'll have Welch's guts for what he did."

A stare. A small, desperate shake of the head. "He d-d-didn't hurt me. Don't."

"Let me judge that."

"No." A second shake of the head, eyes despairing. Brutus' mouth firmed in a convulsive effort. "I'm all r-right. He didn't d-do anything." Through chattering teeth. It was stark terror.

Of what? Of me? Of death and hell? Why—plead for Welch?

"You can get anything out of me," Julius said softly. "You know that."

A softening, then, a relaxation of the mouth, the eyes, till defenses crumbled and there was only vulnerability. "You won't, then."

"I won't. Are you all right?"

"I'm all r-right. . . ."

Julius opened his arms. It was due. He had calculated it to exactitude, what was needful with the boy, if it was Brutus, if Hell had not deceived him. He took a chance. And the boy took his, cast himself into that absolving embrace, a chilled, taut body trembling against him till he locked his arms the tighter and felt Brutus steady.

Gods, it felt too good—to have a son, to have one son who loved him, after all eternity. He patted Brutus' shoulder, stroked his hair, turned his head to lean against Brutus' head, knowing all the while that he was holding the enemy's weapon, that even as much truth as he had told was a seed that would grow in Brutus' mind, and that even Lethe-water could not hold back the truth forever. There was no weapon he had in this private war but love. To turn the blade barehanded—he had tried that, the day they had killed him. It had not worked then.

At the end, Brutus had died a suicide. But it was Augustus and Antonius who had driven him. It was all they had left him. They were all Julians, even Antonius, in his grandfather's blood. Augustus, Antonius, Caesarion and Brutus and himself. All Julians, all damned, and Brutus the patricide damned the most of all—whose hell was innocence.

"He's still in there," Klea said, taking a careful and worried look around the corner of the upstairs hall, and with rare familiarity Niccolo Machiavelli seized her petite pale hand in his and drew her back again to prudence.

"Caesar will handle it," Niccolo said softly. "*Prego*, do not hasten things. It is very delicate."

Kleopatra gazed up at him, piquant face and short blond curls and dark eyes, *dio!* which could have launched armadas—Which had, in point of fact, launched two, though the little queen had led one of them herself. She was dressed in a black pleated skirt, 1930s mode; in a cream silk blouse; in black heels which did little to bring her up to Niccolo's lank height. And he, creature of habit, wore scholar's black, a doublet of fine, even elegant cut, a little accent of white here, of red at the shoulders. He had so recently come from things less elegant and less comfortable than Augustus' sprawling villa. He so dreaded a mistake or miscue that might send him out again; and he found the chance of that in the lovely Ptolemiades' distress over her own son, imprisoned below, and over Julius, who lingered tonight with young Brutus.

Julius had said—that he would speak to the boy. And Julius had also said to keep an eye on Klea, which, gratifying task that it was, made Niccolo very nervous. He had run afoul of Julius' well-known temper in matters not minor at all. And doubled as he was between Julius and Administration, Niccolo Machiavelli felt the heat indeed.

"He never should have let the boy go!" Klea cried softly. "Niccolo, I am going to see my son. Whatever he says, I'm going to talk to him—"

Niccolo caught a pair of shapely, silk-clad shoulders and faced the pharaoh of latter Egypt toward him again . . . huge eyes, dark with indignation, mouth open to protest this violence. He laid a cautioning finger on his own lips. "*Prego, prego, signora,* not now. Later."

"Later, when Julius—!"

"*Bellissima signora.*" He took firm hold of her shoulders and kept his voice very low. "At least, at least wait. I beg you. Do not put me in a position. *Ecco,* I will help you, majesty, but be calm, do nothing rash. We are all in sympathy. Believe me."

"Believe *you!*"

It stung, it truly did. Niccolo straightened somewhat with a little gesture at his heart and a lifting of his head. "*Madonna,* your servant. One who has your interests and Julius' at heart."

"One who has his precious hide at heart."

"One and the same, *madonna*. Come, come, let us go." Against her fury he made his voice soothing, his manner quiet and reasoning. "I cannot leave you."

"What, is it my bed next?"

"*Madonna*, I should perish of such a favor. In the meantime, I cannot permit, cannot—do you understand? Come. Come, let us go downstairs, let us talk among friends. Please! I assure your majesty—we are all concerned."

"*Because my son is in chains in the basement!*"

"An exaggeration. I assure your majesty. Please."

She spun on a neat French heel and started walking, back the way she had come, determined sway of hips and black pleats, the squared resolution of silk-clad shoulders. The vanishing perspective was enchanting, and not lost on Niccolo Machiavelli, amid a relief in one direction, that she had not made a try at Brutus, and alarm in the other, that those stairs for which the little Ptolemy was headed, led equally well to Caesarion's makeshift cell in the storerooms. He hastened, then, waved his hand at a sycophant which had picked up his distress. It wailed and trailed its substance out of his path. Damned creature.

Then: "Find Hatshepsut," he said on inspiration. "Quickly. Quickly."

The creature fled. It had a mission. It might find favor. It fairly glowed in the air as it streamed for the floor and through it, under Niccolo's hurrying footsteps.

He was only a legionary, dodging in and out the slow movement of supply vans and trucks and jeeps, in the sodium-lit darkness of the East New Hell Armory . . . a great deal of grumbling of motors, slamming of doors, squealing of brakes as a third-line centurion walked up and down the rows checking off one truck and another. The convoy was headed out for the patrols that kept the hills clear, the villas and New Hell itself free of attack. Some of the Tenth was out there, and the Twelfth . . . so he had heard. He did not ask. He had not asked for this summons that involved driving his car out to a certain dirt road in the woods near the armory and transferring to the hands of legionaries who dressed him in a khaki uniform and dumped him yonder, from a troop truck, to make his way through this maze with a notebook in hand—a notebook, that badge of men entitled to go crosswise through the chaos of a moving unit, and right up the steps of the armory itself.

Down an unremarkable hall, the ordinary plasterboard and paint of 20th century architecture. He found his door, showed a pass to the rifle-carrying guards who stood there, and walked on with one of them for escort, measured tread of boots on cheap green tiles in a nasty green hallway, but one which had real light fixtures, government issue, and the smell of recent paint in a wing which he had never, in all his career, visited.

More doors, double, this time; windowless, painted steel, that gave back on a dim room in which metal glittered all about the walls, bowed, rectangular shields, staffs, bannered and not, staffs that bore golden hands, and circles in various arrangements, all massed at the end of the hall, where fire burned. And among them, taller standards, winged and gold, sending a chill through the blood, a gathering of Eagles that flung their winged shadows about the room. About the walls, rectangular shields, legion shields worked not in leather but in gold, hung one after the other in their precedences, the thunderbolt of the Tenth, the Jupiter and Bolts of the Twelfth Fulminata centermost to the Eagles and the standards. A single space was vacant. A set of standards and an Eagle would be with it: Victoria Victrix, it might be, which was on duty on the southern coast.

Napoleon Bonaparte knew what it was he saw, to which outsiders were not admitted; and the Emperor of France felt his shoulders tighten as the legionary-guide brought his rifle to rest with an echoing rattle of modern weapons. *Why am I here?* he started to ask; and heard the second set of footsteps clicking from behind those sounds, saw the officer advance down the hall

from which they had come—a man he would see in the
legions as identical to a dozen others, as Roman, as
stern and hawk-nosed and lean as a wolf in winter.

No display of brass, no panache at all. But when that
man walked in, the guard braced up stiff; and when that
man lifted his hand that guard brought his rifle up and
took himself outside, closing the door behind him. At
this range Napoleon knew him very well indeed.

"Decius Mus," the Roman said.

The redoubtable Mouse. Caesar's personal shadow.

"Napoleon," Napoleon said, for courtesy's sake. "Bonaparte. To old times, is it?"

Mouse's face hardly varied. But he walked further
into the room, so that it was the legion shrine which
backed him, and the fires that leapt and flared on gold
did the same about Mouse's figure. This was a Roman
older than Caesar. This was the man who had volunteered for Hell, and *chose* to be here, having sent a
good part of an enemy army ahead of him. This was the
man—they said—to kill whom was worth a deeper hell
than this, and Napoleon thought of this as he looked
into that old-young face, among the fires.

"Caesar sent me," Mouse said. "I speak for him." It
was English the Roman spoke, with an Italian accent.

"I don't doubt," Napoleon murmured, and there was
the most terrible feeling of a call-to-arms, that summons which he had most zealously avoided. "But I have
expressed to your emperor that I am retired, that I
remain most ardently retired, *m'sieur le souris,* and a
man who bumps my car in traffic and murmurs assigna-
tions and gives me rings with his apologies is not the
way I prefer my mail, *m'sieur,* which you may tell to
Julius, with my profound regards. How am I to know
who asks me out on a deserted road, how am I to know
whose Romans they are who expect me to get out and
undress in the dark?"

The least humor touched the hawk-nosed face. "The
ring, *m'sieur.* Julius does not often part with it."

Napoleon scowled and slid the heavy gold signet

from his last finger. Easy done. His ring size was smaller.
Mouse slipped it on. Figure of Venus intaglio on that
ring, Venus Genetrix, patron of clan Julia. God knew
he had seen that ring and its impressions through the
centuries. And there was no question, no question that
he had to come, or *why* he had come on this fool's
venture, alone, on this outer edge of town, beyond
which was wilderness and worse.

"Retired," he said.

"There was a set-to in the hills," Mouse said, "very
recently. Che Guevara has taken the Trip."

"Good riddance."

"Louis XIV is planning an event. A grand ball, you
would say. A very elaborate affair."

"A damned—" *Tedious* stuck in his throat. Tedious,
looking into the Roman's implacable face, did not seem
the probable word.

"Exactly your *consocii*. Your associates."

"I have nothing, *nothing*, in common with that crowd.
I maintain no contacts, none whatsoever—"

"You will receive an invitation. Accept it. You will
not be compromised."

"Not be compromised."

The Roman walked a pace or two and looked at him
again, faceless against the light and the glitter of ancient
gold. "There is a delicate situation. Say that a well-
placed source is in possession of papers. He wishes to
change allegiances, East to West, shall we say?"

"Then, dammit, let him bang my car and pass the
damned paper!"

The shadow bent its head. Locked its hands behind
it. "*M'sieur*, I would much prefer it. But this is a very
well-placed source. This is a very cautious source, with
a great deal to lose. He wants to do this very indirectly.
A third party to our third party. He has known Julius.
He wants to be courted."

"Well-placed."

"One name is Tigellinus."

"*Mon dieu!* Nero's pet!" Napoleon flung up his hands. "I refuse. The man is filth, is—!"

"—is doubled. Considerably. He may achieve cabinet rank. He's presently up for appointment. Do you see? Tigellinus is the key Mithridates is using to Tiberius' villa; he already has agents in the ministries. The murderer of Romans is courting certain Romans, is establishing ties within Tiberius' household—"

"I don't want the names!"

"—and in Louis' society. Very close to home. But the debacle in the hills has left a certain paper—fallout, I believe in the expression. Certain papers are in the hands of a very disillusioned man. Whose agents will find you there, to pass you a certain original document. Suffice it to say, Tigellinus will not want that to come to light."

"I don't want to know these things."

"Without these things you will be vulnerable. Be assured: Caesar is detaching Attila to your assistance."

"*Dieu en ciel.*" There was a sinking feeling at Napoleon's stomach. A small lurch of panic.

"The contact will come. You have only to receive the paper and take your leave, all very smooth. You'll have a string on you all the way. No problems. You'll find your drop where your car is now. And you will have done Caesar a great favor."

Napoleon clenched his fists. But the damned arrogant Roman turned his back and walked away, to stand before the standards, shadow still. As Mouse's speech went, it had been a major oration. And now Mouse was done. Stood there, facing the Eagles, leaving the emperor of France to find his way from the room.

"I take it you are done with courtesies."

"Caesar has done you a favor." Not a twitch. Not an inflection. This *servant* of Caesar's had delivered his speech and was out of courtesies. Republican Roman, Caesar had warned him about Mouse. Not tolerant of outsiders. Nor of emperors. "Attila will contact you."

"*Mon dieu*, the man *has* no discretion!"

"More than you would imagine, *m'sieur l'empereur*. But you do not need to know that part of our operations. I would not advise it."

Shadow before the fires, broad-shouldered and modern in its outlines, against the shields and the standards. Devotions? Napoleon wondered. But this was a man who had delivered himself to Hell, a willing sacrifice to the darkest of his gods.

Napoleon drew in a sharp and furious breath, and turned and strode out; but he was glad to be back in the light, back in modern surroundings, more akin to his age than what lay behind those doors. He rubbed his finger from which something only moderately ancient had parted. Something which belonged to a man he had thought he knew. He had thought all these years that he had known.

But the smell of fire and antiquity stayed with him, out the doors and into the keen night air.

"There, there," Hatshepsut said, leaning across the glass and wire table to pat Klea's hand. The interception, for which Niccolo was profoundly grateful, had been swift and sure, and the distraught latter-age pharaoh sat with a glass of excellent Piesporter before her, the stem in one listless hand, the strong, darker hand of Hatshepsut holding the fingers of the other. Sargon had come. The short, stocky Akkadian had a beer in hand, his broad face all frown: an ancient of the ancients, bare-chested, kilted and with a dagger at his belt, while Hatshepsut of Egypt wore a silver jumpsuit, *most* distractingly transparent here and there in shifting patterns as the light hit it. Gold and brass and silver adorned her wrist and circleted her black, bobbed hair, *uraeus*-like, but the serpent wound its tail right round beneath that coiffure and into her ear—not engaged, now, Niccolo thought: mere decoration. But one never knew.

"Don't give me advice," Klea said. "I know, I know

all Julius' reasons. Does it mean that he's *right?* Because Julius wants it, is it always *right?*"

"Listen to me, kit."

"Don't take that tone with me!" Klea snatched her hand back, and the wine sloshed perilously in the glass. Her eyes, suffused with tears, turned to Sargon, turned to Niccolo. "You said you'd help. Who's on watch down there?"

"Regulus' guard. Not bribable, *signora.* But if you want me to reconnoiter I will. I will try to carry a message. Understand—" Niccolo cleared his throat. "Caesar has *me* under surveillance. This will not be without personal hazard. But if you will write this out—if you can be clever about it—I believe I can persuade Caesar himself to permit it."

"Damn you, you have an opinion of yourself."

"Tssss," said Sargon. "Niccolo is *not* the boy's mother. He has far more chance of reasoning with Julius."

Kleopatra took up the wine glass and took a healthy slug of it. Moisture threatened her makeup. "Paper," she said. "Pen." There was a chittering in the air, a rushing here and there among the insubstantial servants. Hands materialized to dab at a little spilled wine, to fill the glass again, but Niccolo swatted at the latter—"*Vatene*, let the bottle alone." He topped off the glass himself, spilling not a drop, while the requested paper and pen materialized and flurried across the room to arrange themselves in front of the little Ptolemy.

Kleopatra seized up the pen and set it to the paper, lifted it without a mark and bit anxiously at the cap as her brow furrowed in thought.

"A sentiment," Niccolo said, "that will be easiest to get through. An expression of concern. *Your mother is here.* I can persuade Julius that *that* has value."

"Of course he knows I'm here! That's the problem, dammit!" Klea lifted the glass and drank. Her hand shook and spilled a straw-colored drop on the paper. "Damn!" A fierce brush then at the moisture.

"Maternal tears," Niccolo murmured. "Very effective."

Kleopatra glared at him, then set pen to paper, hesitated, wrote, and hesitated again, wiping her cheek with a pale hand. The hand when she set it back to paper, trembled violently, her frail shoulders hunched, and her head lifted with a wide-eyed, open-mouthed stare at Niccolo.

"Oh, damn you, damn you—"

"Don't just sit there," Hatshepsut said, thrusting back her chair, a scrape of metal on terrazzo. She took Klea by the shoulders; and Sargon was hardly slower, taking the pen from Klea's unresisting fingers, supporting her drooping head.

"A fine help you are," Hatshepsut snapped at Niccolo.

"They always blame me," Niccolo said in genuine offense. "Why do they always look at *me?*"

It was a narrow hallway, down among the storerooms. In fact the room had seen such use before, was a prison with all the plumbing, inescapable, for Caesarion had tried the door, probed the windowless walls, had examined the cot for materials for weapons and paced and paced till he knew it was useless and until the anxious sycophants that came and went through the walls of the place began to crowd upon him with chittering admonitions to be still, to give in, a hundred whispering voices, touching hands, contacts which brushed against him until he flung his arms about and yelled at them for silence.

It only diminished the volume of it. The voices maintained a continual susurrus, *give up, give in, hush, you'll only harm yourself* . . . till Caesarion tucked himself up in a corner of his cot against the wall and held his hands over his ears, breathing in great gasps. Still the touches came at his body. He flailed at them and screamed aloud, great inarticulate screams of outrage.

Then, quietly, huddled amid the blankets in a fetal knot: *Mother*. But that was only in his mind, because he had had his tutelage in the courts of Egypt, and the hall of mad Tiberius on the lake, where sycophants were ordinary and betrayal was matter of course; and where only great fools opened up their hearts in a matter of sentiment. There was no one, finally. His half-sister Selene and his half-brothers Alexander and Ptolemaios, Antonius' Eastern brood, had made their accommodations with their destiny—Selene and Alexander Helios at Assurbanipal's court, Ptolemaios at Tiberius' court, lost in his library and his pretensions—oh, and there were the Romans: half-sister Julia, who was lost, he had never met; Antonius' daughter Antonia and her mother Octavia were Augustus' kin, and lived in retirement, in decent shame, it might be. His nymphomaniac remote *cousin* Julia was in and out of Tiberius' court, off lately with her darling daughter Agrippina, in Tiberius' disfavor (in this case tasteful) of Caligula and all his hangers-on—Zeus and Bastet! it was a household. But he would rather face the devils he knew than face the ones here, in this house, his father, and his two damned brothers, the one who had murdered him and the one who had murdered his father.

He clenched his hands against his eyes and gritted his teeth and tried not to hear the voices counseling surrender. He hid his face in the blankets and turned over finally, scanning the ceiling for convenient places for a rope made of bedding—There were none. And there were the sycophants, who would bring alarm, who would—

He relaxed, sprawled wide on the bed, staring and thinking of that, that there was one way out and past the guards.

What are you doing? the voices wondered as he rolled out of bed and applied his teeth to start a tear in the sheet. He grinned at them, tucked up barefoot as they had left him—barefoot and beltless and without his jacket, just a tee shirt and pair of jeans, well-searched. He ripped another strip and began to tear a third.

Sycophants were not an intelligent breed, but they smelled disaster. They began to tug at the sheet. Voices reached a whispering crescendo as they tore at the strips in his hands, pulled with less success at him, and sycophants by the hundreds began swirling about and through the walls—*Help, help!* they cried; and *Not our fault!*

It took about a quarter of a minute to have a key turning in the lock and that steel door opening; and Ptolemy XV Caesarion launched himself with a drive of his heels, knocked a startled legionary into the door frame, and used karate on a second as he barreled toward the last guard who, he was betting, dared not shoot him.

"Halt!" the man yelled, and swung a rifle butt at him, but Caesarion sucked his gut out of the way and slid past, pelting for the door at the end.

Which was locked.

"Oh, shit!" Caesarion moaned, and turned back to face three irritated and oversized legionaries in a hall with one exit only.

One legionary crooked his finger at him.

Then: *No, no, no,* a lone sycophant wailed, materializing between. *Caesar* wants! Caesar wants!

The magic word. The legionaries glared and Caesarion, feeling his knees weak, slumped back against the door.

"It was stupid," Julius said. "I don't say it wasn't a good try."

"You want to take the cuffs off—*father*."

Sullen look from under too-long black hair. Cheekbones and coloring his; the mouth Klea's, full and giving Caesarion a girlish handsomeness. Gods *knew* what Tiberius' house had taught the boy. Not that swagger, not that dark glare from under the brows; that did not go well with courtiers. Julius watched his youngest son walk over and drop himself, hands chained behind him, into a slouch in a fragile chair, curl the toes of his bare feet under him like a small boy and stare at him with the surliness of a defeated general.

"No," Julius answered, regarding the chains, "I don't, particularly."

"I'm a Roman citizen."

"Fine. That entitles you to one appeal and a beheading. *Venus cloacina, quoadmodum insaniam petisti? Nonne Antonius te meliores instruxit?*"

"Sure, he taught me a lot of things. Taught me everything an old sot could. Tiberius too."

Julius stopped his hand, not before Caesarion flinched and shut his eyes. *Damn, that's what he's after, that's what he wants, that's what he believes in.* He turned it into a gentler gesture, patted Caesarion on the shoulder. Caesarion jerked the shoulder aside, and glared through a fall of black hair. Klea's mouth, set in fury.

"Look." Julius put a few paces between them, sat down on the desk edge. "You could have come here any time. Nothing ever stopped you."

"Sure."

"*Quid petis?*"

"Enough with the Latin. It's not *my* language."

"You're a spoiled brat. Damn, you're spoiled."

"Sure. Coddled half to death."

"You're damned lazy! You don't think! How far in Hell did you think you were going to get till you found a door?"

Shift feet and hit him with a specific off the flank. Caesarion's mouth, open to shout, shut while he regrouped.

"How far in Hell," Julius threw after that, "did you think you were going to get with the losers you were running around the hills with? Peace and justice? Overthrow the Administration? I know. It's Satan's place you're after."

"I'm looking at him."

"I *have* looked at him, which is a damn sight more than my fool youngest son can say. I've worked in the Pentagram, which is a damn sight more experience than you have, son, and if you think that was an army you were with, if you think that was the grand army going

to liberate Hell and take on Paradise, you are a damned
shortsighted fool! Look at yourself!"

"You killed them." The chin, firm till now, quivered.
"Men, women, kids, you blew them all away. No, they
didn't have a chance. No more than me."

"*Than I,* dammit, you grew up illiterate to boot."

"Split grammars with me. Is that all it means?"

"Means. My gods, means. We're at that age, are we?
The meaning of life. Look at Curtius, he died young,
but he *changes,* for godssakes! Man looks eighteen
and thinks like three thousand. Put him in the field,
you know he'll do his job, he'll think it through. Damn,
you're a thundering disappointment."

"Then fuck you."

"What did you say?"

"Fuck—"

This time Julius came off the desk and the hand did
not stop. It cracked, ring and all, backhand across
Caesarion's cheekbone; and the chair rocked. Caesarion's
head went over, his body did, and it was a moment
before he lifted his head, with a welt started white and
red, and the mark of the signet a split in the skin. His
brain was rattled. It could not but be. And the front
was gone. The bluff was called and the boy did not want
to be here now, in this situation, facing more of the
same with his wits addled.

"Boy," Julius said, pulling Caesarion's chin up. "You
don't insult a man from that position. That's real stupid.
That's what I'm talking about. You don't expect real
consequences, you don't live in a real world, you go
and do things you're bright enough to know won't work,
but you're not living, you're writing little plays that
don't come out that way in real life, son, and they get
people killed, the same way Che Guevara got his people killed, the same way lousy tacticians all over Hell
get their followers sent back to the Undertaker like
cordwood, and the same way they'll always find sheep
to bleat after their causes and pigs to swallow the swill
they put out. You want to say that again, son?"

Caesarion's face was set in fury, red except for the white mark on his cheek; the eyes ran tears and his whole body quivered. But very judiciously he tipped his chin up in the old Med *no*.

"That's a hell of a lot better," Julius said. "Hell of a lot. I'm relieved. I thought I'd sired a fool."

"You'll find not. Sir."

Hate. Outright hate. But much better control.

"That's fine," Julius said. "Next time you break for a door, I hope to hell you counted 'em on the way in."

Caesarion's eyes flickered. It was genuine embarrassment.

"Damn," Julius said, "there's so much you could learn."

"I'm not your son! I never had a chance to be. I never knew you. And I'm not Roman."

"Doesn't matter. Sorry about getting assassinated. I didn't plan that, you know.

"Then *you* made a mistake, didn't you?"

"Son, I do occasionally make them. I'm generally good at fixing them."

"Except me."

"Your mother wrote you a note. I didn't want her down there." Julius picked up the wine-stained paper. Held it out as if he had forgotten about the cuffs, then fished the key out of his pocket. "Here, well. Let's be rid of those."

Caesarion turned in his chair, offered his hands meekly enough, rubbed at his shoulders when he was free and then took the offered paper.

Your mother is here, Klea had written. *I love you.*

Caesarion's hand trembled. He wadded up the paper and clenched it in his fist. "Touching. Where is she?"

"You'll see her when you manage that mouth of yours. *That* may take some time."

"I'm not staying here."

Julius shook his head wearily. "Son, if you're going to escape, *don't* announce it."

"Damn you!" Caesarion came out of the chair.

Julius blocked the blow left-handed. His right sent Caesarion back into the chair and the chair screeching back against the wall.

"You're no better with your hands free," Julius said.

Caesarion put his hand up to his jaw and looked toward nothing at all.

"Going to be a fool all your life?" Julius asked him. "My gods, boy, you've got a brain. Are we playing games, or are you here, in my study, with my guards out there, and the damned Dissident army funded and run by the Pentagram—"

Dark eyes came up to his, wide and angry.

"Run by the Pentagram," Julius said. "Officers installed. Paid for. Guevara's betrayed. It's a damned *front* for a Pentagram split, son, your great revolutionary leader is either in their pay or he isn't, and if he isn't, he's been had. If he is, he's had you. Which will you bet?"

"It's a lie."

"It's a lie. Of course it's a lie. Guevara's brilliant. There aren't any mercs coming into the cause. Just all purity of purpose. *Di immortales*, boy, Guevara's taken the Trip so often he just waits for the next, comes out like a puppet and staggers through the motions and damned lunatics follow him. You think the Pentagram couldn't crush that headless snake? It's damned useful having it thrash about, lets them maneuver where they want, crush their real enemies—"

Caesarion's eyes were still wide. But the anger began to lack conviction. "Meaning you."

"Mithridates is running it, son. Your precious Dissidents didn't capture Hadrianus, the fool was set up by his own staff, was *thrown* into their hands. You're playing Mithridates' game. Never mind Rameses. He doesn't know what goes on. I pulled you in here because I didn't want you into Reassignments. Die out there and gods know where you'll end up. Or in whose hands. Mithridates', for one. With your mind laundered. Is your English up to that? Do you follow me?"

Long silence.

"Do you follow me?"

"Not that far." Caesarion rubbed his jaw and shook his head. "Wasn't it not to be a fool you were teaching me?"

"Hell, you still haven't got it."

"You've got a mouth your—" Caesarion started off hot; and with a nervous flicker of his eyes upward, swallowed it, frozen like a bird before a snake.

"Right." Julius folded his arms and contemplated his youngest.

"Tiberius failed," Caesarion sneered. "He tried to break me too."

"There you go again. For godssakes I've got men could peel you like an onion. Let's don't lay bets. There's nothing you've got that I'm after. It's yourself I wanted back. For your mother's sake. For mine. Dammit, I've *been* your route. I hoped time would cure it. But this last I can't tolerate. Attach yourself to a ragtag like that, a fool like Guevara—you're too damn smart to believe that crap they hand out. It's my name you're after. To make me any damn trouble you can, and you were so damn smug you walked right into a trap two thousand years in the making."

"What are you talking about?"

"One foot in Roman territory, one in the East—oh, they do want you. Freedom isn't what you're bargaining for. Look at it. You wonder what you'll be worth to them—if ever you get out of line. Where's your independence then?"

Caesarion thrust himself to his bare feet. Tee shirt and jeans, like his other son, but darker. And the flush still showed on the left side of his face. "So what place have I got?"

"That's negotiable." It was as much as could be gotten. "Depends on how convinced I am. But that's your job." Julius walked to the door, shot the inner bolt back and opened the latch. Two legionaries waited outside. "Mind your manners."

"Back to that place."

"Son, we just haven't got a lot of secure accommodations here."

Caesarion straightened his shoulders. "Sir," he said. And walked out, quietly between his guards.

Stopped then, dead in his tracks, at sight of the toga-clad, freckled man who stood across the hall. One half heartbeat.

Then Caesarion ran, broke from his guards and pelted down the hall as the legionaries reached for guns.

"Damn!" Julius hit the first-drawn pistol aside and blocked the second, shoving the legionaries into motion. "No! Catch him!" As Augustus himself hesitated and fleet bare feet headed around a corner. The legionaries ran after the boy; Julius sprinted for the stairs to head the boy off from the downstairs main hall.

Down and down, his boots less sure on the marble than bare feet would be. Down into the main hall and around the turning as he saw Caesarion coming down the hall between him and the two legionaries in hot pursuit.

A door opened midway down the hall. Dante Alighieri stared in profoundest shock as he stepped out carrying a sandwich and a glass of milk.

"For the gods' sake—" Julius yelled, but Caesarion bowled the Italian aside on his way out the offered door to the kitchens, and Julius hit the poet from the other side, rattling the French doors and leaving a second crash of glassware—legion oaths then, as the GIs followed, on a crescendo of Italian imprecation. But with the lead he had gained Caesarion sped ahead, down another, darkened corridor toward the dining rooms, toward the turn that led round again by a row of windows. He snatched up a bronze bust off a bureau one-handed and sent it through the window in a shower of glass and wood, himself leaping after it without ever, the thought came to Julius in a fit of frustrated rage, even knowing what damned floor he was on.

Julius got that far, leapt up with his foot on the ledge

to try the eight foot drop to the flower garden, before
the legionaries grabbed his arms and pulled him back,
risking that jump themselves, one and the other landing in the bushes and staggering across dark bark chips
where glass shone.

There was one thing in which a fit seventeen year
old, even barefoot, had the advantage of a pack of thirty
year olds. Caesarion was on his feet in the halflight of
Hell's night, running like a deer across the lawn and
toward the hedges—gods knew how cut, or bleeding.
But the legionaires with their gear and their guns could
not catch him. "Track him!" Julius yelled into the dark,
and at the flicker of a sycophant that came to the
broken glass: "APB," he said. "Get Horatius."

Horatius, Horatius, Horatius—the creature whispered,
and went for the security chief.

Damned little chance, he thought, seething. And
heard the agitated apologies of the poet down the hall-
ways, protestations of innocence . . . Dante had heard
the commotion, had come out in all good faith to see
what the trouble was. . . . Augustus' voice then, no little
agitated on its own. Julius looked, hearing footsteps,
and found Augustus coming toward him in haste down
the hall.

"I'm sorry," Augustus said. "*Pro di*, I'm sorry."

Julius stared at his adopted son. The Emperor, who
after effecting Antonius' and Klea's earthly deaths, had
lured Caesarion and his tutor to Alexandria and into his
keeping, from which neither had come alive.

"Sorry for which?" Julius asked. "Then or now?"

Augustus said not a word.

BY INVITATION ONLY

Nancy Asire

Light spilled down the stairs leading to Louis XIV's palace. Napoleon helped Marie from the big Mercedes and tried to erase the frown he knew he had worn during the entire ride across Decentral Park. Narrow face touched by just a hint of a smile, Wellington stepped back from the driver's side of the car so the valet could park it.

Napoleon straightened his uniform, tugged at the collar and mightily wished himself elsewhere. *Damn Wellington anyway. Probably enjoying himself. Here we are, going to this damnable party or whatever it is Louis throws in his place, playing spy and courier for Caesar, and he's enjoying it.*

A quick glance at Marie: she looked beautiful tonight, yet her eyes told him she knew this outing was more than it seemed. Napoleon cursed under his breath—her presence would make it easier to explain why he had come to a party, but he disliked exposing her to possible danger.

Before the valet drove off, Wellington took a quick look into the outside rearview mirror, set his cocked hat at a different angle, and adjusted his cravat. Napoleon sighed.

"That's the fifth time you've looked at yourself since we left, Wellington. I don't think anything's out of place."

Wellington snorted. "You're upset because you had to dress up, that's all."

"Damned right I'm upset about it. I *hate* dressing up, I hate parties, and—" He shrugged. "Oh, well. It can't last forever."

"One hopes." Wellington motioned to the stairs. "Shall we?"

Napoleon offered Marie his arm and walked up the steps beside Wellington. *A simple in and out. You'll have a string on you all the way, Mouse says. All very smooth. Huhn. Damned Romans! It'd better be.*

The entry hall was a sea of brilliant uniforms, gowns, and jewels. As the valet took his and Wellington's hats and Marie's shawl, Napoleon glanced around, seeking familiar faces. He had little to do with those who frequented Louis' parties, even less with those who turned up at a God-forsaken ball. Dilettantes, all of them! All he asked was to be let alone on *his* side of the park. He bothered no one and expected the same in return. But the game had changed.

To say nothing of the rules.

Louis' chamberlain glided across the marble floor, some trick since he was wearing three-inch high heels. His elaborate wig was redolent with perfume. Napoleon frowned and Wellington sneezed.

"Shall I announce you now, *majesté*?"

Napoleon nodded briefly, put on a smile for Marie's sake, and shot a glance in Wellington's direction. *In and out, Wellington. No loitering.*

The chamberlain stepped up to the doorway leading to the huge ballroom and rapped his staff three times on the floor. "His Imperial Majesty, the Emperor Na-

poleon. The Countess Marie Walewska. His Grace, the
Duke of Wellington."

Heads turned as those already present stared in their
direction. Napoleon tried to remember the last party he
had been to and gave up. It had been years, at least. If
nothing else, his being here would be the topic of
conversation for days to come. He shrugged, sighed
quietly, and walked into the even brighter room beyond.

"I must say," Wellington murmured at Napoleon's
elbow, "you do look smashing tonight. It's the new
uniform, don't you think? Aren't you glad I talked you
into wearing it?"

"I'll get you for this, Wellington."

"Now, now."

A tall, ruddy-faced man dressed in a Prussian uniform approached them. Napoleon sought the fellow's
name, but could not conjure up much more than Fritz.

"*Kaiser.*" The man bowed formally. "It's been a long
time since you've been seen at a grand ball."

Napoleon forced a smile. "That's true. You've not
met Marie, have you?"

"Your servant," the Prussian said, bowing and clicking his heels. He gestured to the end of the cavernous
room. "Wine, champagne, and hors d'oeuvres are down
there. Try some of the caviar. It's quite good."

"Thanks." Napoleon nodded slightly, took Marie's
hand, and started the interminable drift toward the
refreshments.

Wellington caught up not more than halfway down
the room. "Interesting," he said in a hushed voice. "To
your left."

Napoleon glanced in that direction. Several Arabs
stood clustered against the wall, their white robes brilliant in the lamplight. Arabs at the Sun King's ball?
Interesting, indeed.

"Drift, Wellington, drift. See if you can pick up
anything. You're far better at this inconsequential chit-
chat than I am."

Wellington lifted one eyebrow. "If I didn't know better, I'd consider myself insulted."

Napoleon glowered.

"I'm going. Save some hors d'oeuvres for me."

And Wellington walked off across the mirrorlike marble floor, nodding to various people he passed. Napoleon shifted his shoulders in his new uniform jacket and ignored the urge to scratch.

"You may hate dressing up," Marie said, her blue eyes twinkling in the lamplight, "but I agree with Wellington. You look wonderful."

"Damn fool thing itches like hell," Napoleon growled, scanning the refreshment table and its various culinary delights.

"Maybe if you washed it again—"

"Again? I washed it six times. Any more and it'll fade." He reached out for a cracker loaded down with some sort of cheese. "Have one, Marie. We may not get to eat for a while."

Something flickered behind her eyes, again telling him she was aware this was not a normal social call. Napoleon frowned and glanced off across the ballroom. Wellington had accepted the news that Augustus and Caesar wanted "observational" help from across the Park in return for continued retirement. After all, he had said, one has to know which side one's bread is buttered on.

And Marie?

As of now, she knew nothing, or at least that was Napoleon's fervent hope. With any kind of luck, a commodity usually lacking in Hell, the evening would pass without him having to tell her more than he thought she should know.

He chewed on his lower lip, remembered to keep his expression bland, and looked at the crowd. *He* was Caesar's friend, not Wellington, not Marie. *He* it was who should have come to this ball unaccompanied, keeping those he was fond of uninvolved. Yet here the three of them were, waiting for a contact from someone in this room—anyone—and the transfer of certain highly dangerous papers.

Who was their contact?

Where was Attila?

Round One was drawing to a close.

Wellington glanced over his shoulder as he moved in and out of the crowd, exchanging greetings and idle words; Marie and Napoleon still stood by the refreshment table. Napoleon truly looked Napoleonic tonight—bottle-green uniform coat with gold epaulettes, white pants, black boots. But the frown on the emperor's face told everything.

Napoleon was, to put it lightly, pissed off.

When Napoleon had said he had accepted Augustus' and Caesar's protection for them both in exchange for future favors, Wellington had thought it an excellent move. He could sense the shifting in the balance of power that seethed in and around New Hell. Allies, in such situations, were invaluable—especially powerful allies.

Wellington stopped at the edge of a group of people and listened, all the while looking suitably bored. There was a way to these things: information was best gathered if one seemed disinterested by everything one heard.

And then a name. One of the names Napoleon had whispered to him before the party.

Che.

"—heard he's taken the Trip again."

"Oh?" A portly gentleman, straight out of Louis' century and wearing enough lace to start a shop, looked at the woman who had spoken. "I heard differently. He's back with the Dissidents again."

"That may be true, but he had to come through Reassignments to get there."

"Ah, *mais non!*" An aesthetic face above cardinal's red smiled slightly. "Not necessarily. One *can* escape before that."

Wellington stared. The man who had just spoken had been hidden by the others in the group, his churchly robes out of place amidst this secular splendor. Richelieu! The Cardinal stroked the surly-looking gray cat he held in his arms, murmured something to it, then looked up.

"Surely he had help," said the man in lace.

"Perhaps." Richelieu smiled enigmatically. "Perhaps not."

Wellington moved on, keenly aware his time of anonymous eavesdropping was over. Che. Now that *was* news of a sort. Taken the Trip. Wellington shuddered, trying not to remember his own experience with the Undertaker. But the lace-clad man had said Che was back with the Dissidents. As tightly guarded as the Undertaker's level was, Wellington found it hard to believe Che had not had help.

"Ah, Wellington!"

The Iron Duke froze and glanced in the direction of the voice. Who did he know who would be at Louis' party? The guests were mostly French and, bygones be bygones, after Waterloo, Wellington had hardly been popular with the French.

A man dressed in bourgeois finery came to Wellington's side, his pear-shaped face flushed with excitement. Louis-Phillipe. The Citizen King.

"I haven't seen you in years," Louis-Phillipe said. "Where are you living now? Still the penthouse uptown?"

"No, actually. I've moved. The opposite side of the park." Wellington motioned vaguely in that direction.

"Do you know the news?"

Wellington lifted an eyebrow; Louis-Phillipe was a gossip and a treasure store of who was doing what to whom. "What news?"

"J. Edgar Hoover's been moved out of the Undertaker's. Got caught smuggling drugs in the cadavers or something like that."

"Oh." Wellington lost interest. "Bully for him. Can't say that I ever had anything to do with the man."

"And this is even juicier." The Citizen King glanced around and, satisfied there was no one within earshot, murmured, "You heard Che took the Trip?"

Wellington put on his most bored expression. "Old news, I'm afraid."

"Ah, but did you hear that he's back with the Dissidents again? And that somebody tweeked the Master Computer to send him there?"

Tweeked the Computer? Wellington rubbed the end of his nose to hide his expression. "No," he drawled, "can't say that I'd heard that."

"You *are* out of touch then. Everyone's been talking about it."

"Oh, well. We don't get much news on my side of the Park. Rather refreshing."

"And what about Tigellinus? Surely you know he's up for appointment to a cabinet-level position? That Tiberius is backing him?"

Wellington's heart lurched. Louis-Phillipe was proving himself a gold mine again. Tigellinus. The second of Napoleon's names. The second, and possibly the most deadly.

"Now that *is* interesting," Wellington commented in a slightly bored voice. "Do you think he'll get it?"

Louis-Phillipe shrugged. "I just hear things, Wellington. I don't decide them."

A servant threaded his way through the growing crowd, carrying a silver tray on which lay a number of hors d'oeuvres. Wellington nodded toward the servant.

"Something to eat, Louis?"

"Ah, why not." The King gestured grandly. "Over here, fellow."

The servant turned, came to their sides, and bowed. Wellington looked over the assortment of hors d'oeuvres, while Louis-Phillipe snatched up the two largish crackers heaped with cheese and some kind of cold meat.

"If I may suggest, Your Grace," the servant said, "do try that pizza roll closest to you. It's excellent."

Wellington glanced quickly to the servant's face, then

down again. *Your Grace, is it? And where do I know you from, man?* He took the pizza roll; the servant smiled slightly, bowed, and walked off into the crowd.

Louis-Phillipe brushed the crumbs from his lips. "What have you got there?"

"Pizza roll." Wellington popped it into his mouth and bit down. And nearly choked.

"Wellington? Are you all right?"

A piece of paper in a pizza roll? Surely not— Wellington shoved the strip of paper between his cheek and gum with his tongue and swallowed the rest.

"I'm fine." He straightened. "Well, Louis, I must be off. I'm sure we'll bump into each other again tonight. There are others here I'd like to talk to, I'm sure."

"Keep your ears open, Wellington. You might hear something even *I* haven't."

Wellington nodded, tongued the piece of paper gently, and walked back toward the refreshment table where he had left Napoleon and Marie.

Napoleon stood behind a particularly bushy potted palm, Marie at his side; it was the perfect place to escape from others. He peered out from behind the fronds: Wellington was headed their way, and from the expression on the Iron Duke's face, something with a capital "S" had happened.

Napoleon's shoulders tensed, but he waited until Wellington drew near.

"Sssst! Over here!"

Wellington paused, glanced around as if utterly bored, then slipped in behind the palm. Napoleon stared at him, trying to judge just how much he could say in front of Marie.

"Find out anything interesting?" he asked, watching Marie from the corner of one eye. Her face was puzzled, nothing more. His heart ached with longing— longing to open himself to her, to tell her everything he knew and suspected.

"Uh . . . interesting? You might say so." Wellington

glanced at Marie and his ears turned red. "Your pardon, my Lady," he said, and reached into his mouth to take out a small piece of paper.

Napoleon drew a quick breath. "What the hell's *that*? And where'd you get it?"

"I haven't the foggiest idea what it is, and I got it out of a pizza roll."

"Well unfold it, for God's sake," Napoleon said, leaning forward to see. "That can't be what we're looking for."

Wellington unfolded the soggy piece of paper. There, written in pencil (thank God) was the word "BATHRUM."

"Bathroom?" Wellington guessed, his forehead furrowed.

Napoleon rubbed his chin. "That's what it looks like. Now what does that have to do with—" A sudden lurch of his heart. Whoever had written the note could not spell in English. And that could only mean. . . "Wellington. There's a bathroom on this floor, isn't there?"

"Through that other room, behind the refreshment table."

"Napoleon—"

He winced. He had heard that tone in Marie's voice before.

"Marie," he said, taking her hands in his own. He met her eyes, saw the questions there, and swallowed. "Trust me, Marie. You don't want to know. Believe me, you don't."

"I think I do," she said calmly. "I've known you too many years not to read you right, and if I'm not mistaken, you and Wellington are up to your ears in something dangerous."

"Well . . ."

"Napoleon." She leaned forward and her voice fell to a whisper. "You asked me to trust you. Can't you trust *me*?"

"*Dieu!* Don't, Marie, don't make me tell you. If you know, you'll be in danger, too."

"And when haven't I asked to share your danger?"

He squeezed her hands and tried to smile. "Never. I know that. But—"

She stood there, waiting for his answer, and his throat tightened. Whose plant was she? Who had arranged for them to meet after so long? Augustus? The Administration? The Dissidents? He shuddered slightly. Did it go even beyond that: was she a plant within a plant? Or was she a plant at all?"

"All right, Marie," he said quietly, dropping her hands. "Things are changing in Hell. I'm sure you've noticed. To put it simply, to ensure our own protection, Wellington and I have agreed to work for—certain Romans on this side of the Park." Her eyes flickered with sudden understanding and he plunged on. "It's not supposed to be dangerous, but—" He shrugged. "You know Hell. Things are seldom what they seem."

"Now it begins to make more sense. I didn't think there was any power save duty that could make you come to an event like this ball." She drew a deep breath and straightened her shoulders. "What can I do to help?"

Napoleon held her eyes, all his doubts and fears poised on the edge of reason. The moment came and passed, and his decision was made.

"Right now, Marie, I want you to stay here, out of sight and quiet. Wellington and I are going to the bathroom. If anyone asks for us, try to keep them occupied for a while."

"How long will you be in there?"

Napoleon glanced at Wellington and shrugged. "God only knows. It shouldn't be all *that* long." He leaned over and kissed her forehead. "Be careful, Marie."

"Me? You and Wellington are the ones to take care."

"Oh, come now, my Lady," Wellington said lightly, "how much trouble can one get into in a bathroom?"

Normal coloring was returning to Marie's too-pale face. She smiled, reached for Napoleon's hand and held it briefly. "Knowing the two of you, quite a bit."

*   *   *

The only problem with Louis' guest bathroom was that the men's room contained just two stalls. A line had already formed outside the door: five men stood leaning against the wall, looks of patient suffering on their faces.

Napoleon tugged at Wellington's sleeve and came to a dead stop across the room from the line.

"We're in trouble now. It'll take some time to get everyone in and out."

Wellington shrugged. "Not much we can do about it."

"Huhn." Napoleon glanced up at his companion. "How sick do you think you can look?"

"What?"

"Sick, Wellington. How sick can you—?"

"Oh. Fairly sick, I should think. I'll have to work up to it."

"Hurry, then."

Wellington turned away and walked to the corner of the room. Napoleon resisted the urge to watch and instead stared at the five men who by now had begun to shift uncomfortably on their feet.

"Napoleon."

It was Wellington's voice, sounding thin and strained. Napoleon turned as Wellington walked unsteadily toward him, and smiled slightly. The Iron Duke's face was now a pasty white, the dark eyes looking even darker against the pale skin.

"God, Wellington, you look awful!" Napoleon said as he took Wellington's arm. "Is it something you ate?"

"Pizza roll," Wellington moaned. "Damned thing!"

Napoleon glanced at the five men who were now watching, their own discomfort momentarily forgotten. "Could you give us some help? My friend's eaten something that's made him sick."

"Uh . . . there's already two fellows—"

"I know." Napoleon led Wellington toward the door. "See if you can hurry things up, will you? I doubt Louis would like his carpet messed up."

"There *is* another bathroom upstairs," a second man said. "Why don't you—"

"Why don't *you!*" Napoleon snapped. "Can't you see Wellington's sicker than a dog?"

The first man rapped loudly on the door. "Hurry up in there! We've got someone out here who's sick!"

One toilet flushed, followed immediately by the other. Wellington moaned dramatically as two bewigged men walked out of the bathroom, both looking extremely put out. Those waiting in line whistled and clapped as they walked by, one calling out a lewd proposition.

"Come on, Wellington. You'll feel better in a while." Napoleon gestured to one of the men who pulled the door open. "Take it slow, Wellington. You'll make it." And over his shoulder: "Thanks. We may be a while."

"Damn!" the man at the rear of the line said. "I'm going upstairs."

He turned and walked back toward the ballroom, immediately followed by the other four. Napoleon led Wellington into the bathroom, and waited silently as the door shut behind them.

A grin spread across Wellington's narrow face. "How'd I do?"

"Damned fine. You even had *me* fooled." Napoleon glanced quickly around the bathroom, looking for any hint of a contact.

"Now what? The note said bathroom. Well, we're here."

Napoleon spotted a high window at the far end of the bathroom. If he had his directions straight, it overlooked the garden behind the palace.

"You're tallest. Get over to that window and see what you can see. I'll guard the door."

Wellington nodded; Napoleon turned back to the door, grabbed hold of the doorknob with both hands, and braced himself for any incoming traffic.

"What am I supposed to be looking for?" Wellington asked, his voice muffled.

"How the hell should I know? Anything odd."

"Anything odd. Huhn. That means everything around—Hello! What's this?"

"What's what?" The doorknob jerked and Napoleon threw his weight backward, holding onto the door. "Hurry, Wellington. We're getting company."

"Someone's out in the bushes, I can't see who—They've got a flashlight. Damn! It's code, Napoleon. Two long flashes, followed by one short."

"Hey! Op'n up in there!" a furious voice bellowed on the other side of the door.

"Go away!" Napoleon yelled back. "My friend's sick in here! You want the flu or something?" He glanced over his shoulder as the door jerked again. "Two long, one short?" he whispered to Wellington. "That's Attila! He's telling us everything's set up outside. He'll cover us when we leave."

"There's more."

"Dammit!" the voice on the other side of the door roared." 'M drunk on m'ass an' you—"

"Then use the bushes outside!" Napoleon looked back at Wellington. "What is it?"

"Three short, two long."

"O God! Our shy contact wants to transfer the papers now." The door jerked again. "The light switch, Wellington! Blink the lights off and on twice."

Wellington hurried to the light switch while the drunk outside kept pulling at the door, cursing at the top of his lungs. The lights in the bathroom flickered twice.

"Good job. Let's get out of here."

"My God, Napoleon . . . how our reputations will suffer!"

Napoleon grinned and let loose of the doorknob: the door flew open—the angry drunk yelled an obscenity and fell flat on his back.

"Come on, Wellington. Some fresh air ought to do you good." Napoleon stepped over the drunk, Wellington right behind. "*If* we can get by the riff-raff."

*   *   *

Once again, Marie's hand in his own, Napoleon drifted in and out of the crowd on the ballroom floor. She had come out from behind the potted palm, her eyes troubled, but the smile she wore would have disarmed anyone. Napoleon glanced sidelong at Wellington, who had contrived to still look a bit unwell, and shrugged slightly. If the exchange of papers was to take place soon, it would be before the ball began. The orchestra had not come to its box yet, and the guests were still eating, drinking, and talking.

Several people stopped him and Marie, but Napoleon kept his exchanges with them brief and to the point. No sense in falling out of character now. To act like he was enjoying himself (which he was not) would do harm to future appearances.

Wellington nudged his side and Napoleon looked to his right. The Arabs again. Only this time there was a blond-headed man with them, clad in the same white robes. Napoleon recognizied him: T.E. Shaw (a/k/a Ross), best known as Lawrence of Arabia. He thought Lawrence and his companions eyed him with more than usual curiosity, but he had had little to do with the modern sort of Arab. Egyptians he understood, to a certain extent—at least those he had known during the Egyptian campaign in 1798. But that was decades before the Middle East crises that rocked the world in the mid-1960s and after. He looked away from the Arabs, for some reason uneasy.

"Where the hell's our contact?" he whispered to Wellington. "We've been walking around in circles for ten minutes now."

"Why don't we head over there?" Wellington suggested, pointing with his chin to an extremely crowded section of the ballroom.

Napoleon sighed. "I don't know how much more of this I can take. If I have to tell one more person why I'm at a party, I'll strangle them." Suddenly it hit him. "I get you. The more crowded it is, the better chance of a transfer."

Wellington grinned. "You would have never made a spy. You're too damned direct."

"Huhn. Now you, on the other hand, seem to have missed your calling."

As they approached the thick crowd, Napoleon could catch a glimpse of what it was that had drawn the guests to this corner of the room. Richelieu's cat had gotten away from its master and was darting in and out from under the chairs along the wall as the Cardinal followed, trying to coax it out again. Richelieu was enamoured of cats and always had several near him, but that made no difference now. Just whenever he got within grabbing distance, the cat dashed off again.

Napoleon grimaced. He still was not all that fond of cats, but had outgrown his Corsican superstitions long ago, and had been known to pick up strays himself. But this cat—gray, surly, and mightily pleased with itself—looked like the devil incarnate.

Reaching the end of its patience with sitting under chairs, the cat made a mad dash toward the crowd. Laughing and calling out advice, the guests backed off, giving the Cardinal more space. A big fellow dressed in court clothes bumped into Napoleon, nearly knocking him off his feet.

"Oh, so sorry. How clumsy of me." Hard, capable hands reached out to offer assistance. "Are you all right?"

"I seem to be," Napoleon murmured. The guests were laughing again, even louder than before, jostling one another to get a better view.

"Here . . . you dropped this," the big man said, and shoved two thick folded pieces of paper into Napoleon's hands. Dark Arab eyes glittered in a swarthy, hooknosed face. "Good luck," the man whispered, then turned and shoved his way through the crowd.

Napoleon stood frozen for a moment, his hand trembling on the papers. No one was paying him the slightest attention. *O God! This is it!* He folded the papers once again, careless of what that might do to the

contents, and shoved them under his vest. Drawing a
deep breath, he looked around.

Marie was watching him, a small frown on her face,
but Wellington was caught up by the cat chase and was
laughing with the others. Napoleon reached for Marie's
hand, nodded back toward the entry hall, and poked
Wellington in the side.

"I thought you weren't feeling well," he said pointedly. "Don't you think you'd better go home and get
some rest?"

"Uh . . . yes," Wellington answered, flushing slightly.
"Jolly good idea."

"I think the evening's done for all of us." Napoleon
cocked an eye up at the Iron Duke. "If you know what I
mean."

Wellington's eyes took on a wary expression. "Do
you—?"

"Yes."

"I see. Let's go."

Leading Marie by the hand, Napoleon followed Wellington across the ballroom, the transferred papers crinkling against his shirt with every movement. So far, so
good. No one spared them much more than a curious
glance. A clean getaway proved to be in the offing.

Until his eyes met those of a toga-clad man who
stood, backed by several burly fellows, next to the
doorway leading to the entry hall. Ice was in those
eyes—ice and an intelligent animal cunning. Napoleon's
heart lurched.

Tigellinus!

And the woman on his arm, clad in a gown that
exposed more than it covered: she was equally dangerous. If he knew anything at all about Romans (and he
did know a considerable amount), Napoleon recognized
her for none other than Claudius' third wife, Valeria
Messalina.

O bon dieu en ciel!

Napoleon tried to guide Marie out the door, giving

Wellington a soft shove as he went, but escape was not to be. Not now.

"Ah, Bonaparte," Tigellinus drawled, stepping into Napoleon's path. "It's been a long, long time, hasn't it, since I saw you last? Retired, are you? Living the quiet life?"

"Trying to," Napoleon said, amazed that his voice was steady. The man was filth, was slime . . . was undeniably deadly.

"And attending a party. How curious. I thought you disliked them, especially the large, ornate ones."

"Wellington dragged me here," Napoleon said in a suitably miffed voice. "But he ate something that made him sick, and we're going home."

"One always has to avoid eating much at parties," Messalina said, a thin smile touching her lips. She leaned up against Tigellinus and ran a lazy fingertip down the line of his jaw. "One can never be sure, can one, of what lurks in the food."

"Napoleon." Wellington's voice trembled. "If I don't get out of here soon, I'll soil the floor."

"Right." Napoleon turned to Tigellinus. "Sorry. We really *must* be going."

Trumpets blared; rose petals descended in a shower from the ceiling. The Sun King was making his entrance at last.

"Oh, Tigellini, *amor mi*," Messalina cooed. "Let's go see Louis. Pu-leeze!"

Nero's security officer turned away and Napoleon quickly led Marie around him, Wellington coming close behind.

"Valet!" Napoleon called once he had reached the entry hall. The fellow looked up from where he sat by the cloakroom. "Bring His Grace's hat, the Countess' wrap, and my hat. And send someone for the car. It's the black Mercedes."

The valet was a young fellow, his full white wig

looking ridiculous above a pimply face. "You mean Papa Doc's car?" he asked, his eyes lighting up.

"That's the one. Make it fast. His Grace is sick."

The boy hurried to the front doors and hollered something out into the night. Napoleon stood with Marie and Wellington at his side by the cloakroom as the valet returned and retrieved the two black cocked hats and Marie's shawl.

"I'm sorry Your Grace isn't feeling well," the youngster said to Wellington.

"My Grace will feel a lot better once I'm out in the open air."

Carrying his hat, Napoleon led the way to the front porch just as the big black Mercedes pulled up at the foot of the steps. Yearning to make a mad dash for it, he nodded to the valet, walked slowly down the stairs, and waited for Wellington to join him.

"Do you feel well enough to drive, or shall I?" he asked for the benefit of his listeners.

"I'll make it," Wellington said, as the other valet exited the car and stood holding the door open. "You're too short to drive this thing properly anyway."

Napoleon lifted an eyebrow. "You're pushing it, Wellington. Really pushing it."

Wellington got in the car and tossed his hat into the rear seat as the valet held the door open for Marie and Napoleon. Once the door had slammed, Wellington started down the long drive from Louis' palace to the street which ran on the north side of Decentral Park.

Napoleon sighed and set his hat beside Wellington's; leaning his head back against the seat, he shut his eyes, letting some of the tension drain away.

"You got them, eh?" Wellington asked. "No problems?"

"No problems." Napoleon glanced across Marie at Wellington. The Iron Duke was frowning. "I know. No problems *there*. We still have to make the drop."

"Napoleon," Marie said. "What's going on? If you brought me along in spite of the danger, I think I'm entitled to know something."

He put an arm around her shoulders. "Believe me, *amore*, it would have been far more dangerous to leave you at home."

Wide with surprise, her eyes met his in the dim glow from the car's console.

"Trust me, Marie." His doubts concerning her clawed at him again, but he remembered his decision at the ball. "When we get home, I'll tell you."

Wellington turned onto the street, headed west. As he did so, Napoleon noticed a car fall in behind them, a car that had obviously been waiting all this while, its lights off, parked to one side of the street.

"Attila?" Wellington asked, his eyes flicking up to the rearview mirror and down again.

"It's supposed to be." A chill crawled up Napoleon's spine. "Wellington. Did the Romans tell you how fast this car can go?"

"No, only that it had good acceleration." Wellington grinned mirthlessly. "I can't imagine Papa Doc having a car that wouldn't perform well in a quick getaway."

"Huhn. How about armor plating?"

"That too, I was told. Standard accessory for a petty dictator."

Napoleon shrugged. "Our guns?"

"They should still be in the glove compartment."

"Let's hope so." Napoleon released Marie and opened the glove compartment: two .45s lay gleaming in the dim light.

"Merciful God, Napoleon," Marie whispered. "Are *those* necessary?"

"I hope not."

"Uh . . . Napoleon." Wellington's voice sounded strained. "Check the rearview mirror."

Napoleon looked and his breath caught in his throat. There were *two* cars behind them now, not just one.

"O God." He glanced at Wellington. "I've got a feeling Attila's not following us."

"Then let's see how fast this car is," Wellington growled, and stepped on the accelerator.

"Marie," Napoleon said. "I want you to keep down. Don't argue with me. Keep down."

She nodded and slid into a position where her knees turned sideways on the floor, placing her feet nearly under Napoleon's. He shifted position and glanced up into the rearview mirror, then down at her again.

"Put your head down and hang on. I don't want you hurt."

As Papa Doc's car picked up speed, the cars following matched it. Wellington cursed.

"Where's Attila?"

"You're asking me?" Napoleon watched the following cars over his shoulder. "You know, Wellington, we *could* be in big trouble."

"Huhn."

The road was dimly lit by the sodium glare of too few street lamps. The Park stretched to their left in a tangle of undergrowth, small bushes, and twisted trees. The Cong ruled there, practicing a warfare of utter confusion, shooting at anything that moved, sometimes even each other.

Napoleon watched the Park streak by. Despite their speed, the two cars were gaining on them, and an escape route—if it came to that—was of utmost importance.

A loud burst of automatic gunfire sounded from behind.

"O God!" Wellington hissed. "They're shooting at us!"

"Then stomp on it!" Napoleon opened the glove compartment and reached for the pistols. They would be of little use unless the other cars drew within range, but they were better than nothing. "What *else* did the Romans tell you about this car?" he asked, checking the safeties.

"Not much." Wellington's voice was ice-calm. He drove wildly down the street now, swerving from side to side. More shots rang out. There was a loud snap to the rear of the car: a bullet.

"Jesus! They're aiming for the gas tank! Here!" Napoleon shoved the loaded .45 across the seat to where it rested against Wellington's leg.

"Napoleon." Marie's voice was muffled. "Something's under the front seat."

He glanced down. "Something what?" Then drew a deep breath as Marie slid a long, blackened gun under his feet. "*Mon dieu!* It's an Uzi!"

"Well, don't just sit there with your teeth in your mouth," Wellington said, swerving the car back and forth. "Use it!"

Napoleon picked up the Uzi and checked the safety. It had been years since he had fired one, but some things are never forgotten.

"Marie! Look for extra clips!" He rolled down the window and shifted around on the seat to get a good position.

Wellington swerved the car again, more shots rang out, and Napoleon lost his balance. He reached behind, caught himself on the dashboard, his hand pressed firmly on a large flat button beneath it.

"God, Napoleon!" Wellington yelled. "What did you do?"

"What did I do *what?*" Napoleon answered, shoving himself away from the dashboard.

"Look behind!"

Napoleon looked. The car following immediately to the rear was fishtailing back and forth on the street as if floating on ice. It veered off to one side, straightened, then turned completely around.

"Oil! You hit the release for oil!" Wellington crowed.

The other car just managed to avoid running into the first, but in doing so skidded off the road and into the brush by the edge of the Park. A volley of shots came from the darkened undergrowth.

"The Cong!" Napoleon whispered. "Damn! The Cong have got them!"

"Bully for them!" Wellington replied. "The other fellow's got his car under control now."

"How close are we to where we're to make the drop?"

"A few more turns of the road."

The car behind was gaining speed again. Napoleon flipped the safety off the Uzi, and gently leaned out the window.

"For God's sake, Napoleon, be careful!" Marie said.

"Huhn." He braced his knees against the seatback and the door, hoped it was locked tightly, and tried to get a good aim.

Wellington swerved violently as shots came from the pursuing car. Thrown off balance again, Napoleon squeezed off a round into the night.

"Shit, Wellington! Let's not overdo it!"

Wellington cursed. "The devil with the drop spot! I'm headed for the armory!"

And possible Roman assistance. Napoleon remembered his own trip there, clad in the khaki uniform of a legionary. It was not much farther to the armory and, if Attila had not been seriously hurt, he should have gotten a message through that events had deteriorated beyond control.

Wellington turned the car sharply to the right, skidded on gravel, and sped down the armory parking lot. Napoleon leaned out the window again, the Uzi steady in his hands, as the pursuing car followed, its occupants shooting as they came.

"*Merde!*" Napoleon jerked back inside. "That was too damned close for comfort. I *heard* the bullets go by my ear." He reached behind and pushed on the large button again. Nothing happened. The oil was obviously used up.

And just as Wellington took another quick turn down between a wide row of parked vehicles, a large truck rolled out of the night behind the Mercedes. The car following slammed on its brakes, skidded and plowed head-on into the truck.

The explosion that followed shook the Mercedes. Napoleon ducked, pushed Wellington's head down, and thought briefly of Marie, squashed on the seat. Easing on the brakes, Wellington brought the car to a halt.

The glare of flames lit up the parking lot and some-thing exploded again, showering burning pieces of metal in all directions. One clunked off the roof of the Mercedes and rattled into the darkness.

"My God!" Wellington breathed, looking over his shoulder. "That truck—it must have been filled with explosives."

Napoleon nodded, turned around in his seat, and reached down for Marie.

"Are you all right?" he asked, snapping the safety on the Uzi and slipping it back under the seat.

"I think so." Her hair was mussed, her face drawn, but she tried to smile.

"O God, Marie." Napoleon hugged her tight.

"Napoleon." Wellington touched his shoulder. "We're getting company."

He lifted his head and looked: a jeep drove toward them around the burning truck and car, garishly limned against the hellish background. The occupants were faceless, but Napoleon thought he knew the stocky man sitting next to the driver.

"It's Attila. I'd recognize that set of shoulders any-where."

He let go of Marie, smoothed her hair back from her eyes, and opened the door. His knees were shaking but they steadied as he stood up. Wellington had gotten out of the other side of the car and stood with his hands behind his back, the .45 held ready just in case.

The jeep stopped with a squeal of brakes and Attila jumped out.

"By the Sky, Napoleon!" he grinned, striding for-ward. He slapped Napoleon's shoulder. "That was some chase!"

Napoleon felt relieved that he had left his gun in the car: the temptation might have been too strong.

"Where were you?" he grated.

"Some fool sneaked up on me in the dark," Attila said, rubbing the back of his head. "Nearly brained me,

he did. Fortunately, I was carrying a field phone and
was able to get the message out that things had gone
wrong."

"You're a master of understatement," Wellington said,
coming around the car to stand by Napoleon.

"Why, thank you. I try." Attila looked back at Napoleon. "Do you have them?"

Napoleon glanced at the driver of the jeep, a young
Roman clad in fatigues. "Who's he?"

"He's all right. The courier. The papers should be in
Caesar's hands within the half hour."

"Huhn." Napoleon reached under his vest and withdrew the papers. By now, they were limp with sweat.
Let Caesar worry about that. "Here. I hope I never see
them again."

Attila grinned, trotted over to the jeep, and handed
the papers to the young Roman. The man stuffed them
down the front of his shirt, saluted Attila, and drove out
of the parking lot in a shower of kicked-up gravel.

"Don't worry about him," Attila said, coming back to
Napoleon's side. "He'll have support all the way to
Augustus' villa."

"Damn sight more than *we* had," Napoleon growled.

Attila managed to look highly offended. "You mean
the Cong didn't help?"

"The Cong?" Wellington asked. "What the hell has
the Cong got to do with this?"

"More than you suspect," Attila said, his slanted eyes
crinkling in a smile. "And if you don't know—"

"We won't ask," Napoleon inserted. "God *knows* we
won't ask."

Marie had gotten out of the car and now stood by
Napoleon, brushing the dirt and wrinkles from her
gown. Attila nodded to her, then turned to the Mercedes.

"I see they managed to wing you several times," he
said, running a blunt fingertip down a scratch across the
trunk. "I wonder what Papa Doc's going to say about
this?"

"Let Caesar explain it." Napoleon walked to the car,

opened the back door, and retrieved Marie's shawl, Wellington's hat, and his own. "You're driving this, then?"

"I'm sure as shit not going to walk," Attila grinned. "A Hun on foot? Never."

"Huhn. Where's *my* car?"

"Over behind the trucks." Attila pointed off to his left. "I'm going. Still on duty. I'll see you people later."

Napoleon bit down on his lip to avoid saying anything else as the King of the Huns got into Papa Doc's car, threw it in gear, and drove out of the parking lot.

"Well, I'm certainly glad *that's* over," Wellington said, as Napoleon and Marie started toward the car. "And it's so good to see you dressed up and getting out again."

Napoleon glared. "Three, Wellington. That's three!"

THE GOD OF THE GAPS

Gregory Benford

Courage will not save you; but it will show that your souls are still alive.

—George Bernard Shaw

1.

The dirt road had turned to mud long ago beneath the slow gray drizzle and the tramping of feet. Gregory Markham watched the straggling line of men and women. They moved steadily but without obvious fear, as if fleeing a customary and sluggish foe. They were a herd, bothered but basically docile, moving on. Some who had horses rode them along in the ditch, which was firmer than the road now. Others had hitched them to lumbering, poorly made wooden carts.

Markham saw a lumbering water buffalo, head down and huffing as it pulled a long wagon. Its owner had piled furniture and mattresses, lumpy bundles and wooden boxes into the wagon—even his family, too.

The buffalo had to drag all that and the wheels kept clogging with mud. The owner would climb down and shave the mud off the spokes and rim with a short shovel and then kick the animal to get it started again. Markham didn't think the buffalo had long to go.

He stood in the cover of bushes fifty meters away and just watched. Horses and water buffalo in Hell. Well, why not?

Since this place was somewhat like Earth, why not throw in precise details?—be sure the buffalo didn't have three horns, or its owner walk on all fours. Might as well get that right.

And the lazy light rain fell straight down from the perpetual overcast and hit the ground, rather than going the other way around. Markham was sure that it could have been otherwise if whoever or whatever was in charge here had wanted to diddle with the specs a bit.

He looked at his own hand. It was a little blue from the chill but there were five fingers and the thumb worked all right. All the little details in place. He was wearing rough cotton pants with a draw string and the vaguely Mexican-style shirt, no collar. He had awakened this time, after his last death in Hell—just opened his eyes and there were sodden pine trees overhead and rain falling in his face. His clothes weren't wet yet so either the rain had just started or else he had materialized—he couldn't think of any other words for it—only moments before.

At least this time he hadn't had to go through the whole disgusting business with the Welcome Woman again. Or the elevator. This time was easier and maybe that meant something.

He had a glimmering of an idea, something about the fact that a single death got you out of "life," whatever that had been, but apparently an infinite series of deaths still wouldn't let you escape this Hell.

Would anything? Moral heft? Spectacular brutality? Three Hail Marys and a sour fart?

Ignorance wouldn't, that was obvious. So he had to

observe, learn. That meant staying out of the local cat
fights and madness.

He had to maneuver, though, see how things worked—
without getting captured, used, recruited into the seem-
ingly endless and pointless causes here. He remembered
the legions of troops he had seen, marching off to
interminable battles, fighting out of habit or zest or vast
ancient despair.

Everybody here seemed to have more street smarts
than he did. Unsurprising, since he had been a clois-
tered physics professor, but humbling and irritating.

He started walking through the low bushes, parallel
to the road but opposite to the traffic. Something in
him didn't want to join that bedraggled, hollow-eyed
bunch. They were listless, forlorn, hopeless. Cattle.

And if these refugees were fleeing something, it might
be interesting.

Markham kept close enough to hear the grunts and
occasional swearing from the road. He crossed several
gullies where deep ruts cut into the red clay. He leaped
over them, trying not to expose himself to view. He
didn't know what these people were fleeing, or whether
they were on one side or another of the rebellion Che
Guevara had started. Or restarted . . .

He began to sweat despite the spattering rain. He
was already soaked but a warm wind came from the
hills above and he didn't mind. He remembered reading in *Scientific American* that merely being chilled
didn't increase your likelihood of getting a cold. On the
other hand, that might not apply to Godless microorga-
nisms devilishly devised to keep the ecology of Hell
running.

That was the problem—he had severe doubts whether
what he had learned before meant anything here. He
smiled without pleasure. He saw now that he had been
a man who depended on knowing things, understanding, standing at the center of an orderly world. The
quest to uncover some small new fragment of the un-
derlying Mystery had propelled him blithlely through

Life—that first run-through, that opening scene in a play that now promised to run forever.

Hell wasn't fire and brimstone. Far worse, it was chaos.

He heard popping noises from the right, toward the road. Far away, but they had the characteristic thin spatting sound of gunfire. He stood still and listened. No shouting, just more popping and then the soft *crump* of an explosive.

He angled away from the road. The rain turned to a spitting mist and then stopped. He saw no one. Hell certainly wasn't overcrowded. He tried to remember if anyone had ever mentioned any boundary to Hell.

He pondered the point, trying to view the issue scientifically. At least doing that took him away from the weary present.

There was Earthlike local gravity. Ok, that meant space-time was curved. Well, it couldn't have an indefinitely large surface—that would imply a highly curved space-time, which would appear as a crushing local gravity. Still, this could simply be an enormous world of low density, or a cutoff space-time, ingeniously adjusted to yield a local gravity of one G.

He remembered a student's joke slogan at the university, years ago:

WHITE PAPER IS GOD'S WAY OF REMINDING
US IT ISN'T EASY TO BE GOD.

Designing any environment implied awesome powers. Presumably the Devil had abilities rivaling God's, or else there would be obvious flaws.

"*Alto!*"

Startled, Markham ducked into some brushes without looking at whoever had shouted. A loud report boomed in his ears. He crouched down and saw a man come running toward him, leveling a rifle.

" *'ey! 'ey!*"

Pointless to run. *Crap. Caught within an hour.*

He stood slowly, showing his hands. The man trotting toward him was dressed in loose cotton too and said something in rapid Spanish. Markham shrugged, indicating incomprehension, and remembered someone telling him in one of his previous lives in Hell that classical Greek and modern English were the working languages here. Well, this guy hadn't done his homework.

More Spanish. "No comprehende," Markham said.

The man scowled, brushed back his ragged black hair, and poked Markham with the rifle. Markham began walking as the man directed and they wound their way up a deep arroyo.

Pines hid them. The rain had brought out the crisp scent of the pine needle mat they walked on and Markham fell into a rhythm, working his way up the clay hillside. The man jabbed at him with the rifle, apparently the major method of communication around here.

He had seen nothing but woods and small towns in Hell, and his mind turned to using that fact somehow. Maybe he could estimate the size of this place. How many people should be in Hell, anyway?

He remembered reading that the lifespan of people before the coming of agriculture had been about twenty years. Nasty, brutish and short, indeed. Archeologists had gotten that average number from disinterred bodies, and had found universal signs of broken bones, vitamin deficiency and early arthritis. So much for Rousseau's noble savage.

So if indentifiable humans had been around for a million years or so, what percentage went to Hell? Say, about one half. He also recalled that until people were forced to invent agriculture—because the big game herds were running out—the whole planet had supported only a million or so people.

Okay, then with a lifespan of twenty years, keeping that population steady at one million people . . . for a million years . . . meant about fifty *billion* souls had shuffled off the mortal coil. If half went to Hell, and you added in another ten or so billion to cover the time since agriculture dawned, that was thirty-five billion people.

He smiled. The Earth itself would be jam-packed with such a population. Hell wasn't. That meant the place was huge, maybe ten times the surface area of earth. A giant planet.

Or else that far fewer people came here than he estimated.

Maybe, he conjectured, Hell was a byproduct of organized religion. What a laugh, if theologians *invented* it, gave the Devil the idea!

Perhaps it arose *because* of the idea of moral order, of good ol' right 'n wrong. So when you died, this place attracted the doubters, the sophisticates, the intellectuals . . . the physicists.

The idea made him smile. What a fitting end for the subscribers' list of *The New York Review of Books*.

2.

Distant rumblings, full of menace, rolled down from the far hills. Markham slogged on. Distant cries of agony came and went on the fitful wind. He wondered if he would see Hemingway again. It had been sheer good luck to stumble on Hemingway shortly after arriving here.

Hem had understood at least how to get through the routine horrors of this place, had forged an internal refuge from it all. The point, Markham saw, was to endure without accepting, to never let it break your spirit. That was a good path to follow in their previous lives, of course, but it had taken Markham at least a long while to see that. When you started out, the essential nastiness of life itself was hidden by the zest and dumb joy of youth. When friends started dying, felled by disease or dumb accidents, it sobered you. Hem had seen that early and gotten it down on paper. What he claimed for his own was a territory of the spirit that you recognized in the gut, nothing to do with intellect at all. Even in Hell, Hem strode like a giant, because most of these ragdoll actors still hadn't comprehended what would get them through. It was one thing to understand your predicament and another, far greater thing entirely, to get through, to not let it blunt your senses or rob you of joy.

His captor shouted, jerking Markham back to the gritty present. A hoarse reply came from the trees above them.

Markham scrambled up the steep clay slope, grabbing at bushes to keep going. When he stood up at the top, panting, a voice said clearly, "Mierda."

"Anybody here speak English?"

"Sure I do some," a tall man said, stepping from behind some eucalyptus trees.

"Who're you?"

"Person."

Markham glanced at his guard, who came wheezing up the slope, and then back at the tall man, who carried an automatic weapon with a long curved box clip. "What else is there?"

"Devils."

"I'm no devil."

"You fight on side devils?"

"Don't fight at all."

"What you do here?"

"I was born here. *Re*born, you comprehende?"

The tall man laughed lightly, his eyes never leaving Markham. "You do it with Welcome Woman?"

"God no."

"Devils say God too."

So they didn't believe he was just a mortal. "You with Guevara?"

"Maybe."

The tall man rattled off some Spanish to Markham's guard and the guard started back down the arroyo. "Hey, you come." A prod with the automatic.

"Look, I saw Guevara just before I was killed, last time." Markham omitted that Guevara had personally ordered his execution.

"I not see Guevara many days. Where he was?"

"Near the supply depot, that's all I know. He had lots of wild-eyed followers with him, I think."

The tall man stopped. "That was one, two month ago."

"Really?" Then patching up his body and bringing him back did take time. It was oddly reassuring that even the Devil could apparently not merely snap his asbestos fingers and do everything.

"Come! Commandante speak."

The tall man marched swiftly up the stony hillside and they came out of the trees into a flat area. Men were resting around campfires, cleaning their weapons. In the distance, down-slope, Markham could see more men crouched behind makeshift barriers of rock and felled trees. They had automatic weapons trained downhill. There was no sun, there never was, but a warming glow seeped down through the ivory clouds that seemed closer from the top of this hill.

Markham was prodded forward until they reached a tall man who was shouting at some others. Abruptly, firing came from down the hill and bullets ricocheted among the boulders higher up. Everybody hit the dirt except for the tall man and Markham. The man noticed this and laughed. "You not afraid to die again?"

"Who wants to know?"

"I Joaquin," the man said, holding out a hand to shake. "From Spain."

"When?"

"Time of revolution."

"Which one?"

"Anti-fascist."

"That was over half a century ago, where—when—I come from."

Joaquin nodded grimly. "Sí, we lost. I did not know this for some years in Hell. But hear Franco gone now."

"Yeah." The firing had stopped and the men around them got to their feet, brushing off dirt.

"What is position of church?"

Markham frowned. "In Spain? I don't know, I wasn't much for politics."

Joaquin's eyes narrowed. "Then you renounce the Church?"

"Huh? I don't give a damn about it."

Markham noticed several men nearby bringing their rifles up to ready.

"Say the rosary."

"I don't know it. I'm not Catholic."

"Then are demon." Joaquin smacked his lips and nodded sagely to his men.

"Hey, *no*—"

Somebody seized him from behind and pushed him downhill. There were three things that looked like telephone booths behind an outcropping of rock and a line of men and women waiting nearby, their hands tied behind them. As Markham stumbled down the hillside he saw that each booth had an open back wall on the downhill side and beyond each was a heap of bodies.

"Jesus, no, I—"

Joaquin ordered him bound and as two men tied his hands from behind Joaquin stepped over and casually punched him in the face. Markham's nose began dripping blood and he grunted with pain but he didn't mind that as much as the pile of bodies downhill.

"Demon feel hurt?" Joaquin asked sarcastically.

"Yeah. Look—"

"*Hay que tomar la muerte como si fuera asprina!*" Joaquin called to his men, laughing. Then to Markham he said in heavily accented English, "You have to take death as aspirin."

"Look, is there some kind of test I can—"

"Demon bleeds. Must be special demon," Joaquin said.

The men laughed. There was a mean edge to the sound.

"Dammit, I'm no demon at all!"

"Then swear fidelity to God."

"Which God? The Catholic one, or—"

They wrenched him away. "Okay, I vow by almighty God—"

Someone punched him in the stomach and he fell, dust filling his nose. He struggled up and hands thrust him into the line of forlorn people waiting to enter the booths. He gasped, then sneezed. Guards talked in Spanish, making some joke, and prodded him forward.

"Jesus, if they'd only listen . . ."

"Ah, that's expecting calm logic from a fevered mob," a man in front of him said. He was about Markham's age, with bushy hair, a sharp-nosed incisive face.

Markham recognized him, vaguely. Had he seen him in that grimy town, the one he found just after dropping into Hell? Everything was running together, like a watercolor. He had met Hemingway somewhere, yes, and some Romans . . .

He shook his head. "I just got reborn. I damn sure don't want to go through that again."

"Nor I." The accent was British and the man's blue eyes darted about with piercing intelligence. He wore a badly cut but recognizable three-piece suit which looked ludicrously out of place. "They grabbed me while I was trying to cut cross-country."

"Getting away from the battle?"

"Yes. Messy things. I thought isolation in these hills was clever, but there's some infernal war on."

"It's a revolt. Che Guevara against the local police and the demons."

A pained expression. "Oh, not another."

"There've been some before?"

"I've heard such. No one writes down anything, there is no history—just rumors."

"How come they think we're demons?"

"There have been a lot around lately."

"Fighting?"

"Precious little I know of that. I try to stay away from the endless battling."

"I'm no demon. Can't they tell?"

"They seem to think, these baby bolshies, that anyone human should've rallied to their cause already."

"Therefore, we're not human."

"A slippery syllogism, but enough to knot around our necks, I'm afraid."

The man was slight and precise, an aristocratic sparrow. His hawklike triangular face seemed to seize upon each new morsel of fact and try to wring from it every savor of significance.

Markham looked up the line of hopeless, dejected captives, to the booths beyond. "What're those things?"

"Delightful little telephone booths? Electrocution chambers, actually."

As Markham watched, two of the guards took a stiff-faced man out of the line and slapped him. They they spat questions at him in heavily accented English. The man was fat but was well muscled, too, with a quick intelligence in his eyes. He licked at some blood that trickled from his lip, eyeing the two guards with contempt. Markham wondered if the resemblance to the Spanish dictator, Franco, was coincidental. Apparently none of the others noticed it. But this figure had a certain dignity, a sturdy patient endurance that bespoke a past of authority.

"Where you from?" a guard asked the bleeding man.

"I live down the valley."

"Where that?"

He told them it was near the river that ran down on the other side of the far hills.

"Why you come here?"

"Trying to get away from the rest of you. You burned my house."

"You stay where you are, you okay. Why come here?"

"I thought the fighting would be down below."

"Why you think that?" the other guard asked suspiciously, prodding the fat man with the rusty barrel of his Springfield rifle.

"I thought you'd be brave enough to attack the demons. They were all along the river."

"You think we run?" the guard demanded sharply.

The fat man smiled with undisguised disdain and said nothing.

The guard spat out angrily, "You work with demons."

"Bullshit."

"You not demon maybe but you work with."

"Did you see them tear some of your friends apart? Back there on the road?"

"You there?"

"Sure. I saw a lot of you run away."

"Not us!" the guard said too quickly, too loudly.

"The big yellow ones, they pulled the hands off first. Then they broke the elbows and then the knees."

"We not retreat!"

"Somebody did."

Markham noticed one guard was clenching and un-clenching his hands, breathing hard, eyes white. "You from demons!"

"No."

"You let demons give it to you in the ass."

The fat man said slowly, "If you are going to kill me, do it without all this. This is stupid."

"You like the way they make you take it, face down in mud?"

The fat man said with dignity, "I hope your little trick with the wiping works. I do not want to remember you at all."

The guards both swore at him and grabbed him by the arms. They dragged him to the head of the line and thrust him into the tall booth. They attached a lead to his right foot and then pulled a kind of wire cage down over his head, making contact with the back of his neck. The fat man looked at them disdainfully, as though this was an irksome social encounter with his inferiors and he would be glad to get out of it and back to something interesting. Markham could not tell whether the man was being brave or just acting. Either way he kept it up right until the end, when a guard tripped a switch and abruptly the fat man jerked and twitched and his tongue shot out, huge and purple, his eyes bulging, like a grotesque gesture of final contemptuous farewell. He stayed erect until the harsh rasping buzz stopped and the body collapsed, a puppet with its strings cut.

Markham blinked. "I wonder if he was . . ."

"Right. Franco, I'm sure of it," the Englishman said with clipped certainty. "I saw him in person once."

"He didn't want these guys to know?"

"They'd have tortured him."

"Electrocution? Why not just shoot him?"

"At first I imagined this bizarre device was to save ammunition, but I think not. The diesel, the electrical wiring—no, too complicated." His face wrinkled into a grim mask. "That wire cage around the head is the point."

"What's it do?"

The guards were dragging Franco's body through the booth. They threw it downhill, its arms flailing with false life, muscles still jumping. The eyes showed only white, the tongue lolled. It rolled into the pile of corpses, jerked a few times and lay still.

The Englishman said abstractly, gazing into the distance, "I gather from overheard talk that the booth destroys memory."

"*What?*" Markham felt a cold horror.

"It runs current through the easily accessible lobes. The high current then burns out the short-term memory. It may even affect the personality—not that these lot would care."

"So what? We'll be reincarnated somewhere else."

"Ah, but there is some evidence that you carry your mental information with you." The man's impish eyes danced. Markham had a vague memory of this face, as though he had known of him in his past—his *real*—life. But where?

"Well, sure—"

"We retain our memories, else how is one to make progress?"

"Who says we do?"

"If we don't, what's the point of reincarnating us with all past memory of Hell intact? Otherwise, the Devil or Pseudo-God or whoever—*what*ever—runs this place might just as well begin each of our little Hellish 'lives'—" his eyebrows arched in exaggerated humor "—fresh. Anew. Straight from our earthly graves."

"So you think there's a purpose to . . . this place?"

"A man's reach should exceed his grasp," the man cackled, "or what's a heaven for?"

"I . . . see." Markham was unsure if the man was merely antic, or insane. With British intellectuals it was not always obvious.

The Englishman said with grave calm, "They plan to wipe our frontal lobes."

"Jesus . . . why?" Markham shifted uneasily. Up the line the guards took a swarthy young woman in black and strapped her into a booth. She didn't seem to care, just stared out at the gray sky of endless roiling clouds.

"Apparently they regard us as minor functionaries, trivial demons sent to spy. If they kill us and erase our memories, then we cannot bring information back to the devil and his cohorts."

"And if we aren't . . ."

"Right. Brain damage."

"I won't!"

"Haven't much choice."

"Oh yeah?" Markham shook a fist at the man. "Watch. As soon as there's—"

Without waiting for him to complete his sentence, Hell provided what he wanted. A shriek echoed across the broad hillside, from somewhere below. The cry held absolute terror and pain, mingled with a despairing surprise that transfixed everyone. It was a human wail confronting something from the deepest recesses of fear.

Everyone stopped and turned toward the sound. "The demons come," someone whispered.

Markham stepped out of line. A guard saw him and came running over and Markham spread his hands, as if

in explanation. He put an expression of submissive
anxiety on his face and set his feet and waited for the
right moment. The guard pointed the rifle, jabbering.
Markham slapped his hand around it and jerked it free.

*They think a cat in the hand means the world by the
tail,* he thought sourly, and before the man could react
Markham slammed the butt into the guard's face.

Shouts.

Shots.

Markham instinctively ducked. He grabbed a belt of
ammunition from the guard's shoulder and rolled away.

It had felt *good* to do that, finally take some action.
He reversed the Springfield and fired off a round in the
direction of the booths.

"Let's go!" he shouted at the Englishman. He ran for
the nearby pines, jacking a cartridge out of the breech
and slamming it closed again, feeling the new round
slide home from the clip.

Good stuff, he thought in a detached, lofty way. *Old
tech. Dependable.*

He reached the trees among a peppering of shots
trying to find him, a *tisssip* passing by his ear and
singing grand elation in his feet.

He crashed into something sharp, felt a biting cut in
his left leg, and rolled downslope into a hollow. Shots
snapped by overhead. More distant screams. He brought
the rifle up to cover the trees, but no one advanced
toward him.

He crawled back up the slope and saw that what had
cut him was a small crashed aircraft. Its shell of slick
shiny aluminum gave him back his own face, and he
was surprised to see he was heavily bearded, with long
scraggly locks of brown hair.

The aircraft was light, carrying cameras and a small
pilot's seat that would have fit a monkey. On its stubby
nose it carried an odd emblem: a swastika from which
bloomed a vertical trident. Satan's pitchfork?

Rounds cut through the nearby trees, ricocheted *spang*
off rocks, but Markham was transfixed by his own mys-

teriously transformed self. When he had died in Hell
before, he had only a thin beard and short, servicable
hair. Now, reborn, both were long.

He felt this must mean something, but before he
could think it through, a figure broke from the nearby
trees and ran toward him. Markham brought the rifle
up and sighted along the barrel and then saw that it was
the Englishman.

"Thought—I might—join you," the man gasped as he
slipped on pine needles and crashed into the gully.

"What're they doing out there?"

"You confused them. They expect ordinary people in
Hell to take whatever comes along."

"Huh." Somewhere a machine gun opened up, rak-
ing the trees above with heavy fire.

"Not surprising, is it? Most are frightfully confused
and numb. They've been so quite a long while."

"How do you know?"

"I've talked to a few in Greek—I learned a smattering of it at university."

"Yeah? What do the Greeks say?"

Rounds thumped into the branches.

"Oh, not only Greeks. All the older ones had to learn
Greek."

"Older ones?" Markham studied their situation. How
could they get away?

"Oh, Egyptians, Babylonians, even hunter-gatherer
types from prehistory."

"*They're* here?"

"Indeed. They may be the majority."

Markham remembered his estimate of the population. Fifty, maybe a hundred billion. "This isn't a solely
Christian Hell, then, huh?"

"Not at all. The Babylonians think they're in some
sort of staging area. Any moment a winged chariot
trailing a glowing sun will descend and make this into a
lush forest, they say, a heaven rich in date palms and
fresh springs and easy women."

"Heaven? This?"

"Compared with scratching out an existence in a bleak dry plain, using a wooden plow? Yes."

"Not my idea of even a pleasant weekend."

"Nor mine. I say, what are you planning?"

"Nothing."

"When you dashed away, I thought—"

"Well, I didn't think. I just wasn't going to get my brains fried."

"Nor I."

"Why didn't you do something?"

"I am not the, ah, active type."

"Who are you?"

"A philosopher, Bert—"

"Fine, look, we've got to maneuver away from—"

Something flapped lazily overhead. As Markham looked up he saw it bank and turn, a thing ponderous and scaly and unmistakably interested in them.

3.

Its head was huge. Yellow eyes, with fractured red irises like shattered glass. They peered down at the men from behind a pig snout with inflamed fleshy nostrils. Below these, flaring red-rimmed holes that dripped a bile-green pus. Where a mouth should have been there was a crusted band of hairy warts, sickly white cysts and brimming brown sores. Its head was shaped like a bulldog's, blunt and squat and massive. As Markham watched, it hovered on languidly flapping wings and surveyed the area, its head swiveling completely around, as if on ball bearings. Then it fixed upon them again, selecting them from all it could see. Its eyes locked with Markham's. A moment passed between them, the yellow eyes flashing with malevolent lust and appetite, the fevered ancient communication of carnivore and prey.

It began its descent. The vast body was scaly, triangular, and its six-fingered claws grasped the air in anticipation. It brought bony arms up for the attack, sharp nails of crimson clashing and scraping together.

It came down on unseen currents, heavy and lumbering, its skin like aged brass. Then its swollen neck opened and Markham saw that he had been wrong: the apparent skull was only the upper half of some grotesquely misshapen head. The neck yawned greedily, showing orange teeth that came to glinting points. Muscles knotted, splitting the mouth into a thin, rapacious grin.

"My . . . word," the Englishman whispered.

"Yeah."

The thing was heavy and inexorable. It looked aerodynamically impossible, a huge mass suspended aloft on gossamer wings of coppery reptilian sheen. And it thrust these wings forward and back as though it were batting at the air, not trying to skim through it. The things could move easily and swiftly while high up, but descent seemed difficult.

It doesn't seem to be maintaining an air flow over the wing surfaces, Markham thought. *More like using the wings as oars. Maybe Bernoulli's laws don't work in Hell. But then something else must . . .*

Slow but sure, it came.

"Run!" the Englishman cried.

"No, somebody'll just shoot us." Markham tried to think clearly.

"They'll be aiming at *that.*"

"They already are."

They heard the *thunk* of bullets hitting the side of it. The leathery hide buckled in waves, spreading away from the impact, and then oozed back into place.

"No penetration," Markham said thoughtfully.

"If even machine guns can't puncture it, I fail to see what we—"

"Say, right—puncture. That's it."

"That's what?"

"It isn't flying at all. The thing's a damned balloon."

The Englishman named Bert looked doubtful. "It is a supernatural beast. You cannot assume the same laws—"

"Hell I can't. Or do you want to wait for it to come down here and eat you?"

"We should *run.*"

"It moves sideways too fast." Markham assessed the monstrous bulk coolly. "Even if we got across the clearing, through the machine guns, it would keep up."

"Then what—"

"We let it come to us."

"We're hopelessly—"

"Get some dried pine branches, quick."

The thing filled the air, ponderous and making a slobbering noise of greedy anticipation. The mouth split wider, purpling lips bulging, teeth gleaming a vibrant orange. Its eyes glowed with stupid energy. From the leering lips came a snakelike hiss. Abruptly the thing bellowed a high piercing attack note, a sound like a dozen blaring trumpets filled with spit.

The two men gathered some branches and squatted in the lowest part of the gully. The demons flexed rippling muscles and its distorted head lowered to bite.

"Got a light?" Markham asked.

"A *what?*"

The Englishman fished a worn book of pasteboard matches from a pocket. It tore when Markham opened it. He tried three of the thin matches and each time the head crumbled away. He felt wind fluttering his hair.

"Where'd you get these?"

"I . . . off a . . . dead person."

"Oh great. Been out in the rain—" The fourth match lit, flared, and then the beating of monstrous wings blew it out.

"Stand over me!"

"But—it's so—"

"*Do* it!"

The spindly man stooped over Markham and the fifth match split in two. Markham cupped the sixth—and last—match and struck it carefully. It burst into welcome orange and he quickly touched it to the pile of

pine branches. They caught. Flames jumped through
the pile, aided now by the fluttering wind of the beast.

"Into the mouth!" He had to yell against another
moistly triumphant trumpet blast.

"Those teeth—"

"Now!"

The misshapen head struck down. They pitched the
hot branches directly at it. Most struck the lips. A few
lodged in the corners of the yellow eyes, the crisp
flames sending up quick puffs of steam. Fewer still
tumbled between the snapping sharp teeth and down
its gullet.

"Go!"

They scrambled back as the head jerked and swung.
A wet blue tongue flicked out and caught the Englishman
by the wrist. It started to draw him in, toward the
mouth. Markham chopped down with the Springfield
and the tongue bristled suddenly with needle-point
poison shafts. These tiny swords stabbed the rifle with
demented verve, as if it were the enemy rather than
the man who held it.

The Springfield started smoking. Markham dropped
it. A sour stench made him choke. The tongue slipped
back into the mouth and the Englishman wrenched
free.

"Jump!"

They both dropped to the ground and rolled away
from the lashing, aimless thrusts of the head. The beast
flapped languidly above, six feet from the ground, its
head seeking them. A gust of wind blew it sideways,
bringing into view an underside corrupted by fungus
and open sores.

Markham crawled uphill. If they ventured out from
under the thing, it could catch them as they fled. On
the other hand, once it realized they were hiding under
it, the demon dragon would simply land on them.

He heard a *crump* of something igniting. The beast
shuddered and Markham rolled under the heaving, brassy
scales of the belly. Small, skinny, almost vestigal legs

hung there. They ended in stubby webbed duck feet of a delicate, pale tan.

"Grab on!"

"But—" The Englishman followed Markham's lead and grasped the feet. "Your fire idea certainly didn't frighten it."

"Helium wouldn't give it enough lift, so I figure—"

The beast twisted, struggling.

The Englishman's eyes widened in delight. "Ah! Hydrogen."

They felt rather than heard a dull, heavy *whump.*

"Then—"

The demon dragon lifted. Slowly, then faster, the igniting hydrogen deep in its belly blended with oxygen to yield a pure blue flame that shot from the head, cramming it back into the muscled neck, against the bulbous body. The escaping gas acted like a rocket, driving the demon skyward, ass-first.

The Englishman screamed and Markham shouted, "Hold on! We'll get out of this mess!"

They arced above pines and rocky ridgelines, the venting gas driving them in a blunted parabola above the crackling rifle fire below. Wind whipped them against the steel-solid plates of the beast's coppery underbelly.

Markham felt them slowing, sensed the exhaustion of hydrogen inside. As pressure eased in the beast the rocket effect lessened. The thing curved downward, fuel spent.

They were high, but maybe not too high . . . He had already died several deaths in Hell, and falling seemed to be an element in every one. This time . . .

"Swing the way I do!" Markham yelled.

"I—can't—"

"Just *do* it."

The demon was falling. Its wings flexed weakly. Trees below swelled and Markham hoped they would come down in ones with high branches. Otherwise . . .

"Harder!"

They swung, clinging, Markham feeling his arm muscles knot painfully. The demon barked angrily and a wing batted at them.

"Make it tumble!"

"I don't see—"

Their timed swinging caught the beast off balance. It squawked with brassy rage. Flame leaped from its mouth but it could not spit past its own distended belly.

At their outermost extension, the weight of the two men was enough to send it tumbling sideways, wings ineffectually whacking the air. The thing kept falling and now it turned slowly in air, all skillful vectors lost.

The ground rushed up. The dragon spun over, belly-high. Markham slid down onto it. His shoes thumped into the mica-thin plates and he shouted, "Hang on!"

He had just enough time as wind whistled by him to grab a spindly thrashing leg.

The demon hit the trees with its face turned impotently skyward, yellow eyes blazing with dumb rage. Boughs broke beneath it *crack-crack-crack* and pine needles stung the men on faces and arms as they swirled downward with it, their world a mass of rushing green and shrieking demons.

It struck with a solid *thunk*. The belly bulged. It burst with a liquid *poof*.

A last branch lashed Markham across the face and he pitched forward onto soft humus.

He rolled over in time to see the demon give a quiver, a foul belch of hydrogen sulphide, and close its stormy eyes. The Englishman lay sprawled like a rag doll beside it, blinking and wheezing as if these both were new experiences, rich with sensation.

Markham brushed himself off. "Devil of a ride," he said.

4.

The great demon-blimp had splattered scarlet gobbets among the pines and elms, speckling branches and leaves so that the very forest seemed to bleed. Mark-

ham kicked the crusted plates of its side and read the
lines inscribed there in ornate Germanic script,

THROUGH ME YOU ENTER THE CITY OF
LAMENT
THROUGH ME YOU ENTER INTO PAIN ETERNAL
THROUGH ME YOU ENTER WHERE THE LOST
ARE SENT.

"Dante," the Englishman said.

"Must be like those people who wear sweatshirts that
say, Property of San Quentin Prison—pure bravado."

"True, this demon didn't do very well at inflicting
pain eternal on us."

"What's the rest of it say?" Markham tried to shove
against the sagging belly plates and see the next line,
buried under a wall of quickly purifying flesh.

"If I remember correctly, these are the famous words
chiseled above the entrance to Hell. A few lines on are
the famous ones,

'ABANDON EVERY HOPE, ALL YE THAT ENTER.
These words of colour louring and obscure,
I saw inscribed on high above a gate.'

Or so as I recall. Defunct languages weren't my passion."

"I knew I should've gotten a classical education."

"Rubbish. No use to you here. This isn't Dante's
Hell."

"Whose is it?"

"No theologian even remotely dreamed of something
like this. No rules seem to apply."

"Not entirely," Markham said with a slight smirk.
"Physics did this one in."

"The little trick with the hydrogen?" A begrudging
smile. "You burned his buoyant gas, yes."

"I figured the dragon couldn't let much oxygen into
its system, because hydrogen and oxygen explode. But
it *had* to have a metabolism that involved oxygen—after
all, it was breathing the stuff. But the two gases mingle
safely—"

"Ah yes, I recall. Unless they're heated . . ."

"You bet!" Markham said, eyes bright. "So our burning branches ignited the mixture, deep down in the demon's belly.

"But there was limited oxygen . . ."

"So it detonated slowly, pushing the hot residue out the throat."

"Which acted like a rocket."

"Yeah, luckily. I couldn't figure whether the exhaust would go out the mouth or the ass. So I grabbed on below. But if the hot stuff had come out the ass, we would've had to jump or get scorched."

"Clever, I'll grant."

"Better than that—it proves that there are physical laws that work here. Hydrogen combined with oxygen in the presence of a hot enough flame makes them unite explosively."

"Oh, I'll agree to that, on Earth. But you haven't shown that's what happened *here*. Or that it will ever happen again."

"Look, we just rode this dragon to safety. How—"

"Only careful experiments can show—"

A furious flapping of wings startled them to silence. Above the trees a dark angular shape cruised, searching.

"Hustle!" Markham whispered.

They scrambled away, slipping on pine needles. Through the dark and clotted brush of the forest the heavy regular beat of wings rose, then gradually died as they made progress. Markham listened carefully.

"Maybe that's just the cleanup squad, come for the body."

"They do appear to have missed us."

Markham noted a strange silence in the woods ahead. No bird calls, not even the subtle brush of wind.

"Something funny over that way. C'mon."

They crept through tree-lined paths, angling away from the brooding zone of sepulchral silence. Markham was reasonably sure this was not the same hill where the battle had occurred, though it was hard to gauge distances when you were tumbling through the air on a belching, foul-breathed dragon.

They came to a gouged-out area that seemed the site of some past disaster. Pillars and caved-in buildings poked like jagged teeth from the undergrowth. A snake slipped around a Doric column, eyed them, and left a trail of green slime as it moved off. The emerald line formed a written line, a message. Markham gestured at the slimy numbers silently: 666.

"Ah, the number of the Beast."

"Does that mean he knows everything that's going on?"

"Perhaps. The Devil's supposed to be omnipotent."

"I thought that was God."

A cackling laugh. "Is there a difference?"

"I hope so." Markham sat on a ruined wall of ancient red brick which reminded him of Greece. He felt suddenly tired. Yet in Hell he could not sleep.

"You're a physicist?"

"Was. And you?"

"A philosopher."

"I think I remember your face. From the back of a book . . ."

"I died in 1970. Bertrand Russell."

Markham blinked. Why was Hell so densely populated with the famous? "Of course. I read a book of yours."

"*History of Western Philosophy*, I'll wager."

"Right. I'll bet you're surprised."

"Why?"

"You dismissed ideas of an afterlife as pure bullshit."

Russell again laughed like a cross between a barking dog and a clucking hen. "True enough. I was a neutral monist, holding that personalities were collections of events. An aggregate, like a cricket club."

"But we're here. Some motivating personality makes the world run, and it cares about your particular cricket club. And mine."

Russell's eyes sparkled. "Never feel absolutely sure of anything."

"Come on. You can't peddle that positivist doubt any more."

"Oh, can't I? Just because we have wakened to a comic book Hell?"

"Dragons with Dante written on their hides? You think they arose from natural selection?"

"I do believe someone with a great deal of power has ordered this odd place we're in."

"Not the Devil, though?"

"Oh, I don't know his *name*, mind you. He can call himself whatever he likes."

"But you don't think this is a supernatural place?"

"I believe we are in the grip of a superior intelligence, that is all."

Markham preferred believing in the rule of physical law. If a capricious Devil ran everything here, there was no hope of doing anything independently. All human effort could be overruled by fiat. "You could explain our escape as just something the Devil *let* happen?"

"Of course."

"Even a Devil needs to make his Hell work with *some* order."

Russell leaned forward, rubbing his palms together as if relishing a good talk for the first time in quite a while. "You're a scientist. Let me put it to you: Isn't it perfectly possible that the old world we came from was the product of intelligent manipulation of a purely natural kind?"

"Until I woke up here, I'd have said yes. But now—"

"No no, let me be more precise. For example, our galaxy *could* have been made by a powerful mind who rearranged the primeval gases using carefully placed gravitating bodies, controlled explosions and all the other paraphernalia of an astro-engineer. But would such a superintelligence be God?"

"Well, as far as we're concerned, yes."

"Not so! God was not supposed to be some mere

galactic architect. Clearly, no being who was obliged to operate within the universe, using only pre-existing laws, can be considered as a universal creator."

"I see." Markham didn't know whether he liked this line of argument. It had been strangely reassuring to die in Hell several times and be reborn, none the worse for wear. Even if you weren't hugely pleased with the place—to say the least—it *did* guarantee immortality. Death had been the deepest, most disturbing problem humanity faced in the old, "real" world. Its remorseless coming motivated the pyramids, vast rich art, all the grasping after tatters of immortality that lay behind great works. Awareness of it was just about the only remaining feature which separated humankind from animals, far more important than language or tool-using or the opposable thumb. And each mortal faced it, finally, alone.

"If you as a scientist are to believe in God, you must hold that He created space-time. Eh?"

"Uh . . . okay."

"But modern physics—or what I can glean of it from people passing through—holds that mere humans alone could accumulate enough matter in a small enough region to create a black hole."

"So?"

"Well, a black hole is a closed-off space-time, is it not?"

Markham chewed at his lip. Russell's legendary quick wit was accompanied by a ready grin, a concentrated, almost wolfish gaze, a lust for the intellectual hunt. "No, a black hole *destroys* space-time at its center. That's what the singularity is. The whole idea of space-time no longer works there. Anything that falls in enters that point, where our ideas of space and time and event itself no longer makes sense."

"To us." Russell said briskly.

"Yes, to us." Something was bothering Markham, plucking at his awareness, but he brushed it aside.

Russell nodded, still enjoying the pursuit. "Of creating space-time, admittedly, we know nothing. But in a sense the mathematical discovery of black holes—and how to annihilate space-time at one vortex-like point— brings us halfway to Godhood ourselves."

"You mean if we were just smart enough, or had enough time to work on the problem—"

"Exactly. *We* would become gods."

"Rulers of space-time," Markham said sardonically. "Masters of the sevagram."

Russell sniffed with donnish primness. "Similarly, there is absolutely nothing which requires that we attribute this Hell to anything more than a *natural* God or Devil. He—or It—could quite simply have arranged the galaxies to form, or life to begin, for example. No need for creation out of nothing, *ex nihilo*. Indeed—"

"You're just stuffing everything we don't know into a box and calling it God."

"Ah, quite right. At Cambridge we called that the God of the Gaps. Then, every time you physicists turned a new leaf, brought light on some subject, God retreated."

Markham nodded, still somewhat troubled by the silent forest they had found. He studied the trees nearby, melancholy drooping willows. Was there a dead zone in the woods to his left, a curious noiseless region like the one he had noticed before? He felt jumpy.

Russell said with lordly reserve, "I do not wish to make this God the friend of ignorance. If we are to find God here, it must surely be through what we discover about things, rather than through remaining ignorant."

Markham said fervently, "Damn right. If we can just do a few experiments, try to—"

"No, wait, you misunderstand. Let me frame my point more precisely. You surely accept the possibility that in the remote future, humanity might be able to place great regions of the universe under intelligent control."

"Well . . ." Markham had always been rather leery of wild-eyed speculation, of what-ifs piled atop one another to dizzying heights of absurdity.

"Then such a zone would be totally technologized. Why, then, is it so difficult to suppose such a super-intelligence cannot have existed *before* us?"

"There's no evidence—" Markham stopped.

"Exactly. *This* may be such evidence."

Some innate sense of what science was about forced its way forward. Markham said irritably, "Look, intelligence comes from the upward evolution of matter. That means—"

"Yes yes, matter first, mind later."

"All the science we have—"

"Assumes that the universe is *not* a self-observing, self-organizing system."

"Sure, because—"

"Of bias, pure and simple."

"No, it's . . ." Markham's voice trailed off. "You . . . you've thrown every basic proposition into doubt. If mind comes first, and organizes matter now . . ."

"Note that the universe didn't have to start this way. You can have your Big Bang or this new Inflationary Universe scenario I've been hearing about. Cherish whatever *beginning* cosmology you desire." Russell beamed happily. "Clutch it to your bosom. But in this catch-all Hell, you must at least admit the possibility that somewhere in the last ten or twenty billion years— that *is* still a good value taken from the Hubble constant, isn't it?"

Markham nodded silently, thinking.

"In those billions of years, somehow mind came to the fore, at least in our little neck of the universe."

"And it moved upon the waters and made Heaven and Hell."

"Well, Hell at least. We have no evidence of Heaven."

Markham blinked. "You . . . think this might be *all*."

"Why not?"

"But there must be something better . . ."

Markham saw sourly that Russell could easily be right. This place might be a mild improvement on the "real" world, since you couldn't die, but nobody had said anything about any place better, now that he thought about it. The best anyone could envision was a return to the old world itself.

"In a way," Russell said dreamily, "this is a philosopher's paradise."

"I think I'd prefer the Moslem one, with houris and infinite banquets."

"No no, that would be hopelessly boring."

"I could sure as hell use a stiff drink right now."

Russell waved away such base pursuits. "Actually, this place reminds me in a way of why I took up mathematics. I wanted something that was not human and had nothing particular to do with the messy Earth, or with the whole accidental nature of the universe. I wanted something like Spinoza's God, which wouldn't love us in return."

"Ha! Here everything hates us. Very personally, too."

"I prefer to believe that in this place Mind rules, not brute Matter."

"Gee, that makes me feel better already."

"Sarcasm?"

"Demons chasing us, horrible deaths every time you look around, you can't screw or eat or drink with any pleasure, or even sleep—"

"Well, admittedly there are some sensory details missing."

"*Details?* You call—" Markham was on his feet, fists balled into hard knots, feeling the frustration in him about to explode—when something made him freeze. The silence . . .

It had reached the nearby trees now, a ghostly enveloping deadness that clasped the air in clammy cold. A fine mist seemed to hang suspended on a crystalline inert nullity.

"Run!"

Russell dashed away as quickly as Markham, his spry step belying the generally thin and delicate look of the man. His absurd three-piece suit flapped as he ran, his tie streaming behind.

They crashed through brush and thickets, oblivious to stinging scratches and painful poking limbs. And abruptly stumbled into a meadow, where a figure in white coasted along above the ground.

"What?" Markham gasped.

"It doesn't appear to be a demon."

"But he's flying."

At the sound of their voices the figure swerved and glided toward them. Alabaster blades of light streamed from his flowing robes. He held up a hand, palm forward, and called, "I beseech you, which way did you come?"

"Back there." Markham gestured. "There's some kind of dead zone."

"That would be a timetrap the Beast has sent for me."

Russell said piercingly, "A trap in time?" He stepped forward and deftly felt the hem of the man's flowing robe where it rippled lightly in the air.

The floating figure said airily, "A place where—temporarily, though that is not only a bad pun, but a positive confusion—all space-time vectors are very nearly wholly spacelike."

"In other words," Markham said, "time slows."

The being nodded. "Time becomes as syrup. One swims through it with only muted, mudlike motions."

"Are you a poet?" From Russell's intent expression Markham gathered that the philosopher either disliked the alliteration or else thought this hovering creature was somehow important.

"No," the man said simply, "I am an angel called Altos."

"In Hell?" Russell demanded.

"We labor where we must."

Altos had begun drifting downhill, away from the direction of the timetrap. Markham trotted to keep up and felt in the wake of the angel a breath of warm, tropical air. He breathed in a scent of sweet wildflowers and a rich, spicy aroma of meat turning on an open spit.

His stomach rumbled. An avalanche of images smothered him in sensual longing. Pink-nippled breasts. Prime rib, marbled with fat. Ivory thighs slowly spreading in silent invitation. Incense burning in shrouded rooms where cries of pleasure drifted. Milkshakes. The grunting squeezed pleasure of a good, full shit. Crisp lettuce. The heavy smoke of a Cuban cigar. Lunging shudders between a pair of high-heeled shoes. Musky lamb curry. Dozing in golden sunlight halfway through a winter's morning. A lingering moist kiss in a darkened hallway. Ripe olives—

He felt a stirring, a building of lust long denied. All his senses collided and he could barely gasp, "Heaven! Is there a Heaven?"

Altos looked with mild, distant curiosity at the two running men, as if they were a bothersome detail. He was gaining speed and they had begun to pant as they dashed in his wake across the green meadow, wet grass slipping and squeaking under their shoes.

"Why, I believe so. I am not a framer of definitions."

"But, look! You must have been there," Markham shouted as the figure picked up velocity and began to rise at a steady angle to clear the trees ahead. "Who gives you your orders?"

"Oh," the receding voice called out blandly, "I do not receive orders. I respond to the will of the world."

Altos rose into the perpetually troubled sky, his robes trailing a last faint aroma of distant pleasures, and waved langorously.

"What the Hell did that mean?" Markham gasped, stopping.

"Bloody angel is just as big a fool as we all," Russell said sardonically.

"Well, at least he doesn't have to walk."

5.

They tumbled into the ditch together, spattered with grime and wheezing for air. It had been only an hour

since the angel lofted free and clean and serenely into
the air, leaving them to pick their way through brambles.

"I wonder if we could've grabbed his legs, hung on,
gone to Heaven."

"If he's like most archbishops I've known, he would've
shaken us free." Russell hugged himself, his suit now
shredded and stained almost beyond recognition.

"Wish this rain would let up."

"It keeps down the visibility. That's the only reason
we eluded those fellows with rifles."

"They looked like Guevara's."

"Ah yes, baby Bolshies on the march." Russell shook
his head in wonderment. "How they can think simply
potshotting at demons will topple a being who has been
at this business for a billion years or more—"

"How do you know how long this has been here?"

"I assume it predates all religions."

"Maybe it *caused* them?"

"Perhaps religion is simply an early idea which has
been found wanting. This place may be a failed experiment."

"So we're abandoned here?"

"Or waiting for further examination by a busy, dis-
tracted God."

Markham found this idea disquieting. He took refuge
in physics. "The idea of time may not mean much in a
place where it can be slowed down."

"Or speeded up. Yes. I've thought much upon these
matters. It has been—oh yes, when did you die?"

Markham wiped the drizzle from his face and shivered. It didn't seem right, being chilled in Hell. "In
1998."

"It doesn't seem so long a time—some twenty-eight
years have elapsed since I died. Perhaps time is mallea-
ble here, in much the same way 'they' managed to give
me my body as it was when I was fifty, despite the fact
that I died at age 98."

"Mine's the same as when I died—fifty-two."

"Evidence of some pleasant intention, then, or else we would all be dragging about as cadavers."

This struck Markham as an unexpected shaft of light. "Yes, and we don't seem to get sick, either. I probably won't even get a cold from this rain we're in, and—"

A hideous shriek split the air. Through the roiling fog that shrouded the trees they saw a yellow thing like a huge hornet swiftly zoom into view, wings beating like some gargantuan hummingbird. Its beak was long and pincerlike, and in it a man wriggled, screaming. The long twisted body of the beast wriggled as if in a vast sensual orgasm of anticipation. It jerked its head eagerly, steam spouting from holes in the beak, eyes fevered and flashing red. Wails of torment shook the man in helpless delerium. The hornet-beast eagerly reared its head back and with quick, convulsive gulps bit the man into thirds. Its muscled throat knotted and swallowed and in ten seconds the man was gone.

"So much for the theory of a kindly providence," Russell said mildly.

The contorted yellow thing did not hear them, for which Markham was thankful. It hovered, eyes rapidly scanning the terrain, and then darted away on humming wings.

"This ditch seems quite homelike, compared to the open," Russell said.

"I'm afraid we're going to have to move," Markham said, pointing. From the nearby fog emerged a line of men, rifles and machetes at the ready.

"If we can see them, they'll see us when we leave this ditch," Russell said.

"If we—"

Something big and bile-green fluttered down from the clouds. Its grasping claw plucked one armed man up by his head, and called like a shrill bluejay. The bloated thing was all feathers and foaming hunger, with a mouth like a cut throat and five feet that clutched at the soldier with hot purpose. It tore a leg free and stuffed the blood-gushing morsel into its grinning mouth.

The man screamed once, hopelessly, and then went slack.

"Come on!" Markham leaped over Russell and ran swiftly down the ditch.

They went fifty meters before shots began to snap and buzz above them. Markham reached a stand of trees and lunged for cover, scrambling among the wet aromatic leaves. They were out of sight of the men behind and he ran faster, watching the sky above for something awful to descend.

Instead, he ran into a tall man in fatigues who slugged him casually in the stomach with the butt of a submachine gun.

They huddled among a ragged band of other prisoners and tried to stay out of the rain. Gunfire cracked nearby and flights of ornate flying demons scudded across the sky. Anti-aircraft rounds exploded among them like dark flowers blooming, making distant hollow thumps. Some of the chunky blimp-types took hits. They wheeled and veered and tumbled out of the sky, trailing smoke.

"At least Guevara's giving them something to think about," Markham said.

"Meaningless." Russell sniffed disdainfully. "Thinking is exactly what *isn't* going on. And surely the Devil can conjure up an infinite supply of such creatures.

"Nothing's infinite except to mathematicians," Markham said pointedly. Russell had spent decades in the pursuit of perfect, immutable knowledge by plumbing the foundations of mathematics, only to find that such certainly was impossible. Godel's proof that there were unprovable axioms in any mathematical system had laid to rest this splindly man's quest.

Russell ignored this jibe and pursued his lips. "Did you ever wonder why the Devil permits rebellion?"

"Boredom?"

"Perhaps . . . but equally likely, he likes its distraction value."

"Throwing us off the scent of something?"

"Ummm." A mirthful expression flashed across the wrinkled face. "Give mankind's nature, if you ever try to get people to not think, you will surely succeed."

"You think this fighting is a sideshow?"

"Hell doesn't seem a place designed for learned reflection, does it?"

Markham looked at their bedraggled lot, squatting in ankle-deep mud. Another of the silvery aircraft, apparently used by the Devil for observations, lay smashed nearby. In the cockpit lolled a wizened monkey-man, head caved in on impact. On impulse Markham inspected the wreck, pulling it apart to see how it flew.

"Standard piston engine," he murmured in the drizzle. If there were no physical laws, and everything ran by devilish intervention, why bother with cam shafts and carburators?

Cables for the TV cameras and electrical controls spilled out like shiny intestines. An idea flickered. Markham coiled up some cabling and wiring, tying them around his waist. In the somber gloom of the rain their guards, laughing in a shack nearby around a roaring fire, took no notice.

"I must say, I don't like the look of those," Russell said tightly.

Markham saw approaching them the fate he had been dreading. Horsedrawn carts lurched up the hillside, bringing the field generator and two of the mindwipe booths.

"That's our little Lenin, is it?"

On horseback, riding with a clear air of authority, came Che Guevara. He shouted directions at the troops in a harsh mixture of Spanish and English. Uniformed men and women scurried to set up the booths.

"Amazing, the types you see here," Russell said bemusedly. "I ran into a crazed scribbler of popular fictions a while back who thought this was all run by some primordial God named Cthulhu." Russell pronounced the name as though it were an involuntary prelude to active nausea. "Poor chap was keeping a diary. He said that when he returned to the real world he would publish it and become rich and everyone would at least know that he had been right." He shook his head.

Markham whispered, "Here, if you want to keep on trying to understand, take this."

Russell watched as Markham snaked a cable down his pants leg and into his shoe. Beneath his locks he affixed the cable to some bands of bare wire.

"Thoughtful of the Devil, giving me this long hair."

"I don't—"

"Quick!" Markham whispered instructions as Russell slipped the cable around himself, the etherial philosopher all elbows and fussy bother when confronted with a real-world problem. Markham stepped between Russell and the others to shield his movements.

Scowling troops were pulling the prisoners together, prodding them toward the booths. "This means they're falling back," Markham whispered. "They'll mindwipe us to keep information from falling into the Devil's hands."

"Typical," Russell said ascerbically. "That Guevara is armed to his mad teeth and stupid as a stump. This isn't the way to cause real damage to the Devil. Only by—"

An impatient guard applied his boot to Russell's backside, sending him in an abrupt trot downhill. Markham moved along quickly, watching for an opportunity to escape. But Guevara was near the booth crew and they were on the alert. If Markham bolted they would simply catch him, beat him, and shove him into the booth anyway. In the scuffle they might well find the cabling, too.

He stepped forward when his turn came. A woman in fatigues and looking bored roughly attached the wire cage to his head. She seemed completely unconcerned, as though these bodies were mere meat to be processed. *The banality of evil*, Markham thought. Far more chilling than all the technicolor monsters of this place. Far more . . . human.

She jabbed him in the side with a dull knife and shoved him onto a metal platform. A thin mist began settling through the trees. He smelled the pungent taste of pine and thought of his childhood, when he had run through southern woods and sucked in that wonderful smell and knew he would live forever.

They tied him securely. Elementary circuit theory, with Markham as the resistor.

He inched the cable forward with his right toe, poked it through his shoe and into firm contact with the ground plate. Now if only they didn't notice—

"Aha!" Guevara called, seeing Markham. "This time you not get away."

Markham smiled without humor. "You can run but you can't hide."

Guevara frowned, puzzled, which was just as Markham had intended. It gave him a moment to shuffle slightly to the left, inching the wire cage around his head into close contact with the cabling. He had never thought about Ohm's law in a personal sense. $V = IR$ with himself as R meant that, unless he shorted the V to ground, his skin would carry the I, seizing up his heart. And frying away all capacity for speculation, thought, redemption.

They delayed a moment to tie Russell into the next booth. The man had a birdlike dignity, his soiled suit flapping about him in the drifting drizzle as he defiantly regarded Guevara.

"*Scoundrel*," was all he said, the word summoning up all the dislike of an ivory tower moralist for those who are pinned to the muddy world.

"We're either going to wake up as morons," Markham whispered, "or in a pile of corpses. Either way, keep quiet."

He saw Russell's eyes flash momentarily with defiant anger. The bored woman pulled a switch and Markham felt a jolt snap through him, heard a crackling, smelled a sharp rank odor of burning hair.

His muscles jumped, his eyes bulged. But though a

myriad rippling threads swam in his eyes, he did not black out. An eternity of surging, enfolding pain made him dance and writhe. Then it was over and his legs gave out and he sagged. Dumbly he remembered not to gasp for air as hands untied his arms. A foot caught him in the chest and he tumbled over backwards. A soft cushion stopped him. He felt cold flesh under him. Squinting an eye open, breathing shallowly, he saw a tangle of bodies and, nearby, the hideous contorted face of a Negro woman, eyes staring at him in the perpetual blank reproach of the dead.

6.

When the killing crew had moved on, Markham crawled from under the pressing weight of still-warm bodies. He stumbled away and only stopped when a familiar voice hissed, "Wait!"

Russell bounded into view. The rain had stopped and dim light suffused the land.

Markham said happily, "I told you it would work! Physics rules."

"You may have a point." Russell rolled up his shirt and displayed a cable wound round his scrawny belly. "I got it all the way round, as you said."

"What about your feet?"

"I got the wires round my head and down to here."

"Not to your feet?"

"Well, no, there wasn't time." Russell displayed how the cable ran halfway down his body, no more.

"That wouldn't short-circuit a voltage. It would just kill you a little more slowly."

Russell thought. "I see, one needs a complete connection. I didn't understand that point."

"But you're here, alive."

"So I am. I don't suppose . . ."

"No. The way you had it rigged, it shouldn't have worked."

The thought struck both men at the same time.

"Something *else* saved me," Russell said.

"But how?"

Russell smiled wolfishly. "Something intervened to save my dear fragile thinking apparatus."

"What you said earlier, about God being the stuff we can't explain . . ."

The two rumpled men stared at each other.

Russell said hollowly, "Yes. All that fatuous talk about God's being present in those physical phenomena which science hasn't touched on yet. Wedding ignorance with the miraculous. A comic idea, back among the fellows at Trinity. Just the thing to bring a derisive bray of donnish doubt."

"Then it's . . ." Markham did not like the conclusion, somehow, but he was forced to it. "You were saved by the God of the Gaps."

"Right. Only here, He is made manifest."

"To us."

"Yes. Somehow, to us. Not to the poor souls who had their very selves blotted, back on that decaying pile." Russell's famous sadness for the blighted human predicament filled his haggard yet undaunted face.

"And so we were given a sign . . ." Markham was not entirely comfortable with this thought, but he found no way around it.

"Hold on, that reminds me . . ." Russell walked back to the piles of corpses. They were already turning blue-green. Markham gathered that if flesh decayed here as on Earth. Russell pointed at a naked woman who had already started to bloat.

"I noticed this as I was waiting for Guevera to move on," Russell said.

The woman had been stripped and beaten before her electrocution. Starting below her breasts and winding around the body were scrawled words, inflamed, as though written with a blowtorch:

Lewd did I live & evil I did dwel.

"Ummm. Guevera's work?"

"I think not. Notice that it's a palindrome?"

"What's that?"

"A phrase that reads the same whether read forward or back."

"But *dwell* is misspelled."

"Indeed. To fit the palindrome form, a bit of cheating is winked at. Perhaps this *dwel* is an old English form. And using an '&' mark is not greatly sporting in the palindrome game. In any case, such a thing is quite beyond the capacity of those thugs."

"Then who. . . ?"

"The electricity seems to have played over her skin, scorching it."

"My God, the pain . . ."

"Yes. All to send a message." Russell's great eyes were sad.

"To who? Us?"

"Who else would see it?"

"From the Devil? Or Altos?"

"Before we become positively Biblical, might I point out something?" Russell held up a finger.

A distant rumbling and snapping, punctuated by hideous mournful cries.

"What's that?"

Russell nodded. "We'll be given no respite to ponder this latest morsel of fact. The demons are coming."

Markham listened, nodded. "Yeah. The God of the Gaps wants us to obey the oldest rule."

"What's that?"

"Keep moving. Think later."

Russell laughed heartily and they both slipped into the woods, off on more adventures that could be, for all they knew, without end.

Several hours of hard slogging through muck and mire sank them back into the cloying, persistent awfulness of Hell.

Russell finally collapsed, exhausted. He sat staring at an impassible lake of mud and said pensively, "Odd, isn't it? People who farmed and labored thought of

Heaven as primarily a place to rest. Hell was pain, flames, torture. And here we sit, resting in the rain."

"And nary a demon with a pitchfork in sight." Markham settled onto a somewhat dryer spot, beneath a willow tree. Even in this depressing gray drizzle, its lovely limbs bowing to the ground were the most beautiful things he had yet seen in Hell. He wistfully recalled the crisp look the old world had, its sense of flavors and unexpected, casual loveliness. Though he had never thought about it while alive, the world then seemed to promise a presence, sources of surprising order, a guiding overall principle. He suddenly missed that terribly.

Hell displayed the same general landscapes, but its spaces seemed empty, its vistas the bare product of mechanical perspectives. No haunting beauty arose from its forests and hills, no thrust of burgeoning, willful life. Amid such yawning vacancy he felt desperately alone.

Russell wrapped his ragged suit around himself to ward off the chill. "Quite so, the demons appear to merely happen by. They don't rapaciously, continuously seek us out."

"Yeah. Can't figure it . . ."

"I wonder if a Hell invented by intellectuals would simply be a place which they couldn't explain."

Markham laughed loudly. Russell looked startled, eyes wide, blinking. "I was being *serious*."

"Uh, sorry. Beg pardon, m'lord."

"And what's that mean?" Russell gave Markham the full force of his famous scowl, his nose like a beak beneath glaring eyes.

"Well, you were a lord, after all."

The philosopher was startled again. "I was?"

"Of course. Lord Russell. You inherited it from your father, I think."

Russell sat down slowly, his haughty air of indignant affront turning to puzzlement. "I . . . did?"

"Can't you remember?"

"Well . . . no." Russell looked embarrassed.

"You won the Nobel Prize, too. For literature, some essays or something."

"Really? Not for peace? I seem to recall working for peace."

"No, they usually give that to people who negotiate treaties."

"Like Mr. Kissinger, you mean? I saw him a few disasters ago, being carried off by a talking black snake."

"Wish I'd seen that."

"I rather enjoyed it, yes. But I've been thinking about an earlier remark of yours. It has been 28 years since I died, but I can remember very little of my life before that. It's been fading gradually. The longer I'm in Hell, the more foggy become my recollections."

"You can't expect to keep stuff from the nineteenth century fresh at hand."

"Usually it's the other way, isn't it? That you remember the name of your favorite teddy bear but cannot recall last week?"

"That's just aging. We're *dead.*"

"Ummm. Good point."

"Still, you're just as feisty as your writing was. I wonder how your personality survives, if your memory doesn't?"

"Perhaps that's my *soul.*" Russell rolled his eyes in donnish jest.

"Y'know," Markham said sarcastically, "ritual irony and Brit class postures won't get us anywhere."

"I assure you—"

"You can't 'assure' me of anything! You've been here 28 years and learned nothing!"

The two men glared at each other, Russell drawing himself up into his ostrichlike dignity. His suit was a wet, begraggled thing. "You can scarcely expect anyone to make sense of this madness, this meaningless chaos."

"Not unless we can do something concrete," Markham said, "an experiment."

"Ah, the old scientific ethos," Russell said sardonically.

Markham decided to take a different tack. He hunched

forward, hands outspread. "Look, if you're right, memory fades with time around here. That means our technical knowledge will slip away. Use it or lose it, I'll bet."

"I'm not dotty, if that's what you mean," Russell said primly.

A distant bellow rang through the foggy arroyo where they huddled. It sounded reptilian, trailing off ominously into bone-crunching bass notes. Markham waved it away and kept on earnestly, "Look, you remember lots of theology and stuff, maybe you can piece it together and find some kind of clue, something we could apply rational analysis to, get—"

"I'm surprised you haven't considered the implications of that time trap, then," Russell said archly.

"How so?"

"The ability to suspend time surely implies some tinkering with casuality, no? If time can stop or even run backward, then what's the sense of moral action? There is no guilt if effects do not even follow from causes."

Markham frowned. "I don't . . ."

"Then such a time snare must be the creation of something that stands outside the realm of morality, theology, of everything."

"Look, we need something practical, not some abstract—"

Russell's eyes flashed. "If you want to do some—" a disdainful drawing-down of his mouth—"*engineering*, then look to whatever causes those traps."

Markham blinked. "Y'know, that might actually tell us something. Come on."

He surged to his feet and set off into the mist. Russell scrambled after him, calling, "I only framed it as a hypothesis."

"Hurry up. The time trap might go away."

They tried to find their away back through the shrouded hillsides, but bearings were hard to keep in the shifting gray banks of fog. They stumbled among stunted trees and tricky, sandy slopes. Just as Markham began to think any effort was futile, the cloying wet mist lifted. A faint *mmmmmm* grew as a warm white cloud enveloped them. "What's this st—"

An insect buzzed past his ear, another flew into his eyes. He batted them away. Three more landed on his arm.

"A swarm!" Russell called.

"Head downhill. We'll—"

A wasp-thing hovered in front of his eyes, gossamer wings humming. A tiny voice cried, "Help us!"

He looked closer. The wasp body was a series of slender, jointed tubular sections, connected with a bulbous abdomen by a slender waist, A sharp green stinger dripped clear fluid at the tail.

But this was far larger than any wasp he had ever seen, and covered in a crusted blue sheen. Spindly forelegs were held out toward him, beseeching. Atop the body was not the normal insect's bulging eyes but instead . . .

"It's a woman's . . . face," he said wonderingly.

The tiny features were pinched with anxiety, the eyes large and white. She cried forlornly, "Help!"

Horrified and intrigued, Markham suddenly realized that the low hum of the insect hoarde was not merely the beating of myriad wings, but also a thing chorus of pleading voices, each shouting different messages as they hovered around the two men. Some buzzed angrily at his ears. Others attempted to attract his attention by flying up his nose or into his loose-fitting clothes. He felt a thousand minute pinpricks as small hands grasped his skin. He shivered with disgust.

Without thinking, he slapped at them. Tiny bodies tumbled from the air, screaming.

Small things struck the ground. Some survived, but scuttling brown insects dashed from under leaves and stones to attack the wounded survivors. Markham bent down, confused by the welter of tinny voices, and watched a black beetle close sharp pincers around the neck of a swollen fly. Blood spurted. Markham thought irrelevantly that insects did not have red blood. As the fluid oozed from the plump little body he studied the small contorted face and felt remorse.

Until one bit him.

It had settled on his neck and plunged a sharp pinprick snout into a vein. He slapped at it, which only drove the point further in.

"Damn!" He slapped at others, and saw Russell was dancing madly, beating his suit with flailing hands.

"That's right! That's right!" called the woman-face, still hovering before him.

"Call them off!"

"They are of the mad," she explained reasonably.

A blue mote nipped his nose painfully. He squashed it, wiped his hand on his pants.

"Good," the woman-wasp called. "Send them to the other shore, great general."

He looked around wildly for some escape. The swarm seemed larger, a dense white cloud orbited the two men. A spherical galaxy of insectoid things, he thought, each with an obscenely mismatched head. Markham saw match-head sized faces of all races, some churning in endless loops, others with eyes closed as if in sleep or prayer, still more screaming incoherently in strident bursts. Some made droning speeches or gave hoarse mad barks. Another flitted into Markham's face, as if demanding attention—but when he looked, the head lolled, yellow eyes frozen, skin a putrid decaying mass, worm-ridden. Yet the thing buzzed on, a doomed soul harnessed to a brute insect engine.

Markham slapped it from the sky in revulsion and pity. Most of the motes simply wheeled about the two men, their voices like tiny saws, neither threatening nor giving ground when Russell and Markham began walking rapidly downhill.

Again the tiny woman's voice called, "Lead us! Show us a way, giant prophet."

"I don't know any," Markham said.

"Give us sup with devil-juice."

"If I had a fly swatter—"

"Yes! Yes! Thousands of us crave it." Her tan wings beat in an almost sexual frenzy.

A tinny cry went up from the swarm: "Free us! Free us!"

Russell slapped at several of them and barked, "From what?"

A welter of piping voices called out to Russell as they spun and fluttered about his head:

"Accursed form!"

"Hunger eats like worms in belly!"

"Want suck demon!"

"Crush me!"

"Inhale me!"

"Hot kiss of frog's tongue!"

Markham caught a foul scaly thing crawling into his ear, crushed it between his fingernails, flicked it away. "What do they mean?" he asked the wasp-woman.

"Some are beset by hungers. Others wish to leave this foul form."

Russell caught in midair a large one which was pleading for death. He popped it in two and a rank acid odor turned the air blue. The men trotted away from the spreading murk, but the swarm stayed with them, humming with feral desires Markham could sense but could not name.

"Those who would die, please crush," the wasp-woman pleaded, flying nearly into Markham's eye.

"If you'll leave us, yes," Russell bargained.

"I would travel in your wake," she answered, darting around Russell's wrinkled neck.

"Why?" Markham asked, methodically smashing his cupped hand into the path of all who ventured near. When they understood that he would accommodate them, dozens of hornet-people dove directly into his swinging hands. They died with sharp, brittle cries of almost sensual agony.

The wasp-woman hung by his ear. "I would suck the green blood-pap of a demon."

"We don't want to tangle with them."

"But you are a world-strider, and so so will cross them."

"Not if I can help it." Markham panted with exertion.

"They come to test you, yes, vast man." The wasp-woman seemed sure of her prediction.

"Try to follow us and I'll knock you from the air," Russell said imperiously, patience gone.

"If I suck the green-gore pap, I can become a frog or rat," the wasp-woman explained as though this were a laudable and common enough ambition.

"Bravo," Markham said sarcastically.

"Get away!" Russell shouted.

"If will not lead to demon," the wasp-woman cried, "then crush me."

"Well, no, I . . ." Despite his horror, to Markham this careening mote was a person, even if it was a dreadful perversion of nature.

"Is chance I return as worm to sup shit! Or be weevil," the wasp-woman pleaded.

"And you would rather be *that*?" Russell was puzzled.

"Would rest from endless gyre!"

The wasp-woman's passionate plea bothered Markham. He could not bring himself to swat her into oblivion.

Russell pointed at the air. "Look!"

The weaving flecks united for a long moment, hovering, forming letters that drifted lazily before the men:

Emit

no

evil;

live

on

time.

"Why are you doing that?" Markham asked the wasp-woman.

"Do what? We fly, we seek."

Russell said slowly, "They don't know what they're doing. Something else is using them."

"To write little epigrams?" Markham snorted.

"It's another palindrome."

Markham blinked. "Time. Time trap. We should keep going."

"Thirst for blood juice!" a small keening came in his ear.

"Dammit! We can't stand this!" He smashed a few more of the eager suiciders. His hands were thickly spattered with gore now, and stung.

"Then I will banish them!"

She turned and wove a pattern over their heads, spewing a milky fluid behind her. It curled into orange smoke as it descended, scattering the swarm. They fled, sobbing and calling curses at her.

"I don't . . . are you their ruler, somehow?" Russell asked.

"I hold sway," she said, wings beating the air with a tired drone. "I have been among the cursed and the crawling for centuries now, and have learned their vexed arts well."

Russell observed, "But not well enough to escape the form."

Her slit of a mouth pouted forlornly. "I must suck the green-pap five times, so a frog told me."

"A frog?" Markham wondered if animals talked in Hell. So far he had seen only domesticated animals and birds.

"It promised me knowledge, if I would approach to be eaten."

Markham said, "So you . . ."

"Gladly made my way into its mouth cavern."

This shook even Russell's aristocratic demeanor. "All to discover that drinking demon blood five times will do . . . something?"

"Will make me a *person*! Like you." She said this with awe and desire.

Markham asked, "You were once?"

"When I came, a shepherdess I was. Then I transgressed. Spread thighs and made sup with a snot-eater.

It gave me ram and at its spurting moment pierced my brain with its prick-sucker."

Russell paled. "Well, at least the sins are more picturesque here. I'm sure . . ."

"Then was I cast among the crawlers and flyers. *Please* let me come with you. I see knowledge, a path from this vile station."

Markham wondered if this implied a sort of reversed transmigration of souls. The Hindus had imagined that they could work their way up the chain of being, eventually attaining nirvana. Here you could easily slip down evolution's slick steps, end up a bug. And the Hell of it was that you *knew* what you were. Was this a parody of Earthly beliefs, a joke? Or the truth? Perhaps both . . .

Russell eyed her with hooded eyes, as though he were examining a student in oral exams at Cambridge. "Ummm. You were a Christian?"

"Oh yes, sir. A humble and devout servant."

Russell said wryly, "At last, a religious person. Very well." He nodded preemptorially at Markham. "We are all seeking knowledge. Let us travel together."

7.

Markham had explained his thinking to Russell, and the philosopher showed a quick ability to get through the thickets of jargon and find the kernel of physics. Markham had wondered how the time trap could work, and in pondering the riddle realized that perhaps the trap itself was a huge clue. After all, if the God of the Gaps intended them to figure anything out, He—or She, or It, or whatever—would have to allow them some ability to experiment. They certainly couldn't deduce the essence of Hell by abstract thinking alone. "Like Descartes crawling inside the famous stove, to deduce the properties of the world by pure undisturbed thought alone," Russell had remarked when Markham brought up the point.

So, to Markham, this meant they must be able to

experiment in some way. Russell's survival of the electrocution was perhaps a hint, a gesture, an encouragement. To learn more they had to try something different, not just slog around in the mud, waiting for demons or Guevera to find them again.

So Markham had been thinking of the time trap, and how it might work. In Einstein's relativity, the basic unit was the space-time interval. He had scribbled this out for Russell—and, resting on a tuft of grass nearby, the wasp-woman—in a patch of sand:

$$(ds)^2 = (dx)^2 - c^2(dt)^2$$

"See, ds is the length of an interval in space-time," Markham said, expecting to have to step through the equation slowly. He started to describe in his familiar professorial cadence how the notation dt meant a small, differential change in time. But the philosopher waved away his explanations, remarking that he had himself written a book about relativity and its implications well before Markham was born. Daunted, Markham went on to point out that the only thing which had the differential ds = 0 was light itself. Ordinary matter couldn't move fast enough—at the speed of light, *c*—to do that.

Markham felt a forgotten pleasure, the muted joys of the orderly classroom. He went on with assurance, "Now, let's assume general relativity applies to this space-time, shall we? Then—"

"To suspend time means making dt = 0," Russell said crisply.

"Uh, yes. To do that, there has to be a region where the differential of physical lengths, dx, changes sign. Then—"

"What is a negative length?" Russell asked acidly.

"It's a mathematical way to say that measurements made in such a vicinity would show a warpage. A region where length measurements make no sense.

"Impossible," Russell said.

"I can show it's true by integrating over the manifold," Markham said with irritation. *No wonder this guy didn't get the Nobel for peace*, he thought.

Russell screwed his lips around, squinted at the sand, and nodded grudgingly. Markham was glad to finesse the point, because he was a little rusty with this area of mathematical physics, and anyway it was hard to do calculations in the dirt. The majestic authority of mathematics lost a lot in this medium.

"I fail to follow," Russell said. "A physical distance can't change from positive to negative."

"Right. That means there must be some singularity there."

"Where?" the wasp-woman piped in.

"I'd say at the boundary of the time trap. Inside, $dt = 0$ and dx is a real, ordinary quantity. But *not* if we pass from ordinary time into a time-frozen state."

"Magic not work in devil's paw," the wasp-woman said. "I see many who try, they shrunk to toads."

Markham shrugged. "I've always wondered what it would be like to be a frog."

Russell said, "I assuredly have *not*."

"If you were, wise one," the wasp-woman said, giggling, "would you eat me?"

Her tinkling laughter made the Englishman redden.

8.

They were tired and dejected long before Markham spied a twisted tree and a crumbling flank of rocky ridge that had stuck in his memory. From there he was able to work their way around the broad sweep of a hill, across a roiling rain-swollen stream, and down into a low range of scrub forest. In there, somewhere, the time trap had nearly snared them.

But someone or something was blocking the way.

Red flares lit the canopy of milky clouds above, paling the dull sunlike glow overhead. Sudden rattling reports rolled down from those clouds, like news from an Olympian struggle.

A strange low *wooong wooong* answered from the pines nearby.

"Rather odd," Russell remarked, blinking owlishly.

"I'm pretty damn sure the time trap was that way, down a gully and up in some ruins. Remember?"

"I've never been one for spatial relationships."

A clanging from the clouds, like a vast cracked gong.

The wasp-woman's tiny voice called, "Demons? I drink!"

"Stay with me. You might be useful," Markham said.

He crouched down the way he had seen men do in combat movies and ran across a small clearing for the cover beyond. It had never been obvious that running bent over was actually effective. It kept you out of the way if they shot a little high, but on the other hand it slowed you down, too, exposing you to fire longer. Halfway across the *wooong* sound came and something rushed over him. There was no loud report, nothing, just the wake of something huge passing by. It cast a sudden cold stab into his back.

He reached the other side and plunged into the trees. He felt the wasp-woman inching across his neck. It made his skin crawl, but she wouldn't be able to keep up if she didn't hitch rides. To him she seemed a woman, human, someone he in his old fashioned way felt instinctively should be protected . . . not a mere makeshift insect. He was doubly sure that back in Life, he would never have felt this way. He could not quite understand why; was Hell changing him this quickly? He had been here only a few weeks, at most.

There was movement ahead. Markham watched vague ivory forms glide among the trees. He studied them carefully. A cool light refracted around them in waving strings, giving a watery sensation of multiple surfaces, of solid bodies that were nevertheless in constant flux. Alabaster light seeped among the branches. Shadows shrouded their ghostly passage. Markham noticed there was utter silence here, as though nature were holding its breath.

"What's on?"

Russell thumped down beside him, panting from his run. His hearty salute had seemed to boom in the stillness, making Markham jump. But the gliding, blocky, wavering things did not seem to notice or change their stately movements.

"What are those?"

"Not dragons."

"Maybe the Devil's come up with something new."

The wasp-woman called into Markham's ear, "Hoar Gods."

"What're they?"

"I saw before, ere I came to six-legged perdition. Hoar God bring frost. Banish devils." She held onto his ear with six spindly legs and underlined her description by stamping on his earlobe in some kind of tattoo signal.

"But they're not from, er . . ." Russell seemed reluctant to use the word. "Ah, *God*, are they?"

"From Hoar place," she said.

"Do you have any notion of what god they represent?" Russell went on. "What were the gods of your time?"

"I come from when Caliph ruled, awaiting the return of Mohap. Christ was boy, Mohap big man with red member." She seemed pleased to be addressed so seriously.

"Um. Some ancient era," Russell said, losing interest, and with a sharp clap the tree next to him dissolved like a melting candle.

"Down!" Markham cried.

Wooong—and trees behind them turned to glassy, sliding waterfalls.

The two men pressed themselves flat. Another *wooong* rippled through the air. Markham turned and studied the patchy damage in the forest, trying to triangulate the source.

"Funny," he said quietly. "There's no pattern."

"Not coming from one place?"

"There's no design to it, as near as I can see. Just random gulps taken out of the trees."

"Perhaps they're not firing at us at all."

The wasp-woman's small buzzsaw whine persisted, "Hoar Gods will chill all."

Markham chuckled, despite a keen sense of threat. "How long does it take for Hell to freeze over?"

"Hoar Gods try. Come, go, try!" She rasped out her displeasure at his levity, whirring around his head. He remembered the long stinger and caught the clear glint of paralyzing poison at its tip. This sobered him more than did the dissolved trees.

Russell commented pensively, "It does seem quite as chilly here as on an Oxford morning. I can't recall Hell being this damp, either."

Markham studied the shifting, quilted radiance ahead. "We can't be far from the time trap."

"Can this be part of it?" Russell asked.

"They can't be inside the trap, or they wouldn't be moving at all."

"Hoar gods come from stillness!" the wasp-woman explained, as if to demented children. She buzzed him again, spitting at his eyes. Markham began to see why she might well have deserved to be sentenced to insect-hood. Whoever she had been in a past life, it certainly wasn't Salome.

"Come *out* of a space where there is no change in time?" Russell shook his head. "What can that mean?"

"Look, there's got to be a zone where the spatial interval approaches zero. Maybe these Hoar Gods come from that . . . whatever it is," Markham finished lamely.

"We could try to speak to them, discover—"

"Forget that. They might try out their *woooom*-gun on you, instead."

"Well, I think it is worth the—"

"We've got to get around them, reach the time trap itself."

"I still believe—"

"I help," the wasp-woman called eagerly.

"How?" Markham asked disbelievingly.

"I can make them think only of me."

"Well . . ."

"If I can prick them, they die!"

Markham eyed the sharp needle she carried and decided this was as good an idea as any he had. Her mood swings were enough to put him on edge, and he would be glad to have that outsized weapon pointed at someone—or something—else.

"Good, I like that. Look, we can try to work our way around . . ."

9.

It all happened so fast Markham had to rely on pure instinct.

One moment he and Russell were creeping forward, trying to flank around the watery alabaster radiance. The wasp-woman had droned off among the bushes, to distract the entities she called the Hoar Gods, but could not further describe. Russell had remarked that he thought that she had simply affixed a folk-theology term from her own era to a phenomena she couldn't understand. Markham didn't care. To him the rumblings ahead were an obstacle to his first true chance to learn something *real*, something physical, about Hell. He had heard enough conflicting tales and mad hypotheses. He wanted data.

So he carefully duck-walked through the low thorned bushes, waiting for a sign that they could make a break . . .

And the world split.

To their right a vibrant line ran straight down from the clouds, white-hot and sky-searing. It was like slicing a canvas, peeling back the rustic scene and exposing beneath it the crude cardboard backing. The air was scooped away from the scratch-line and behind was . . . nothing. White void. Endlessness.

It happened in seconds—soundless, without tremor of warning. Markham watched as smoky white nothingness spilled from the cut in reality. He started to get to his feet—

—and noise crashed about him, swarmed over his back, hammered his ears. He whirled. To his left the trees were broken off, leveled, bare ragged stumps. Beyond them lay an open muddy field. On it masses of men and animals clashed in crazed final combat.

A glistening ebony elephant trampled bronzed warriors into the mud, snorting and bellowing. Arrows found targets, mortar rounds burst among clotted knots of struggling figures.

And among the hooting of victory and hopeless moans of defeat strode white blocky structures, oblivious to the chaos about them, never deviating in their slow stately glide. Beneath them an invisible weight slammed warriors to the mud and ground them into it, spattering blood in the air. Behind them, a purpling wake choked the men and woman who had survived their massive passage.

Markham spun back to the right.

The seam that split Hell widened. Milky stuff diffused from it. He felt a cold bristling at the back of his neck and knew the cascading torrent was death, and perhaps worse.

To the right, the battle roared and hooted and waxed bloody.

"Russell! Run!"

The Englishman stood transfixed. "Wait—I've seen something like this before. Give the insect a chance to—"

One of the massive blocks dimpled. A dark brown wave spread from a single point in its hard sheen. It wavered.

Markham frowned, fighting down his impulse to flee. "Is that . . . ?"

"Yes," Russell said professorially, "the little woman. She explained to me that these 'Hoar Gods' can fend off attacks from large, slow-moving things, like man or beast. And also small, fast-moving arrows or bullets or the like. But not a small, slow-moving creature, she said—such as herself."

"Sounds like they have limited their response time windows."

The angular shimmering thing turned, as if wounded. The battle around it quieted. Fighters stopped, lowered spears and bulky guns to watch the gravid chalk-mountain death.

Markham waved his hand at the panorama, where only moments before there had been deep woods. "This battle, what . . . ?"

"These things simply appear suddenly, huge armies materializing, dying, then vanishing. I've watched them from afar. And there are those levitating white objects, too," Russell said. "I've seen them before, at various foolish contests. Perhaps they seek out such events."

"Look, let's—"

The muddy field stretched far into the distance, and above the fray floated at least a dozen of the milky oblong things. They had been coasting among the carnage, but now as the nearest block veered from its path, crippled by the spreading brown stain, so did its companions. They converged on their wounded brother.

Markham heard—but in his mind, not his ears—the rasping voice of the wasp-woman. "I go! Am eaten! Go you!"

The split sky to his right yawned larger.

One of the effervescing white blocks began to shower the struggling ranks below with quick bursts of sprinkling, fine-grained amber light. Again came the *woooom* and again an answering thunder roll, this time from the forest on the next hill.

"Dammit, run!"

He could see a wedge of the amber glow projecting toward them.

He took two steps and a something burst inside his head.

White.

Light.

—liquid rainbows sparkling—

—booming musk melody—

—impaled on shrill sharp shafts of vinegar—

—granite flowers imploding—

—slide and splash and wrenching fire-pain chorus—

He sat down heavily amid mud and crushed, blood-stained grass.

Russell cried, "What's wrong?"

"I . . ." Markham did not know how to describe the sudden avalanche of blistering sensation and swarming, scattershot knowledge that had rushed through him.

"Get up!"

"I know who they are—the white things."

"Demons?"

"No. Aliens."

"Seems a fine distinction, here."

The wasp-woman had somehow done her deadly work. The radiance from the wobbling alien rippled, shifted colors—and it abruptly crashed into a phalanx of troops, throwing bodies in high arcs.

"Let's go to the right, where the thunder was," Markham yelled over the rolling din of battle.

"The wasp-woman—"

"She's gone. She'll be a dog in her next incarnation."

Russell ran after Markham, who was ducking among the trees at a steady lope, trying to avoid the slabs of amber luminescence that rained down. "How do you know that?"

"I have no idea. Those aliens projected a lot of information directly into my memory. But it's not an experience I want to repeat."

A rank of women carrying pikes spilled pell-mell by them, shouting in some strange tongue.

"They're aliens," Markham panted, "not just from another planet, but somehow from another space-time."

"Why then these battles?"

"They're *using* them. For training. A sort of military exercise."

Russell ducked around a bewildered, dazed man with an antique pistol, its charge spent. "More madness."

"No, there's a point. Those white things are living creatures. They test their war games here, with human cannon fodder. They come through the edge of the time trap, visit Hell, and go back."

"To where?"

"The images . . ." Markham shook his head to clear it. He wanted to stop, sift through the myriad sensations he had received from one brief brush with the amber glow.

Men and women came scattering pell mell through the forest now, trying to escape the white gliding aliens. They still carried on their mindless fighting even as they fled. A short fat woman in a toga and carrying a crude iron short-sword came at Markham and he dodged her awkward thrust. He grabbed the cuffed hilt from her and tripped her with his left foot. She squawked and cursed and Markham ran on, holding the weapon. The sword was heavy and ineptly made, but he felt better to have it.

"There's a glimmering over there," Russell called. Markham saw through the trees a curious wan blue glow and headed that way. The time trap might give off Doppler-shifted light, if his suspicions about the space-time singularity were right. Blue light would be up-shifted from some other place, maybe from the land of the Hoar Gods.

"They're here to practice on us, then?" Russell asked, panting heavily. His suit flapped with his loping stride and he had not even loosened his tie.

"I got the impression we were vermin as far as they cared. Maybe they're pest exterminators from Alpha Centauri."

"The Devil's not an anthropocentric twit, then," Russell wheezed. "Makes Him, or It, more believable. I wonder if Hell is built to a galactic scale?"

"Let's go see," Markham said, trotting down an incline toward the shifting zone ahead. "There's a dead spot over there."

"For once I agree with your empirical approach. There is so much structure to Hell, there *must* be a larger design. Something planned to—"

A squad of women in yellow canvas suits spread through the trees, attacking fleeing men. The women used only their rigid hands and feet in a sort of smooth-flowing karate. Yet they felled large men easily. With each lunge they barked out a quick animal noise of jubilant victory.

Markham ran faster, but one of the women came charging down a gravel slope and cut them off.

Russell did not hesitate. "Get on with it!" he yelled, and simply threw himself at the advancing woman. She swatted at him, connected with a solid thud. He grunted but scrambled to his feet.

"Go on! Find out! I'll see you somewhere in this mare's nest!" Russell struck an archaic pose, like a nineteenth century boxer squaring off, and glared at the yellow-suited woman. She frowned in puzzlement. Markham slipped into a stand of trees and kept moving quietly away, looking back as the two circled each other, an absurd match.

But there was nothing amusing about the way the woman kicked Russell expertly in the belly. She whirled expertly and sent a heavy blow to Russell's neck. Markham could hear the loud solid snap.

He felt a stabbing sense of loss as the rickety figure crumbled into the mud. "I . . . I'll come back for you," he whispered. "When you reappear, I'll . . ."

But there was no way to keep promises in Hell. He felt a building rage, but nothing to vent it upon except the milling, fighting ranks of humans. That was the way the Devil liked it, Markham was suddenly sure. *Hell is other people,* Sartre had said, though surely not anticipating this.

No, the point was to fight down your anger, and do something the Devil didn't expect.

The women in yellow were spreading into the woods, calling out orders to each other, searching. Markham got his bearings and slipped away, following an old stream bed that somehow was not filled by the earlier rain.

As he trotted along the sandy rut he found it was nearly bone dry. Somewhere up ahead the rain had not fallen.

The scent of mouldering pine needles reminded him of the games he had played in the Alabama woods when he was a boy. Form two armies, ambush your enemy in dirt clod attacks, capture their castle. And do it silently, flitting through the woods with scarcely a whisper, a mere flicker of motion. Think like an Indian, strike like a storm.

He used those skills repeatedly in the next hour, working his way around maurading bands whose only amusement seemed to be death and torture. He passed inpromptu crucifixions, the nails driven so as to bleed the victims slowly, letting the weakness steal over them so that they slumped on the cross and suffocated. There were group impalements, long shafts driven up the fundament of one, out the mouth, and into another above him. Women turned helplessly, descending by slow inches on thick shafts that skewered them by agonizing inches, rough barbs checking the rate of their skewering. He kept telling himself that their deaths were in fact liberations, and kept on, concealed in dappled pools of brooding shadow.

10.

A land of frost. That was the way the time trap looked as he approached, weary and scraped by brambles in a hundred stinging spots.

The blue-white wall was translucent. He could see sheets of chilled air fall away from it, giving the illusion of motion, but the wall stood frozen. Beyond was an airy landscape of contorted gray hills, all angles and pivoted streamers and scooped-out, yawning bays—a world twisted into a vast handiwork. In the valleys moved more of the alien ivory blocks, some sprinkled with silvery wafers. They seemed to drift and sway at the command of some unseen wave, like motes on the ocean bottom.

Markham stepped to within centimeters of the flat cool wall. A cutting scent like ammonia hung there.

He picked up a pine limb and stuck it into the blue-tinged fog boundary. It went smoothly. He watched the murky world beyond the barrier and saw the tip of his stick emerge. Was there some optical trick? In the frostworld his stick was of normal width, but impossibly long, protruding what seemed to be hundreds of meters among the softly lit, sea-blue arctic hill-sculptures.

He pushed it in further. The pencillike image extruded further, lancing a kilometer into the flat iceworld. He dipped it and struck a high, graceful arch. Layers of green jewellike stone fractured, fell. He twirled the stick and chopped at a warped monument of flinty rock. It flew apart.

The ivory aliens began to dart and hover in a manic insect pattern. They were huge in his zone of Hell, but in theirs his simple pine limb stick could crush them.

Markham remembered their blind indifference to the pulped bodies they bestrode on the battlefield. He grimaced. What better than to smite a few now?—to repay a blood debt mankind as a whole owed these motes, who now swarmed about his stick, milling, uncertain.

His pine limb was a straight hard line, now, a stretched abstraction that could kill. Markham started to bring it to bear on a cluster of the aliens . . . and stopped.

It would merely be more of the cycle, he saw.

Unending malice. Roiling, empty chaos.

He withdrew the limb gingerly. It looked all right except for a layer of frost. He touched it. Searing cold made him jerk his hand away. He picked up a stone and tapped the limb. The wood sheared off at the frost line. It hit the ground and shattered with an explosive clap.

Passing into the frostworld, the stick had undergone Einsteinian swellings along its length, growing like Pinocchio's nose. But it had not been in some abstract place: very real air had frozen it.

Markham had to shove it in a few feet before the tip emerged in the ice-blue landscape. That suggested there was an invisible slice of space-time between the two worlds. A zone of refractions, Doppler confusions, perhaps portals.

There had to be some way to use that effect. But not here, where a slip into the frostworld would freeze his lungs solid.

Markham went to his right, following the slight curve in the porous barrier. The alien land gradually faded into a vibrating haze shot through with pink lightnings. As he walked a glow seeped into the territory beyond the invisible sheet and he could see ordinary pine forest again. He was about to try the pine limb experiment again when he noticed a bird just beyond the barrier. He had not seen it at first because it hung in air, glittering eyes fixed ahead, wings arced upward to begin a downward, propelling plunge. But it was utterly motionless.

There was something between him and the still forest. A wavering in the air, a yellowing fog swirl, a strumming sense of convective movement.

He saw nothing beyond the shimmering region, no scaly dragons or belching demons or cartoon ogres to snare him.

A shout. From behind he heard the pursuit of some hoarse voices, even—was this a memory from Alabama childhood?—the distant mournful baying of hounds. These were running dogs, on a scent. When they found prey, treed it, their yips and yelps would signal the coming slaughter.

Well, he wasn't going to be chased any more. He picked up a hefty stick and probed through the barrier. If nothing happened—

The shock wave traveled up his arm, sucking in the stick. It came so fast he could not let go before its accelerating jolt jerked him forward, through a velvet-light breath of corrosive air, into—

Falling.

Again. His cotton clothes flapped in the rushing air.

The old phobia swarming up into his mind. For an instant he went rigid, squeezed his eyes tight. He sensed an endless gulf below him. Bile rose in his mouth.

But he forced down his panic and opened his eyes. *Get off the wheel. End the cycle. Don't let the bastards get you down.*

He was in a shaft. Smooth white slabs on all sides, ceramic-hard.

He looked up and saw, dwindling far above, pine trees. Like the years of his childhood, rushing away.

He had fallen straight down the boundary sheet that separated the two sections of forest. Like falling into a crack. And now plunged toward the center of . . . what?

More blazing whiteness. The shaft walls expanded away from him, opening into a vast chasm. Still he fell.

But somewhere in him came the strength to relax, to still the screaming childlike fear.

He spread his arms, caught a sweet warming breeze.

Banked.

Swooped.

Flew.

His spread arms and legs stabilized him, provided wind resistance, slowed his fall.

Markham the kite, sailing the fevered winds.

His eyes brimmed with hope. He felt the first true elation he had enjoyed in a great while. At last, he could *do* something.

The shaft walls were mottled with dark caves. At the entrance of each a hideous brown-red thing crouched. Orange eyes followed his gliding fall, as if eager to intercept his flight.

Markham heard a shout and looked up. A black-haired woman tumbled out of a silky sky. Her yellow canvas coveralls fluttered and slapped. She cried out for help and beat her arms. She was enveloped in pure blind panic and shot downward like a stone.

She passed Markham, eyes rolling at him, mouth jagged and red. He watched her dwindle away below.

Then one of the cave-creatures leaped from the side and somehow snared her. Together the two veered to the side, the woman's screams higher pitched now and forlorn, as though she glimpsed her fate.

As Markham sped by them, the rusty-skinned thing was picking apart the woman, using three of its legs to hold the still-shuddering corpse.

Don't let the bastards get you down, he reminded himself.

He had slid down a thin wall in the time trap. This was the layer where space contracted, admitting flaws and tangles. Some passing whorl of casuality had sucked him in.

The Devil had mastered space-time so deftly that he could freeze time, and stuff the snarled loops of space into a mere slice. Through that wedge the Hoar Gods had penetrated into the human Hell, and surely had provoked Satanic glee. Maybe the land of frost he had glimpsed was an alien Hell. Why not a plurality of Hells, to match the plurality of worlds? And let the inmates disembowel each other . . .

But was such a practice entirely Devilish?

Maybe Russell's phrase was literally true—in the interstices of Hell there were thin sheets of Godliness. Openings. Opportunities. Gaps.

When Russell speculated out loud, did some eaves-dropping Entity take him up on it? That would explain his surviving the electrocution—the Entity, leaving its calling card?

If so, God had a sense of humor. Russell had meant a gap in knowledge, but this tube Markham was plunging down was a physical gap, a wedge . . . an exit.

So God made puns. That made a certain wonky sense. After all, the Devil kept leaving his signature in unlikely places: the snake that wrote out *666*.

And something had left those two palindromes . . .

The Devil would have no interest in prodding him and Russell into further explorations. But perhaps other forces than Satan operated here.

Was there some God in this Gap? He swooped sideways, enjoying the sensation of buoyancy, of at last controlling the fear of falling that had plagued him all his previous Life. He banked past the spider-things that crouched in their caves. He came tantalizingly close, provoking them. But they saw he had his bearings, could veer away if they sprang. So they gave him red-eyed glares and watched him descend.

To what? To fall implied a curved space-time, a geometry rounded by mass or . . . He remembered Russell's speculations. A geometry shaped by Mind?—some massive intelligence from the primordial ages of the swelling universe?

Did *that* lie below?

He felt both joy of release and a sullen, brooding fear.

What had the angel said, that Altos? *I respond to the will of the world.*

Falling was a sort of response, though not voluntary. Had the physicist's Mass been replaced by Will?

It was the kind of question Russell would have liked. And Hemingway, too, if you could phrase it to him right. A lot of the souls Markham had seen here would like to know what lay waiting below him.

And he owed it to Russell and the poor wasp-woman and all the rest who had given of themselves, to try, to make it through.

11.

He had been falling for at least a day. The cave-things had tried again and again for him. He had evaded the last one by inches, banking sideways and finally going into a sudden, balled-up plummet.

Now below something slowly grew. He spread his arms further, cupping the wind, slowing himself more than mere Newtonian laws allowed. Markham saw a patchy land rise toward him, a quilted place of hills and deep blue lakes.

He spread his legs, his pants snapping in the breeze. Then the whipping of the warming wind abated. He slowed still further. He thought of a billion worlds that the time trap boundary might enter onto—alien planets, eras of history, the fantastic contorted geometries of mathematicians . . .

He drifted down into the courtyard of a shadowed sandstone ruin.

It had once been a temple with Corinthian columns. Now the roof had caved in and half the columns sprawled, cracked and scavenged.

Two men sat on the broken flagstones of the square, talking.

Markham landed with a mild bounce. The land was rich and verdant. Grapes hung in bunches bigger than a man's head. From orderly rows of stakes grew plots of tomatoes, of ripe wheat, of odd globular fruit. Men and women worked the fields. Some strolled, hand in hand.

If this was Hell, he wouldn't mind.

The two men were old, heavy-browned. One wore a sweater, shorts, sandals. The second wore nothing and was quite hairy.

Markham walked over to them, easing the kinks out of his knotted muscles. "I wonder if—"

The sweatered man looked up. "Oh, it's you," he said in heavily accented English. Markham couldn't spot the accent but the man was swarthy, full-lipped, Mediterranean, almost Asiatic.

"W-what?"

"We heard you were coming."

The nude man nodded. Markham felt a shock as the shaggy head lifted and wise old eyes regarded him. "I heard you ver bringing my friend Russell," Einstein said with a thick German accent.

"*You*? Here?"

"I haff been waiting for my friend a long time."

"But you were a *saint*! How could you end up in Hell, when—"

Einstein smiled broadly, eyes crinkling. "Do not bother with questions we cannot attack."

"Yes," the clothed man said solemnly, "we have learned that here."

"Where *is* 'here'?" Markham demanded.

"We are in a quiet zone," Einstein said.

"A Gap?"

"If you vish." Einstein shrugged away matters of definition.

"We are beneath the Rude Lands, where you were," the other man said.

Markham felt a sudden flush of joy rush over him. "Then I've . . . I've escaped?"

"From Hell? No," the swarthy man said slowly. "And how long you or any of us will remain here, no one knows."

"Is . . . God here?"

Einstein chuckled. "*Nein*, but every one thinks that when they first come here. I haff not seen the gentleman."

His mind aswirl with speculations, Markham turned to the other man. "Who . . . are you?"

"Thales of Miletus." The man held out his hand, but flat palm up, not in the traditional handshake. Markham pressed his palm into that of Thales, remembering that the handshake formality he knew was a Roman custom. Thales had died centuries before the rise of Athens, much less Rome.

Markham tried to recall his undergraduate smattering of Greek history. Thales had introduced abstract reasoning into science, devised the method of deductive reasoning, and claimed that everything was in essence made of water, the one substance he knew had both solid, liquid and vapor forms. The Athenians had regarded him as the greatest of the early philosophers.

Markham sat down unsteadily on the chipped flagstones. One gave him a hard jab, as if this world were reminding him of its persistent, gritty, painful reality.

"You . . . were both mathematical reasoners," Markham muttered, staring into the two faces that beamed at him. "I suppose I am, too, though I'm really a fly on the wall compared to you . . ." He smiled wanly. "Have I come to some sort of refuge?"

Thales's mouth twisted in disapproval. "You dismiss me as mere numerologist?"

"Well, no—"

"I remind you that in the city of Miletus I once humiliated the so-called 'practical' men by cornering the market in olive presses. When the crop came good—as I had calculated, a half year before—I charged them, great and often. I laughed muchly while they scowled, and thus made my fortune. No mere abstract reasoner, I."

"I'm sorry, sir. I didn't mean . . ." His voice trailed off. It had been millenia since Thales died.

"You can remember that far back?"

"Of course. Oh, I spy your intent. In the Rude Lands memory rubs away on the stones of agony."

Einstein said, "Here, not."

Markham said eagerly, "In all that time, have you found out what's going on here?"

Thales blinked. "Why, no. It is barely possible to learn this fool tongue."

"English?"

"Yea. It is ripe with tangle and contort."

"But you've had—"

"A year, no more."

Markham gaped. Einstein said, "*Ja*, and I haff been heir perhaps a few months."

"That's—"

"Vee know vye you are disturbed," Einstein said. "Vee are in a pocket, a leftover is maybe. A drain which collects junk, I denk." Einstein chuckled agreeably.

Somehow Markham had never thought of Einstein as a stooped little man with a broad, comic accent. Yet here he was, no icon, but a cheery figure brimming with life. Markham found he was blinking back tears. To come to this, a green and warm paradise, in the company of the greatest minds in history . . .

Thales said stubbornly, "I cannot ponder this point of singular points, Einstein, when you persist in saying that there *are* no such things as points."

Einstein shook his shaggy head. "Let us go back to time, eh? You here, me here, this new *Junge* Markham—*proves* that *gedanken* experiment is right. All time arrows here can go forward *or* back. Only solution to field equations, I say, is a singularity *in time*. Not space!"

Thales slapped his palm to the stone. "A single time would mean frozen time, as up there!"

He jagged a finger at the filmy blue sky. A few yellow puffball clouds coasted by lazily. Looking up into it reminded Markham of the open simplicities of childhood.

"*Nein!* Field equations are clear."

"Not so. Your third derivative term—"

"One haff to interpret the intergral convergence—"

"You look for God in equations!"

"Vee haff proved that in Hell, time radiates from a non-temporal center, *nicht wahr?*" He scowled at Thales.

The Greek replied, "A possibility, yes. But the center may be God, or may be Devil—cannot tell from physics, not yet. We need more *data*."

Markham said wonderingly, "Then we *can* figure this out, if we just reason together . . ."

Both men looked at Markham with pity. "So that is vat you denk?" Einstein said. "*Nein!*"

Markham sputtered, "But, but—"

"*Nein*, you are coming for harder task," Einstein said gently. "Hier there are *real* problems. Come, we must get down to the truly difficult werk."

Markham smiled. Russell and the wasp-woman had paid a price to put him here, and yet he had reached no plateau of the spirit. The whirl of Hell would go on, revealing new levels, and he would go with it.

But what could be the *real* problems? If Einstein hadn't solved them . . .

Somewhere, he thought he heard the keening, malicious laugh of the angel, Altos. And a low bass one, as if from Satan himself.

What if, Markham thought, they were two faces of the same coin?

SPRINGS ETERNAL

David Drake

"Here we have hope," said Sulla to Sulla's Luck who lounged across the table from him. Either of the two could have been the other's mirror image, except that Sulla's Luck wore a peculiar smile. "As they do not anywhere in this—cosmos—except for this Pompeii we have founded."

"They have the hope we bring them, my Lucius," said Sulla's Luck in a tone too mild to be an objection. His thumb and forefinger pinched powder from the heap on the low table, raised it in the air, and brushed it off again.

Illumination from the roof opening of the adjacent reception court entered Sulla's office through a lattice-work door. The light of Paradise was usually a murky red from piercing the clouds which covered even this place that could almost be home— but now, for an instant, a shaft of clear light pierced the sky to scatter from the decorative pond in the center of the court.

The powder drifted down, as white and pure as an infant's soul.

"Hope," repeated Sulla's Luck.

Sulla stood up, a motion that began abruptly but hitched as the ghost of a pain reminded him of the gout he once had. He thought that agony was over, now—here, wherever *here* might be. Still, the memory hid somewhere in Sulla's mind or in the muscles themselves; and it seemed to recur whenever long absence had let him hope that it was gone forever.

Sulla walked to the window that opened onto the garden of his house and threw back the shutter. He favored his right foot, even though the twinge was gone and there had not been any real pain anyway. Behind him, he heard his Luck rise from the opposite couch, but the mirror figure did not join him at the window for the moment.

The plants in the walled garden grew well, though they tended to flower less fully than they should—than they would have in the sunlight and breezes of the real Pompeii. In the sky, Paradise struggled with the lowering clouds and won through as nothing brighter than a baleful orange.

"Nearly perfect," said the man who was Dictator here, as he had been Dictator of Rome before he chose to abdicate and die a private citizen. "That I could found *this* town in *this* cosmos was your doing, my Luck."

"It's unusual in the Underworld," said Sulla's Luck, fingering the trophy that hung on the wall above boxes of scrolled accounts, "for the parameters of existence to seem as familiar to men as they do here on Adam's Isle. Elsewhere, they may be quite different."

The trophy was a bronze plate two inches thick. A bullet was imbedded in the bronze, a coppered-steel jacket over a steel core. It had been shot from a weapon at velocities enormously greater than could have been achieved by a slinger in one of Sulla's armies in life, but the plate was thick enough to stop the missile and hold it in the center of an inch-wide crater in the softer metal.

Pompeian fishermen had cut the plate from the breast of a huge creature which actually flew, buoyed up by light gas in its belly, until it drifted across the shore of this place. Then, acted on by physics similar to those of the upper world, the huge mass of metal had crashed to utter ruin.

Sulla's Luck traced with an index finger the motto engraved on the plate: All hope abandon, ye who enter here.

Dante had reported accurately, though of course he did not understand. Even now.

"They're happy, don't you think?" said the Dictator in a tone of harsh demand, though he did not turn his eyes from the window. He had not painted his garden walls with hunting scenes or foliage to expand the apparent space for planting. Instead, Sulla's walls bore a frescoed bird's-eye panorama of the town he ruled. The orange-red roof tiles glowed with a semblance of reality, but the shifted spectrum of Paradise turned the painted gardens into splotches of purple.

"No, I don't think they're happy, my Lucius," replied Sulla's Luck in a voice more wistful than ironic. "But they have hope."

"Why shouldn't they be happy?" snapped Sulla, turning his head with the jerky suddenness of a fish engulfing prey. "What do they lack that matters?"

"Has Theodora succeeded, then?" asked Sulla's Luck with a smile that would have brought anyone else's head from his shoulders as soon as the Dictator's guards arrived.

Sulla's complexion was mottled even at rest. Now the blotches of red and white stood out as distinctly as badly-painted stage make-up, and his grip on the sill and jamb of the window made flecks of sand crumble from the stucco.

He turned his face deliberately toward the garden.

"And after all," continued Sulla's Luck in a conciliatory tone, "they don't have what you have. The opportunity to return to the upper world."

"It's always possible to come to an arrangement," said the Dictator. His voice was ragged and husky at first, but he gained control of it and his breathing by the time he had completed the sentence. "Even with an enemy. And I'm no enemy to the—powers there."

He would not say, "to the Gods," but he lifted his head in a tiny jerk toward the cloud-wracked sky and Paradise beyond.

"I helped you make peace in life with Mithridates," said Sulla's Luck approvingly, "though the price was Asia where he had slaughtered a hundred and fifty thousand of your fellow citizens—and would kill more in the future. But the arrangement gave *you* peace, and the freedom to capture Rome from your enemies—with my help."

Sulla walked back from the window. He was calm again, but there was an expression of concern on the features which anger had left. "When I've handed over the shipment, on behalf of—" His fingers toyed with the white powder on the table, making a crater like the maw of a volcano in the smooth cone.

"On behalf of the powers who wish hope to be spread as widely as possible throughout this Underworld," Sulla's Luck encouraged, pausing then with tented fingers.

"Yes," said the Dictator and swallowed. He met his companion's eyes. "Will *we* leave this place? Will *you* still be with me?"

Sulla's Luck laughed. "Oh, my Lucius," he said. "I'll *always* be with you. As I was on the day you, though only a youth, took the surrender of Jugurtha and Rome proclaimed you his conqueror—for anything Marius your commander could say in his own right."

"He never forgave me for that," Sulla said, smiling in relief and at the memory. He twisted the ring on his left little finger, a signet carved with the scene of Jugurtha's surrender. "But Marius died, didn't he? And *I* ruled Rome."

He met his companion's eyes.

"Of course," agreed his Luck. "Though all men—"

He laughed instead of finishing the caveat, as if oblivious to the shadow his words had drawn across the face that had in life been that of the all-powerful Sulla.

"And now," Sulla's Luck resumed in a different vein, "the terms are quite clear. If the drugs are delivered today to the caravan you have arranged to distribute them, you—we, my Lucius—will return to the upper world. Perhaps even to Paradise." He smiled. "We can hope, after all."

"Yes," said the Dictator in forceful agreement. "They need have no concern . . . but let's go check the warehouse once more."

He strode out of the office, almost colliding with a servant who cringed away on an errand for his mistress.

"Benito!" Sulla was shouting. "Benito!"

Pausing for a moment in the office, Sulla's Luck murmured, "Oh, I'm sure they aren't concerned, my Lucius," as his fingers teased the powder back into a perfect cone.

The mirror in which Theodora watched her hairdresser work had an ivory handle carved with the figure of Chastity—right arm covering her breasts, left palm over her pudenda. Theodora's hand sweated every time she gripped the warm, slick carving, but she had never demanded that it be replaced.

Once she had attempted to masturbate herself with the statuette—just in case—but that hadn't worked. Either.

Theodora's bedroom was on a front corner of the house, across the reception court from Sulla's office and the room they nominally shared at night. Through the pair of high windows, slits that flared into the room to admit light but nothing larger than a sparrow, she had heard a woman talking to the doorkeeper in a husky voice, but the sounds were empty of meaning.

Her hand squeezed the mirror until the peaks of her

knuckles were as bloodless as the ivory. It was not a good idea to consider what things were empty of meaning. The list could become very long.

But it was not a complete surprise when Benito, the chamberlain, slipped into her bedroom, and said with a slobbery attempt at portentousness, "Mistress, there is a matter which may be of the greatest concern to you."

Theodora did not turn toward the fleshy eunuch immediately. Instead, she held the mirror out at an angle so that she could see Benito past her own face and the plaits of incredible delicacy into which her hair was being woven this morning and every morning.

The chamberlain's swarthy complexion was accentuated when viewed side by side with the alabaster of Theodora's own skin. He began to sweat under her scrutiny. The heavy brocades he had chosen for his robes of office could scarcely have been less comfortable if they were designed to torture him. Benito continued to hope—against the evidence—that they would increase the honor in which other residents of this place held him.

"Speak, then . . ." said Theodora softly. She left unspoken the promise—not a threat—of what she would have done to this cringing lickspittle unless the reason he interrupted her toilet were indeed of the greatest concern to her.

"Mistress, a woman has been admitted to the house," Benito blurted. His eyes, fixed on hers in the mirror, held the abject terror of a man who has learned the difference between bluster and an iron will—and who knows that he is only bluster.

"Do you think I care who my husband sees?" Theodora snapped, the pitch of her voice belying the intended content of her words. If Sulla's *Luck* ever procured him a woman who could do for him what his wife could not—and what he could not do for his wife—Theodora would. . . .

Well, to begin with, there would be two eunuchs in this household.

The hairdresser continued to work, weaving strand on strand into a lustrous black embroidery. It might have been worth her life—here—to leave off without being directed to do so; but more than that, her work was the only thing in which she could pretend to find meaning. Her fingers moved in patterns, though she knew her art was as empty as the motions of men drinking and gorging and flinging hollow boasts that led to hollow battles.

Nonetheless, she shifted to the left side of her seated mistress, in order to avoid the eyes that sparked with an anger which threatened to melt the mirror's polished silver face.

"Mistress," said the chamberlain, "it's not—that is, the woman wishes to see you. She has an offer for you that could, that could. . . ."

Benito swallowed, then swallowed again. His concern went beyond the normal fear of talking to Theodora— and that went far enough for almost anything.

Theodora laid the mirror flat on her lap and turned to look at the sweating eunuch over the bronze-sheathed wooden back of her chair. Her loins gave an anticipatory stir, though there was no *reason* as yet for the hopeful warmth. "What offer, Benito?" she said in a voice that was almost calm.

"Mistress," replied the chamberlain, no less terrified by the woman's present aspect than he had been by her former one, "I really think it better that she discuss the matter with you alone."

Benito glanced around the painted wall of the bedroom with the skittering panic of a rat in an endless maze. At last, he locked his eyes with Theodora's. A rope of saliva started to drool from the corner of his mouth, but he recalled it through an effort of will.

"Mistress," the chamberlain went on. "I think you should know that this woman once had a child with her. Here."

For a moment, Theodora's mouth and eyes were open. They gave no sign to the outside because of the pressure of what remained within. Then she said, "Perhaps I can arrange she go where the brat is. But send her in. Perhaps. . . ."

She waved imperiously to the hairdresser as Mussolini bowed and backed himself from the room. "Leave me, Penelope," Theodora said. "I may want you later, for a touch-up."

She was surveying herself critically in the handmirror as the chamberlain and the hairdresser disappeared together.

Instead of ushering the woman properly into Theodora's presence, Benito stood in the reception court and waved the visitor through. He clacked shut the slatted wooden door loudly, but Theodora knew he would hover near it, listening to whatever went on in the bedroom.

That was desirable. The chamberlain would keep away all lesser servants and would provide a warning if Sulla himself approached.

And she had nothing to hide from Benito, who had been her go-between in the only part of the business which she might wish to conceal from others.

The visitor who entered Theodora's bedroom was short, swarthy; plain even without the pockmarks sprinkled across the nose and right cheek. She had survived that disease and presumably childbirth as well, but her features were more youthful than the look in her eyes.

Well, appearance was not a trustworthy guide to age in this place.

"Lady?" said the visitor. Her fingers played tremulously with the knotted fringe of her shawl, but she kept her voice clear, albeit respectful.

"You have business with me, then?" Theodora asked thinly. She squeezed all emotion but mild distaste from her voice so as to give away nothing.

"I didn't come until I had something to offer you," said the other woman softly. She laced her fingers together, but her thumbs continued to toy with her drab garment. "The caravan that just arrived, it—a friend

of mine in it, he's procured a gift for you, lady. From—
not here."

Her tongue dabbed her lips, not so much a nervous
gesture as a practical one, moistening the dry skin so
that it would pass the next syllables flawlessly. "A couch,
lady," she concluded.

"A couch?" Theodora repeated, surprised out of her
pose of nonchalance. She had expected an elixir, possibly, or an amulet. Not a couch. . . .

Instead of answering the implied question, the visitor
looked at her thumbs and said, "Lady, they tell me you
might be able to help me find my child."

"*Who* tells you?"

"Lady," said the visitor, raising her steadfast eyes to
Theodora's fury. "I would do anything to get my child
back. The couch I offer you will serve your needs."

Theodora had been an empress in life, while here she
was in name and appearance wife to a dictator of unbri-
dled power. She had learned haughtiness as she struggled to eminence from her beginnings as a child
prostitute, and it was with regal grandeur that she rose
and sneered at the other woman, "What do *you* know of
my needs?"

"Lady," the visitor repeated, "the couch will serve
your needs."

Theodora rested her left palm lightly on the lathe-
turned bar of the chair back, but her sweat marked the
bronze slickly. In this place there were few children
and no infants, she had thought, until the morning a cry
in the street outside had driven her to the door
half-dressed—

And reminded that this place was Hell.

"It wasn't his fault that he was here," continued the
visitor as if making a prayer of contrition. "*I* brought
him, the innocent, because I loved him too much. . . ."

"He should not have been . . ." whispered Theodora as her mind stared in horror at its memory of the
child she had carried to term while she was an actress.
Its face, uglier than a monkey's and smeared with blood—

her blood—had scrunched up as the brat wailed. It was a boy, but that didn't matter: she would have paid her doorman an extra gold *solidus* to drop the infant over the seawall in a weighted bag whichever its sex. She had never in her whole existence hated a thing as much.

Until she heard the wail of the child in the street: *this* woman's child.

"I have no reason to believe you," Theodora said in a distant tone as her mind began to recover. "What can a couch do?" She walked toward the one on which she slept, a mattress of firm horsehair on a low frame of curly maple.

Movement gave her an excuse for breaking eye contact with her visitor.

Theodora had become empress—and died in that rank—because she fought, no matter what the odds or the means she had to use to even them. She had not lost that ruthless will when Fate placed her here. Benito had his instructions within minutes . . . and by that night, he had shown his mistress a tiny hand, to prove those instructions had been carried out.

Death was not necessarily final here; but thus far, it had proved final enough for Theodora's purpose. No infant had bawled outside her window since.

That permitted her to hope that the cries in her mind would one day be stilled as well.

"Lady," said her visitor softly, "I will have the couch brought to you. All I ask is that when you succeed, you return my child to me."

The dead did not come back in this Pompeii. At least Theodora could hope so.

Aloud she said, "If the couch has the virtue you claim for it, woman, I will—use my authority to have your brat located. *If* the couch—"

Theodora shuddered and broke off, shocked by a leering recollection of the one to whom she had been married in life.

"My husband was a demon," she blurted, trying to

clear the thought by spilling it out in words to this nonentity. "Justinian, the emperor. I think that's why I came to be here. My—my life was hard, but not so very evil. . . . Except for wedding a demon."

"Lady," said the visitor with a gentle smile, "they thought that of Solomon, too; many did. He was quick-minded and so shy that he covered it with pride hugely greater than that of other men. But Solomon *was* a man, Lady; I knew him. And your husband was a man. Men aren't demons."

"No, but demons can wear the faces of men," replied Theodora in a ragged voice, for the face in her mind was again that of her own squawling infant.

She shook herself, empress again and a dictator's wife. "Go on, then," she said clearly and with open disdain. "If you care so much about your child, then—provide me with this couch that suits *my* needs and get him back."

The cries echoed in Theodora's mind as her visitor bowed deeply and left the room.

In the kitchen located in the other front corner of the house, Apicius worked with something closer to happiness than he had managed to achieve for—who knew *how* long? Not that he had any *real* confidence in the way things would turn out; but the situation was so unusual—even for here—that he couldn't help feeling at least a little hopeful.

Hopeful enough to keep a pot of seasoned water simmering on the range while he began to crush the available spices in his mortar: pepper, mint, rue; a little vinegar to moisten it; cumin, coriander—

"*Wak!*" screeched a voice at the grated window. "Laser root! Laser root! Said I would, *wawk!* Said I would!"

The parrot, a large blue and red Macaw, squirmed through the grating with the grace of tumbler executing a trick. For a moment he paused with his body in the kitchen, left leg clutching something to his gorgeous scarlet breast and the other clawed foot gripping a bar.

Then the parrot hopped so that his tail, red and blue and as long as his body, cleared the bars.

"*Wak!*" he repeated as he landed on the counter in front of Apicius. "Laser root!"

His left foot opened and dropped a scrap of something vegetable onto the tiled counter.

There *were* gods. And they had found him, Marcus Gabius Apicius, even in this place.

"You let me go," the bird squawked. "I bring you laser root from caravan. Wawk! Laser root!"

Apicius picked up the bit of root with a care that he would not have wasted on the most delicately-worked gold filigree. He sniffed, still afraid to believe.

It really was what the parrot had promised: Cyrenean laser— silphium to the Greeks—and of first quality besides. Laser was the king of spices, and the one spice which Apicius had been unable to locate throughout his bleak sojourn in this Underworld.

The bird strutted down the counter, clicking his beak and preening himself. When he turned, he flicked up his beautiful tail to keep from singeing it in the fire beneath the pot of seasoned water. "*Said* I would," he muttered. "*Said* I would."

Apicius had thought he was being a fool—his master would have been furious if matters had not worked out, and Sulla's fury was never something to discount. But the parrot had spoken to him, *real* speech and not just the miming of syllables.

The parrot had promised to bring laser root from the caravan which had just arrived to pick up the shipment of drugs that Apicius knew his master had procured.

Men could eat and drink on this island, and the food passed through them in normal enough fashion—the smell of the house's open privy, here beside the kitchen range, was proof enough of that. But meals didn't have a real savor. Even the ignorant commons knew that, while to educated palates like those of Apicius and his master; well . . . one might as well have been eating sawdust.

Pine sawdust, reeking of turpentine.

Now, with the crucial spice which had been missing, it was possible that Apicius could construct a truly perfect dish. If he could burst that dam of frustration, his whole existence here took on new meaning.

The parrot dipped his torso over the edge of the counter, balancing himself with a flick of his tail which neatly avoided the leeks and coriander waiting for a later stage in the meal's preparation. "Well," he said as he hung upside down. "*Well.* I go to Hellywood. *Beautiful! Beautiful!*"

He hopped upright again and spread his wings, twisting his head so that he could see the way they took the sun through the grated window. The feathers of the parrot's head and shoulders were orange-red and separated from the royal blue of his wingtips by a band of yellow as pure and distinct as the decoration of an Egyptian tomb.

"Well!" repeated the bird. "I go—"

Apicius, flawless in his timing here as in any other phase of cooking, shot out his hand.

"*Wawk!*"

The bird's beak was an ivory white above and black beneath. It looked powerful enough to disjoint a man's hand, and it was certainly capable of drawing blood. Apicius pinned the halves safely closed with his index and middle finger while his thumb clambed firmly around the lustrous throat.

"*But our bargain!*" cried the parrot, its shrieks muffled but surprisingly distinct. Its wings buffeted Apicius' wrists, but the cook was holding his captive out at arm's length where its struggles could do no real harm.

"*But our—*"

Apicius snapped the bird's body in a quick arc while his fingers kept its neck from rotating normally.

"*Wak!*"

Humming to himself, Apicius set the gorgeous corpse down on the counter and fed some more kindling to the fire. He wanted the seasoned water to be at a full boil before he scalded the parrot. Quite an unusual creature, that one.

But while the laser root was necessary to the preparation—so was the full-flavored meat around which the entree was designed.

Additional primping could add nothing to Theodora's toilet by the time she heard Sulla return to the house. She was ready—almost too ready: the muscles of her lower belly had, by working against themselves, brought her to a state of almost unbearable lubricity.

As Benito greeted his master with his usual slobbery exaggeration, Theodora stepped once more to the new couch and touched it with a thrill of hope. The couch was like nothing she had ever seen before; and, now that it had been delivered to her bedroom, she found it easy to believe that a piece of furniture had the virtue which the stranger had claimed for this one.

In shape, the couch was normal enough—a low frame with a mattress. The coverlet of silk, striped red and yellow on a blue ground, came from Theodora's original bed, as did the down-filled cushion at the head.

But the mattress was sprung instead of being stuffed like the one it replaced, and there were additional springs of coiled steel in the bedframe where the other had rigid wooden slats.

Details like that shouldn't have mattered. In her youth, Theodora and her partners had reached climax often enough while standing in an alley or even bending over the starting gate after a horse race, roughly screened by a dozen or so happy men awaiting their turn.

Here, though, everything mattered. And perhaps this one detail, resiliance instead of softness beneath the buttocks or thighs, meeting and then redoubling the gentle shock of the thrust—

It should work. Theodora had been so close, so many times and in so many ways, that she *knew* this would be the final step to the heights of splendid orgasm.

With a smile that could have meant anything but weakness of purpose, Theodora strode to the bedroom door to greet her husband.

Sulla had just entered the reception court. Servants bowed obsequiously in front of the walls painted with false columns, and Mussolini continued to babble in terrified cheerfulness despite the obvious attempts of his master to brush him away.

Sulla's Luck had paused at the ornately carven marble table beside the ornamental pond, waiting for the Dictator to free himself from the rancid emptiness of his chamberlain. There was a faint smile on the face of Sulla's Luck. By now, the expression was as familiar to Theodora as the ache of failed climax—and almost as unpleasant.

"Good evening, little heart," called Theodora from her doorway. "May I speak with you for a moment?"

Sulla turned, scowling. His mouth was poised to say something devastating enough to silence Benito. He saw his wife, and his eyes lost their distraction while the planes of his face cleared.

The only make-up which Theodora wore was the rouge which turned her lips into a Cupid's-bow of brilliant carmine. Her outer tunic was of black silk with a rippled pattern which echoed her hair and set off the perfect white of her skin.

Her undertunic was silk as well, but diaphanous.

Theodora stood with her left arm raised on the door jamb and her right hip shot out so that only the toes of that gilded slipper touched the mosiac floor. Her right hand rested on her hipbone and it tugged the upper tunic just high enough to hint at her pubic triangle as well as displaying the marvelously-detailed muscles of her dancers' thighs.

"I—" said the Dictator. No one else spoke or moved, though Theodora glimpsed the cook, Apicius, poised at the kitchen door like a squirrel frozen in uncertainty as to which way to jump.

Sulla turned.

His Luck shrugged and smiled more broadly. "Who knows?" said Sulla's Luck to the question that need not be spoken to be asked. "So long as one tries, there's hope."

"Begone, then," Sulla barked to his retainers as he stepped toward the bedroom with a haste he had not shown in ages, as time was reckoned here.

Apicius hopped back into the kitchen to lower the fire beneath his braising pan. The rest of the servants would wait and titter hopefully, in corners of the reception court and leaning over the rail of the loggia above, but the Dictator cared as little about that as Theodora did.

She closed the door as Sulla stepped past her, but she eluded his grasp with a hand and a pirouette which made his face darken at what he thought was ill-timed coquetry. He had already shrugged off his toga and flung it to the top of a clothes press.

"First, little heart," the woman whispered huskily as she guided Sulla to the new couch, "let me show you what came with your caravan."

"What?" said the Dictator in amazement. Emotion left his face again as his mind grappled coldly with the new data and decided how to respond. "I was just at the warehouse. Why haven't I been informed?"

The curse that Theodora's mind ripped out at her verbal misstep would have been enough by itself to threaten her soul's salvation, but she kept her lips smiling as she protested aloud, "There'll be time for that later, dearest. Sit here for just a moment."

"Woman," snapped the Dictator, "this is important!"

"So," said the woman, her eyes sparking like flint and black steel, "is this."

She had already undone the clasp of the filigreed pin which fastened her upper tunic. When she twitched her shoulders now, the black silk cascaded to her feet, licking across the surface of the transparent undergarment.

Paradise was setting with a creamy, almost golden

glow beneath the cloudbanks. The light turned Theodora's skin to ivory and darkened the cones of her fiercely erect nipples.

Sulla allowed himself to be guided to a seat on the end of the couch. His mouth was slightly open, and his left hand fumbled repeatedly as it undid the sash of his tunic.

"What?" he muttered as the springs lifted with a soft moan beneath him.

"It's from Paradise, my heart, my dearest dear," said Theodora, embroidering what she knew with what she believed. She lifted both hands to the throat of her tunic and ripped the garment with deliberate strength. Her breasts were firm here as they had remained throughout her life. The nipples described a pair of flat arcs as the muscles beneath them tensed to tear the silk.

Sulla reached for her breasts, half rising and subsiding again, charmed by the springs, as the woman knelt and lifted the hem of the tunic he still wore. His member was erect, and the head of it was fiery red as she stripped back his foreskin.

"Little heart," Theodora murmured; licked the tip of the penis; and changed the angle of her head slightly so that she could engulf most of the thick shaft in her mouth while her fingernails tickled Sulla's scrotum.

The couch whispered, and gave, and gave back. Such a little thing, but the visitor had been right. . . .

Sulla was kneading one breast with a harshness that many women—other women—would have found painful, while the fingers of his right hand were buried in the shimmering hair which alone covered Theodora now. His muscles were matching the rhythms of his body and hers and the softly creaking springs.

Theodora's flared nostrils caught the sudden hormonal change of her partner's odor into something goatish and male and intensely aphrodisiac to her. A vein at the base of his penis throbbed.

She lifted her head away and stood, her eyes filled with rapture.

"No, *no*," cried the man in dizzy amazement. The twist of her head had freed it from his fingers, so that they closed only on her black, rippling hair.

"Not *that* way," said Theodora in a voice that was a promise, guiding Sulla to his feet by leaning back and clamping his hand to her breast more savagely than he had done himself.

She twisted, then rose onto her toes and arched her pelvis forward to receive him. The tunic flapped, a momentary obstacle, but both of them together snatched the hem out of the way.

He would have the garment off before the next time—but there could be any number of 'next times,' now, and this was delight mounting to a bliss greater than godhead.

Theodora tipped them back onto the couch, her buttocks sliding on the warm, slick fabric while Sulla's member thrust as deeply within her as a man could reach and the springs squealed like a terrified infant.

Theodora's scream overwhelmed the other sound everywhere but in her mind. It was at the wizened face in her memory, streaked with placental blood, that she clawed—

But it was Sulla who leaped upright, howling in fury and amazement. His left hand covered his eye and cheek, but the reddened triple scratches extended well across his forehead.

The Dictator leaned forward again and slapped the vacant-eyed woman as she started to rise. Then he swept out of the room, bellowing for his Luck.

Theodora lay sobbing on the couch whose springs chuckled beneath her.

Benito was the only servant visible when the Dictator tore from his wife's bedroom. The chamberlain was sweating so furiously that the breast of his cloth-of-gold outer robe bore dark stains. Through the lattice screen

of the office, Sulla saw with his good eye that his Luck
was standing with a concerned expression. Benito tried
to say something, but the Dictator brushed past him.

Apicius strode from the kitchen into his path. The
cook carried a covered silver serving dish by its han-
dles, and his face was wreathed with an ecstatic smile.
"Master—" he began.

"Idiot!" shouted the Dictator as the two men collided.

Apicius' shriek was too much like the cry Theodora
had given as she lashed out. Sulla struck the cook with
his clenched left fist as the man bobbled the platter
desperately.

Apicius sprawled. The lid rang like a bell on the
stone flooring, and the platter itself jounced from his
hands despite his despairing wail. The fowl skidded
over the lip of the ornamental pool. It floated there,
cooling and staining the water with the flavorful sauce
with which it was to have been eaten.

Water seeping into the body cavity made the bird
chuckle.

Benito was so distraught that his right hand reached
out as if to pluck his master's sleeve. The chamberlain
wasn't *quite* in such a state as to touch Sulla as he
knocked down the cook, but Benito did trail the Dictator unbidden into his office.

"What have you heard about the—" Sulla shouted to
his Luck before motion and the gleam of gold cloth
spun him again.

"What are *you* doing here?" the Dictator asked with
anger the more terrifying for being offered in a voice of
normal volume. He pointed with his whole right hand,
palm down and trembling with eagerness to clutch the
fat throat before it.

Sulla's left eye was bloodshot. The scratches traced
scarlet furrows across a visage otherwise the complexion
of mulberries in clotted cream.

"Ma—" stammered the chamberlain. "Ma-ma—" The

fingers and thumb of his left hand were pinching the air, miming the nervous emptiness of his lips.

Sulla balled a fist to strike him. Then he would summon guards and have them—

"I'm afraid you'd best listen to him, my Lucius," said Sulla's Luck in a voice that was the Dictator's in every particular save in the mouth from which it issued.

"No time for that!" said Sulla harshly, but the voice of his alter ego relaxed him. He turned again, lowering his arm and letting his face smooth into the gentler contours of normal intercourse. "The caravan's come in, and—"

"The caravan's been destroyed," squeaked the chamberlain in a voice that could have summoned bats. "Everything's burned, everyone's dead. The guides you sent to meet them, they saw it all happen, everyone dead."

The Dictator did not look back at his servant. His left hand began very carefully to rub his stinging, tear-streaming eye.

"I'm afraid he's right, my Lucius," said Sulla's Luck. "The guides reported here while you were—otherwise occupied. There can't be any doubt about what happened . . . though *why*, of course, that will require a great deal of sorting out."

"You may go, Benito," Sulla said quietly.

The chamberlain bolted, but he reached an arm back to slide the door lattice closed before disappearing toward a staircase and a place to keep out of sight on the second floor.

"How does this," said Sulla, watching his fingers extend toward the white powder heaped on the table, "affect our agreement?"

His Luck shrugged. "The terms were very rigid, you know," he said. "By today, the shipment was to be placed in specified hands for distribution. I can only presume that there *is* no agreement any more."

"*I* couldn't help that!" shouted the Dictator, animated again. He would have struck out at any face that showed itself at the moment, but the only features he could see were his own.

"Well, of course I can inform them of that, my Lucius," said Sulla's Luck, turning his head tactfully so as not to watch the Dictator being reduced to puling incapacity. "But—well, you must realize that results rather than intentions are the, ah, coin they require."

"Wait, wait," blurted Sulla, raising his hands as if to grip the other figure by the shoulders but sliding them away from the touch at the last instant. "Tell them I *will* put the shipment out. It's all safe, all safe. I'll go right now and start to make arrangements!"

He sprinted to the door; but as his fingers touched the wood, his body convulsed with a great shudder. Sulla looked back at his Luck and said, "A few days, a week perhaps—it shouldn't matter. But it does, doesn't it?"

Sulla's Luck smiled regretfully. "Well, my Lucius," he said. "I'll pass on your offer. Who knows? Perhaps in time they might be willing to come to another arrangement with you, on the former terms." He shrugged.

Sulla moaned and rested his forehead in the crook of his elbow for a dozen heartbeats. Then he slid the lattice open and staggered across the reception court. He was muttering, "I'm sure they'll be reasonable. After all. . . ."

Sulla's Luck closed the lattice again and walked back to the table. The filtered light of Paradise was a red as deep as pulsing anger. It would not have been sufficient to limn the writing on the bronze plate for human eyes—but anyway, Sulla's Luck knew it very well.

They had never understood, the damned souls or the living—Dante as little as the rest. *All hope abandon*—because if you have no hope, you cannot be tortured. Only the possibility of release can make interminable pain interminably painful.

Sulla's Luck reached slowly toward the heap of white powder. The latticework through which the light seeped distorted his shadow, making it seem now that of a woman hunched within her shawl, now that of a bird with a great clacking bill.

he lifted a pinch of the powder.

Hope for success, thought Sulla's Luck. Hope for surcease, hope for *something* besides damnation to a place where he knew well he did not reign.

He snorted the powder of hope into one upturned nostril. Horns quivered on his shadow. Where his eyes should have been were two glowing drops of hellfire.

SNOWBALLS IN HELL

Chris Morris

When his horse started dissolving under him, Alexander the Great was riding along the shore of a wine-dark sea.

Though the beach he cantered along was no longer the beach of Troy, it had been that, once. Alexander had fought here then, with Achilles and Diomedes by his side. Or he thought he had. He remembered it.

The horse under him was the noble Bucephalus, long lost and now found again. For Bucephalus' sake, for the mighty heart beating under that black hide, for the mane that whipped now in his face and the soft sweetness of a kiss from that velvet muzzle, Alexander had left his new-found Achaean friends behind. Friends were hard to come by in Hell. But Bucephalus, the war horse of Alexander's Earthly life, had been reunited with him and the choice between staying with the horse or returning to a higher hell had been no choice at all.

So he'd stayed behind, here on what was once the

battle plain of Ilion but remade itself anew, periodically. He'd stayed with Bucephalus, alone.

And now, on a canter to nowhere for no particular reason, Bucephalus was starting to leave him. To dissolve. To decompose. To scream and become ectoplasmic and . . . *gone*.

Alexander too was screaming, though he didn't know it. He was crying and this he knew. He couldn't see clearly but he could see—and feel—the horse between his thighs becoming dust and air and sand and . . .

Bright white light came from somewhere, burning away the sea mist and destroying everything in its path. Alexander twisted his fingers in what remained of Bucephalus' mane and yelled, "I love you Bucephalus. I'll never forget you. I'll not rest until we find each other again!"

By the time he'd howled the last words he was falling, unseated by a ghost horse who might never have been there. Falling forever. He didn't hit the ground. He fell and fell.

Trying to brace for a concussion of flesh and ground that would not come, his tears dried. Dried in the wind and the white light and the grief that emptied his soul. And still he fell.

He fell through white wind and soon he fell sideways. He opened his eyes and squinted into the light and noticed that he wasn't the only one falling: he saw others, shadows passing at a distance, dark dapples in the light. And then he realized, by the way his hair was whipping around his eyes, that he wasn't falling downward. He was falling *up*!

How can a man fall up? He couldn't understand it. He clenched his fists and brought them to his eyes. And there he found, wound among his fingers, long, midnight strands of Bucephalus' mane. He laughed a defiant laugh, clutching those strands to his face.

And fell some more, until at last he began to sense that he was falling downward. Through the white light he could see dark plateaus. He could see clouds below him. He could see lands far and wide, with rivers and forests.

Forests toward which he was falling at a terrifying rate. Doubtless, he told himself as he pinwheeled in the air, he would hit the ground and die instantly. Death, in Hell, meant the Trip: he would suffer, he would crash and crumple and shatter like faience; then he would awake in New Hell on the Undertaker's table, subject to the foul jokes of the Chief Mortician. And then he would be Reassigned.

Next to losing Bucephalus, it was a minor horror. He was Alexander the Great. He was not afraid of Hell's bureaucracy, only of himself—of his capacity for love and his capacity for rage.

So as he fell ever more quickly toward a stand of trees among which wound a series of roads, he clutched the strands of Bucephalus' mane more tightly, and tied one end of the strands to his chiton's clasp, the other to his wrist.

No matter what happened to him, or where he woke, he would have that talisman of love and luck when he lived again. For Alexander, who had been separated from Bucephalus for millennia, those strands were all the luck and all the hope he needed.

Death was a mere inconvenience.

Or so he thought, until he began falling through a stand of pines. Every branch that broke under his weight stabbed him. Every bough that bent slapped him. Every trunk rebounded him like a pinball in that game the New Dead played. Every pine needle pierced him.

And then he began to wonder *where* he was dying: if you died in certain deeper Hells, like that of Troy, rumor had it you never found your way back to the Undertaker. You experienced nothingness. Forever. Or you *didn't* experience anything. Ever again.

Suddenly the pain of his fall became precious—it was experience. Alexander had stayed sane in Hell because he *was* Alexander—was always Alexander, would always be Alexander.

The idea of "not being" terrified him. What had happened to Bucephalus? He shook his head, falling with his eyes closed, and his skull hit a tree trunk. Hard.

The last thing he thought, before his body hit the ground in a marsh and a rush of reed and water, was that if Bucephalus was really gone forever, he must face it. And face a similar fate with courage.

But that much courage, Alexander the Great did not have. "No!" he screamed, at the top of his lungs, until those lungs filled up with marsh water and his battered body sank in the mud.

It wasn't easy, being the only volunteer angel in Hell, but Altos was doing the best job he could. He'd been co-opted into the rebel camp, into the Dissident movement, by men of low degree for foul purpose—those who followed Che Guevara, those who took orders from a Pentagram faction headed by Tigellinus and Mithridates.

He'd come to the Dissidents for reasons that none of those who'd brought him even suspected, until it was too late. There had been an air strike called on the Dissidents' camp by the Devil's Children. Altos had gone among the rebels to save whomever he could.

Not "save" in the sense of salvation, manumission, or ascension to heavenly estate, although he could and would offer true salvation to any he found deserving—it was part of his job. But, among the Dissidents, before the cleansing fire of the air strike, he'd found none ready for salvation.

He had, however, found many ready for mercy, many who might feel the hand of God if it touched them, even here. So he had gone into the camp in full awareness of the napalm soon to come, of the cluster bombs and area denial munitions which were among the Devil's favorite tools. And he had denied, as was his mandate, Satan's will.

For the sake of the souls here who were worth tempering, of those on the path toward redemption, he had spread a warning in the camp and urged the Dissidents down into their ubiquitous tunnels. Many had heeded him, and many had been saved from the Devil's crucible of fire. Temporarily, of course.

Now, walking along a wooden path toward the marsh by which the refugee Dissidents were encamped, Altos contemplated the meaning of salvation, when applied to the damned. The salvation he could offer the Dissidents was not complete because they were not ready. They were not yet good. Some of them, however, were increasingly less bad. Thus, he had managed to keep them from the Undertaker's table, from disbandment and Reassignments. Reassignments, more than any other bureau among Hell's proliferate bureacracy, was Altos' antagonist. The Reassignments computer and the souls who manned it strove to keep the damned lonely, bitter, venal, and horrid. Altos strove to teach them community, hope, sacrifice, and generosity.

When Satan dispatched his Children with their fighter-bombers full of hellfire, Altos had been among the Dissidents to shepherd them out of harm's way. He had even confronted one of the Devil's Children, an agent named Welch, face to face.

And that had been wrenching, because Altos was an angel and thus subject to the occasional unsolicited Revelation. Looking into Welch's eyes, he had had one: the Devil's agent was not committed to evil; this man who did Satan's will was closer to salvation than Che Guevara, than many of the Dissidents. Welch thought of himself as a soldier in the service of order, and of order as an ameliorating factor in the suffering of the damned.

It had been disconcerting to meet the pragmatic gaze of a man who had made an accommodation with his fate that allowed him to serve the Devil—well—without becoming Satanized. In those eyes for the angel to see was a life spent on earth in similar circumstances. Welch had personal standards to which he adhered and a perception of the evil around him that made the man, in his own mind, almost a comrade in arms of the angel.

Only Welch, being human, took the failings of his fellows more personally. Not only did the agent believe that he himself belonged here, but that everyone he met did. In fact, Altos had learned in that cataclysmic locking of eyes, Welch didn't believe that there were any better men in heaven. It was his catechism that real men went to hell.

The member of the Devil's Children had no designs on a pass to heaven. The Child merely did his job. When Altos had gone back into the camp to save the Dissidents in the face of the air strike, Welch's pity had followed after the angel like a balm.

Pity from a damned soul? An irredeemable? For Welch was surely that, as an agent of Satanic will. It troubled the angel still, so long after.

It had troubled him while he hustled the Dissidents down into the tunnels. It had troubled him when Che had refused to run, hesitated to hide, dug in his rebellious heels and kept a score of men with him on the surface.

All of those were back, now: the Devil's Reassignments bureau knew its job. Che and his staunchest followers had been returned to the Undertakers, debriefed, their hearts and souls gleaned of all they knew and planned and schemed. Then they'd been returned to their band, having betrayed everyone and everything that supported them.

Che Guevara knew this, and he sulked in his tent, weakened in mind and body. He had betrayed Mithridates and Tigellinus and even the hired mercenaries who served him as long as the Pentagram faction's gold held out. Che couldn't help it. He'd been through the System, taken the Trip.

The Devil was impressing the fruitlessness of revolution on Guevara, the hopelessness of hope itself. And it was working. Che was nearly broken. He was listless and uncommunicative. His lieutenants covered the change in their leader as best they could, but Altos knew: Guevara, the leader who inspired the Dissidents, was drained of inspiration, merely going through the motions.

And so, Altos could not leave the band of rebels: if Che did not recover and no new leader took his place, the entire Dissident movement would dissolve. At such a moment, the volunteer angel must witness Satan's victory and the final damnation of these many souls.

You're not truly damned until you accept it. You're not lost until you lose hope. You're not irredeemable until you lose faith in redemption. Like Welch.

The angel shook his head and hiked up his robe as his sandals squished, sinking into boggy ground, pushing thoughts of the Devil's Child away. Here the cattails were as high a his blond head and the smell of putrefaction was like that which blurts from a man's rectum: the marsh was near at hand. All around was white gas rising, opaque and cloudlike, making it hard to see your hand before your face.

The gas eddied and hung low in the air, in patches and whirls and swirls. Somewhere out there, creatures lived: he could hear insectlike chittering and froglike croaking and the calls of murderous owls and hawks and gulls. And then he heard another sound, and stopped.

It was a moan of pain, a human moan, from a throat in torture. Altos hiked his robes above his knees and headed toward the sound.

His ankles sank into the mud. Fetid water swirled about his knees, scummy and dotted with algae, larvae, and worse. Mosquitoes the size of hummingbirds dove at him, veering at the last instant: he was an angel; the smell of his flesh, sweet and clean, repelled the suckers of impure blood.

On he struggled, stumbling so that his white robe soaked up mud and became an impediment. He tore it at the knee and cast away the lower part of his garment, pressing on toward the moans, which were fainter, though he knew he approached the moaner.

A soul in torment could draw the angel like filings to a magnet, if it were the right sort of soul. Altos could not fail to find this man if the whole of Upper Hell were in between them, for the man was calling on God for help.

The words were garbled, but the intent was clear. The man was delirious—the damned did not call on God, in Hell. Not if they were in their right minds. But this one was in such pain that he didn't know what he was saying.

When Altos broke through a stand of reeds and saw the distant battered body in its pool of blood-stained mud and scum, there were already predators about, waiting with slavering jaws and open beaks: jackals and ospreys and wolves and vultures.

"Shoo!" called Altos, his arms waving. "Get away!"

The carrion-eaters scattered, but did not disappear. They retreated and reformed, lurking, curious, their nostrils full of the odor of an incipient feast.

This man might be eaten alive, a particularly unpleasant fate here, where death would not come early, and memory would linger through resurrection and beyond. Might be, if Altos couldn't help him.

The angel paused, thinking as he did so that he was out of earshot of the camp. He would have to drag or carry this man to the Dissidents, if he could be moved. Or simply sit with him until his soul bled out, until sleep came, if he could not.

More, Altos had no power to do. Preparing a soul for heaven wasn't something one could do in minutes. Everyone here was here for a reason. Altos could not commute a sentence out of hand, no matter the heart-wrenching plight of the sufferer.

So he cautioned himself, hastening toward the wounded man. And as he got closer, and the footing beneath him became more treacherous, his steps began to lighten. Soon he was treading water, then walking upon it.

Then his sandals skimmed the marshy surface. And, as he approached to within ten feet of the moaning man, the angel was levitating freely.

Altos could only levitate under certain conditions. The condition here which lightened his heart sufficiently to allow the angel's body to rise, and float, was inherent in the soul whose body he approached.

Floating freely, Altos settled slowly toward the man, his knees bending, his mind full of questions. Who could it be, who faced death with such equanimity? Who could it be, who had such passion for life and such love in his unrepentant soul? Who could it be, who met his fate so boldly that merely being in his presence caused Altos' heart such joy?

Kneeling as he descended, Altos settled by the body and brushed mud and blood from the battered face. The countenance revealed was beautiful even in its pain. From split lips no words came now, only rattling breath and occasional groans.

At Altos' touch, one eye opened—the other was swollen shut. The eye, blue as the Mediterranean, regarded him, and the lips tried to form words. The head tried to rise, but fell back with a splash into the mud which was its pillow.

Broken reeds had jabbed him; some terrible fall had bruised him. His flesh was torn and flies crawled freely over open wounds.

But the single eye met the angel's two eyes, and held. Held long enough that Altos learned why he'd been drawn here, and why he'd levitated in this man's presence.

This battered soul before him was Alexander of Macedon, who'd given up salvation to bring the light of civilization to the darkest corners of the ancient world.

Altos gathered up the man in his arms and it was as if Alexander weighed nothing. Floating with the Macedonian toward the Dissidents' camp, the angel was moved to send up a paean of praise and thanks. Even in Hell, the proper tools were delivered unto him, that the angel might better perform God's work.

Among the Dissidents was Judah Maccabee, and when Maccabee saw Alexander, with whom he'd fought at Troy, the Israelite was filled with joy. He demanded that the angel give the Macedonian into his care, which the muddied Altos, staggering through the camp with Alexander in his arms, was glad to do.

"Just Al," said the Israelite, calling the angel by the name the Dissidents used for him, "where did you find him?"

"Ah, out there," said the angel, cocking his head vaguely to indicate the swamp. Altos did not admit to his high estate among the Dissidents. Some knew; some suspected; some disbelieved. But none would ask him to his face, because if Altos was really an angel who could grant salvation and deny it, then all hopes of the questioner were in jeopardy of being dashed eternally.

It was one thing to be sent to Hell by mistake, another to have an agent of God tell you that you belonged here. No one wanted to hear that.

Not even Judah Maccabee, who was on speaking terms with many of Hell's movers and shakers, including the redoubtable Welch.

"Out there?" Maccabee's intelligent eyes narrowed; his tall frame stooped to draw back his tentflap. He motioned Altos and his burden inside. Once the flap was drawn and Alexander laid on Maccabee's pallet, the Israelite said, "Last time I saw him, he was . . . in a deeper abode. Troy. Ilion, if you like. Or if you don't." White teeth flashed in the gloom. "He couldn't have gotten back up here by himself. I know. I made that journey. And where's Bucephalus? That's what he stayed for, the horse . . ."

"I don't know what to tell you, Israelite." A careful answer, for Altos had seen in Alexander's eyes all that had transpired. And more, for the angel understood what the Macedonian did not. "There was no horse, just the fallen man. Perhaps the horse ran—"

"Bullshit." Maccabee had been long among the New Dead, the likes of Welch. "You know; you don't tell me. Why not?"

Altos spread his hands. "Let us see if we can keep this man from the Undertaker—cheat fate. You're an expert at that, aren't you?"

"First aid? Yeah, I can probably manage. But how is it you're so interested in keeping him alive?" The Israelite stroked his bearded jaw. Eyes that had looked upon the Roman army and dared to oppose it defocused, then sharpened. Maccabee said: "What do you want from this, friend? What does your sort want? Why not let him go back to Reassignments? Or did *you* bring him here—for your own purposes?"

Too smart, this one. Too smart and too contentious. Altos answered the safest question: "I didn't bring him. There are . . . temporal disturbances. Do you understand? The very fabric of Hell's before-and-after is troubled. Someone went . . . down . . ." Altos pointed to the ground beneath his feet and as he did so, Alexander groaned softly, stirred, and then was still again, ". . . down abruptly, to some deeper 'abode,' as you call it. And Alexander was . . . thrust up. Pure coincidence." Altos shrugged.

"I bet. But not coincidence that he'd appear here, when Che's not exactly *compos mentis*, I'd wager. Don't you have to play fair? Or is this just more punishment? Alexander's not up to these sorts of games. I know him." And, rather than tending the battered Macedonian, Maccabee crossed his big arms over his chest and stared hard at the angel.

"I know him, too," said the angel softly. "And he's capable of whatever he asks of himself."

"You might as well be working for Satan, if you separated him from that horse of his just to stick him in with these limp-dicked weekend wonders," said the Israelite in colloquial English. Then he switched to Attic

Greek, speaking softly to the wounded man as if Altos weren't present.

The angel left the two men together, wondering why, when God's ways were so mysterious to him, the very sword of Heaven in Hell, they were so obvious to an Israelite whose main distinction in life had been teaching Jews how to die for their ideals.

Of course, that had been Before Christ. It occurred to him then that Maccabee might be jealous—might have wanted to take over the Dissident's; leadership himself. But he could still do that. Though Altos didn't think that he would.

The Macedonian would change everything among the Dissidents. Where Maccabee could have engendered only sacrifice—suicide, in Altos' terms—Alexander could generate passion, belief, personal loyalty.

If Alexander wanted to, he could launch a crusade and every man and woman among the Dissidents would be his willing crusaders. A crusade against the Devil such as had not been seen since the Middle Ages on Earth—and never, in Hell.

If the Macedonian chose to, he could bring the revolution to the Devil's very doorstep in New Hell. *If*. Assuming, of course, that Che and his followers mounted no opposition.

Altos, outside the tent, was wandering among dozens of other, similar tents under cammo netting, not watching where he was going, absorbed in his thoughts. Thus it took a moment for the commotion to penetrate his abstraction.

As a matter of fact, he didn't notice the ruckus in the camp (Dissidents were always bickering) until a blond woman who had been a twentieth-century news reporter came running up to him, tape recorder in hand, thrusting a microphone toward him.

"A chopper's crashed on the other side of the marsh!" she proclaimed. "Number of casualties, destination, and cause of crash unknown. Would you like to make a statement?"

"A statement?" Altos frowned. "No, I wouldn't. Why would I?"

When the woman scowled and stalked away, he slipped between two tents and ran toward the marsh. It was another result of the temporal wind shear, he was certain. But someone should have warned the pilot.

Unless, of course, Satan was already countering the insertion of Alexander into the Dissidents' camp with some players of his own.

In the ravine, the helicopter lay askew, one skid bent sideways, leaning on its rotors against the upward slope. Smoke still came from it, and the slight, red-headed figure of Achilles could be seen darting hither and yon with his fire extinguisher.

"Hold him!" Welch said again to Nichols, who had his gun pointed steadily at Enkidu's hairy chest. That chest was heaving, as if Enkidu had run a long, long way. Which was what the captive wanted to do, would have done, if not for the watchful eye of Nichols' gun.

The crash had been terrifying, a dizzying descent, an onslaught of spinning and jolting, men yelling and being thrown against the great bird's insides. Now, safe on solid land, Enkidu crouched low, his hairy knuckles nearly brushing the ground, and awaited his chance. Sometime, Nichols must blink. Beyond him was clean country, trees and bog and hills. A place to hide. A place to run.

The woman called Tanya brushed blond hair matted with blood out of her eyes and went to Welch, pressing her cheek against his arm. "Are you all—is the chopper all right?" she said, changing her mind in midsentence.

"You mean, can we fly it out of here?" Welch looked around, past Nichols, guarding Enkidu, to the people peeking over the ravine's crest and a few, braver souls straggling down it. "Ask Achilles, it's his mess."

Enkidu fully expected the woman to stride up to the red-haired man who fussed over his wounded bird and do just that, but she did not. She said to Welch, "Achilles said it was wind shear from a singularity. . . . What does that mean? Were we shot down?"

"He doesn't know what he's talking about," Nichols spat without taking his eyes from Enkidu's chest. "The only thing 'singular' about the crash was that damn fool's pisspoor performance."

Enkidu wanted very much to run. His entire person was rejecting everything around him—everything he'd seen and heard, the whole concept of having flown in the bird's belly. None of it had happened. None of it was real. Somehow, he'd had a bad dream that transported him here. A dream, that was all. A dream that had separated him from Gilgamesh and transported him here.

Yes, it was easier to believe in the power of a dream than in a bird that had flown him hither in its belly. He looked beyond Nichols, whose black-clad, threatening person was all that kept Enkidu from the beckoning forests, and his eyes alighted upon the woman, Tanya.

The woman was a sorceress, a priestess of hostile gods, a wielder of powerful dreams. He must remember to warn Gilgamesh about such women. When he saw him again.

Right now, it was perfectly obvious to Enkidu's wilderness-trained ears and nose that people were sneaking up on them: he could smell their excited sweat on the downwind; he could hear their secret whispers on the breeze.

But this man with the fire-spitting weapon before him did not hear the voices approaching, nor the tread of furtive feet or the crack of broken branches as they came. The square-jawed man with the short hair like a beard upon his head looked only at Enkidu, thought only of Enkidu, and waited with a taunt in his eyes that dared Enkidu to break and run.

Enkidu did not. He hunkered down where he was and watched. The red-haired owner of the bird tended it with occasional gesticulations and curses that reconsecrated him and it to Hell. The sorceress with the beautiful blond hair hung upon the arm of Welch, the heavy-set leader, and they spoke in tones they thought Enkidu could not hear.

"What about the ape-man?" Welch whispered to her. "You think you can control him long enough to get him back in the chopper? If Achilles is right and we can get it flying again?"

"Have we a choice?" she answered with her own question. "We're supposed to bring him back to Reassignments. What's the penalty if we go back without him?"

Welch's shoulders rippled up, and then down. "Maybe none. 'Enkidu and Gilgamesh separated'—depends on how you want to interpret the orders. We can always shoot him, that'll get him back to Slab A quick enough." Welch bared the most perfect white teeth Enkidu had ever seen on a man. Then the pleasant features of his pale face hardened as he looked straight at Enkidu. "If I didn't know better," he said to Tanya, "I'd think he could hear us."

"—Use all that muscle of Enkidu's to help us right the chopper," Achilles called out, his short legs scissoring blurrily as he hurried toward Welch and Tanya. "We'll be out of here in short order. Nothing's irreparably— *shit*! Y'all see that welcoming committee?"

Now the entire group, even Nichols, looked past Enkidu and he saw his chance. Without hesitation, he lunged to his left, where the ravine was met by trees and boulders, not even taking time to come erect, but scuttling away on all fours, his callused knuckles helping to push him along the ground.

"Nichols!" he heard Welch yell from behind him, but he didn't look back.

He didn't hear Nichols' laconic, "Yeah, boss; gotcha," either, because the sound of the gun going off behind him followed almost simultaneously, and in its wake came a mighty hand that thrust Enkidu from his feet, face down into oblivion.

*   *   *

"Back the fuck off," warned Achilles in a voice that had trumpeted over the battle of Ilion. His M14 quested among the ranks of the armed men who had halted twenty feet away. Before the helicopter, the little Achaean stood, spread-legged, as if, single-handedly, he could defend it all: the chopper, the woman whom he'd grabbed and thrust inside it and who now peeked out the open door, and Welch and Nichols, who'd taken cover behind its fuselage.

The fifty-odd men and women who had come down over the ravine were all armed to the teeth, but they hesitated when Achilles brandished his assault rifle.

None of 'em wanted to go back to Reassignments, Achilles realized. So once again, Welch was right: *We can hold them off if nobody panics,* the sortie leader had assured them, and given Achilles an indefensible position he was too proud not to take.

But it was working. Or at least, it worked for a minute. Then the ranks parted like a drill team and a slight, bearded man with soulful eyes and waxy skin came forth, a grenade in one hand, the pin in the other.

"Hello, fighter," said the man in accented English. *"Comienzen fuego?"* A taunt, incomprehensible. "No? Then surrender. Or we return you to your base of operations, the hard way." He raised his fist, brandishing the grenade. On that signal, other men pulled grenades (pineapples) from their belts and pulled their own pins, so that if Achilles fired, the ensuing explosion would wreck the chopper, and his body.

"Shit," said Achilles under his breath. Men weren't usually this careless of their own lives, even in Hell. "Well, Welch, got any more bright ideas?"

"It's Guevara," said Welch calmly, from only a few inches behind him.

Achilles, startled, flinched and a ripple of laughter ran through the opposing ranks. "Bastard, don't sneak up on me. So what, it's Guevara? I'm Achilles."

"We know," said Welch with what might have been a sardonic tinge in his tone. "But even Achilles wouldn't want to waste the Trojan Horse. Go back with Tamara. I think," and his voice lowered to a whisper, "we're going to surrender. For the nonce."

"Nonce, shit," said Achilles through tight-locked jaws. It was like giving in to the Atreides. He couldn't abide surrender. He wouldn't. He'd jack himself up into the chopper and hold out there. Even without operational cannon, he could give these sons of whores a—

"And don't try anything cute. One casualty on this is all I'm willing to take the blame for." Welch came up beside him and nodded toward the pile of smouldering flesh that had once been Enkidu, and now was just another self-combusting husk on its way to the Undertaker's. "If J. Edgar's still got connections in the Mortuary, you or me or anybody involved in that interdiction sure wouldn't want to come under an unfriendly knife there."

Achilles shuddered. One could be in worse shape than Achilles was—his whole body worked; every limb did its job. He'd seen men whose resurrection had been botched, for less reason. "Yeah," he said, retreating. "I heard that." And promised himself silently that he'd find some way to blame this whole mess on Welch, when he got back to New Hell.

Got back alive. After having surrendered. It wasn't something he could take with equanimity. He slung his rifle over his shoulder and jumped for the doorsill of the canted chopper, then pulled himself up and sat on it.

Tamara looked up at him from inside the chopper and said, "Well, at least they're asking, not shooting."

"Achilles didn't have a thing to say to that New Dead slut. He just crossed his arms and wished she wasn't there. If she hadn't been, with her nasty little side arm pointed casually at him from the darkness of the chopper's belly, he'd have barricaded himself inside.

But Welch, as usual, had everything covered. He surrendered their party with grace, poise, and good manners to the Dissident leader known as Guevara, and there wasn't a damned thing Achilles could do but go along. For now.

"We ransom you, gringo, back to your slimebag masters," Che said with a wave of farewell, and ducked through the tentflaps before Welch could respond.

Alone in the interrogation tent, Welch tried to ignore the pain in his bound wrists and ankles, the complaint of muscles strained and skin chafing against the tentpole. He had some time to consider his options. He ought to take it.

Guevara was an old pro at this. He'd stripped the captives naked, made a number of lewd suggestions as applicable to men as to women, then separated them. Welch's main concern was for Tanya. He should have known that, when Guevara realized who the woman was, there'd be no reasoning with him.

He had no doubt that Guevara would ransom him, and Achilles, and Nichols, but he had a feeling that Tamara Burke was going to return to New Hell the hard way. He felt bad about that, he really did. It surprised him *how* bad he felt about it. But there wasn't much he could do; not tied to a tentpole, there wasn't.

Guevara would ransom them back, eventually, but until then, it was going to be mind-fuck and interrogation, lots of it. If Welch had anticipated this mess correctly, he'd have shot his people himself, to spare them what was coming.

But he'd screwed up—he'd forgotten about Che and Tanya and their long history of kill-me/kill-you—the sort of history that got repeated endlessly in Hell because people never learned.

If you could keep from making the same mistakes that got you here, you could probably get out, at least to Purgatory. But nobody ever could. Or, at least, nobody ever did.

Welch spent an interminable interval staring at the tentflap that shivered in the wind—the same sort of

wind the chopper had run into. Hell's heaviest weather,
complete with thunder and lightning: there'd been no
anticipating that. Things screw up. Perfect planning
prevents pisspoor performance, but nothing was ever
perfect in Hell.

Only some sort of screw up on Che's part, something
Guevara hadn't planned for, was going to get them out
of this anytime soon. He hoped Tanya was thinking
about that. If he could have reached her, he'd have
suggested she try to make Che . . .

"Pardon me, do you mind a visitor?" said a man who
poked his head into the tent. A blond head. A slightly
glowing countenance in the dim light. A perfect, beautiful smile that made Welch's heart ache.

"Hello, Altos," said Welch calmly, because all he had
left now was his inner arsenal—apparent calm, clear-
headedness, incisive analysis of his own plight. "Come
to save me from the Dissidents?"

In came the angel, who wasn't about to do any such
thing. Blue eyes lowered and Welch was glad enough
not to meet them. It had hurt, the last time he'd looked
this supernal errand boy in the eye.

"Not exactly," said Altos very quietly.

"How about alleviating my suffering? A quick cut, a slug
in the brain—me and Tanya. Yeah, Tanya first. Do her a
world of good. Good's what you're about, here, right?"

"Don't tease me, Welch. I *am* here to help." A
flicker of darkness crossed the angel's face like a storm
cloud scudding before the moon. "Alexander of Macedon
is here. He would speak with you."

"It doesn't look to me like you need my permission,"
said Welch, giving a desultory pull against his bonds.
"You want it, then loosen some of these ropes. I'm all
pins and needles."

"I can't," whispered the angel with something like
real despair. "Not yet. But Alexander needs only to
know that you wish to be rescued. For the rest, honor
will exact its due."

Welch began to see where Altos was headed. "Tell

Alexander I'm waiting for him to make his move. I'll gladly see him. But I want somebody to check on Tanya—she's in more danger from Che than you know."

"Perhaps more than Alexander knows," said Altos wearily. "I, unfortunately, know exactly how much danger the lady is in." He shook his head. "I shall bring Alexander to you, as soon as possible. And . . . thank you, Welch."

"Don't thank me, friend. You could have just said I . . . oh, I see, you couldn't: can't lie, I bet. That so?"

The angel nodded glumly and turned to go, shoulders slumped.

Welch watched without another word. The angel hadn't been able to loosen his bonds because he'd promised not to. Altos couldn't spring him personally because he'd given his word to Guevara. He couldn't even go to Alexander on Welch's behalf unless Welch expressed the need himself.

Much be tough, in this crowd, having to walk the straight and narrow.

As the flap fell, cutting off Welch's view of the angel and the ruddy light beyond, Welch was grinning. He wasn't that bad off. He could be working for the same agency Altos was—*that* would have been torture.

Alexander lay on his friend's pallet and listened while Maccabee talked. Judah Maccabee would never lie to him and Maccabee said that Che was doing evil upon the persons of men who had fought at Alexander's side.

"So," said Judah, with the light of the lion in his eyes, "we have only one recourse." He sat back, his muscular shoulders gleaming in the cookfire's light.

"Which is?" Alexander was barely recovered from his fall—every muscle still hurt. Oh, he was bandaged and clean, but whenever he wanted to turn his head, he had to do it very carefully. So very carefully he propped himself up on one elbow. "Speak plainly, Judah."

"Force Che to turn the prisoners over to us—to you, Alexander."

"To 'us' will do." Judah was a guestfriend, and more. Judah was his Hephaestion, the man to whom he was closest. "But how, and on what grounds?"

"Will you see the one called Just Al, my lord?" said Maccabee then.

When Judah called him "lord," he wanted something. And Alexander thought he knew what Judah wanted. Judah wanted what Judah had always wanted: a way out of Hell; power over his own fate; a conduit to God, whom Judah knew was just testing him. And minions, to cleave a way to Heaven through force of arms.

"See Just Al, the one who saved me, the . . ." Alexander knew, because Judah had told him, what the Israelite perceived Just Al to be. He did not believe it, but he would not hurt Maccabee's feelings by saying so. And he should thank the one who'd saved him from the Trip. "Yes, bring him here. And see that, if he and you know a way that we may release our comrades from bondage, this is told to me."

You had to be careful with minions, even beloved ones who were friends. You had to let them know that you were who you were—Alexander the Great. Thus, no matter how close he wished to be with Maccabee, he kept this shred of distance. He was a living god, or had been. Judah was merely a guerrilla fighter of infinite courage and unshakable resolve.

A fighter who believed in angels. It was a bit disturbing. But someone had brought Alexander back from the Trip's door, in the swamp. Some one or some thing. Judah was not omnipotent. He might have been fooled. This Just Al could be an agent of evil.

But whatever he was, he glowed softly in the firelight when he entered. And Alexander found the strength to sit up completely, and the need to be erect in this one's presence.

Judah left them alone, although Alexander protested it was not necessary. And Just Al said, "A man named Welch to whom you owe a debt, and one named Nichols, and one named Achilles, petition you for aid and comfort. Guevara will not release them as long as he leads these Dissidents, because of a woman they brought with them."

"A woman?" said Alexander cautiously.

"A Tamara Burke."

Alexander nodded as if he were not surprised. "I see. What would you have me do? Between those two, man and woman, much blood has been spilled. Bad blood."

"Che has lost faith, and hope. He merely goes through the motions. He has let himself be compromised by factions in the Pentagram. The entire Dissident movement is imperiled because of him."

"I didn't think your sort mixed in infernal politics." Alexander wanted to see if this curious being would proclaim himself as a divine agent, face to face.

But Just Al did not. He shrugged. "Surely you have come among us for some great purpose, Alexander of Macedon. Surely there is good reason you are called Alexander the Great."

"But you are alluding to . . . suggesting that . . ." Alexander shook his head and it hurt. "I'm in no shape to wrest control of these Dissidents from the man they've followed so long."

"But declare your willingness, and Providence shall aid you. Your loyal servants shall smooth the way for you. Only accept the honor."

"Hold. I know only what Maccabee has told me, and Maccabee thinks God is everywhere, under every bush, in every storm and rock, in every corner even of Hell." Alexander leaned forward, into the fire's warmth, even though it hurt his neck. "Do you too think that this is so?"

"God is."

"I need more."

"Then you must provide what you need yourself."

"If I allow you and your . . . compatriots . . . to remake these Dissidents in my name, when it is done, they are mine. Command is mine. Control is mine. I owe you nothing."

"This is acceptable," said the one called Just Al whose eyes were as blue as the sky over Parthia.

Alexander wanted, then, to make a further bargain—to say that, if he did this thing, became embroiled in the affairs of the Dissidents, freed Welch et al, then in exchange, Altos must reunite him with Bucephalus. But he couldn't. He was too proud to ask a favor, too much a king to admit a weakness, and too much in love with Bucephalus to chance that the steed would be brought here, into so squalid a hell as this.

So he did not, just waved his hand. "I am tired. I must rest. Do what you must to free the captives in my name."

Just Al inclined his head and arose, then slipped from the tent. Outside, Alexander soon heard the whoop of joy he knew to be Maccabee's, whenever action was in the offing.

Weeping quietly, Homer was sitting crosslegged before the interrogation tent in which Torquemada was questioning Achilles when Judah Maccabee and a dozen others materialized out of the rufous mist that cloaked the camp.

"What's this?" said Maccabee, reaching down gently to lift the old bard from the dirt and sand. "Tears for your noble savage, Achilles? Don't waste them. We're here to loose the ungovernable anger on which the whole Iliad turned." Maccabee grinned.

Nichols, letting the bolt of his old Thompson slap home, pushed his way forward. "That's right, old man. Don't sweat the small stuff . . . meaning that fool in there." Nichols' stubbly chin jutted toward the closed tent, out of which only an occasional grunt wafted to join the smell of seared human flesh. "We've got a saying where I come from: 'Everybody goes home.' One way or the other. You read me?"

"Read? Of course I can read," protested Homer, unsteady on his spindly legs. The bard pulled at his long, crooked nose and his sunken eyes searched the crowd.

Nichols didn't miss the confusion there, or the dawning suspicion that followed, or the certainty that made the sharp-featured antique square rounded shoulders. "I see. What can I do to help? I am with you, to the death!"

"Probably won't take that," Nichols replied before Maccabee could. (Best to make it clear who was running this show.) "Just stay in the back, with Fat Boy there, and write the action report after."

From the rear of the volunteers, Confucius called softly, "Yes, honorable Homer, come fight by me. 'The king uses him to sortie forth and chastise. The superior man must kill the leaders and capture the followers. There is no blame in this.'" The oriental beamed beatifically and held out a pudgy hand.

Nichols watched Homer stumble by him and signalled Maccabee. "Now, before we go in there, I gotta make this clear: them's we kill, we can't control. So we ain't killin' anyone if we can help it. Till we get to Welch and find out what he wants to do, anyways. Clear? In the ranks, and all?" Nichols turned on his heel then and faced the volunteers Maccabee had collected—Meds and Third World mercs, Hittites and Kurds, and a couple of Brits with shoulderboards. "Take prisoners, got that? We c'n always kill 'em later, after Welch sorts 'em out."

A rumble went through the men, and Nichols had to take it as assent. There wasn't time to do anything else. Like the outmoded submachine gun he carried, produced before its maker changed to open bolt, there was no refinement here, just overcomplication.

But brute force was something Nichols understood better than many of these banana politicos. He rotated the cocking handle back, taking the weapon off safe, and raised his left hand in the air.

When he lowered it, these dogs of counterrevolution would be loosed. For just an instant he hesitated, wondering whether Welch would have approved this action, if Nichols could have asked him. But he couldn't. Welch's tent was too well guarded. Only a crisis like the one Nichols was about to foment would draw those guards away so that Nichols could get to his commander. Which he had to do, before Torquemada got to one of the Devil's Children.

Thinking to himself that putting the revolution in Alexander's hands was one way to stop Che, and that, if Welch had any objections, he wouldn't have said what he had to Altos, Nichols took a deep breath, clenched his sweating fist, and brought it down.

As the group of fighters lunged forward, Nichols had only a second to wish that fate hadn't decreed that he must save Achilles too. But Achilles was necessary to rally the Old Dead, to make the whole thing work.

Then Nichols dived for the tentflap, calling out hoarsely, "Okay, girls, let's rock 'n' roll!" as his finger squeezed the trigger and his M-10 began to bop.

Both Che and Tanya heard the semi-suppressed chatter of auto fire from some distant part of the camp.

The woman tied to Che's tentpole looked toward the sound. The man, nearly as naked as she, stepped forward and took her chin between his fingers, forcing her to look again at him.

"Tell me," said Che Guevara raggedly, "why you did it. The first time. For whom, and why?"

"Got you killed?" said the woman he'd known as Tanya. "It was my assignment. You were. And the second time, it was you who— "

"*Don't lie to me!*" Guevara said loudly, just short of a shout. "Tell me, was it real? Was everything a sham? Did you not—"

Love me, she realized he was going to say, and cut him off before he could. "It doesn't matter, not now. It can't matter. Look at you—there's nothing left. You're a shell, a simulacrum. The Devil's got you on the run." She spoke as quickly as she could, because she knew what she was hearing, and she could guess what it meant. Welch. You couldn't hold Welch. You could murder him, to slow him down. But you couldn't hold him. Not unless you were smarter than he was. And what was left of Guevara, this lovesick wetback, this husk all eaten up inside with twisted ideals, couldn't hold his own against a stiff breeze.

The eyes of Guevara burned with all the self-consuming passion of a zealot. He was a martyr, thrice over. He was a cynic who'd lost his center. He believed in nothing; he was exhausted, disgusted by himself and what he'd wrought.

She understood why: on the Undertaker's table, and in Reassignments, he'd betrayed everything—himself, his cause, his loyalists. They always did. And so it made sense that he'd clutch at her, grab for the last shred of self-definition.

What he wanted to know was who'd betrayed him, in life: what she'd done, how she'd done it, and who for—CIA or KGB. As if it mattered to anyone but him. But if he could exonerate her as a player, he could pretend that there'd been love there. Or remember that there had.

She wasn't sure there hadn't been, but love wasn't an excuse for anything. It solved nothing. It answered nothing. It was only a torment.

The man who should be interrogating her with hot pokers and sensory-deprivation hoods was trying to do so with memories, with guilt she didn't possess.

But he had enough for both of them. And he had enough lust . . . perhaps obsession . . . where she was concerned that he could even ignore what was obviously gunfire in the camp.

Instead of reacting to it, he moved close, very slowly, and his face broke out in a sweat as his hand raised toward her naked breast. He was going to fondle her into submission. He was going to bring her to her knees—and his cause—with the power of his personality.

It might have worked, in life, if she'd been desperate

or stupid or not . . . what she'd been. It couldn't work here, because *he* wasn't what he'd been. Suddenly Guevara reminded her of an aging sex queen, a two-hundred pound geriatric tart who'd never realized that flirtation served only to point up what had been lost.

Che was ludicrous, a parody of himself. His liquid eyes, eyes that had inspired so many to give their lives for an unformed cause, inspired only a shadowy remembrance of himself.

As his fingers closed on her nipple, his lips said, "Tanya, you love me. Say this. Say it's so, blanca, and we will make a new world here together—"

Bam! Blat-blat-blat! Thud. And yelling, outside the tent, which shivered as struggling men fell against it.

"Che," she said, "for your own sake, run." She said it flatly. She didn't know where it had come from. She couldn't afford to feel what she was feeling for this addled Quixotic soul. "Go on, go!"

"Not until you say you did. Do. Or no. *Si. Nada.* Say . . . something."

Something for him to remember. Something to make it all right that she'd been killed while he watched, the last time through here. Something to make it easier for him to look at all the souls his teachings had brought here, every dim-witted rebel who used Che's words as an excuse for his basest crimes, and not shrivel with guilt.

If she'd loved him, if she'd been forced or compromised to betray him, then it wouldn't be empty. It wouldn't all have been a mistake. He'd have something to live for, here.

She stared him in the eye and his hand ran down her belly, onto her naked thighs. His breath came fast.

Hers did too, but because she could see the tent behind him, where firelight beyond it threw shadow-play on the canvas, so that she could make out strugglers in silhouette.

"Che, you're a fool. A dangerous one. You always were. No matter what I felt for you, I always knew I could never trust you. Your dick got you killed—that's not my fault."

"No! No!" he said and closed his fist on the soft flesh of her inner thigh.

She closed her eyes, wishing the men outside would hurry.

And thus she missed the nearly silent storming of the tent, the slitting of its sides with knives, the sneaking of the men through the slits.

Until two men spoke and her eyes snapped open.

"Hold it, asshole. Freeze!" said Nichols, not even breathing hard, his Thompson easy on his hip.

And Achilles, brushing by him, pushing Che roughly from his feet, yelling "Briseis! Briseis, my love," as he came toward Tanya.

Great! That was all she needed, was one of the Old Dead hallucinating that she was some long-lost love.

More men were crowding in now, and Achilles was cutting her bonds. Someone handed her a robe and she flung it over her shoulders, rubbing her wrists, watching Guevara, still on the ground where Achilles had thrust him.

Watching Guevara, the great revolutionary, who had buried his head in his arms and was sobbing like a baby.

The coup was relatively peaceful, as coups went. Welch, once he'd been freed by Nichols, asked for a body count that Nichols gave proudly as, "Zero, sir. That's the way I thought you'd want it. Though we can always remedy that now."

"Nice going, soldier," said Welch and slapped his adc familiarly on the arm. "Let's check the wounded and sort the players out."

The players, in this case, were those who secretly harbored real sympathy for Guevara. Three hours of interviewing Dissidents didn't turn up a single one who'd admit it, and Welch sent Nichols and Maccabee to "see how Achilles is doing and bring me Tanya."

The first personal question he'd asked had been how Tanya was; the first observation Nichols had volunteered was that Achilles, though "mussed up some" from his interrogation at Torquemada's hands, was "fit to fly, sir."

So it was going to be all right. As right as anything got, here. Or he thought it was until, instead of Tanya, the frigging angel poked his head into the tent Welch had commandeered—the one that had been Guevara's.

Welch had just been congratulating himself on breaking the back of the Dissident movement. It might even make up for having to shoot Enkidu. Express Trips were always a last resort. In more controlled circumstances, he'd have been able to call in an alert, so that somebody'd be ready for Enkidu when he arrived.

Welch was about to do that—send somebody to the chopper for a field phone, or have Achilles call in on the bird's radio, when the angel said, "I hope I'm not disturbing you, Welch."

"Not unduly. I heard you were a real help in all this. Want to tell me why that was? How could you throw in with Authority and against the Dissidents?"

The angel walked as if his feet hardly touched the ground. When he was an arm's length away from Welch, who was sitting on a feather pallet in scrounged fatigues, Altos said in his velvet voice, "You proceed under a mistaken assumption."

Oh-oh. "Well, then, why don't you sit down and clarify the situation?" Welch kicked himself for letting wishful thinking seduce him. *You didn't get this lucky. Not in Hell, you didn't.*

The angel sat and a sweet smell like spring in a field of wildflowers wafted from his garments. Coup or not, hand to hand combat or not, the angel didn't have a golden hair out of place. He played with the ragged hem of a short, once-white robe as he said, "The Dissidents will be led from now on by Alexander of Macedon." And his stare was fierce and full of God.

"Crap," said Welch, and rubbed the back of his neck. "I can't have anything to do with—"

"You did not, if I may interrupt. You were a prisoner, a helpless victim, until moments ago. Now you are free to go."

Fuck you, buddy, and the wings you rode in on. But there was no mistaking the angel's certainty. "Alexander's a friend of mine. You can't compel him to do anything against his will."

"That is so. But he has agreed. And it is done, in the sight of—"

"Don't say that, not Down Here." Welch got to his feet and nervously began to pace, his head bent toward the angel. "Look, I don't want to have this conversation with you. Why don't you just disappear? Go somewhere you're needed."

"I was needed here." The angel rose too. "Thank you for your help. I couldn't have—"

"Fuck-all, if you say you couldn't have done this without me, I'm going to find out what it takes to dismember one of your type." Few things frightened Welch, but this just might be one of them. "I don't need to know any more about what you're doing. If you're not trying to treble my torment, you're still doing a damned good job of it."

"Damned, yes. But not without free will," said Altos as the angel glided toward the tentflap.

"A lot of good that's going to do me with the Agency when I try to explain this."

"Don't," said the angel, and the parting word of advice hung in the breeze long after Altos was gone. Hung there, in fact, until Tanya arrived, her eyes full of shadows and Che's plight on her lips.

"Look, Tanya," Welch said, "don't talk to me about your old boyfriend. You do whatever you want, where he's concerned. Send him through the System again, if you want. Anything. Just don't bother me with it. I've got to see Alexander."

"Send Che through the System? But then Authority will know what . . ."

"That's right," said Welch savagely. "What happened here. I'm just glad I didn't give the damned orders.

And I've got to make sure we can say that about Nichols, too. Suss it out. Prove to yourself that Maccabee and the angel cooked this up, that we were just pawns. I'd rather have the whole Admin building know I got caught with my pants down than take the blame for this one."

"I know," said Tanya, rubbing her eyes with the back of one hand. "I know. Nichols was right, though—no casualties. We're all okay. Achilles says the chopper can make it back to New Hell . . ." Her eyes were pleading.

"And your boyfriend?"

"Come on, Welch, you know that's not fair. He can't hurt anyone, the shape he's in. Reassignments didn't keep him off the playing field the last time; we don't have to. Let's just go home."

"Fine. Get everybody packed into the chopper—just the team, no passengers. I'll meet you." He ducked out of the tent.

"Where are you going?" Tanya called after him.

"Got to see a man about a horse."

Alexander of Macedon lay in Maccabee's tent, listening to the triumph in Judah's voice more than to his words.

Alexander had made a bargain. He had a task to accomplish, men to lead. Judah assured him that this was so. And it had been relatively bloodless, because of Welch's people. Bloodless was always better, when men are brought together by ideals.

He'd made bloody mistakes, in life, at moments like these. He appreciated the restraint that Welch's forces had displayed. So when Welch came to thank him, Alexander allowed the New Dead leader a private audience, even though Maccabee scowled and said, "I'll be right outside if you need me, Alexander."

"I won't," said the Macedonian. And, to Welch: "Sit. We have much to talk of. Old wars on the beach at Ilion. New wars of liberation. There's no need to thank me."

Welch did not sit. The man in tiger camouflage put his hands on his hips and said, "Tell me you're not going to get sucked into this mess. You're too good a strategist to be the next sacred cow here. Look what it did to Guevara."

"Guevara did that to Guevara. And perhaps the woman called Tanya helped. Women can do that to some men. But I am Alexander. These men need me. I have given my word to lead them."

"Lead them *where? Why? How? For how long?*" Welch was nearly shouting, an odd thing in a man whose voice tended to drop when he was intent. "You're too smart for this trick, no matter which side's at the bottom of it. Don't do this, Alexander. I don't want you for an enemy."

"Nor I you," said the Macedonian, and rose because his guest would not sit, so that Welch would not be guilty of standing in the presence of a reclining Great King. And held out his hand in the New Dead gesture of friendship. "But as I said, I have given my word. These men want a leader. They have chosen me."

Welch did not take Alexander's hand. "Again, where're you going to lead them? To what end?"

"Freedom is what they want. A fairer, more just land in which to . . . live." Alexander's hand, extended in friendship, did not waver. He thought of the one called Just Al, who had called upon him to champion the Dissidents' cause. And Maccabee, who loved causes.

"You fool," Welch said, shaking his head. "I shouldn't waste my breath. . . . Look, what're you going to do, ride into New Hell and camp on the Devil's doorstep? Join the government? Even that won't do it. These bastards have got exactly the Hell they deserve. And I've got a chopper waiting." Finally, Welch met Alexander's hand with his, and shook it, his grip manly in its strength.

"Go with luck," said the Macedonian as he broke the clasp. "Remember, you have friends here. You may count on that."

"Yeah, and you can count on us, too . . . when you have trouble with Mithridates and Tigellinus and that lot." A sour grimace crossed Welch's face. "Look, Alex, you're a good fighter, a brave man, a—"

"Living God."

"Right. You don't know what you're getting into. Politics, around here, is a deeper sewer than you know. And it leads right to the Pentagram. You haven't got a snowball's chance in hell of making this thing work."

"This is not what Just Al thinks," Alexander said as Welch, without another word or a proper farewell, turned to leave.

Alexander watched the swaying tentflap that had fallen back in Welch's wake, and wondered if what the New Dead agent said was true, until Maccabee called him out to attend the celebration in his honor and meet his new and loyal followers.

There were so many of them, and the celebration was so noisy in its gaiety, that Alexander didn't even hear the chopper as it flew away.

C'MON DOWN!!

Is the real world getting to be too much? Feel like you're on somebody's cosmic hit list? Well, how about a vacation in the hottest spot you'll ever visit ... HELL!

We call our "Heroes in Hell" shared-universe series the Damned Saga. In it the greatest names in history—Julius Caesar, Napoleon, Machiavelli, Gilgamesh and many more—meet the greatest names in science fiction: Gregory Benford, Martin Caidin, C.J. Cherryh, David Drake, Janet Morris, Robert Silverberg. They all turn up the heat—in the most original milieu since a Connecticut Yankee was tossed into King Arthur's Court. We've saved you a seat by the fire ...

HEROES IN HELL, 65555-8, $3.50 _____

REBELS IN HELL, 65577-9, $3.50 _____

THE GATES OF HELL, 65592-2, $3.50 _____

KINGS IN HELL, 65614-7, $3.50 _____

CRUSADERS IN HELL, 65639-2, $3.50 _____

Please send me the books checked above. I enclose a check for the cover price plus 75 cents for first-class postage and handling, made out to: Baen Books, 260 Fifth Avenue, New York, N.Y. 10001.

TRAVIS SHELTON
LIKES BAEN BOOKS
BECAUSE THEY TASTE GOOD

Recently we received this letter from Travis Shelton of Dayton, Texas:

> *I have come to associate Baen Books with Del Monte. Now what is that supposed to mean? Well, if you're in a strange store with a lot of different labels, you pick Del Monte because the product will be consistent and will not disappoint.*
>
> *Something I have noticed about Baen Books is that the stories are always fast-paced, exciting, action-filled and seem to be published because of content instead of who wrote the book. I now find myself glancing to see who published the book instead of reading the back or intro. If it's a Baen Book it's going to be good and exciting and will capture your spare reading moments.*
>
> *Another discovery I have recently made is that I don't have any Baen Books in my unread stacks—and I read four to seven books a week, so that in itself is a meaningful statistic.*

Here is an excerpt from Tempus *by Janet Morris, coming in April 1987 from Baen Books:*

A dozen riders materialized out of the wasteland near the swamp and surrounded the two Stepsons; none had faces; all had glowing pure-white eyes. They fought as best they could with mortal weapons, but ropes of spitting power came round them and blue sparks bit them and their flesh sizzled through their linen chitons and, unhorsed, they were dragged along behind the riders until they no longer knew where they were or what was happening to them or even felt the pain. The last thing Niko remembered, before he awoke bound to a tree in some featureless grove, was the wagon ahead, stopping, and his horse, on its own trying to win the day....

Before him he saw figures, a bonfire limning silhouettes. Among them, as consciousness came full upon him and he began to wish he'd never waked, was Janni, spreadeagled, staked out on the ground, his mouth open, screaming at the sky.

"Ah," he heard, "Nikodemos. So kind of you to join us."

Then a woman's face swam before him, beautiful, though that just made it worse. It was the Nisibisi witch and she was smiling, itself an awful sign. A score of minions ringed her, creatures roused from graves....

She began to tell him softly the things she wished to know. He only stared back at her in silence: Tempus's plans and state of mind were things he knew little of; he couldn't have stopped this if he'd wanted to; he didn't know enough. But when at length, knowing it, he closed his eyes, she came up close and pried them open, impaling his lids with wooden splinters so that he would see what made Janni cry....

All he heard was the witch's voice; all he remembered was the horror of her eyes and the message she bade him give to Tempus, and that when he had repeated it, she pulled the splinters from his lids....The darkness she allowed him became complete, and he found a danker rest-place than meditation's quiet cave.

288 pp. • 65631-7 • $3.50

To order any Baen Book by mail, send the cover price plus 75 cents for first-class postage and handling to: Baen Books, Dept. B, 260 Fifth Avenue, New York, N.Y. 10001.